PRAISE FOR I, CARAVAGGIO

"*I, Caravaggio* is a trip, is an erudite hoot, is art and lust and immortality and loss: this book is a fucking party."

— KATHE KOJA, AUTHOR OF *THE CIPHER* AND *DARK FACTORY*

"What a talent Eugenio Volpe is! One of the freshest new voices around, I always look forward to reading his work!"

— ANN HOOD, BESTSELLING AUTHOR OF *THE OBITUARY WRITER* AND *THE RED THREAD*

"Volpe's outrageously inventive novel recreates Caravaggio and early modern Rome with a post-modern spin, all the while asking shockwave questions: Who is art really for, the masses or ourselves? Are we our own Gods? Whiplash smart, this novel did what the best books do: it changed the way I see not just Caravaggio, but the world."

— CAROLINE LEAVITT, NEW YORK TIMES BESTSELLING AUTHOR OF *PICTURES OF YOU* AND *WITH OR WITHOUT YOU*

"*I, Caravaggio* is a breathtaking portrait of the artist with all the dirt, swashbuckling, violence and reverence Caravaggio himself would crave. It pulsates with wit and pathos while shedding a raking light on the themes of the corrupting power of patronage, the myth of genius and the redemptive power of art."

— LORRAINE TOSIELLO, AUTHOR OF *THE BEE AND THE FLY THE IMPROBABLE CORRESPONDENCE OF LOUISA MAY ALCOTT AND EMILY DICKINSON* AND *ONLY GOSSIP PROSPERS*

I, Caravaggio

Eugenio Volpe

CL⊲SH

Copyright © 2023 by Eugenio Volpe

Cover by Matthew Revert

matthewrevert.com

Troy, NY

CLASH Books

clashbooks.com

All rights reserved.

ISBN: 9781955904759

For Sara. Forever fading into you.

I.

Rome, 1604

Some call me a libertine. Others call me a genius. I make love to lads. I fuck women. I'm a New Man in the oldest of worlds. I'm primeval, homicidal to boot. I'm Michelangelo Merisi, the Lombard hick who prefers butter, not olive oil, on his artichokes. I prefer my Christian name, but the Divine One, Michelangelo Buonarroti has minted that denomination, so friends and enemies alike have dubbed me *Caravaggio*, named after the plague-ridden town of my origins. Caravaggio. Michelangelo. The two names have scored a cross within me. I'm a pleb. I'm royal. I'm a heretic and a believer. I'm at odds with myself. Michelangelo with his defiant, proletariat rage comes naturally. Being Caravaggio is arduous, the ascetic dedication and strenuous concentration. He's always reflecting, always in his own head, especially during sex. His tireless superiority complex has made Michelangelo the lesser man, but we accept Caravaggio's dominion. Genius must be served.

That's where yours truly comes in. Behind every great artist is a greater psychosis. I'm the nameless, faceless beast yoked to the dueling egos of Michelangelo and Caravaggio. I'm the middle child of this inflated self. Michelangelo was born first, punchy as baby Hercules. At the age of five, his working-class fists caught thunder when a plague ate the flesh of our father, grandfathers, and paternal uncles. Then I entered the world, fatherless, spawned by Michelangelo's grieving head, nursed on our widowed mother's shattered nerves. I was born to fear death. I was born to protect Michelangelo from himself. Don't pick fights with older boys. Don't throw rocks at the marquis' guards. Don't hunt wild boar alone. He seldom listened. It was the tallest of orders, and then, at the age of ten, we painted a still life that put the art tutor's cornucopia to shame. Our prodigy was born. Another inner child to feed. My tall order was demoted to a fool's errand. Protect the genius from the libertine. Keep Michelangelo from sabotaging Caravaggio. It's been hell, refereeing Romulus and Remus, constantly prying the fingers of Cain from Abel's throat. Fraternal battles are the bloodiest, but there's nothing more destructive than a warring self.

So here I am attending Mass, the dull fluorescence of a cloudy Sunday morning emanating through the central dome of the church. It's the perfect light, intensifying the darkness of my work. All eyes are on them, my two pictures hanging in the chapel left of the altar—Peter's upside-down crucifixion and Paul's ecstatic fall from his horse. Only three souls mind the mumbling priest, two servers kneeling on either side of him and a third kneeling wide flank. The priest bows woefully low, confessing his sins to almighty God. The servers ask God to have mercy on the priest, to grant him everlasting life. I've partied with the man. I know the sins he's committed, most of them venial. His soul can be saved, unlike mine. All my sins are mortal, but I'm not here for absolution. I'm here to be witnessed, and to witness the power of my work on the wretched. I'm an idol who can recognize his dependence on fandom. Without worshippers, a god is just a baseless psycho.

I look over my shoulder to count stargazers. Thirteen. None of them wretched. Most have more money than God and dress like it—shiny satins and patterned silks tightly fitted to both sexes. Some turn a head to cough. Others itch their noses against a shoulder. Any old trick to steal a glimpse of the maniacal genius.

I feign a stiff neck and slowly twist my head, a ploy to see who's stargazing from the other side of the nave. I count twelve. One looks like a thuggish bureaucrat, his stark black doublet, the starched point of his beard. He eyeballs me as if auditing my soul. I don't know him, and he certainly doesn't know me. If he did, he'd know better. I've bled men for exhibiting friendlier looks, but I'm currently unarmed. I never carry a sword to Mass. Don't misjudge the piety. I'll punch his lights out just the same once we've exited the church.

Here in Santa Maria del Popolo, I can only stab him a menacing glare. He averts his eyes but returns them moments later with a softer inquisition. Maybe I misjudged. Maybe he's praying for me. Maybe he recognizes me from *Sacred Love and Profane Love*, a crap painting by my enemy Baglione that portrays yours truly as a cock-munching goblin with mangled fangs, gasping in humiliation as Sacred Love beats me aside with his exquisite wings, rescuing a traumatized Cupid from my lap. It was painted in response to my blockbuster *Love Conquers All*, a full-frontal portrait of Cupid as a ruddy, happy-go-lucky lad with bad teeth and working-class wings. My Cupid poses alone, fisting two arrows, straddling a draped stool. The lad is having a blast, and why shouldn't he? Love is a fun business, and he calls the shots. He's no knockout. He's not even a god. He's every other lad on the street, ordained by the powers vested in me, tickled by the act of having his picture painted, his darling dick dead front and center.

My picture and Baglione's painting both hang in the gallery of the Giustiniani brothers, Vincent and Cardinal Benedetto. If the bureaucrat has visited their palace, he's surely heard my name not only mentioned, but revered. He would have also seen my apprentice Cecco on their walls. Cecco is my Cupid. He's also my full-frontal John the Baptist, the most copied picture in Rome. Friends and enemies alike have dubbed him *Cecco del Caravaggio*, his name married to mine. We're going on four years. He calls me *master*, but only in the company of others. He's hardly my servant, and much more than an apprentice. He's my heart. He's a sensation. He's a budding star. Cecco del Caravaggio is the next best thing after me.

Cecco is my young lover. He stands beside me, our kneecaps smooching behind the pew. Footsies at Mass—we play this game every Sunday, but today I'm not in the mood. I have a headache. I'm exhausted and remarkably sad. Caravaggio is no longer interested in painting Cecco. He has Virgin commissions and a final John the Baptist to paint. Cecco isn't manly enough for his new vision of John. If not painting Cecco, God will finally take exception to my loving him. That's how He works, like any self-seeking king or pontiff.

I turn to Cecco. He flashes me that crooked smile I've made famous, but more than fame, my Cecco deserves love. I can't give him that. God forbids it, yet He made me this way. Why punish the lad for succumbing to my superpowers? I resent God's duplicity. He's a user. He hates Michelangelo, and barely acknowledges my existence, but Caravaggio is His pride and joy. Like the cardinals and aristocrats who pull strings to pardon my crimes, God keeps me around for my pictures. Without them, Christians would have limited perceptions of His greatness. I have a good mind to destroy myself, let Michelangelo's proletariat ire burn our genius to the ground. That would show Him. Without the likes of me, He'd be just another idol with a bloated sense of self. By cutting Cecco loose, I'm free to fail at my job. I could walk away from Michelangelo and Caravaggio, letting all hell break loose. I'm in no hurry for that, but I'm preparing it as a last defense against Rome's army of horseshit Holy Rollers and two-faced users.

We sit. We sign the cross. We stand. Cecco sensually probes my ribs with his elbow. I pretend not to feel it. I fake focus on the priest. He ascends to the altar and places his pinkies upon it, praying over the relics of an anonymous martyr. This is the part of Mass where God forgives the priest's sins, the ones I've seen him commit at Madama Palace. I look for an outward sign of his absolution. No halo. No aura. No ecstatic shivers. Cecco grazes a knuckle against my thigh. I shiver. It's not ecstasy. More of a frigid ambivalence. When the goosebumps subside, I glance over my shoulder. The thuggish bureaucrat appears to be making a mental note. He's onto me. No matter. He can't report what Papa Clement already knows. What Baglione painted. What I've confessed in my own pictures. The shameless joy of *Love Conquers All*. The dewy sensuality of *Lute Player*. The brutal passion of *Isaac & Abraham II*. Noblemen and cardinals buy up my man-love pictures. They order copies. They want my pictures more than they want my head. Patronizing yours truly buys them immortality. I'm the only one selfless enough to persecute Michelangelo Merisi da Caravaggio. It'll kill me, but it's time to squash my indomitable love for Cecco. Save the lad's soul. A new tall order to complicate my fool's errand.

The priest makes wine. He signs the cross. My goosebumps return. He washes his hands. The servers kiss them. Cecco blows in my ear. My remarkable sadness sinks to a new nadir. Sacrificing my love for this lad. The throb of my headache quickens. I clench my sphincter to relieve the pain. The priest transforms bread and wine into the Body and Blood of Christ. It's a minor miracle, but boring nonetheless. The sanctus bells are struck. My stomach growls for donuts. The priest and servers exit the nave. The congregation flocks to my pictures. I listen to them wow out, low moans and loud whispers from groupies, fanboys, and collectors. Cecco steps from the pew into the aisle and tempts me with his mischievous *John in the Wild III* grin.

"Donuts?" I ask.

"Mass and donuts, master. Our Sunday ritual."

He makes a perfect circle with his mouth. Its circumference perfectly matches my girth.

"One small happy family," I say.

I distance myself from Cecco as we exit. I don't get far. I'm slowed to a straggle by a procession of lollygaggers staring up at the stucco saints standing on the cornices of the arcade. I turn to evaluate the breadth of my separation from Cecco, but he's right there, happy-go-lucky as ever, oblivious to the motive of my queer pacing.

"Don't worry, master. The donuts aren't going anywhere."

I want to compensate my ex with a consolatory smile, but the bureaucrat is a few faces behind him. I've seen his acquisitiveness in the eyes of thousands. He wants blood or paint from me. Deciphering which requires superhuman paranoia, but the headache and remarkable sadness have disarmed me. I'm in no condition to fight or haggle so I flip him the bird and push past the lollygaggers toward the exit. I don't look back until reaching our favorite donut cart halfway across the square. Of course, Cecco is there behind me, standing so impossibly close that our souls become superimposed. Severing our bond will be the hardest thing ever.

The entire square stargazes as we stand in line. Caravaggio and Isaac. Caravaggio and his Cecco. Sick Bacchus and Cupid. The sun has triumphed over the clouds. The morning's glumness has brightened into a perfect Sunday. We have all the light in the world. Sacred and Profane love, not a shadow at our feet. I raise the hood of my cloak to hide from it, a wounded animal backed into its cave, glaring out at the world. We order donuts and take them to the fountain. I devour mine as if the dough was kneaded from Christ's flesh.

"Have you eaten since last Sunday's donuts?" Cecco asks.

"A few heads of chicory."

"You curse your days of apprenticing for that tyrant who fed you only greens. Now you're a superstar and feed yourself the same diet?"

"What doesn't kill me," I say.

"You barely sleep or eat. You consume nothing but claret and poppy seeds."

"This superstar is superhuman."

"Superhuman on the inside." Cecco jams a thumb into my fat oblique.

"Minus the love handles, my body is looking swole. I'm going to paint a nude selfie. Haven't done one since *Matthew Killed*."

"Selfies are dead. You killed them a decade ago with *Sick Bacchus*, the god of intercourse and wine yellowed with jaundice."

"I had malaria. Thought I was dying before my time. The deathbed selfie was a parting shot at God."

"A selfie to end all selfies, denouncing all forms of worship. Brilliant, but why the sudden need to resurrect them?"

"Documentation. I'm dying of something. I don't know what. My insides feel toxic. I don't think I'm long for this world."

"It's the poppy seeds and claret," he says.

"Probably, but either way I'm toast. Powerful men want me dead."

"Who?"

"The usual suspects. Captains. Cardinals. Maybe Papa Clement. Definitely God."

"You're too valuable. They need your pictures."

"Why do you think I've been dragging ass on the Virgin commissions?"

"Caravaggio, you're depressed."

"*Master* Caravaggio. Someone might hear."

"Over the spewing fountain?" There's a fair amount of conjecture in his voice.

I shrug, nod, and shake my head.

"I can't get used to calling you Caravaggio. You were Master Merisi my first year of apprenticing. Michelangelo for two years, and now Caravaggio. What'll it be in 1605?"

I can't answer, not here in front of everyone. His heart deserves privacy while breaking it. I'm his master, which means I can walk away from the question without him reading into it. I swallow the last of my donut and push through the crowd, traffic slowing to a shuffle as we near Via del Corso where two coaches are causing a major backup. One of the coaches is the slickest in Rome. It belongs to Costanza Colonna, the woman I call *Mamma*. She was wife to the late Francesco Sforza, the Marquis of Caravaggio. An architect by trade, my father was steward of his estate. Holding my father in high regard, he and the marchioness stood witness at my parents' wedding. I was born nine months later, on the feast day of the archangel Saint Michael, but more importantly, a week after Catholic superhero Marcantonio Colonna blew the Turkish Empire out of the water at Lepanto, the greatest Christian victory since David plunked Goliath between the eyes. Marcantonio was Costanza's father. The marchioness deemed my birth a Colonna family blessing. When the plague wiped out every adult Merisi male known to God, she helped the steward's widow by appointing herself a parental role in raising the punchy Merisi child. My mother didn't refuse given her meager resources and fretfulness. She had two younger mouths to feed. I practically grew up on the Sforza estate. The marchioness paid for Michelangelo's sword training. When our inner genius revealed itself, she paid for Caravaggio's training and arranged his art apprenticeships. I had lost a father, but gained a second mother, every poor Italian boy's wildest oedipal dream, especially when she's the daughter of Italy's most glorified patriarch. Costanza Colonna has been wiping my messes since. I only wish I could call her *Mamma* to her face.

Assuming there's been an accident or altercation, I shuck my hood and rush to Mamma's rescue, shoving aside anyone with a penis. Cecco slipstreams in my ego. Some jackass femme-fop in a curly wig tries standing his ground. They're all over Rome these days, puffed-up nouveau riche pilgrims dressed like the second coming of Duke Dildo. His cosplay doesn't fool me. He hasn't a drop of noble blood in his veins. Michelangelo enjoys hunting these wannabes for sport. I sturdy my core and run an elbow into his solar plexus. He crumples. Cecco giggles through his nose. That laugh once made me rock-hard. Now? Little more than a chubby.

As I near Mamma, it becomes distressingly clear that she doesn't need saving. Zero drama surrounds the traffic jam caused by her conversing with Lady Mattei from their respective windows, coaches headed in opposite directions. The stalled drivers behind them wait patiently. Bottlenecked pedestrians keep any grievances to themselves. A few pursed lips at most. The coats of arms dangling from each coach do not need fortification from the likes of yours truly.

"Speak of the devil," Lady Mattei says with an agnostic smile.

The marchioness looks me up with disappointment and down with concern. She has always seen through the vigor of Michelangelo and Caravaggio, preferring to view the torment of yours truly. An emotionally even me makes her job of mothering the maniacal genius easier.

"My Michele looks paler than Mantegna's Christ cadaver," she says.

"I'm picturing Dante's Fifth Circle and the choked rage of those fetid hotheads mauling each other amongst the scummy surface of the Styx," says Lady Mattei.

She thinks she's entitled. She somewhat is. Lady Mattei is also a mother of mine. I lived at Mattei Palace for three years. Lord Mattei commissioned Cecco's full-frontal *John in the Wild III*, the namesake of their eldest son. The other two Mattei brothers, the marquis and cardinal, also lived at the compound. It was one hugely rich happy family. Nevertheless, they were cheap fucks, paying squat for my pictures. The living, however, was superb, my most lawful, peaceful, and maternal years to date. Mamma visited almost daily. She and Lady Mattei spoiled me with donuts, praise, and claret. A psycho genius can never have too many mothers. My biological mother, let's just call her Lucia, forfeited a superstar to better care for my unexceptional siblings. It was a prudent choice. I'll never respect her for it. Given the chance, Lady Mattei would steal me from Mamma and lock me in her girdle purse. She furnished all my needs at Mattei Palace. It's where Cecco first came to live with me, where I painted him as Cupid, John the Baptist, and ravaged Isaac.

I turn to Mamma's carriage and take a low and woeful bow. She hangs her hand from the window. I kiss it with the diehard slobbering of a naughty son. I turn to Lady Mattei and bow, not much woe.

"I pray that you've been a good boy," says Mamma.

I turn to Cecco and encourage him to answer for me.

"Mezza mezza, my lady," he replies, bowing deep.

"I haven't bludgeoned anyone since that waiter rubbed my nose in buttered artichokes."

"Haven't bludgeoned anyone but yourself," says Mamma. "Your face is stewing with self-defeat. Don't do this to me. I already suffer the disappointment of one son, locked behind bars, his ancestry squandered on barroom duels. Don't you dare squander God's grace. Don't you dare squander my investment and love."

Whenever Mamma guilts me like that, I double down on the woe.

"I'm dying from something. Headaches. Exhaustion. Bouts of remarkable sadness. Powerful forces want me dead. Claret remedies the aches and depression."

"Sadness? I'll give you sadness. My father forced me into marriage at twelve. You romp around Rome with whomever pleases you."

Not looking at Cecco takes all my strength. Keeping quiet about the ass-fucking I received at twelve requires little strength and mostly love. Mamma arranged the apprenticeship for her prodigious foster son. She didn't know that my master was a chicken-plucker, or maybe she did. She too subscribes to the cliché of serving genius. Lady Mattei changes the subject. She has always had the wettest of soft spots for Cecco.

"Everyone's dying to see your Virgins. What's taking?" she asks.

"I hear you're also late on a John in the Wild commission," Mamma says.

No one, not even the patron's wife, knew of the commission, a surprise anniversary gift. Her omniscience is up there with God's.

"You always know my business," I say in wonder.

"I'm a mother. Knowing is my business."

It's true. She knows everything. Mamma, Cecco, and God are the only ones who know that I exist. Everyone else thinks it's just Michelangelo and Caravaggio in here. I wonder if Mamma can see me scoring this emergency escape tunnel in the shadowy corner of my skull. I wonder if she'd abet my getaway. I'd like to think that she would.

"I'll paint the Virgins if you help me find one. I don't want any old model. I want to employ some wretched soul. Save her from the streets. Launch her into stardom."

"Ginger or brunette?" Lady Mattei asks.

Again, I encourage Cecco to answer for me.

"It was acceptable for Magdalene to be a ginger, but the Virgin should be a downright brunette," he says.

"Tar black or burnished wood?" Mamma grins as if sitting for da Vinci. If twenty years younger or at all immaculate, I might cast her as my Virgin.

"I trust our marchioness to recognize a worthy tint of Virgin," Cecco says.

Both ladies blush. He's the Machiavelli of salty humor. His lowly status be damned, Cecco once made the Marquis di Giove glow. He gets away with murder. It's the soft lips and cherub jawline. I'm already jealous of his next lover.

"Hurry. Find a Virgin. I'm tired of lesser artists stealing your thunder. Stay clear of the taverns. Lock yourself in the studio. You're your best self when painting, peaceable and astute. Besides, you're my favorite. Act like it," Mamma says.

Favorite what? Artist? Son? I don't have the balls to ask but let the record show that she has never bought a Caravaggio. Regarding my *best self*, she's referring to yours truly, the one who keeps Michelangelo and Caravaggio from canceling each other. She witnessed my neurotic birth, Michelangelo hatching me from fatherless heartache. Like God, I'm reluctant to show myself. There are people out there who would kill for the opportunity of being Caravaggio's inner voice. As self-preservation, I keep a low profile, but without Mamma there'd only be Michelangelo. She fostered all three of us. She deserves a rare glimpse of me. I doff my cloak and unlace my doublet, baring my physique to the Marchioness of Caravaggio.

"I'll repay your investment and love with immortality, but I must self-destruct as my creative process dictates. The younger I die, the rarer and dearer my pictures become. Therefore, I'll enkindle my violent ways and flame out pronto. Tell friends! Tell family! Buy me up quick! I'm getting dangerous, physically *and* artistically. I'll paint Virgins, but first I'll paint a swan song series of naked gory selfies. Ponderous decap-itations and epiphanic screams. Get them while my blood is still hot! Get them while my abs are popping like Christ's on the cross!"

I bow and flog my back with an imaginary lash. Mamma finally smiles. I inherited my morbid sense of humor from her.

"You're a piece of work," says Lady Mattei. "Come to the palace for dinner. I mean it."

She doesn't mean it but loves me just the same. Like me, Lady Mattei is a state-of-the-art Roman. She was not born a lady. She was born a disgrace, her mother one of Pope Alexander's many bastards. Like me, she was raised on the fringe of nobility, willing herself to power with that terrific bod. Anyone can make it in Rome. All it takes is some combination of beauty, brilliance, strength, charm, moxie, luck, nepotism, back-stabbing, cut-throating, and/or patricide. If only Lucia had a single one of those talents. Her superstar son wouldn't be ghosting her ghost.

Mamma and Lady Mattei blow farewell kisses before riding off in opposite directions. Neither offer a lift, but the traffic is finally purged. I turn to Cecco. The poor lad stands there, carrying all my shit, the city gushing around us.

II.

After three wordless miles, we arrive home. There is a note tacked to the front door. Cecco reaches for it. I know what it's going to say, but it's news to him.

"Three months late on rent?" he asks.

I shrug, nod, and insert the key.

"Paint that John and those Virgins. You've only finished two paintings this year. At that rate, we'll be on the street by winter."

I finally offer that consolatory smile. He doesn't want it. I open the door and wave him in. He hesitates. His only other option is the artist commune at Campo de' Fiori with his parents, but they wouldn't take him back. He's outgrown them beyond repair.

Cecco kicks off his boots and heads upstairs. I wander the downstairs rooms, closing shutters, drawing curtains. When it's good and dark, I retreat to the kitchen for my flask, the same one at Joseph's feet in *Rest on the Flight into Egypt*. I sit at the table, the three-legged one in *Matthew Called*. The plates and carafes are from *Supper at Emmaus*. Everything in my house is from a picture. Caravaggio lives inside his pictures before, during, and after their making.

I drink and listen to Cecco's footsteps. He's up to something in the studio. I could guess but take another drink instead. I guzzle the entire flask and hit the pantry. I refill the flask. I reach for my bottle of poppy seeds. I munch a few handfuls and take another swill from the flask. I top it off again and return to the table. I listen for God. Nothing. I listen to Cecco's bare feet prancing about. It's a veritable wonderland up there—costumes, swords, and props from my pictures. I take another drink and keep at it until I'm certain that my cock won't work. The poppy kicks in. Minutes, maybe hours later, Cecco's feet patter down the stairs. He enters the kitchen naked, wearing his Cupid wings from *Love Conquers All*. He also holds an arrow. He presses it to my throat. The right side of his face is gone, erased by shadow. Michelangelo is turned on. If I let him, he'd throw it inside Cupid while staring God right in the eye.

"You need to start sleeping in your own room," I say.

"I've been waiting for you to end it." He withdraws the arrow from my Adam's apple.

"Since when?"

"Back in April when you painted *John in the Wild IV*."

"Because I didn't cast you as John?"

"That's insulting. I'm no prima donna. It was the way you painted him, the exact opposite of your other Johns. The picture is erratic and grim. You nixed the ram. There's no sexuality in it. No love of any kind."

I raise the flask. Only some of the claret finds my mouth. I leave the dribble on my chin. Cecco drags a chair next to me and sits. His wing tickles my neck.

"I love you, but God will ruin you for succumbing to me," I say.

"That's not you talking. That's Michelangelo."

"I can't paint Virgins and love you at the same time," says Caravaggio.

"You can't do this to me." His tone is defiant. I was expecting heartbroken. I can't say that I'm not hurt. Luckily, I'm too numb to feel anything.

"Of all the things I've done to you, I can certainly do this. God wants it this way."

"That's still Caravaggio talking. Let's hear *you* banish me to the streets."

"I'm not banishing you to the streets. I'm moving you to the spare bedroom. It's a nice room. Spacious. You're your own man now. We'll get rid of the cot. I'll buy you a nice bed."

"Do you want a blowjob?" he asks. "For old times' sake?"

"Never again."

"How about you give me a blow job for old times' sake?"

I stumble out of the kitchen, flask in hand, already missing his delicate lips. We'll never make love again. Worse, I'll never paint him again, especially not his ears. I love those ears! Deeper and more baroque than a vagina! Jesus Christ shut me the fuck up I'm so fucked up.

I cross the hallway to my bedroom, shutting the door for the first time in our two-year occupancy of the house. I undress and stagger to the window. In the process of closing the shutters, I spot the bureaucrat standing across the street. His stance is nonconfrontational. It's the posture one assumes while observing my pictures. He's taking it all in, the entirety of my house and my bearing inside of it. I smile and wave to him, a ridiculously cordial gesture that says *Hi! I'm super wasted! Come on in and kill me. Please.*

My sword and armor are stacked in the corner of the room. It's the armor at Cupid's feet in *Love Conquers All*. The same show-stealing suit of armor in *Christ Taken*. I don the plackart and pauldron and take to bed, sword by my side. I close my eyes and sign the cross. I pray to almighty God, to the Blessed Virgin, to Peter, to Paul, to John the Baptist, and to the archangel Michael. I listen for them. Nothing. I try envisioning my Virgin. Nothing. I pray for Michelangelo Merisi da Caravaggio to outshine the names of Pope Clement VIII, Ferdinando de Medici, King Felipe III, King Henry IV, and every Mattei, Giustiniani, Costa, Sforza, and Colonna past, present, and future. Amen.

III.

Late Tuesday morning, ascending Capitol Hill with my posse. Four of us on foot. Onorio atop his charger. Eight servants in our slipstream. We round the road eastward and the sun blindsides us. I squint and trudge skyward, pacing my steps to the four-beat clacking of the charger. The left side of my face bleeds sweat. My armpits stink to high heaven. Cardinal Del Monte once re-gifted me a twenty-scudi vase of royal perfume. I only wear it when bedding pros. This morning I absolutely doused my balls with it. We always visit the bordello after a brawl.

I'm strapped with dagger and sword. The armor hasn't come off since Sunday night. I'm ready for my killers. Perhaps this gang of mercs tumbling down the road at us. I clench my already squinting sockets into a baneful glare and they know at once. They couldn't wet me on my worst day. Indifferent to Caravaggio's brush, they fear Michelangelo's sword. They tip their hats to yours truly and my infamous cohorts. Every man thinks his posse is the tightest, but I'd pit ours against any five men in Rome. Mercs, bodyguards, pimps, Spanish pikemen, and punks. We've bludgeoned half of them and scared the rest straight. We've almost run out of opponents. I look back at Cecco. He hikes straight into the sun, taking our divorce like a champ. I'm proud of him and still remarkably sad for myself.

Mario marches alongside me, looking the dapper mercenary, the one I painted in *Matthew Killed*. He bows his head to my crotch and jokingly takes a sniff.

"Michele's balls smell like roses," he announces.

Orazio sniffs at the air. "And civet anus."

I cock an eye through the yellow heat. In the elevated distance, the upper façade of the Senatorial Palace appears. The Divine One designed Campidoglio Square and its two palaces, but he rose to heaven before breaking ground. Onorio's father, the late great Martino Longhi executed the blueprints. He also built the Senatorial Palace bell tower. The sun broods over it, rendering his brilliance into a phallic silhouette. Onorio has to be seeing it that way. In Rome, occupational achievement is everything. Men are appraised by what they design, write, paint, or bank. Onorio has drawn masterful blueprints, but built zilch, not even a public latrine. Nothing in Rome bears his name. Kids? Onorio just had his first. His name? Martino Longhi the Younger. My remaining memory of Fermo Merisi is a small shadowy figure hundreds of feet in the air, standing in front of the sun on a topmost section of scaffolding. He's repairing one of the marquis' tenements, but not the one we live in. My father could have built a Duomo of his own, but he let the marquis buy his stewardship. That too was a prudent choice that I don't respect, but as Caravaggio's custodian, I totally relate.

We're headed to Campidoglio to taunt the man who robbed Onorio of his vocational birthright. Papa Clement has bankrolled construction of a third palace, completing the celestial symmetry of the Divine One's blueprints. Onorio fancied himself a leading candidate for the new project but wasn't even considered. He's the biggest hothead in Rome (Orazio a close second). No one will employ Onorio, certainly not Papa. We can't break the Papal architect's legs, but we can ridicule his craftsmanship, hoping his laborers might pick a fight with us.

"Is God going to let Papa die of gout? You'd think he'd grant him a more dignified death." With his onyx eyes, Orazio looks around for eavesdroppers, spies, or finks.

Pantomiming a yawn, Prospero covers his mouth and speaks into his hands. "God wasn't the one who force-fed him Parma ham for breakfast, lunch, and dinner."

It's dangerous talk, up there with heliocentrism. Four years ago, the pope burned my friend Bruno at the stake for heresy, Bruno kind of asked for it. He aspired to be a Socrates, a martyr of truth, the Christ of math and science. I watched him burn. More so, I smelled him burn. More so than that, I heard him burn. It moved me. I came to recognize myself as the Savior of painting. They'll kill me for it, for my dirty feet and crooked teeth, not for talking blasphemous smack on the street. I'm too big and connected for that. Unfortunately, my friends aren't.

"Ishay eathday isyay ouryay ifelay," Mario whispers in hog Latin.

He's the most paranoid among us, a side effect of having two wives. Mario was forced into marriage at fourteen. Months later, a wealthy merchant winked at his wife. Mario cut out his eye and fled Syracuse, leaving wifey behind. He sends money but never word of his new family or flourishing art career. Mario is a capable painter. He doesn't have to be great. I've painted him six meteoric ways to Sunday. He was my first love. My dewy lute player. My erotic boy with fruit. Unlike Cecco, he's the one who broke my heart. He wanted a quiet life. He wanted safe sex. No more looking over the shoulder during intercourse. No more cuddling on high alert. Close your eyes and love freely, unguarded. No God in the room. Caravaggio would have painted Mario and nothing but Mario until Papa finally delivered our decapitated head to God.

I'm hoping Cecco chooses a woman for his next lover. Otherwise my sacrifice will be for nothing.

We ascend the cordonata in double-file lockstep, Onorio leading from his charger, Mario at my shoulder. The servants trail rear flank. Arriving atop the square, we disperse in a squad line to survey the literal law of the land, to see what authorities are present before committing assault and/or battery. What we see alarms even us. Campidoglio is littered with cops, Spanish soldiers. Swiss guards, and two Knights of Malta. In unison, the entire platoon turns its collective sights on us. *This is them*, I think. *My killers*. In avoiding their gaze, I notice a wider and more chilling presence. A sea of cassocks and skullcaps in various colors. Black. Black and purple. Black and fuchsia. A smattering of scarlet galeros. Half the Vatican is here on a Tuesday dressed in their Sunday best. Needless to say, this ain't no place for street-fighting.

"Idday Apapay itshay ethay edbay?" Mario asks.

"We would have heard the Great Bells," Prospero answers.

Prospero is always our voice of reason, but I turn to Cecco for further reconnaissance. He's already read my mind, asking some wretched soul peddling wild mushrooms from a mangled basket about the crowd. He reports back at once.

"The pope is coming to bless the New Palace foundation."

I feel the news travel straight up Onorio's ass. I grimace on behalf of my proudest friend.

"It's why those mercs were huffing it downhill," Orazio says.

Onorio spins his charger toward the cordonata. It's not cowardice. It's sound judgment. His frustration will turn criminal if he stays. Turning to follow his lead, I catch sight of Cardinal del Monte by the statue of Marcus Aurelius. He commands me home with a sanctimonious finger wag. Del Monte is a bear-bodied man of peace and fornication. A young libertine couldn't ask for a better father figure. He's the only man that Michelangelo answers to, the only one that Caravaggio and I have ever known. When gouty Papa does shit the bed, Del Monte will have substantial say in appointing a successor. I hurry after Onorio in an attempt to avoid vocational self-sabotage.

We descend the cordonata and enter Market Square. This time through, I pay particularly painful mind to the racket of hammers and saws, the gay labor of monks constructing banquet tables and makeshift stalls. They've got pep, not toiling with their usual sobriety. Tomorrow is the Feast Day of the Archangel Saint Michael. The low-ranking clergy will be pigging out like cardinals. Tomorrow is also my name day. I will not be celebrating. If anything, I'll be fasting. Celebrating one's name day is asking for it, louder but not lusher than Bruno at the stake.

"Papa pissed on our Campidoglio plans, but God has brought the bordello halfway to us." Onorio's voice booms with vindication.

I pull my head from my remarkably sorry ass to find my ginger Magdalen before us. My Catherine condemned. My cut-throating Judith. My Fillide Melandroni approaches, posing through her most acclaimed Caravaggio roles, a cheeky tribute to her savior, yours truly. She was a street whore before I painted her. Now she's the priciest pro in Rome. Even when altogether quiet and still during modeling sessions, she never stopped talking or moving. So that's how I painted her, a dynamism of courage and wit. She taught me to value the true surfaces of an individual. Before Fillide, I was stuck on Mario's fixed and uninterested glamor. She fucked my genius to its senses. My pictures have bested life ever since. We made something of each other, and then she left me for the high life. Her present dress costs more than I made on *Judith Beheading Holofernes*. Its artichoke pattern sings to me.

Cecco deems *Saint Catherine* my masterpiece. He's Fillide's biggest fan. He keeps the pearl earrings she wore as Judith in a box, in his nightstand drawer, in his new room. Cecco has stood within the personal space of cardinals, dukes, and marchionesses. Fillide awes him most, but she's not the one who currently has him mesmerized. Nor is it Annuccia, the ginger pro beside her, my previous Mary and subsequent Martha. Cecco is gobsmacked by the resurrection of Lena Antognetti, the foxiest pro in Rome. She's there amongst her colleagues looking morose as ever. She was raped and impregnated by a crooked cop three years ago. The cop happened to be her sister Pila's main monger. After winning a scandalous incest trial, Lena fled Rome to bear the bastard in anonymity, but now she's back, bodacious as ever. Ecstatic shivers shoot up my spine, or maybe it's just my sweat turning cold. The sun has taken shelter behind a cloud.

I bow to the pros, holding eye contact with Lena.

"A little birdie told me that you're looking for a Virgin," Fillide says.

She motions to Lena. Her hair is big and slutty, but her gown uppity, imperial black, chichi tight as if sewn to her skin. The neckline is all the way down to Napoli. She would be a Virgin to end all Virgins, but Lena appears as detached as my Mario musician. She wouldn't have me five years ago. My sword was too heavy, my purse too slender. The contrariety of those proportions has only widened. I'm mad and broke as ever.

"Her career needs rebooting. Starring in your pictures would put her back on top. She has a son to feed," Fillide says.

I motion to Cecco. Let him weigh the idea. He nods so hard his neck almost snaps. I turn to Lena.

"Happy name day," she says, perfectly unaffected, maybe a slight whimsicality in the corners of her eyes and small mouth.

"You want to be my Virgin?" I ask.

"A pro posing as the Virgin? They'll kill us both." Her Mona Lisa smile cracks into something more artful.

Mario draws his dagger. "No hope! No fear!"

Onorio dismounts, draws, and echoes the battle cry. Orazio and Prospero too. As lads, we terrorized the streets of Rome, shouting this favorite creed of ours. Hearing it inspires Lena to step toward me. I offer my elbow. She hooks it. I escort her from Market Square to the vulgar cheering of our closest friends. Cecco frontrunning our campaign.

IV.

We sleep in on my name day. Languished by sex, we feel each other out, half-aware of the full reality blooming between us. We're so into each other. She on her side. Me on mine. Her face in my throat. My chin on her forehead. Her arm scooped under my ribs. My leg over her hip. First, it's the smells of the Archangel's Feast. Roasting chestnuts. Burning oak. Scorching pig. The richest foods for the poorest folks. Her stomach growls. Mine whines. She slides her hand over my ass, the same ass in *Matthew Killed*. I bring my knee between her. She presses into it. We drift off, Lena a few breaths ahead of me.

Then it's bells of various sizes from unequal distances. Then trumpets and snares. A drumfire of artillery followed by the hissing gibberish of fireworks. I share my feast day with the celebration of harvest and my virtual grandfather's Lepanto victory. On this particular name day, I'm honored and appreciative. We stir and feel around, squirming into each other, starting up again. By the time we're too sore and numb, it's sometime closer to eve than noon, the room darker than my darkest picture. I can't speak for Lena, but I'm wading in it, searching for a sense of her fulfillment. A sheet of light projects from a crack between the closed shutters, striking my armor that slumps in the corner like some relinquished self.

"It smells like a civet dragged its anus across your chest," she says.

"I paid the civet twenty scudi."

"I hear you go by Caravaggio now. Who's that? That's a town. Such a person doesn't exist."

"It's mostly a stage name. I'm still the same old Lombard hick, only poorer."

"But not angrier?"

Violence sickens Lena. She blacked out when the executioner smashed Giacomo Cenci's head with a mallet at Sant'Angelo Bridge. She slept through the quartering of his corpse and the beheadings of his young sisters, Lucrezia and Beatrice. I carried Lena's deadweight home, cursing Papa under labored breaths. The Cenci kids murdered the aristocratic dad who habitually raped them. Papa should declare a holy day whenever Isaac turns the knife on Abraham.

Lena kisses me on the eye and leaves to care for her son. He's home with his nanny. They live with another man, a lawyer no less. Gaspare Albertini raises her son as his own. He's a decent man, a bourgeois bookworm. I'll probably have to rough him up at some point. For now, I remain in bed, alone, replaying the euphoria I just endured. I'm soon interrupted by my posse singing outside my window, *The Triumph of Bacchus*. Mario tenors. Cecco countertenors.

I sleep like Bordone's Venus and upon awaking, I recline like Titian's, staring at the door, caressing myself. I stay as is for days, listening for Lena's footsteps. I leave bed to fill my pot. Cecco empties it. He also serves me wine and heirloom cos lettuce. He's genuinely happy to see me beaming, but after a few days, he wants me converting that energy into pictures.

"What are you waiting for? Get up. Paint the Virgins," he says. "I've primed a canvas."

"She feels too good. I don't want to muck this up by making art out of it."

"You've always mucked your best models."

"This is different. She's too meta for art. I couldn't even make her fade."

"It sounded like she was fading. I definitely heard you fading. Three times."

I bring my hand from my balls to itch my nose. Cecco drops another rent notice onto my abs. Now we're four months back. I crumple the note and toss it into the pot. I miss. Cecco leaves without picking it up.

I watch the room darken, reflecting on Lena, hoarding her residuals for myself, Michelangelo tries punching his way in. Caravaggio makes loud demands for his Virgin. I fall asleep to shut them up.

Sometime after the curfew bell of Our Lady of the Soul, I hear Lena jiggling the lock of my front door. I gave her the key. She jokingly offered the key to her man's house in return, the lawyer who buys drab dresses, who doesn't know that she's back on the streets. She keeps her chichi work dresses at her sister's. I wonder if the bookworm makes her fade.

The front door closes and locks. She trots the hallway, her steps hurried by love. I feel that energy enter the impossible blackness of the room as she skitters in, kicking the crumpled note on her way to me. She clumsily dives onto the bed, landing ungracefully, a shoulder in my sternum, a knee narrowly missing my groin. I catch her excitement from careening onto the floor. We laugh and roll right into sex. She is soft but the force of her is like nothing I've met save the cop I murdered in Milan. He was punching me dumb until I drove a dagger through his throat. She carries his intensity, but hers is revitalizing. The miracle of Lena is that she exorcises my ghosts. She comes at me all night. I battle back but can't make her fade. She seems fulfilled, or maybe she's being polite.

We sleep heavy and intertwined. We wake and love some more. I try everything. I try everything twice, but she still doesn't fade. She leaves to care for her son. She comes and goes like this for weeks but never fades. The heat of summer rises to heaven. Daylight shortens. Lettuce falls out of season. Cecco brings pomegranates and grapes, ripe as the ones in *Boy with a Basket of Fruit*. My armor collects considerable dust.

The nights she's not here, I lie in bed listening to the traffic, the three-beat canter of passing chargers. When Papa dies, when I land monster commissions from his Del Monte-appointed replacement, I'm buying myself a badass charger. I'll trick the beast out. Teach him to capriole and courbette. I'll train him to kick, strike, and bite like the horses of Attila. On Sunday mornings, I'll park my charger in the middle of a crowded square, sitting high and mighty, eating donuts, getting eye-fucked, looking bored.

Lena comes. Lena goes without fading. She comes back for more and consoles me after I cum.

"Rome wasn't built in a day," she says.

"I need to make you fade." I pillow my head on her armpit.

"You made me fall in love."

"I'd rather you fade."

"Fading makes me cold. It cools my blood. My hands and feet freeze. I need to stay hot."

An almighty knock raps the front door thrice.

"That's a heavy fist for an old landlady. She have a son?"

"Yeah, but he's a wuss," I say.

I slide out of bed and slip into my breastplate just in case. I haven't worn it since my name day. It feels like bumping into someone you've been avoiding.

"You want to put on some pants?" Lena asks rhetorically.

I tiptoe down the hall to the front door with every expectation that it's Signora Bruni. If so, I'll return to bed and let her stand at the stoop another four months. I spy through the peephole. The thuggish bureaucrat. He's unarmed, his beard thickened for the coming winter.

"Fuck you want?" I inquire through the door.

"Is Master Caravaggio home?"

"Duh."

"I am Fabio Masetti, ambassador to the Duke of Modena."

"And?"

"The duke wishes to commission a picture."

"No thanks."

"He's already commissioned your rival Master Carracci to paint a Madonna of the Rosary. He'd like you to paint one as well. A friendly contest. A comparing and contrasting of expression between Rome's best painters."

Kings and queens are terrible art patrons. They pay like shit and bleed you if unsatisfied with the work. Next to popes, dukes are the best patrons. They don't have king money, but close to it. They also don't have the kingly expenses, nor the kingly authoritarianism. Unlike kings and popes, dukes don't care who you fuck.

"How much money you got?"

"I have a blank check from the Duke of Modena...once a contract is signed."

"No. How much do *you* have on you this very moment?"

"I don't know...Maybe twenty scudi."

"Slide it under the door. Down payment. He can have his Virgin after I finish my others."

The coins come sliding under the door. I collect them and gallop back to the room, peeling myself out of the plackart. Lena reclines in the buff like no woman in any painting ever.

"That was an ambassador."

"I heard."

"The Duke of Modena wants a Virgin."

"I heard."

"You've healed my headaches. My remarkable sadness too. I want to deify you and your son."

I offer her the scudi. She evil-eyes the coins and then me.

"Offer me money again, and I'll hex your cock with leprosy."

I drop the coins to the floor. They patter and jangle. One of them whirls for eternity.

"Please be my Virgin. I want to immortalize you."

"But it has to be *you* who paints me, not this *Caravaggio*."

"It'll be me."

"Will it hurt?"

"More than anything," I say.

"Good."

I faint onto the bed. She mauls me half-dead. I don't even try fucking back. Defending myself isn't an option. Let her put me in my place. I have it coming.

V.

I haven't seen Lena in days. Her absence has caused another remarkable sadness to suffuse my being. Nothing too intense. Think bleary twilight of pre-dawn. Only it's dusk. At least I think it's dusk. I'm positive it's Sunday. Church bells don't lie. Nor does the smell of frying donuts. I'm in bed. The shutters are closed. I haven't eaten enough to shit, but I've been thinking nonstop about how to paint my Virgin. For the first time in months, I'm fretting over the time I'm wasting. Caravaggio wants to rise and shine, but all we can do is lie and wait for her. Michelangelo doesn't do women. He's happier to have Cecco sitting shirtless on the edge of the bed, reading the Gospel of Luke aloud by lamplight, Gabriel annunciating the pregnancy of a virgin lass.

"*For he that is mighty hath done to me great things; and holy is his name.* Could be talking about you and me. Or just about anyone gazing into a Caravaggio," he says.

He flashes that smile, hoping to eat Lena's scraps. A quintuple wrap comes at the front door. Onorio's secret knock. Cecco closes the Bible and fetches my breeches, tossing them onto the bed. I kick them to the floor, opting to shame my junk with nearby pomegranate peels. Cecco buttons up his blouse and leaves, returning with Onorio and Menicuccia, a curved and raucous colleague of Lena's. Menicuccia is Onorio's favorite amongst the real gals of Rome, her dander nearly rivaling his. He's dressed in casual velvet. He's also unarmed. It's illegal to carry a sword into a brothel, meaning he came straight here after moistening his pope. Menicuccia is dressed to the nines but looking smeared and wrinkled by sex.

"Now *that's* a basket of fruit," Onorio says, pointing to the pomegranate peels.

Menicuccia has seen it all before, but that doesn't stop her from taking a hard look.

"I've got infuriating news and I've got exciting news. Which do you want first?" Onorio asks.

I look to Cecco, signaling for him to answer.

"We'll take infuriation first," he says, carrying my sword and armor out of the room.

"Ranuccio Tomassoni wants money for all the times you've fucked Lena since your name day," Menicuccia says.

I sit up, the first time since Lena last left. "We don't fuck. We make love. Since when is Tomassoni her pimp?"

"Since he threatened to tell her man that she was back to working the streets."

"He heard about Lena modeling for your Virgin. He knew it would jack her value exponentially," says Onorio.

"That little pecker did the same thing after I made Fillide a star. Recruited her as a client and exchanged her amongst the Farnese crowd for top scudo."

"I broke his hand for that," Onorio says.

Four years ago, Onorio did me the favor of disciplining the conniving pimp. I was deathly ill. The start of my headaches and remarkable sadness, when God unleashed my ghosts upon me.

"This time I'll cut Ranuccio's hand off," I say.

Cecco returns with two apples. He offers them to our guests. Onorio accepts. Menicuccia declines. Onorio takes hers.

"Lena doesn't want to live a Greek drama," Cecco says. "She doesn't want you going all Michelangelo on Ranuccio. Ranuccio will kill Lena. Michelangelo will kill Ranuccio. Papa will execute Caravaggio."

"How do *you* know what Lena wants?" I ask.

"I ran into her at the greengrocer. She wants to love you forever, but that can't happen if Papa beheads you. She needs time to think. She also needs money to feed her son."

I stand from bed. The pomegranate peels fall to my toes. I give Cecco my look of all looks, the psychopathic scowl of my Abraham as the angel coaches him into dropping the knife.

"When were you going to tell me?"

"She told me to wait before telling you."

"Wait for what?"

"The right moment."

"Who told Ranuccio that she was modeling for my Virgin?" I pose the question to the three of them.

"Are you ready for the exciting news?" Onorio's asks with a mania that fingers his favorite pro.

"We're ready," Cecco answers, forgoing my approval to speak.

"A new star has appeared in the sky," Onorio says. "Brighter than Sirius. It's been shining day and night."

The news floors me, but I offer no sign of it.

"A new star? What could it mean?" Cecco asks.

Even Onorio Longhi, Rome's roughest ruffian thinks twice before uttering blasphemy in a shuttered bedroom amongst close friends.

"The heavens ain't fixed. The cosmos moves," he says under breath.

"Maybe it's the signaling of a new messiah," Menicuccia says.

"It can't be a new Messiah. I'm not dead yet. I'm not done setting the cosmos in motion." I bend for my breeches and pull them up.

"Your abs are popping," Menicuccia says.

I accept her flattery as an apology for leaking the news of my Virgin to her pimp.

"Let's grab some dinner and see this so-called star," I say.

Before leaving, Menicuccia helps herself to another hard look. I slip into my cloak and reach for my dagger on the nightstand. Cecco catches my hand. His fingernails are filthy, just how I like them, how I painted them in *Matthew Inspired*, the angelic hoodlum counting off digits, outlining plot points to the author of Mary's immaculate conception.

"Leave the dagger. Make Lena happy. At least this once," he tells me.

The apprentice pounces on his chance to teach the master. I hear him loud and clear. If I want to be Lena's slave, her desires have to come first, annihilating mine in the process.

We walk to the tavern with our chins up, fixated on the sparkling phenom in the dusky sky. The star is brighter than the moon and larger than Alpha Scorpii. We divine its meaning in silence, stepping on each other's heels, pelvises bumping asses in ungainly euphoria. Its mysterious presence is forceful, sexy, but I'm in no mood. Lena has a pimp. Her pimp thinks he's God's gift to selling sex. At least my remarkable sadness is in remission. The ghosts are making space for Ranuccio Tomassoni.

We stop to stretch our necks, eyeing each other, confirming what we've witnessed. The cosmos has a new idol. We return our perceptions to it, but I'd rather be eating something. I smell roasted pumpkin, tonight's special at the tavern. I suggest we keep walking, but Onorio and Menicuccia are captivated. Cecco arches in wonder, his spine defying gravity. Most passersby gawk at yours truly, the superstar, head tilted, baring his throat to God. Others hastily move along for fear of what I or Onorio might do to them, but a chosen few schlep their woe straight by me without noticing a goddamn thing. They wouldn't know Michelangelo Buonarotti from Michelangelo Merisi, and good on them. The wretched have far greater concerns. Rome is leaving them behind as its cranes and scaffolding reach heavenward. Every city block is on the rise. Lawyers constructing handsome villas. Aristocrats renovating palaces. Expanding public squares. Why look at any of it? Rome is metastasizing too, and this so-called star is yet another demoralizing development.

I fear that it's not a new star, but a hole through which God is projecting his illustrious jurisdiction upon Rome, upon yours truly. He's been overlooking me all these years, more concerned with Michelangelo and Caravaggio. God has historically ignored yours truly. In the past, He has chosen to underestimate me, downplaying my role in producing Caravaggio pictures. Maybe He's catching on. Maybe He can now see that I've got my own delusions of grandeur. Maybe He's been watching me chip away at my escape tunnel. He's punctured a channel of his own, a hole in the floor of His kingdom, a camera obscura to capture my escape. He'll off me if I succeed. He'll off me for misusing Cecco, and then He'll take my place as Caravaggio's inner voice. God would love nothing more than to have the genius' ear, but He can't kill me if I'm attached to this being, not without offing his beloved Caravaggio. Maybe I'm better off locked away in this cell.

I almost believe this nonsense. I nearly buy into the self-conceited prophecy. I'm on the brink of falling for my own dogma when two sapient faces emerge from the dying twilight.

"Don't look too long. They'll burn you for heresy," says the man closest, tipping his broad-brimmed, ostrich-plumed pilgrim hat.

He's dressed like a Duke Dildo, but I know him better than that. His name is Ottaviano Gabrielli. He owns the best bookstore in Rome, specializing in banned texts. He sells everything on Papa's Index— Dante's *Monarchy*, Erasmus' *Praise of Folly*, Petrarch's *Babylonian Sonnets*, and of course the entire works of my scorched friend Bruno.

The other man is Paolo Martinelli, the ugliest man in Rome. We call him Fright. We call him Fright to his face. He's a good sport about it. He works the nickname with pros. It earns him their sympathy. "You're not *that* unappealing," they say, staring at the smallpox scars through his beard. Aside from hustling his nickname, Fright is the most honest man in Rome, the city's most reliable courier. He transmits information for Papa and his nephew Cardinal Aldobrandini, who just today was ordained Archbishop of Ravenna. Fright's new Rome-Ravenna route will earn him enough coin for a snazzy new coach. This latest fortuity has already done his face a bit of justice, along with the deepening shadows of nightfall.

"Fright brought me two letters today. One from Delle Colombe. One from Galileo. Delle Colombe says the star has always been there. He says that we're just seeing it now due to some alteration of cosmic clouds. I bet you can guess what Galileo is saying."

Gabrielli doesn't care if anyone hears his blasphemy. He's been jailed before. He'll be jailed again. They'll never burn him for it. Too many cardinals and monsignors buy his books.

"I hear you've accepted a third Virgin commission. Have you finished the other two?" Fright asks.

I look to Cecco to answer, but he's still bending over backwards for the new superstar. I don't know what to tell Fright. God's up there giving me the evil eye, expecting greatness but secretly hoping for sin. Damn me if I do. Damn me if I don't. Fright doesn't take my reticence personally. He's a firm believer in the artistic temperament. Cutting me slack, he lifts his sights to the superstar. Menicuccia fixates on his scars.

"That roasted pumpkin is making my stomach growl."

I say it loud enough for all of Rome to hear, but my friends are too caught up in the glaring evidence. Galileo is right. Caravaggio doesn't stand at the center of the universe, but I'm still big enough to warrant God's surveillance. I close my eyes and listen for Him. I hear nothing but the disappointing quiet of fatherly expectations. I listen closer, beyond the dissipating joy of a Sunday night, beyond the offbeat clacking of well-heeled Romans (the wooden soles of haughty culture). Beyond that I hear Lena fading to the thrusts of her bookworm. I hear Mario playing lute. I hear Isaac giving Abraham all hell. I hear someone call me an asshole from across the street.

"Michelangelo Merisi da Caravaggio has a greasy fucking asshole," the voice repeats as if the entire street hadn't heard the first time.

I grab for my sword. Its absence feels phantom-limbless. Onorio fumbles around for nothing too. Gabrielli is a pacifist. The only blade that Fright carries is a letter opener.

"Hey, Michele! You owe me three scudi," the voice shouts.

"It's Tomassoni," says Menicuccia.

"Three scudi? You only made love seven times. How much is he charging for Lena?" Cecco does the division on his fingers, like the angel in my *Matthew Inspired*.

Michelangelo wants to gallop across the street and trample Ranuccio with his fists and feet, but I reign him in. Four silhouettes lurk in the shadow. Ranuccio has three older brothers, all veteran soldiers and mercs for the Farnese family who would kill for little more than a bowl of cannellini beans, for a Farnese pat on the back. The Tomassoni brothers wear their blades in the bathtub. They wear them to the brothel. They're sure as shit armed right now. Onorio and I are better swordsmen, but right now our only weapon is a letter opener. The Tomassoni assume we're packing rapiers and daggers, otherwise they'd be over here cutting us up.

"Caravaggio gobbles cock!" The voice isn't Ranuccio's. It's too baritone.

I pick up a rock and side-arm it at the tallest silhouette. I lose sight of the rock's trajectory, but see the Goliath fall to one knee, genuflecting in pain. Cecco hucks a rock of his own, and the Goliath falls flat on his face. A rock hums by my ear, and thumps Menicuccia in the tit. She groans, picks up the very rock, and heaves it back from whence it came. Onorio rapid-fires three rocks. Gabrielli drops to the pavers and curls up, arms covering his head. I drag him behind a nearby perfumer's cart. The scent of civet anus makes me smile. I'd rather be exchanging steel, but this is pretty damn fun.

The perfumer abandons his cart, and the others join me and Gabrielli behind the barricade. We throw and duck, but there are only so many rocks to be had, so we sit low, practically in each other's laps, waiting for ammunition to return. The next round comes without anyone suffering a serious wound. As we gather the rocks, someone from the crowd shouts *cops*.

I pitch a final rock at a fleeing Tomassoni. Whoever it is stumbles, but unfortunately regains his footing. We laugh like hell until three cops interrupt our victory dancing, Corporal Malanno blowing his whistle like the excitable hard-on he is. He's been busting my balls since the day I arrived in Rome a naked and starving wretch.

"Merisi, what shit are you stirring now?" he asks, pushing his chest in my face.

"Just defending my honor," Michelangelo answers.

"Defending your honor?" asks the cop I've never seen. He must be a recruit. I barely recognize the other cop without a donut in his fat face.

"Ranuccio Tomassoni insulted his manhood," Onorio says.

"How?" Malanno asks.

"He said I gobble cock."

"Well? Don't you?" Malanno replies.

His shit-eating grin is too much for Michelangelo. Michelangelo is too much for yours truly. He blurts it out before I can censor him.

"Do you suck the recruit's cock between donut breaks?"

Malanno pulls his sword and orders his underlings to cuff me. I don't resist. I offer my wrists. They knot them tight. I smile at Gabrielli.

"Tell the Duchess Olimpia Aldobrandini that I'm at the precinct. She won't be happy, the cops harassing her favorite genius."

Olimpia Aldobrandini is niece to Papa and sister to the new Archbishop of Ravenna. She's also Gabrielli's secret lover. Fright delivers her mail. I look to Cecco and give my first command since kicking him out of bed.

"Go buy some donuts. I'll be home to eat them before they're stale."

Cecco sprints off. I never have to tell him anything twice. I look to Onorio and wink. He winks back and points to the sky. God is still staring me down. I tilt my head all the way back and spit in His eye. Believing that my saliva was aimed for him, Malanno puts me to sleep with the hilt of his sword.

VI.

The donuts are stale. I eat them anyway. Eating my own words tastes like the rotten grapes in my *Sick Bacchus*, and speaking of fermentation, I'm day-drinking, but at least I'm out of bed. I'm actually dressed and sitting up at my three-legged kitchen table. Cecco sits across from me, shirtless, wearing his wings, reading Bruno aloud. Lena didn't visit me in jail. I was there thirty-six hours, and not even a note. I chew on her cold shoulder, rubbing the bump atop my skull. Thanks to Malanno's hilt, I'm obsessing over a lesser, albeit more unnerving headache.

"*Unless you make yourself equal to God, you cannot understand God,*" Cecco reads. "*Make yourself grow to a greatness beyond measure, free yourself from the body, raise yourself above all time, become eternity, and then you will understand God.*"

"*Think yourself immortal. Mount higher than the highest height. Descend lower than the lowest depth,*" I recite back.

"*If you embrace in your thought all things at once, times, places, substances, qualities, and quantities, you may understand God.* Or one could place themselves in the company of a Caravaggio and experience the same magnificence," Cecco adds.

He's not wrong. He and Bruno are being blasphemous for all the right reasons, but I can't believe it, not when I've lost my Virgin and Mary Magdalene to a two-bit pimp. Michelangelo's ego won't accept that. My heart won't survive it. My nerves won't withstand the insurrection of ghosts. Lena wards off Michelangelo's evil, and she's the first woman who's preferred me to Caravaggio. In fact, she doesn't even believe in Caravaggio. She thinks it's just me and Michelangelo in here. In turn, Caravaggio doesn't believe in her. He thinks he can transform any old pro into a Virgin. Nobody, not yours truly or God could tell him otherwise.

"Good thing you weren't carrying a sword the other night," Cecco says. "Otherwise, that rock fight wouldn't have happened. What a blast!"

"I won't leave the house unarmed again. My enemies list has four new names. The Tomassoni brothers are known for ambushing enemies. They specialize in fighting dirty."

"Why leave the house at all? Stay inside. Paint that naked selfie. Paint the John commission. Let's head upstairs right now. I'll model."

Cecco stands from the table and places a hand on my shoulder as if imbuing me with some creative spirit. His feathers shave my cheek.

"Paint the John, but not another mopey John. Your previous Johns. A naked John with ram. Revisit the pagan sexual energy."

I shrug and throw back some wine, giving the swole selfie some serious thought. I'm halfway to convincing Caravaggio when a measured triple knock steals me from myself. The knock is too businesslike for Lena, too courteous for the landlady or thuggish bureaucrat.

"A Tomassoni? Should I get your sword?" Cecco asks, slipping out of his wings.

I stand for the first time in hours. The world tilts. I reach to steady myself, placing a hand on the legless surface area. The table totters. Luckily, Cecco is there to steady it and save my wine from spilling. I take a grateful swig.

"I've got this," I say on my way to the front hall.

I open the door without checking the peephole, fully accepting whoever bringing whatever fate. As God would have it, that person is Cardinal Del Monte's young and dapper gopher requesting my presence at Firenze Palace.

"Right now?" I ask.

"More like five minutes ago," he replies.

The lad is only half as handsome as he thinks and carries Del Monte's imperium up his ass. I'm existentially obligated to heed his summons. I step outside swordless, barefoot, and buzzing. The noontime sun whitewashes the street. Not a shadow to be had anywhere along the tall defensive wall bordering my alley from Firenze Palace. Del Monte works there assisting the French interests of Ferdinando de' Medici, the Grand Duke of Tuscany. It's no coinkydink that I live a literal skip, hop, and jump from the office of my lord and protector. I cross the street and make my way to Del Monte, dragging a hand along the shadeless wall for balance. The gopher slipstreams in my wobbly ego.

We turn the corner onto Via dei Prefetti and I look to the sky. God's eye is there, adjudicating me in broad daylight, searching for a way inside this head, trying to outshine Caravaggio's superstardom in the process. The weekday hustle of every femme-fop entrepreneur is at a standstill, suspended in lofty contemplation of Rome's newest celebrity. They question the worth of their silk shoes and satin capes, oblivious to yours truly, the unshod superstar fresh out of jail. They wouldn't know God if he kicked them in the face with His scuzzy foot.

"Duke Dildos are the worst." The comment is for Michelangelo, but the gopher assumes I'm talking to him.

"They're paying no attention to you. This is the fifth time I've trailed you to the palace. Usually, there are so many eyes on us that I feel painted onto the Sistine ceiling."

"Gaudy Duke Dildos hoodwinked by a chintzy star."

"What do *you* think it is?"

"Smoke and mirrors. The camera obscura of a prankster."

"You ever fuck Del Monte?" he asks plainly.

I can't answer because I don't know, which is to say I can't remember.

"Have *you*?" I ask, keeping my eyes on myself.

"Yes, but only because I thought you did."

I burn the lad with silence. His neediness is not my problem. God made me an idol. He made everyone else susceptible to tyrannization. He made it so for His own amusement. I look up and wink, a sarcastic gesture to the prankster-in-chief, the chintzy goldbricker.

The interior of Firenze Palace is gilded floor to ceiling. Gilded molding and cornices. Gilded cabinetry and furniture. Enough Catholic ornamentation to make Martin Luther combust with indignation. I too am on the verge of combustion as I pass through a series of galleries adorned with the paintings of friends and enemies. There's not a single Caravaggio. Madama Palace houses six, but this is not my lord and protector's home. He doesn't get to decorate his office. He merely works here, assisting Ferdinand de' Medici in his quest to eradicate Protestantism and help the French out-Catholic the Spanish. Ferdinand doesn't live here either, not anymore. He moved back to Firenze after usurping the dukedom by slowly poisoning his brother. He poisoned his sister-in-law too and banished their ten-year-old son. Florentine by birth, Ferdinand de' Medici is the quintessential Roman, his ascendancy a result of beauty, brilliance, strength, charm, moxie, back-stabbing, cut-throating, and fratricide.

Everyone working in the palace is a Medici cousin or in-law auditioning for a role in my next picture. They'd forfeit their pedigree to be an eternal peasant with filthy feet, a boundless vagabond with rotten teeth. The Medici bureaucrats make their best tragedy masks as I pass, hoping I might see something in them, but not even a Caravaggio could render them miserable. They're too polished and blessed. I don't hate them. They're good people. They just don't deserve eternity.

The gopher leads me to Del Monte's office. I genuflect factiously before entering, head down in pretend penitence. I served my time for calling that cocksucker cop what he is, and now I'm here to be dressed down by my lord and protector, but it's not just Del Monte sitting on the cushy walnut sofa. Mamma is parked next to him. My two guardians are sipping pure evil from the finest china, the beverage of choice for Turk and Arab infidels. Last year, Papa legalized coffee after his first tasting. Del Monte has been fiending on it, and now he's got Mamma hooked. I'm disappointed. She can see it on my face. My displeasure causes her great joy. Mamma hates joy, her own in particular.

"My father would kill me if he saw me drinking coffee," she says. "He defeated the Ottomans and for what, so his little princess could slurp their demonic brew?"

Del Monte dips a thumb in his coffee and signs the cross on her forehead. They burst with laughter and collapse against each other. Some wicked current has demented them. Del Monte composes himself and stares down at my bare feet. He shakes his head.

"What?" I ask.

"What." he replies.

"My feet. You gave them a look."

"Yes." He sips more coffee, not breaking eye contact.

Del Monte is a man of peace, fornication, and silence. He banks secrets like the Medici bank banks. Our exchange was chatty for him. Something is up. I'm here for a scolding, but not the scolding I had coming. Michelangelo already feels guilty.

He and Mamma make room for me on the sofa. Mamma pats the space between them. Del Monte pours me a cup. I'm a little terrified. I've never had coffee. Hopefully, it will deliver the best possible evil. I sniff at my cup. The heady aroma percolates my existing wine buzz. Del Monte waves the gopher from the room. Del Monte and Mamma hit me with that pitiable look of theirs, the one I deserve and want.

"Must we give you the speech?" Mamma asks.

"What speech?" I ask coyly.

"The one about you being a supernatural genius. Sometimes we feel as if you get into trouble *just* to hear us say it."

Del Monte places a bear paw on my knee. His hands are immense and heavy as fuck.

"Why are you throwing rocks at pimps and *not* painting a Virgin?" Mamma asks.

I suck down some coffee. All the Caravaggio goes straight to my head.

"Speaking of heavenly celebrities. Why aren't you outside marveling at the new superstar?" I ask.

"We're hiding from it," Mamma says. "I'm not going outdoors until that thing's gone. I'm sure it's something awful. Besides, I'm only concerned with stars that revolve around me."

"I saw you and your cohorts at Campidoglio," Del Monte says.

"A little birdie told us that Longhi was going to assault the Papal architect."

"Let him self-sabotage his career without your help." Del Monte grips my knee as if confirming the ripeness of a melon.

They're talking at a frenzied rate, which scares me into guzzling more coffee, this time singeing my tongue.

"There's nothing noble about jeopardizing your career to avenge a friend's damaged ego," says Mamma

She places a hand on my other knee and tugs it in the opposite direction of Del Monte's tugging. I wish they'd just wishbone me already.

"The brawling. The drinking. The poppy. You're making yourself unemployable," Del Monte warns.

"I'm dying of something. Headaches. Exhaustion. Bouts of

remarkable sadness. I think it has something to do with that superstar in the sky."

"You can't die. The church needs you," Del Monte says to Caravaggio, wholly incognizant of my existence.

"Needs *my* pictures," I reply.

"I need my Michele to *not* get himself shanked by a pimp."

Michelangelo spurs me to stand in protest.

"I could outduel any Tomassoni drunk and left-handed! I could outduel Ranuccio with just my dagger! I could outduel him, headache, exhaustion, remarkable sadness and all! I'm as good a swordsman as an artist!"

"I know. I paid for your art tutor and rapier lessons. By twelve, you were a better swordsman than some of our guards. We thought you were going to be the next Marcantonio. You turned out to be the next Michelangelo."

"You're also brilliant with a tennis racquet." Del Monte pulls me back down on the sofa.

I take a deep breath and an even deeper mouthful of coffee. Del Monte refills my cup.

"The Tomassoni brothers have the entire Farnese militia behind them, thousands of bored mercs itching to kill," says Mamma.

"My posse could cull the entire Tomassoni clan," I reply.

"Yes, and then the entire Farnese militia will come for you," Del Monte says.

"What? The Farnese are more powerful than the Aldobrandini all of a sudden?"

"No, but Papa just avoided a potentially cataclysmic war with the Farnese. He won't risk another over an artist who paints pros and sleeps with his apprentice. It doesn't matter if his niece thinks you're Jesus Christ with a paintbrush. Amity is good for business. Both families are making money hand over fist these days, and even the *Pieta* is only worth so much." Mamma makes a fist and lovingly chips my chin.

"Stay out of prison. Keep your neck off the chopping block. By this time next year, you'll have altarpieces in churches all over Europe," Del Monte says.

"By this time next year, you'll be cruising Rome in your own coach," says Mamma.

"By this time, five hundred years from now, you'll be known as Caravaggio's foster parents."

Del Monte whispers into his cup. "Ethay opepay isyay yingday."

I stand to honor the news.

"Olyhay uckfay," I say. "Let's wait for him to get good and delirious, and then hit him up for a commission."

"Dim and deranged with fever, he still wouldn't patronize you," Del Monte says.

"He knows your name too well," says Mamma.

"How? How does he know so much about me?" I ask.

"He reads the newspapers," says Del Monte. "He knows your violence. He read your dirty Baglione limericks. He knows you throw rocks at cops."

"So, it's useless. I can die. The church doesn't need me. It doesn't even want me."

"Cardinal Alessandro Ottoviano de' Medici wants you," Del Monte says.

The name rings a bell, but the reverberations dissipate before assigning a face, leaving only a silent vibration between my ears that intensifies and throbs behind the eyeballs. I become intensely focused, but on nothing whatsoever. Not the eleven gray whiskers in Del Monte's auburn beard. Not Mamma's off-white incisor. It's not a useful focus. I couldn't paint with it. It's a focus that generates too much reality, even for a phantasmal being like me.

"Which one is Cardinal de' Medici?" I try blinking away the sudden blind spots in my vision.

"The one with the red cassock and skullcap," Del Monte replies.

That's funny. Del Monte is never funny. It must be the fucking coffee.

"Cardinal de' Medici attended Santa Maria last Sunday and saw your *Christ Buried*. It demolished him. Jesus' hulking arms drooping toward earth. He's been hearing the hammering of nails all week," Mamma says.

"Half the city is under construction," I reply.

"He's been hearing it at night in his sleep," Del Monte says.

"I didn't paint the Savior's wounds."

"You did better. You painted his humanity," says Mamma.

"So, what? Another cardinal buys a picture for a few hundred scudi, and three months later I'm behind on rent again. What does this have to do with Papa's gout?"

"Ehay illway ebay ouryay ewnay Apapay," Del Monte says in syllables.

"He wants to be your Lorenzo the Magnificent," says Mamma.

The blind spots protract into dazzling orbs, two in my left eye. I sip more coffee hoping to remedy them. It does not do the trick. The intense focus thickens, and I become overstimulated by some good-for-nothing zest. It's like some hyper-inspiration before death. Papa is dying. The new Papa wants me to be his Divine One. I feel like a Carracci character looks, accentuated, emotionally pornographic.

"I don't feel so hot," I say, unlacing my blouse.

I can't see their reactions. There are filmy holes in their faces.

"Get busy. Stay alive. You'll be rewarded exponentially by your new Papa." Del Monte says it so fast that I barely understand.

"Paint the Virgins. Show that dreadful superstar in the sky who's boss," says Mamma.

"Have you found a model for the Virgin?" Del Monte asks.

I shrug hard. I shrug the blouse right off my shoulders.

"Your Virgin can't be prettier than me. Your Judith. Your Mary Magdalene. She was a spitting image."

"You've always been a second mother to me," I say courageously.

"Your mother was a work of art. You got your talent from her. You get the warmongering from my side of the family."

Caravaggio is insulted. His talent doesn't have a wellspring. But I heartily accept the comment. It's the nicest thing she's ever said. I've been waiting for Mamma to recognize our bloodline since Lucia died when I was nineteen. Michelangelo's been waiting since before that. I wish I was in a better state to receive it. Someone has driven a dagger through my eye. The worst headache of my life. I excuse myself and head for the door, only seeing half of everything.

"Would you rather stand over the pimp or stand at an altar in St. Peter's?" Del Monte asks.

"Perhaps those who pronounce my sentence are in greater fear than I who receive it," I answer, quoting Bruno.

"I'll remember you said that," he replies.

"Go home and paint as if your life depends on it," Mamma says.

"Close the door behind you," Del Monte commands.

I exit, leaving it open.

I pass through the palace shirtless and barefoot, the globules smearing everything in my path. I feel the Medici eyes on me, the aspiring models. Despite the twisting dagger in my skull, I don't shirk the opportunity of a teaching moment.

"This is what an agonizing face looks like. Not contorted and crinkled, but pale and placid."

The comment draws applause, but I'm too anguished to care. I flee the palace and turn onto Via dei Prefetti. The sunlight is brutal. It ratchets the pain ten, eleven, twelve notches. A charger canters past. Some monger's donkey plods forth. The clacking and clopping go right to my brain. I close my good eye and look to God through the kaleidoscopic impairment of my other. I curse Him for this almighty pain. So intense. So located and persistent. I've done so much to deserve it. I close my afflicted eye and hear Lena fading all over Rome. The aching makes me sick. I lean a hand against the great wall of Firenze and vomit against it, splattering my toes and shins with black Satanic liquid.

VII.

When I arrive at my stoop, the landlady is there with her hands out. Prudenzia Bruni is a miserable old cunt, but I only say that because I owe her money. In the real world, she's patient and fair with a kind countenance sexified by jade eyes. Signora Bruni was a serious looker in her day. She can still turn heads from across a wide street. She got her start hand-jobbing Spanish soldiers. Now she owns three houses. She's no older than Mamma, and like my virtual mother, Signora Bruni always gives me the benefit of the doubt. Unlike Lucia, she's happy to have a heavenly wunderkind on her property. She's always wanting to talk shop. *How do you select your subject matter? How did you come to the idea of painting live models? Is it true you hate the color blue?* I usually indulge Signora Bruni, but my current head space is insufferable. I shouldn't be opening my mouth to anyone, let alone the human who owns my home.

"Where's your shirt?"

"I can't afford one."

"The abs look chiseled, but your face looks like wet mortar."

"I'm a dead man walking."

"What's ailing you this month?"

"Coffee. Love. God. You name it."

"I heard you stoned the Tomassoni brothers. I hear they're sharpening their swords."

"Hearing that makes me feel better. Conflict is my raison d'être."

"Caravaggio, I hate to ask, but." She can't bring herself to ask.

"I know. I hate making you ask."

"So, let's not do this to each other."

"I'm sorry. God hates me and I take it out on everyone else."

"God doesn't hate anyone, least of all someone of your genius. Saying he does is a slap to His face, and I know you wouldn't dare think of slapping God's face. They say you're a heretic, but I know better. A heretic couldn't paint *Rest on the Flight into Egypt*. A heathen couldn't paint *St. Matthew and the Angel*."

I close my eyes and groan like a wounded beast. It relieves the migraine just enough. Otherwise, I might have told Signora Bruni how dumb she sounds. Michelangelo has been slapping God in the face since He scourged the city of Milan with plague.

"Three months?" I ask.

"Four months."

"I'll do my best."

"Speaking of your best. Your pictures have introduced me to my *best* self. I stand inside of them, self-reflecting without shame. You're the apple of every Roman's inner Eden. You make our ejection from the Garden of God worth it. I used to make a living with my body. Your pictures inspired me to be better, smarter. I'm buying a fourth property this month. Be your best and you'll own three or four countries."

"Thanks. I'll try."

"How do you do what you do?"

"I don't know. What do I do?"

"I see myself through your characters seeing me. Does that make sense? I didn't even know that I had that kind of a self. It's not a soul. It's not really a being. It's more of an awareness. I'm aware that I'm aware, and that awareness opens my eyes to all the possibilities of my essence, good and bad. Thank you for that, from the bottom of my heart."

She sounds so fucking silly. She sounds like yours truly talking himself into Caravaggio's genius. I can only think to genuflect and kiss her hand. She vacates without payment, without a single scudo, with only the debt of my gratitude to her name.

I enter the house in search of a hammer. I want to demolish my head. I want to punch through my escape tunnel, but the voices stop me. Not the Caravaggio. Not Michelangelo. These voices are coming from upstairs. Mario and Cecco, but there's also a third. I've never heard this particular voice, but I know the garble and slang. It's the talk of a drudge—loud, monosyllabic, proudly obtuse. I can read Cecco's mind through the floorboards. I can hear his thinking through the stabbing in my head. He brought a laborer home, a John in the Wild to paint. It's why he was pushing the picture on me earlier. I lug my splitting headache upstairs to see if this potential John is hot.

I enter the studio and assess the scenario, globules and all. The laborer sits on a stool, a red cloak gathered around his naked lap, the same cloak in my other four John pictures, the curtain in *Judith Beheading Holofernes*. The laborer isn't hot, but he's weathered and sunburnt. His chin is weak, his eyes dumb. His triceps and deltoids are ripped. He's not in the same league as Mario or Cecco, but he'll very much do now that I'm painting men and not fucking them.

Mario and Cecco, the men of my life, stand on either side of John, arguing the same point, that Della Porta bettered the Divine One with a compass. John interjects immaterial facts about mixing lime and sand. He catches sight of me and shuts his mouth. His mouth is his best feature. It looks nothing at all like it sounds. It's dainty and sensual. I will make it my focal point.

Mario and Cecco give me their respective looks, the ones they've co-opted from me. Mario looks younger by the day. Cecco's adorability grows manlier by the hour. I wish I had the nerve to love them again.

"Want to live forever?" I ask John.

"Not as a grunt."

"How about a saint?"

"I'm your John," says John.

"I picked him up at Campidoglio the other day. He's been laboring for stonemasons," Cecco says.

"Will Herod be chopping off my head?" John asks.

"We don't say *chop* when describing the martyrdom of saints. We say *behead* or *decollate*. Dignified words that consecrate the crime," I reply.

"Will my beheading be decollated in the picture?" John asks.

"You seem off," Mario says to me.

"I drank coffee. My head feels like a Roman soldier nailed three spikes into it."

"You drank coffee? I always knew you were half a heathen. Now you've gone full Satan." Mario says.

"Let's get at this John. I stretched and prepared a canvas," says Cecco.

"I can't paint, not with that star outside. It's responsible for this migraine. It's trying to outshine me. It wants me dead."

"To hell with stardom. What has it brought you? Freeloaders, bloodsuckers, and opportunists. All of them ingrates. Stop painting for fame. Paint because you're the best to ever hold a brush. Paint for you and you alone." The last time Mario sounded this fervid he was inciting the beginnings of my first major picture, *The Fortune Teller*.

"Paint the Virgins. Paint this John. Paint them before you flame out," Cecco pleads.

"Had you heard of me before Cecco recruited you?" I ask John.

"I'm stupid, but I don't live under a rock. Is it true you murdered a cop?"

"It's more than true."

"I love *Matthew Killed*. I go to San Luigi every Sunday to see it," John confesses.

The headache is too much for my legs. The two mirrors too. Cecco has positioned them on either side of the canvas. Within the mirrors and globules, there are twelve of us moving about the room, defaced, malformed, and concentered. I take to the floor faceup, forearm over my eyes. I'm in some kind of wilderness.

"I don't suppose Lena has come knocking." I ask nobody in particular.

"I'm sorry," Cecco says, not really meaning it.

"Ranuccio has been hanging around the tennis courts waiting for you," Mario says.

"When this migraine is done killing me, I'll go to Navona and end him."

"After you finish the Virgins and John," Cecco says.

"And after you finish finishing yourself," says Mario.

Their points carry the extra weight of Alessandro Ottoviano de' Medici being my next Papa.

"John, do you have steady work at New Palace?" I ask.

"Another week or two before we're finished setting the foundation," he replies.

"Go back to Campidoglio. Come back when the work dries up. It's hard to come by. You'll need the modeling job when you're unemployed. When you return, bring your lunch bowl. It'll be the only other object in the picture. Your John will have no surrounding story or symbolism. Just you. Shirtless. Your creamy torso poised in darkness, highlighting that sunburn. A portrait of real sacrifice, the sacrifice of slaving for a living. A man paid in chickpeas to build a palace, and damn proud of it. You won't sulk on a cross. You won't bow to a headsman. You'll be straight chilling, contented in hardship. You'll dare Rome's playboy clerics and leisured bureaucrats to take pity on you. You'll show them what a real man looks like. One who works hard and fucks harder."

"Paint me like that, and you'll get us both decollated," John says.

"Ethay ewnay opepay illway avesay usyay," I say.

"You have a hole in your ceiling," John says as if it's been bothering him the entire time. "I can repair it for you."

"Don't mind that," Cecco says. "That's how the light gets in."

VIII.

All Saints' Day and I'm sitting on my backyard veranda in the company of my saints. My Peter. My Paul. My two Jesuses. My *Killed* Matthew and my *Inspired* Matthew, who also modeled my Abraham raping Isaac. My *Called* Matthew couldn't make it. Nor my Martha. Nor my Mary Magdalene. I invited both, but they had to work. Erections don't take rest on holidays. No worries. My fourth John is here. My new John too. He and my Cupid have taken to each other. I spied it in his bedroom a few mornings before starting the picture—John the Laborer hunkered on the edge of the bed, splendidly undressed, sunning his work tan in the post-coital ember of a hearty fuck. I finished the picture yesterday. My Cupid is thrilled with it. He almost loves it better than his John picture. Cupid has fallen on his own arrow once again. Against my warnings and wishes, he has not taken a woman for a lover. His soul will roast in Satan's furnace with mine. I tried sparing him. Our divorce was for naught. I'm too heartbroken over Lena to care, but Michelangelo is fuming. He had Cupid for a lover, and now he's got nothing but his fists. Caravaggio is also a bit peeved. John the Laborer is the first young model he won't fuck, not that he was planning to. It's an entitlement he'd prefer not relinquishing.

And of course, the superstar is there in the daytime sky, keeping me honest, staring me down, failing to outshine my cast party. My saints are reveling in their immortalization, sitting on furniture of my making, eating from my signature dinnerware. In the eyes of my saints, the blip is just another aspiring star trying to make it big in Rome. I wish I had their resolve. The star goads me. God wants Caravaggio for himself. He's behind Lena's ghosting me and resurrecting my ghosts of the past. He's trying to break me, trying to wedge his way in. *When* and *if* I do break out of here, I'll leave my station uninhabitable, and if God doesn't return Lena, I'll burn this place down like the Temple of Jupiter. I miss her something fierce, and sensing Caravaggio's joy confounds me. I'm flushed with his ecstatic shivers. I've finished a picture for the first time in months. The house reeks of resin. My hands are dyed vermillion. Our transubstantiation of oil to flesh always absolves us. From what? I don't want to say with God's eye on me.

I watch Cecco from a discerning and wine-hazed periphery as he and John the laborer peruse the courtyard. The roses are headless and jaundiced, but the ivy is a dark, wet winter-green. The thyme flourishes. The rosemary steeped high. The fennel full-fledged. The pomegranates hang like ruddy family jewels. Cupid picks two and holds them up for both Jesuses, failing to offer me dibs. He does it to hurt me. I'm mostly okay with it, but Michelangelo's been eyeing the readiness of those particular pomegranates all week.

They return to the veranda cradling pomegranates like so many biceps. *Supper* Jesus commands them to portion the fruit equally. Cecco ignores him, tearing them into uneven chunks. He hands the largest one to my Judas from *Christ Taken*. It's a hilariously dickish move. Everyone howls. I smile in mild amusement. I know Cecco. He meant some disrespect toward my *Taken* Jesus. Since having sex without me, Cecco isn't himself. There's no Cupid to him. His fun-loving John is gone. His restrained Isaac ancient history. Cecco's been peacocking around the house like he invented fucking, slinging his salty wit into the open wounds of yours truly. Jokes about my swelling love handles. Jokes about pimps and pros. He questioned my technics throughout the making of *John V*, shifting my model here, redirecting the lighting over there. I wanted to slap the Cupid back into him.

John the laborer speaks to his wineglass as Cecco tops it with claret.

"Being made into art was like seeing my own ghost, but I was more alive than ever. I'm still in a daze over it, but, like, a good daze. You know?"

"It's more of a euphoria than a daze." Peter slaps a handful of poppy seeds in his mouth and licks the clingers from his palm. A few stick to his beard.

"And the euphoria only gets better," says Paul. "It's been three years since that epiphany bucked me from my horse. The elucidation has only magnified."

"What's an *elucidation*?" John the laborer asks.

"You get smarter," says *Supper* Jesus, nibbling at the smallest chunk of pomegranate.

"And then you go viral," *Taken* Jesus says.

"And then what?" asks John the laborer.

"Every artist in Rome wants to paint you," says Paul. "You make a living modeling and save your back for a few months, maybe a few years if you go viral enough. No humping sandbags or fieldstones. No getting harassed by the cops for vagrancy."

"I haven't pounded a single nail since my picture," says *Taken* Jesus, a former carpenter.

"Sounds nice." John the laborer sips and swishes wine as if already accustomed to the finer things.

"Nice work if you can get it," I quip.

"Modeling feels like the end of a hard but satisfying workday," he muses, deaf to my forewarning tone.

"Exactly, but without the aches and pains," says John *IV*, holding out the smoothest palms in Rome. "I haven't toiled in sixteen months."

"But when you *do* go back to toiling, the foreman will assign you the easiest tasks. He will see you as the saint himself. If you want to lift anything heavier than a trowel, you'll have to beg permission." Peter picks a seed from his beard and eats it.

"Toiling isn't the most horrible thing, but fame is the fucking best, especially for an attention whore like me. Bakers throw bread at me. Bartenders shower me with drinks. Pros comp me tricks. Mothers beg me to baptize their sons," says John *IV*.

"You're young." Peter pokes John's pecs with two fingers. "You're strong, handsome. Wait until you're old. Wait until you're ugly and weak. You'll curse toiling, especially after modeling more pictures. You'll dread job sites. Modeling makes you soft. The toiler me has lost all respect for the famous me. Luckily, the famous me could give a shit what some wretch thinks of him."

The saints toast Peter's inner superiority complex. Again, I envy them. I'd give anything to mute Caravaggio for a day. I'd cut off my own head to censor Michelangelo for just an hour. Maybe I don't need emancipation. Maybe I just need a vacation.

John the laborer swirls his wine, staring over the miniature whirlpool like Neptune. I watch the idea arrive over him. Michelangelo decides to hate him on the spot. Caravaggio loves all his models unconditionally. As per fucking usual, it's my job to be the tiebreaker.

"When's my next role?" John the laborer asks as if the paint is already drying.

"Never," I respond immediately.

He coughs on his claret. Cecco snarls, reminding me of Baglione's cock-munching goblin. Cecco suddenly resembles him more than I ever did. He's the one with actual fangs, but judging from the wary expressions of my saints, I'm the one looking monstrous. Knowing myself, I'm probably wearing the wry mouth of *Killed* Matthew's assassin. The courtyard is silent save the shallow whistle of Peter's deviated septum and a faraway roost of bickering starlings. Being virtual saints, my models are prone to shrinking at the first sign of strife. They know me, and they know Michelangelo even better. They've seen his work on the street and in the tavern. They also know what Cecco means to me, what he's been to me. They don't judge. They've bought into the religion of serving genius. The consummate pacifist, *Supper* Jesus changes the subject.

"To our divine creator! For hallowing the likes of us grunts." He raises the very glass in my picture of him.

It's ass-kissy but effective. Michelangelo wants to thrash John the laborer a little less. The saints toast my generosity and evacuate with a jovial efficiency. John the laborer is first to leave. Cecco is angry but doesn't know what to do about it. My indifference is new territory for him. His only option is taking it out on my signature dinnerware. He clangs glasses and slams plates, cleaning the mess of his fellow models. Something breaks. Sounds like a plate. God help him if it's one from a picture. He's never acted the brat, and he's too old for it now. That ship has sailed halfway to hell and back.

I go to the bedroom and don my armor. I haven't worn it since the morning Masetti slid twenty scudi under my door. It feels queer, like a doublet worn backwards. I exit the bedroom in full regalia, sword at hip, and tennis racquet in hand. Cecco appears from the kitchen. I startle him. He takes a defensive backstep. There it is. His ravaged Isaac back from the dead. The lad actually thinks I'd hurt him. How shitty am I?

"Where are you going?"

"The tennis courts."

"Why?"

"So I can take out my anger on someone who isn't you or your John."

He reaches for my sword but thinks twice. He's not that lad anymore. He's lost his sway.

"Don't go. You'll get yourself killed," he says.

"Sounds like a plan," I say.

He drops to his knees and makes prayer hands.

"Think of Lena. Violence repulses her."

"Lena-fucking-who?"

I leapfrog Cecco and goose step toward the door.

"What about the marchioness? Saving your neck is putting her into political debt!"

"Let her go bankrupt. My price for making her name eternal."

I fuck off out of the house and slam the door with the express purpose of disrupting the neighborhood quiet of All Saints' Day. I shoulder through the parade of mourners toting flowers and gifts to the cemetery in honor of dead relatives and their namesake saints. Do any take exception to my bull-rushing? Hell no. Do any stand their ground? Hell fucking no. I'm the superstar genius named after God's arch-general. I can't be stopped. I can't be explained or reasoned. I'm more arcane than that wannabe superstar in the sky shining brighter than the afternoon sun. All that luster yet the star scopes *me* out, envying my fame as I slipstream in Michelangelo's wrath.

IX.

The Campo Marzio tennis court is packed with gamblers, pimps, and mercs. The femme-fops are most likely home with their precious families commemorating dead relatives. Ex-soldiers don't have families, at least none they care about. In this sense, I relate to them. In every other sense, I revile them. I don't acknowledge their bravery or brand of masculinity. Spilling guts for money is weak. Defending Rome. Defending loved ones. Defending your ass from chicken-pluckers. Punishing bad artists. Those are heroic reasons to pull a blade, but the most glorious reason to stick a fellow man and make yourself an eternal ghost enemy? Because you're great at it. Because you're angry. Because your lover. Because an old lover. Because your father died and Lucia forfeited your prodigy for two nobodies.

I know most of the mercs by name and the rest by face. If they weren't so cocky, I'd pity them. I might even paint one or two. Most are unemployed and half-starving. Like Mamma said, money is fast and easy in Rome right now. Patricians don't want to choke the flow with warmongering or even some general jousting for political power. Until two aristocrats decide on hating each other, mercs earn crumbs by bodyguarding lesser aristocrats. Mercs are too high on themselves to wield a shovel or hoe. Otherwise I'd put them to work, not that they'd accept. Mercs don't think much of Caravaggio or art, but they very much mind Michelangelo. Like Del Monte said of my tennis game. I'm fucking deadly with a racquet.

Two Farnese mercs smash the ball back and forth. Dumb heaving overhands. No spinning of ball. No placement. Straight at each other. They're mocking the game, and deserve backhands across the mouth, but first things first. None of the five Tomassoni brothers are present, but there are six more Farnese mercs sitting on the bleachers across the court.

"Someone run and tell Ranuccio that the violent femme is here to get his ass kicked."

"Ass kicked? I hear he'd rather get his ass fucked."

I can't tell which merc said what, so I sprint across the court aiming for the biggest, most Spanish-looking of the gang. He looks like Don Quixote with rabies. His name is either Alfonso or Alonso. Either way, he vaults the partition to greet me, sword drawn and standing guard. I pull my rapier and take a diagonal swing. When he parries it, I punch him in the jaw with the butt-end of my racquet and kick him in the family jewels. Then I kick him in the family jewels again. He drops to his knees, and that's when I slice his cheek. Serves him right for chumming around with those who would call me a femme.

Someone blindsides me with something blunt and heavy. I leave my body and go mental. He hits me again with whatever's in his hand. I wrap my arms around his waist, step behind his legs, and pile him into the lawn, burying my shoulder into his solar plexus. I feel the wind blow out of him. Kneeling on his chest, I hold his head steady and rapidly smash his jaw, going full Michelangelo.

Halfway to committing murder, someone catches my arm. Someone who knows how to handle me. Someone saving me from Michelangelo. They maneuver a half-nelson and dance me off my assailant, who I now recognize as Ranuccio's longtime sidekick Federico Fallacci.

"That turd ain't worth it," my angel says.

I look over my shoulder at Mario. He gives me his soppy *Musicians* gaze. I exhale and limpen, exorcising Michelangelo from my shoulders and fists. The rest of my posse flexes behind us. Orazio stands over the writhing Alfonzo. Coolheaded Prospero talks sense into the agitated mercs on the sideline. Onorio atop his charger, a cocked wheellock in each hand. Cecco sits double behind him, the fun-loving John all over his face.

The blows to the head have me woozy and seeing stars. I look up and around for God's eye, wanting to see His reaction to my performance, but He's gone. The aspiring superstar has disappeared. If it couldn't make it in Rome, it has no chance of making it inside the head of Michelangelo Merisi da Caravaggio, not after seeing yours truly on top of my game, commanding this vessel like a holy admiral. I chased Him out of Rome like my virtual grandfather expelling Turks from the Mediterranean. I raise my hands toward heaven, one crimson, the other vermillion. I raise them just in case He's still looking, just to rub it in.

I awake naked in bed with a wonderful headache. Cecco sits beside me reading Catullus.

"*Because you've read my countless kisses, you think less of me as a man?*"

"Where did you come from?" The reverberations of my voice make my own head throb.

"I come from Caravaggio. Same as you. Did you forget? Are you concussed?"

"The tennis courts. How did you get Mario there so fast?"

"After you left, I ran to his house. They were on their way here to celebrate All Saints' Day. You're the only one of us named after a saint."

"Forgive me."

He rests the book on the nightstand and places his hand over my nipple.

"No. Not yet," he replies with a kinked smile.

"I'll want you back someday. Don't have me. No matter how hard I beg. If you do, I'll never respect you. I'll never treat you right. Your soul will burn in hell."

"I'm never taking you back."

He believes his own words but only because he mistrusts mine. That takes insane superstar confidence. I beam with pride, smiling to my ears. Doing so kills my head.

"You broke Fallacci's face, but he'll live. Ranuccio will double down on the retribution."

I point to Catullus. "Read one of his odes to Lesbia."

"You need a new Virgin. You can't wait for her. Keep your momentum. The new John is swaggering."

"Read some Lesbia."

Cecco flips through the book, pretending to be lost, like he doesn't know the exact page of our favorite poem.

"Lesbia, come, let us live and love, and be deaf to the vile jabber of the ugly old fools,

the sun may come up each day but when our star is out...our night, it shall last forever and

give me a thousand kisses and a hundred more a thousand more again, and another hundred, another thousand, and again a hundred more, as we kiss these passionate thousands let

us lose track; in our oblivion, we will avoid the watchful eyes of stupid, evil peasants

hungry to figure out how many kisses we have kissed..."

I drift off and float back. This time, I'm not so sure of the authenticity. The room is dim and cold. My headache gone. Cecco is gone too. Michelangelo and Caravaggio are also absent. I suppose this is the vacation I'd wanted. Catullus is still on the nightstand. I'm still in my birthday suit. Mamma, Del Monte, and Lady Mattei stand over me. Two of them look royally pissed.

"Time for some tough love," Mamma says.

"I've revoked your license to carry a sword," says Del Monte.

"Every Farnese merc wants your face diced." Mamma pulls the covers up to my waist.

"How will your Michele protect Caravaggio without his sword?" I ask.

"Stay inside. Paint the Virgins. Papa's illness is getting worse," Del Monte says.

"Are you just going to stand there without saying anything?" I ask Lady Mattei.

"I liked the naked gory selfie idea." She strips the covers to my knees.

"With that thing in the sky gone, the shine is back on you. Act accordingly," Mamma says.

"It's only gone during daylight hours. It's still there at night. Stay indoors at night. Stay out of trouble. Paint the Virgins," Del Monte says.

"I lost my Virgin."

"Find another. Find three," he says.

"And not a prostitute," says Mamma.

They sound like Caravaggio. They think the genius can do it alone, that my emotions don't factor. Maybe that was true in the past, but this Virgin is my Caravaggio. All mine.

"I can't *find* a Virgin. I don't work like that. I need maternal lust. You of all people should know." I say it right to Mamma's face.

Mamma pats my penis like a kitten.

"There, there, how's that? Now go find a Virgin," she says.

Del Monte blushes. Lady Mattei makes a sign of the cross over my head, and then they're gone like they were never here. I reach for Catullus, but the room has turned too dark. The words are barely legible. I drift away after *Sparrow, o, sweet Lesbia's bird...*

"Reading Catullus? That's so predictable," Masetti says.

I open my eyes. Sunlight blanches the room. An achromatized Masetti looms over me. I lift Catullus from my chest and spread it over my face.

"How are your brains feeling? They say you took a chunk of fieldstone over the head, twice. Still concussed?"

"I wasn't concussed. I always hibernate after finishing a picture, after however many weeks of depriving myself sleep."

"The new John is a stud. Make the duke's Virgin of the same working-class sensuality."

"Got another twenty scudi on you?"

"I have ten."

"Leave it on the nightstand."

He places the coins down one at a time, and then walks to the window to close the shutters and dissolve into shadow...

Catullus is gone. The coins too. It's the middle of a cool and silvery afternoon. I'm bare but under the covers, Lena sleeping on top of them, adorned in her chichi dress. She appears to be real, but I steal the expression of my *Doubting Thomas* while looking upon her.

"I thought you'd never come back from the dead," I whisper.

She doesn't respond. I touch her arm. I touch her nape. She's ice cold from work, from fading hard and often.

X.

We're sitting on the veranda, on a three-legged bench gifted by Lady Mattei. It had a fourth leg when her servants delivered it, but I kicked it off in a fit while painting *Isaac and Abraham II*. I steady the bench with my right leg as Lena and I lean against each other for moral support. We're snuggled under a blanket, playing footsies, and watching the full moon swing west. She smells like the Tiber. I can barely keep myself from begging. Her body. She hasn't offered and shows no interest. She's said six words all night, three more than her norm. She's content sphinxing the moon. The joy she takes in silence. It's hard not making it personal, but it magnifies her beauty like one of Galileo's lenses. As if she wasn't cosmic enough.

"Someone told Albertini I was working again," she says.

"Ranuccio?"

"He wouldn't. He likes the money too much."

"Then who?"

"Maybe Fillide or Menicuccia."

"Why would they do that?"

"To bring me back to you."

"They want you to star in a picture, but you have no interest."

"Sorry."

"I don't care if you're interested in my pictures. I care if you're interested in me."

"I'm not interested. I'm in love."

She massages my inner thigh.

"Quit the streets," I say.

"I did. Then I didn't. Then I came here."

"How did Ranuccio react when you quit?"

"He blamed you. He said he'd cut off your nose for marking Fallacci and cut off your balls for stealing me. Please don't play his game. Combative men turn my pussy to sand. I'll leave and never come back."

"Del Monte took my sword."

"Good."

"How did the bookworm react to the news of you working?"

She slides her hand from my lap and looks to the moon. The glow burns through her makeup, uncovering the damage above her eye. That motherfucking bookworm.

"He hit you?"

She's back at my thigh, but with consoling pats.

"Is it the first time he's hit you?" I beg with the same compulsion that wants her body.

"I'm not telling you anything. You'll kill Ranuccio. You'll kill Albertini. Papa will smash your head like Giacomo Cenci."

"Albertini doesn't deserve you. Live with me."

"He's a good father. Albertini reads Ovid to him."

"The rape and murder passages?"

"The world is rape and murder. Ovid is no worse than the Old Testament."

She has a point. My house is worse than the Old Testament. It's hardly a home. A prison first and art studio second. No place for a childhood. I've been a terrible father to Cecco. I'm not a bad master, and I have been a loving creator, making Cecco not in my own likeness, but as a facsimile of his own unlikeness to other earthlings. I could do the same for Lena's son. If he can't live in my house, let him flourish in my kingdom.

"Bring your boy to me. I'll make him Christ child to your Virgin. He'll be Rome's favorite Jesus since *Pieta*."

Her hand goes dead on my thigh. She considers the idea long enough for Cecco to come home. He's been out partying with John the laborer, who's been capitalizing on his newfound celebrity. They giggle and raid the pantry, unaware of our presence on the veranda.

"Who's with him?"

"His new lover. My new John the Baptist."

"You're the most understanding ex ever." She then calls out to Cecco and his John. "Hey, lover boys, we're out here."

The giggling stops as Cecco places her voice.

"Lena!" He proclaims her like an unexpected gift.

He wants the Virgin more than yours truly. I just want Lena.

Cecco crashes onto us horizontally, Lena cradling his torso, me cradling his legs. The bench dips. I right it with my right leg. Cupid is lit on equal parts claret and romance. I look at John the laborer. He's wearing my old cloak. Michelangelo's not so understanding, but I grin and bear it for fear of turning off Lena.

"Are you here to model the Virgin?" Cecco asks from her bosom.

"I'm in the process of reclaiming my virginity. Does that count?"

"She is here to model my Virgin and her boy will be Rome's new Christ," I declare from Cecco's ass.

"Speaking of maculate conceptions, I have to go home. The nurse can only watch Ovidio for another hour."

It's the first time she's called her boy by name. It's usually just *boy*. I didn't know that she named him after his rapist cop father, and now his abusive stepfather reads the assaults of Leda, Daphne, and Europa to him. Ovidio needs divine intervention. I'm his fucking man. This is the fucking family I've been missing my entire life. I point an ear into nighttime darkness and listen for ghosts. Crickets.

I swing Cecco's legs from my lap and stand. Cecco sits up, sliding into my spot, buttressing the bench with his leg. John the laborer steps back in fear. He's jumpy around me, his most endearing attribute. My ass is numb. My leg asleep. I bounce on my toes like a fighter to arouse the blood. John takes another nervous step back. I smile. The curfew bell alarms the pros of Navona to clear the streets. Few adhere to the law. It's lazily enforced, easily circumvented.

"Lend me your cloak," Lena says to John the laborer.

Cecco stumbles to his feet, stuttering to explain my clothes on his lover. He urges John to remove it, who's one step ahead of him, already forfeiting the contraband to Lena.

"You haven't worn anything in weeks. You've been naked and bedridden. It was cold. He left his cloak at home."

I wave the excuse off with magnanimity, hoping to impress my dove.

"I'll walk you home," I say.

"I think it's better if you stay. I don't want you bumping into Ranuccio or Albertini."

"We'll take her," Cecco says.

"That's not necessary either. The cops give me a pass when I go drag. They reward effort and creativity when it comes to cheating curfew."

Nearly every cop in Rome wants up her chichi dress. The rest want my newest John in the mouth. They all want my skull cracked open. I stand down for now.

She slips into my cloak and raises the hood. Nothing about her appears masculine, her bosom least of all. Cecco bids her farewell and retreats to his bedroom with John. I walk Lena through the back gate to the front of the house. We stop and face each other on the stoop.

"Promise you'll stay indoors. Promise you won't go hunting for Ranuccio or Albertini."

"Promise you'll quit working. Promise you'll be my Virgin and Ovidio my Christ."

She puts her tongue in my mouth. I take this as a yes. She turns for the alley. I watch my Virgin fade into the shadows of Firenze Palace. I trust God to protect her. It's the first time in recent memory that I've entrusted Him with anything. He never had my full confidence, but when it comes to getting this Virgin right, He'll put his sociopathic ego aside and do something altruistic.

I forgo the liquor cabinet and retire to my bedroom. I'm feeling extraordinarily sober. I would like to maintain this lucidity for as long as Michelangelo allows. Yours truly, not Caravaggio, could paint something masterful at any moment. I might paint a masterpiece this very second if not for the chest moans and belly laughs sounding throughout the walls.

A week later, I find myself in the courtyard under a bright but tepid midday sun, running my fingers through the rosemary, listening to the fabrication of Rome. I hear it doubling, tripling in stories—belfries, cathedrals, and palaces. The pounding of stone and wood. The tapping of stone and steel. The clacking of keratin on stone. Street vendors advertising products. I feel the city growing without me. I'm aggrieved. There are knocks at my door. Most are for Cecco. John the laborer has become a hot commodity, a luminary at the taverns and an art object at palace orgies. The other knocks, the ones for me, I don't answer. She has my key. As for Masetti, Signora Bruni, and Ranuccio, their money is already spent. Not on claret or poppy seeds, but paint and canvas for my Virgin.

At night, I rest, ignoring Michelangelo's demands for wine while listening to Cecco and John trying their damnedest to break the bed.

By day, I busy myself in the studio, shushing Caravaggio, positioning mirrors, conjuring my Lena between them, an amalgam of spirit and hallucination. The Cavalletti family wants a levitating Virgin over the altar of their newly purchased chapel in Sant'Agostino. I won't do flying Virgins. I won't paint an immaculate orgasm haloed by radiant light. Whether painting Mary Magdalene or the Madonna, Caravaggio has always depicted the God-given defects of our models. We don't sell viewers doctored tits or fake orgasms like Carracci. Our wrinkled Peter is sexier than his schmaltzy Virgin. My new Virgin will bitch-slap whatever one Carracci inevitably falsifies in our not-so-friendly contest for the Duke of Modena. My new Virgin will stun Rome. She will halt construction projects. Laborers will drop their tools and flock to her. She will congest Navona Square. She will flood Sant'Agostino with hysterical believers, lavish and impoverished pilgrims, not to mention monsignors, bishops, cardinals, and femme-fops. I'm witnessing her glamour right now, levitating between the two mirrors, my phantasm. She's so tactual I could almost paint her. I'm on the verge of laying her colors, when I hear the very real clicking of Lena's heels against the fieldstones of my alley. She's come back! Did the power of my imagination summon her? Sometimes my process presents such enigmas, and the easiest explanation lies in admitting to my own godhood.

I punch and kick out of my clothes. Cupid's wings are stretched out on the floor. I attach them to my back and scurry downstairs to the bedroom, swan-diving onto the bed, positioning myself in Cupid's likeness. She inserts my key into the front door, and everything inside me opens. She kicks off her heels and tramps into the bedroom. She's wearing my cape over an elegant but none-too-sexy gown. She smiles all over my wings.

"It's been over a week. What took you so long?" I ask.

"I was in jail," she says all businesslike, reaching around herself to unclasp the dress.

"What? How? No cop would dream of arresting you. They all want a piece."

"I left your house that night and turned the block. There they were. I think they were waiting for me."

"Someone has had it out for me. Now they have it out for you too."

"I used to think you were paranoid. Now I think you have more covert enemies than Papa."

"The Farnese family. Ranuccio probably hit them up for a favor."

Her dress drops to the floor. I roll onto my side, careful not to crush my wings. She rolls onto the bed and scooches her buttocks into my lap. She's colder than a dry night in January.

"Please let me kill Ranuccio. I promise to leave Albertini alone."

"I don't want you leaving this house until you're done painting me and Ovidio."

"Then can I kill Ranuccio?"

She doesn't say yes. She doesn't say no. She bends her arm behind her back and takes me in the hand. I'm already hard.

"Did anyone ever explain that star in the sky?" she asks.

"Galileo told Martinelli that it was a dying star."

"Good. I'm glad it died," she says, guiding me home.

"Does that mean you're ready to shine?"

"Only if you make it hurt."

XI.

After a day and two nights of disgusting myself and mildly satisfying my Virgin, I escort her sultry bod to Navona where I hope to cast some wretched pilgrims for her picture. I am to Navona what Romulus is to Rome. I'm always essentially here, my blood, sweat, and piss soaked into the pavers. I've bathed in both fountains, looped on claret and zooming on poppy. The tennis court is still stained with my gore from the October skirmish. When I become Divine One to the next pope, I'll build a palace here among the vagrants, hoods, and pros who call it home. It's one of the remaining neighborhoods not entirely colonized by femme-fops.

The femme-fops are out in full force on this bright cold Wednesday. The February weather has not deterred them. I take cover inside the hood of my winter cloak. Fops are always the first to recognize me. Those who can *almost* afford a picture are always the quickest to crawl up my ass. Fops come here to slum it and rub elbows with Caravaggio. If I'm not here, they buddy up with one of my followers, the men who paint, dress, and grow their hair after me. Collecting the company or work of my followers is a golden ass pursuit. I'm a one-and-only. The addi of Lena on my hip is doubling my usual fanfare. The bigge in Rome strolling Navona with the psycho genius. My fanboys, followers, idolaters, collectors, and haters are losing their shit, swarming us with adoration, gushing in our slipstream.

I steal a peek at Lena. She's Mona Lisaing the fandom as if her picture has been hanging at Fontainebleau Palace for centuries.

A dry voice crackles above the murmurs. "Are you casting models?"

Another voice undercuts it. "Caravaggio! Over here! Look at me! I'm the best wreck you've ever seen."

I don't look. There's a trace of optimism in his voice.

"I'll pay fifty scudi to be in your next picture." This voice sings of itself. I consider jabbing the fop in the nose, but the mob is already butchering him with jeers.

"Those two. I want them," Lena says.

She points to an ancient woman and her battered son, who, if I had to guess, is pushing the wrong side of forty. They're skulking within the crowd, striving for invisibility. She's completely toothless and fully pruned. He's a total loser. They're both shoeless, their feet mottled, purple with contusions and white with cold. They're the only souls in Navona paying us no mind. It's the talent I seek most in casting models, complete artlessness. They're perfect subject matter—a wretched mother-son pair kneeling before Virgin and child. God, I love Lena's instincts. I lower my hood and turn to her. The scantest halo hovers above her head.

I watch the son boggle over Lena as she approaches him. The mother crosses her heart and hopes to die, one withered old pro to a much younger, more voluptuous other.

"Do you know who he is?" Lena turns and points to me, not Caravaggio.

"We don't know our next meal," the son says, his tongue hanging out of his mouth, thick with southern dialect.

The mother says something fast and slangy. The words gallop past me. Lena seems to understand. She responds in kind to the gibberish. I hear the words *scudi* and *Caravaggio*. The son drops to his knees and bows, practically kissing my toes. The mother is unmoved.

"The cops threatened to drag us out of the city if I didn't find work. They threatened to feed us to the bandits. You've saved us," the son says.

"Please. Stand. Save it for the picture. You'll be kneeling before the Virgin and Christ child for eternity."

"How much are you going to pay us?" the mother asks, speaking the Italian of Dante all of a sudden.

"Three scudi each," I answer.

Her face finally cracks, laughing at my Christ complex.

"You look poor as us." She slips a decrepit finger into one of the many holes in my cloak.

I guide her hand into my dearth like my Christ steering the hand of his doubting Thomas. My surrounding fans cheer the allusion.

"Blessed are those who have not seen my pictures yet believe in them," I shout.

The cheering escalates into rowdy ovation. Lena whispers something to the mother. Her ear is curvaceous. The son's too. I'll paint the helix of their lobes as exalted arches. I scan Navona to foresee my someday palace and the vaulted arches of its portico. I try entering, but it's hard daydreaming over Navona without my posse. For ten years, we've bred the square's disorder, and now here it is, perfectly unruly without us. We made recklessness a fad. The square is rife with teen desperados. The desperate youth of Navona emulate Michelangelo. The teenage femme-fops copycat Caravaggio. Personally, I'm mostly Michelangelo here, which is why Navona feels uneven without my posse. I haven't seen them since the tennis court melee. When Mario isn't home seeding the wife, he's hustling to feed the resultant offspring. Orazio loves teaching his teenage daughter to paint like he once loved teaching mercs to bleed. Onorio is more into Menicuccia than Martino the Younger, both of whom keep him from Navona. Prospero lives with his mother, painting grotesques in his bedroom. He's just launched a promising second career as an interior decorator, capitalizing on Rome's real estate explosion. Vocations and wives, the leading cause of fraternal divorce. I'll move my posse and their families into my Navona palace. Cecco and John the laborer too, but their bedroom out of earshot from mine.

We lead our pilgrims home, Lena and the mother hooked at the arm. The son no longer skulks, his spine now straight as his stave, his weak and wispy jawline parallel to the pavers. A procession of fans follows, yipping and barking for immortality. As we approach the Fountain of Neptune, the coach of Ranuccio Farnese Duke of Parma approaches at an excessive speed, its six chargers at full canter. I don't think much of it. He's a spoiled brat who believes in absolute monarchy. He also fucks witches, which I happen to respect. The duke is also an avid art collector, but a Carracci guy. My rival has painted dozens of frescoes at Farnese Palace, pagan porn scenes from Ovid. The duke's aesthetics suck, but I respect his choice of content.

The coach approaches with no sign of slowing. My fans run for their lives. Lena and I hold steady alongside our pilgrims, unphased and a bit amused by the duke's antics. The coach slews and lurches to a halt, a few feet from killing us. The curtain is drawn. I raise my arm to salute the duke's horseplay. My salute is three-quarters hoisted when I realize the humiliation that I've caused myself. Ranuccio Farnese is not in the coach, nor his cardinal brother. It's the duke's unworthy name-sake, the motherfucker of all cocksuckers, Ranuccio Tomassoni. He's riding bitch between his older brothers, Luca and Giovan. The Tomas-soni have worked as Farnese mercs for centuries. Tomassoni fathers have named their sons after Farnese patriarchs for generations, but I'm miffed that these clowns scored a joyride in the Farnese family coach.

I recoil my arm, but it's too late. Ranuccio is gloating over my mistake. His brothers mean-mug me. Ranuccio pulls his dagger and points it at Lena while addressing yours truly.

"You fuck my whore without paying and disfigured my friend without cause. Refund me with blood or coin. Your choice, cocksucker."

I haven't seen him up close in months. He's grown into the Tomas-soni barrel chest, his hand-me-down embroidered doublet straining at the laces.

"Lena, remember that time my dick was in your ass?" Giovan asks.

"Or those times mine was in your mouth?" says Luca.

"My dick will be in that cunt forever." Ranuccio points the dagger at my balls.

I lunge at the coach. Lena drops and clings to my legs for dear life, saving us from Michelangelo. The wretched son hugs my waist, further anchoring me in place. I waddle a few steps, dragging Lena and the son. We look pathetic. I'm pathetic. I can't fight like this. I don't even have my rapier. The brothers yowl. I look for God's eye. It's too early in the day for Him to appear. He doesn't think I have the gall to sin in broad daylight.

Lena pleads from her knees.

"Don't waste yourself on them. They're trying to antagonize you. You're unarmed. They can't so much as scratch you. It'll be criminal. The entire square is watching."

The brothers pile out of the coach, laughing like fiends. Hands on hilts, they form a kill triangle around us. I hoist my dukes. Their laughter is cut at the throat. A shadow has entered the triangle, a shadow of Chiron. I smile. I assume it's Onorio atop his charger, but the brothers salute the rider with rigid submission. The Tomassoni would never salute Onorio, not sarcastically, not with a rapier pointed at their prick. I turn around to see who.

It's no centaur. It's my knight in lavish armor—Fra Ippollito Malaspina. He's gray in the whiskers, a total silver fox. The furrows of his forehead equal seven Mona Lisa smiles. Malaspina is a knight of the Order of St. John's Hospital. He captained a galley at Lepanto alongside Marcantonio Colonna's admiral ship. I honor the war buddy of my virtual grandfather with a high and stiff Roman salute. The Tomassoni slide their hands from their hilts. Lena and the wretched son stand. The mother remains wholly unimpressed.

I point up at the gold Maltese cross hanging around Malaspina's neck.

"I've wanted one of those since boyhood," I say.

Michelangelo has dreamt of becoming a knight since his boyhood, but our father's proletariat blood prohibits it.

"The marchioness and Del Monte have asked me to keep an eye on you," Malaspina says.

"These femme-fops are lost. They were asking directions," I say.

"Should we send them along their way?" Malaspina grins.

"All roads lead to Farnese Palace," Luca mumbles.

The brothers crowd into the coach and ride away, tails up their asses. I'm grateful for the one-man cavalry, but I'm also frustrated, enraged, and ashamed. I wouldn't need protection if Del Monte hadn't revoked my license. If Lena hadn't sweet-talked me into leaving my sword beside the bed this morning.

Malaspina escorts us home. I measure my stride between the four-beat clacking of his charger. I'm too sullen for conversation or eye contact. I'm trying to unimagine all that Tomassoni dick inside of Lena. It's all I think about as Malaspina lubes me for a picture.

"I attended San Luigi Sunday. Your Matthew pictures are staggering. I stared at *Martyrdom* for the entire first half of Mass. I saved Matthew from his assassin a thousand times, disemboweling him, splaying him, decollating him. I spent the second half of Mass lost in *Inspiration*. I saw so much of myself in that Matthew. At my age and rank, I handle a quill more often than a sword. The quill has twice the duties and liabilities. I find myself more startled at my desk than I ever was on the battlefield. I've always known my place, but your pictures put me there, up close and personal with God. I'm a devotee, Master Caravaggio. I could tell by the composition of *Martyrdom* that you know your way around bloodshed, that you know how to wield a sword, but it's better for the world that you chose a brush. Your marchioness tells me that you have some Virgin pictures underway. When you're finished with those, I'd love to commission a St. Jerome. I bought a new villa in Navona. It would centerpiece my gallery."

I don't say yes. I don't say no. I don't want any conflicts with my Virgin so I sphinx like Lena while approaching my stoop. I enter my house without looking back, leaving him in the alleyway wanting more of me.

I hit the pantry for a handful of poppy seeds and a gulp of claret. Mid-chug I hear Lena cry out. I follow her voice to Cupid's room, where he's standing over the bed tending to John the laborer's battered face. He's bludgeoned, barely cognizant, but he'll live. There'll be heavy scarring. Lena turns away from the carnage, nauseous and remorseful. I console her with the full force of my arms. I'm altogether weak in the legs.

"He was on his way here. They rode up in a coach. Three men." Cecco lays his head on John's chest. "No one will want to paint him after this. He'll be back to digging ditches. Why would three noblemen maul a laborer?"

"They weren't noblemen. It was the Tomassoni. I'm going to kill him," Michelangelo says.

Lena protests. I muffle her pleas against my chest. A swift double knock comes at the front door. Lena jumps. I release her to collect my rapier. She tries restraining me. I deflect her arms and make for my bedroom. I approach the front door with my rapier drawn. Before opening it to slaughter whoever, I take a sensible peep through the eyehole. It's Del Monte's gopher. I'm wildly disappointed. I open the door and greet him with a perturbed sigh.

"Papa has taken to bed. He won't live through the week," the gopher says.

"Well ain't that convenient," I reply.

I surrender my rapier. He accepts it with baffled hesitation.

"Give it to Del Monte. Tell him I won't be needing it. Tell him that the marchioness' Michele won't be a problem."

XII.

I haven't been this into a model since Mario. Mario will always be my big was. I'd cry inside of him. I'd cry inside his mouth. I wept at the very thought of him. We were an ideal with nothing to prove. Cecco was all flesh, sinful sure, but the love was easy work, spiritually rewarding, like sweeping dry snow from bricks. Peaceful as death itself. He never got in my head, which is why he'll always remain in my heart. Lena is my afterlife.

Her son is the absolute worst model, a total horror show. Lena is trying to look virginal with the Christ child in her arms, but the little Antichrist won't stop flipping his middle finger at the wretched pilgrims kneeling before them. I doubt that he learned the gesture from reading Ovid with the bookworm. I suspect the influence of a john, but more likely he inherited a hatred for the poor from his rapist cop father. The Christ child has been kicking and screaming the entire session. I'd love to smack him. Michelangelo dreams of strangling him. Even Caravaggio, who loves all of his models equally and unconditionally, wants to teach our Christ child a motherfucking lesson. Most baby Christs are beatific homunculi. Unlike the Divine One and Raphael, I'm painting mine like the sanctimonious brat he is, a burly toddler crowned by a halo of disintegrating dust particles.

It's noon, late summer, but inside the studio, I've recreated the diffuse glow of a shortened autumn evening, and as planned, I've also recreated the Virgin. She's no flying prude, blissful and sexless. My Virgin stands on her tiptoes. She's in the process of elevating, but only to show off her calves and prove she isn't solely dependent on God for miracles. She's got tricks of her own. She's the modern Roman wife, outfitted in bougie velvet and silk. Her gray skirt and sheer shawl are wardrobe donations from Lady Mattei. Her top was doled by Mamma. The top is vermillion, but I'm painting it Renaissance red, the color of the blanket draped over Mario's playing hand in *Musicians*. I'll never paint the color again.

Lena is my ideal Virgin, but a problematic model. Her beauty does not sit well. It needs motion. I can't paint her slow, catlike perambulations around a room. I can't paint her twiddling a tress of hair. I can't paint her sphinxing. She is emotionally challenged. She is removed. I can't bring her to fade in bed. I can't make her shine on canvas. She can hardly hold an athletic pose without tipping over. She is dead gorgeous but fundamentally uncoordinated. I haven't been this challenged by a model since my sick Bacchus selfie. I should probably ask Caravaggio for some advice.

My pilgrims are perfectly obedient, honored to kneel for hours in the dark, getting shit on by my Christ child. Their subservience is further testified when the Great Bells go gonging. My pilgrims break pose, cowering with grief. Papa has died. The silver hammer has thrice tapped his gouty head. His rapidly declining health has unnerved Rome in recent weeks, and now all hell will break loose as the nobility maneuvers for power. The pilgrims stand and weep for the man who wanted their sloven asses expelled from the city. Lena sinks to earth. Cecco bursts into the room. He's been eschewing assistance on my Virgin picture to nurse his injured John.

"It happened! You've arrived!" Cecco heralds.

I accept his assertion with a proprietary smile. My Christ child writhes free from my Virgin and streaks out of the studio chanting *fuck*. Cecco fetches him, returning the spastic Christ child to his mother's bosom. It's nice to have them both back on board.

"Stay fucking still, and I'll take you out for donuts when we're finished," I say.

The promise of fried dough speaks to him. He shuts his yap but offers the pilgrims a middle finger as if feeding it to them. Del Monte's gopher will come knocking any minute, carrying news of my golden moment. Meanwhile, I paint the Christ child's bird into a wagging index finger, the same gesture Del Monte waged against me at Campidoglio the day we intended to haze the papal architect. Del Monte's knock comes as I apply the final touches to the finger. My Christ child squirms and kicks. My Virgin almost trips over herself in the process of restraining him. My pilgrims remain kowtowed for fear of everything. I signal Cecco to the window. He opens the shutters, scorching the scene with daylight. I head downstairs, a dopey glee injected into my cheeks.

I should have checked the peephole before opening the door. Signora Bruni stands on the stoop wearing the mother of all bitch faces.

"A little birdie tells me you're housing whores. I'm so sick of your shit. Five months' rent. I want it now or I'll have the cops drag your sorry ass out of here."

"Can you not hear the Great Bells?" Caravaggio asks.

"Papa doesn't pay my property taxes."

"The next Papa will pay my genius in gold. I'm working on the Virgin picture. Want to come up and see? I'll tell you all about my process."

Her stance loosens. Her bitch face rests. Worshippers of fame and fortune are the most deserving suckers.

"Is the next Papa really a Caravaggio fan?"

"It's time for everyone to see what I see," I say, paraphrasing Bruno.

XIII.

San'Agostino has all kinds of eyes. Small oculi above the aisle doors like
the cloudy whites of a blind prophet. Centered above the entrance wall
is a colossal oculus emanating hot blue light. I see it as an omniscient
globe, an obtrusive planet crashing through the nave. Dazzling
pyrotechnics for the flock. It does nothing for me. Can't read under it.
Couldn't paint by it. The globe projects nowhere and reaches no one,
none of it falling on the congregation. It's just up there in the ceiling
vaults, high on itself, powering its own conceit, and we're down here in
the dusk, cozying to some shockingly domestic idea of ourselves—
Cupid to my left, my Virgin on my right with Christ baby on her lap.
What a fucking foursome.

Father Gonorrhea breaks the body of Christ into threes, roundly
and understandably pleased with his portly self. His church is stuffed
with souls. San'Agostino has always been popular with pilgrims and
pros, but my *Pilgrim's Madonna* has been overfilling the nave with
lowlifes and upper-crusters alike. Everyone under the vernal sun is here.
My entire posse. Fright and Gabrielli. Masetti is over there somewhere.
Lady and Lord Mattei sit front row. Mamma is absent. Del Monte too.
Not one Tomassoni, but Ranuccio Farnese is in attendance, looking
pouty because his pro-Spain candidate lost the papal election to my
benefactor Pope Leo XI, formerly known as Cardinal Priest Alessandro
Ottaviano de' Medici, cousin and former emissary to the Queen of

France. His Medici cousins from Firenze Palace are here. Fra Malaspina prays amongst them. If not infatuated with Lena, I might have a thing for him. I've always fancied silver foxes. I can't get into a Jerome while immersed in my Virgin. Maybe I could paint Malaspina a quick still life, a girthy zucchini or two.

A brood of pros are pig-piled into the pews adjacent to the chapel where Fiammetta is buried, the luminary prostitute and mistress to Cesare Borgia. Pros call her Queen of the Square. She retired richer than some marchionesses, but not before revamping the oldest profession, incorporating dignity and prowess into the craft of pleasing men. She spoke Latin, quoted Petrarch at length. It's said she invented the slowjob. Before Fiammetta, gingers were viewed as homely. She made the hair color exotic. This morning, Lena combed beetroot into her tar-black hair, the red highlights a self-appointed coronation. My New Queen of the Square. My State-of-the-Art Virgin. Far from the Divine One's sorrowful Mother. Nothing like Titian's fish-eyed war hawk Madonna. Forget about Raphael's bloodless goody-goody, my Virgin is a bombshell Roman housewife. She's buxom, swarthy, and barefoot. She's sexed by boredom. Bored of worship. Bored of one-way sex. Everything around her is flat, fixed, and gimmicked. Her run-down stoop. The groveling pilgrims. Her smug tot. Artistically, it's my worst picture ever. Caravaggio has been taking pleasure in my ineptitude, but I'm not completely discouraged. It's my first picture. I'll perfect her in the next one.

But Rome loves this picture. Everyone is geeking over my amorous Mother of God. No one is kneeling or genuflecting along with Mass. No one faces the altar. Everyone is standing and spun around, craning for a view of Cavalletti Chapel, where Rome's foxiest pro revamps God's sweetheart. Their *oohs* and *ahhs* echo off the ceiling vaults, drowning Father Gonorrhea's sloppy Latin. He's far from offended. For two consecutive Masses, his church has drawn the largest audiences in Rome. He slants a gaze toward Cavalletti Chapel while praying for the living, while praying for Pope Leo XI, while extolling the Queen of old. He then names Caravaggio. No *Michelangelo*. No *Merisi*. Not even a *da*. He prays in thanks to the one name. *Caravaggio*. The bigger you get, the less name you need.

The pros fixate on us, their eyes emitting admiration, envy, and everything in between. Lena is dressed to kill, her newly purchased sable draped over a shoulder. She's back on the street, making hand over fist off her new celebrity. The mink's amethyst eyes stare back at the pros. I can hear their thoughts. *Caravaggio's into chicks again*. On the streets, in taverns and bordellos, Lena has been renamed. *Lady Caravaggio*. Her bookworm is none too happy. He's been turning a fearful eye. What else can he do? Defend his honor and get killed? He's too middle-class for that. Ranuccio wants a piece of her new action. I pray she stays clear of him, but I would never tell Lena how to conduct her business. I trust her volition. What else can I do?

Father Gonorrhea pounds his chest, declares his unworthiness, and reverently devours Christ. He drinks his blood. We sign crosses on our heads. A server jingles the sanctus bells. I kiss my knee to Lena's. She allows it, but doesn't footsie back, not even a nudge. She's off somewhere, deeply focused on nothing. Baby Christ flips me the bird. The three servers kneel along the high altar. Father Gonorrhea stands cock-level with their mouths and feeds them.

"Yum," Cecco whispers.

I smirk but he only meant the joke for himself. He's been going out of his way to ignore me. John the laborer's face isn't healing well.

Lena absently rubs Junior's back, sphinxing onward, past the pros, beyond Father Gonorrhea and his cannibalizing servers. She's already regretting immortality. She enjoys the afforded garments but can hardly stomach the stardom. She's hardly lifted her chin the entire Mass. She taken no bow, not the hastiest wink to her clamoring fans. She likes being known and not seen. Only God can have fame both ways, but even He's titillated by her enigmatic stare. She sasses Him with indifference. Her dispassion is mildly abusive, if not entirely sexy. Lady Caravaggio doesn't mean to offend. She doesn't mean anything, far as I can tell.

I place a hand on her knee. Junior kicks it. I don't flinch. Neither does Lena. Junior kicks my hand again. I steal a page from Lena's book and zone out on him. He stomps and stomps as if trying to squish an indestructible spider. I already regret immortalizing this homuncular Antichrist. He strokes the sable's muzzle with his wee thumb. It rubs me the wrong way.

My stomach growls for donuts. I now eat them Sundays, Mondays, and Saturdays. My abs are gone. Relatively happy and fat, I don't foresee those naked selfies happening. I've always abhorred joyous subject matter. Not that I'm all that joyous. I'm joyous enough to scare myself, to loathe myself with renewed purpose. I've made Lena a superstar rivaling the one still dazzling the nighttime sky. She could take it or leave it. She could take or leave yours truly. She says it isn't so, but I can't believe her. I'm not brave enough. Being happy requires the kind of courage an artist can't afford, unless he wants to paint like Carracci. Papa isn't patronizing Carracci. He prefers the graphic woe and heartache of a Caravaggio. He's been Papa for more than a week but hasn't ordered anything. I'll perfect my new despair while waiting for him.

The priest draws a final cross and dismisses the congregation. Jesus has left the basilica. Lena breaks from her own trance and turns to me, closing her eyes as if being kissed. We exit via the center aisle, mobbed by fans chanting *Lena*, and others hailing *Caravaggio*. Lena pauses at the *Madonna of Childbirth* sculpture carved by Jacopo Sansovino, the former assistant to Andrea Sansovino. Jacopo adopted his master's surname along the way of eclipsing him in talent and reputation. I turn to Cecco. He's working the crowd, winking up a storm. He's caught up in the pomp, happy for Lena's celebrity. The Caravaggio name is in good hands. He'll never eclipse me as an artist, but I thank God he already has a human being.

Lena stops to read the sculpture's epigram aloud.

"*Virgin, childbirth is your glory*. Pfft."

"You don't subscribe to that?"

"It's something a man would think to write."

"What if the child becomes the next Divine One?" I ask.

"Who was the Divine One's mother? Tell me her name."

I want to answer that her name *wasn't* Lucia, but don't for fear of sounding sorry for myself. So I stick to the facts.

"The Divine One's mother died when he was six. He was raised by a nanny."

"According to this sculptor, a woman's highest achievement is having her rapist's son."

She releases a sarcastic moan, a melody of labor pain and orgasm. Our fans within earshot cheer. Cecco blazes us a path through the crowd. We follow him onto Navona, locked at the shoulder, baby Satan in her arms, kicking me every so often in the ribs. The traffic is chest-to-back, stop-and-go, pelvises rear-ending asses. People push back, some annoyed, others in fun. The gridlock tightens, a dick-length of personal space on all sides. We're spotted. The superstar, the Virgin, and John. The libertine, the prostitute, and Cupid. A hysteria is leavened. Rich and poor pilgrims. Femme-fops and laborers. Cruddy street whores and posh pros. They crush on us in a stampede of greedy idolization. I hip-check our way through the scrums. Lena clutches my biceps as if enduring some immense pleasure. I refuse to believe that it has to do with me.

A noisy logjam is a good place to voice some unidentified heresy. So, it begins.

"The Earth is round," someone shouts.

"The Earth revolves around the sun," shouts someone else.

"God is dead! Caravaggio rules!"

"The Virgin is dead, long live the Virgin!"

Everyone laughs and cheers. Someone boos. Everyone boos the booing. It's great fun until the cops arrive swinging pikes, singling out those in shabby clothes. Our fanboys and groupies step aside and peruse the brutality. Lena shudders and swoons. I prod Cecco forward and ferry Lena toward the Fountain of Neptune. Her nails dig into my biceps. She claws them all the way to the donut cart. My posse is there waiting, booted, suited, and armed. Their servants burdened with their entire arsenals. Onorio is sans horse but Menicuccia rides his hip.

"Congratulations on the blockbuster!" Mario has an eye on Lena, the other twinkles upon me.

"Not your best picture, but your biggest crowd-pleaser," says Prospero.

"A Virgin like that being worshipped by peasants like those? That could get you both decollated." Orazio angles a frown of genuine concern.

"The new Papa is all about him," Onorio says.

"Not if the Tomassoni have their way," Menicuccia replies.

I roll my eyes. Ranuccio's been in hiding since defacing my John. Del Monte told Cardinal Farnese to chain his goons. He told him that Papa has divine plans for me.

"The Tomassoni brothers only pick fights they can win," Cecco says.

"They've been patrolling Campo de' Fiori, picking fights with anyone who so much as smells French," Orazio is suggesting.

"Let's go there now and defend Papa's supporters," Onorio says.

Lena's nails puncture my skin. I regret not wearing my armor on her promise of a noonday blowjob. I turn to Cecco hoping he'll answer for me. He's talking blades with Onorio's servant with his back to me. I'm forced to speak on behalf of Michelangelo.

"I can't go. Del Monte and the marchioness have forbidden me from fighting. They revoked my license to carry. They confiscated my rapier."

My posse believes me. They know it's true. They also know that it's never stopped me in the past. Mario is the first to offer mercy.

"Your success is my success," he says.

He salutes me. Prospero salutes me. Orazio half-salutes me. Onorio right-faces and gallops away without his pro. The posse stalks after him. Cecco accompanies the servants. Lena forfeits the Antichrist to Menicuccia.

"Thanks. I'll pick him up after the dinner bells."

Lena kisses Menicuccia on the cheek and lowers her puckered lips to the Antichrist. He shuns her lips and mashes his face into Menicuccia's tits, bawling all over them. Menicuccia carries him away screaming. Michelangelo dies a little. My posse is off to brawl, and I'm happier to live by my woman.

The shutters are open, the bedroom blanched with noontide radiation. Our skin cools on each other. She's reading my palm with her ear on my chest. The sable naps at the bottom of the bed. Now that I've made her famous, I'm not so destroyed when she doesn't fade. I tried like hell. She came close.

"Your thumb is Venus. Jupiter the forefinger. Saturn. Apollo. Mercury is your pinky."

"Does it say when I'm going to die?"

"You're between Virgo and Libra, two very opposite signs."

"I'm actually three very opposite thirds. Which one will get his head chopped off first?"

"I've told you, there's no such thing as Caravaggio, and I'm proud of Michelangelo for not marching off with your friends."

"Papa will give us St. Peter's. He'll award us wall space in the Apostolic Palace and Quirinal Palace. We'll draw larger crowds than *Pieta*. I won't misspend our opportunity on a pimp."

It's the sex talking, but the sentiment becomes my every intention now that I've said it.

"I fucking love you," she says.

"I know. I can't believe it."

"I know. That makes me sad. Why can't you believe it?"

"I don't need to believe it. I feel it."

"That makes no sense," she says.

"Exactly, which is why I trust it."

"But you don't trust me."

"I don't know you. You won't let me inside. At Mass, you were just sitting there. I had no idea what you were feeling. I have no idea if I make you feel anything."

"You're inside me all the time."

"No. Inside your *head*."

"I think of you when I'm with other men. I think of you when I'm alone. At Mass, I was thinking of how lucky I am to have you."

"It didn't look that way."

"You read minds? I didn't know your genius included clairvoyance."

"I want viewers to be intimate with my Virgin. I want her dwelling in their heads. Staring into you, I only see me, clearer than my selfies. I thought I knew my fears and flaws, but being with you, I've discovered new ones. It's exhilarating, but I need to paint it out of my system. It's making me fat. It's making me paint like an idealist. Prospero was right. It's my worst picture. I need Caravaggio."

"I don't want to be the Virgin again. She's getting to you, or maybe I'm getting to her."

"Then give me another crack at you. I'll do you justice. That was my first picture without any Caravaggio."

"You made me look like a whore. I've never seen myself that way. I like it, maybe too much. What's the end game to all this? Besides double decollation."

"The end game is making you feel something."

"The feelings of others have always felt more real than my own, but I do have them. I have feelings, but unlike you, I don't believe my feelings."

She examines the fingernail impressions on my biceps as if they're news.

"You're almost too beautiful," I say.

"You're beautiful. *You.* There's no Michelangelo. There's no Caravaggio. There's only you in there. It's suicidal to believe otherwise."

The sable intensifies its stare as if to say *amen*.

XIV.

The gopher escorts me to Del Monte's music chamber. I don't want or need him to. I know Madama Palace better than him. I know it better than Del Monte. I know it like the back of Mario's hand. I know it like the top of his head. Like the Sicily-shaped beauty mark on the small of his back. For five years, we shared a bed here. We also shared a drafting table and easel, two orphans whetting our craft, resting only for sex. We faded in every corner of every room. I made him Bacchus here, my most meta selfie painted into the god of fornication's carafe. I made his superstar lute player at Madama, my most beautiful picture to date. I revolutionized painting within these walls. I made Madama matter till kingdom come. Michelangelo perfected his violence in this palace. Caravaggio came of age in this palace. I was born here.

"That Virgin. I've never crushed on an icon before. A woman no less," says the gopher.

I cold-shoulder the comment. That's not my brand of vanity, praise from a lad decorated in satin and frilly lace. He says something about her hair, but I ignore that too. From the end of the corridor, I hear the familiar strings of Del Monte's favorite madrigal. I step ahead of the gopher and welcome myself through the closed door. Del Monte is there, his scarlet heft squeezed into a Dantesca chair, strumming the lute from Mario's *Musicians* like a Spaniard. Mamma is sprawled on the daybed, dying all over herself with a sumptuous ennui. Standing before them singing "You Know that I Love You" is the former ghost of Rome's secret past. He's nothing but flesh now. Rome's favorite fuck buddy of recent yore, the castrato Pedro Montoya. His silver voice would bring cardinals to tears. His donkey dick too. Noblewomen jumped that bone on the regular. He was his voice, lithe like a rapier, but now he looks like a chubby serpent standing on its tail. His arms are long and misshapen like the necks in Carracci's mannerist porn. I painted Montoya twice. Fucked him eleven times, roughly. I'm sick thinking about it. I smell coffee but don't see any cups. The gopher closes the door behind us.

Montoya's soprano is brighter than snow, his intonation immaculate, the trill stiffening.

"But do you know, yet, I am dying for you,
For, if you did but know it,
You would perhaps have some pity for me."

Montoya left Rome four years ago. I can't imagine why he'd return looking as such. Del Monte smiles, hoping I'll take a wild guess. He repeats the stanza in his raspy tenor. I raise my voice to greet Montoya, but the fucking diva shushes yours truly. His eyes are on me, but he hasn't *seen* me yet. He goes somewhere when he sings, probably to find his balls.

"How this ardent fire is reducing me,
You will see me consumed, little by little."

How can I not think of Bruno? His contralto screams. The funk of his burning flesh. Montoya brings the madrigal to its climactic end. Mamma and the gopher perform their own polyphony of bravos. I give a polite clap. Montoya smiles at me without recognition.

"The Virgin is not your best work, but she's your biggest blockbuster," Del Monte says.

My *Bacchus* hangs on his wall. Del Monte turns to it and consumes an eyeful of Mario. I kneel before Mamma and slobber her hand like an unruly dog. She likes it. Montoya clears his throat. I stand and approach him with open arms, not wanting to deny Caravaggio's fondness for his former model. We loved Montoya when he wasn't acting like a basic bitch. I embrace him with firm affection. His malformed arms do not reciprocate. I withdraw. His cow eyes glaze over me. He doesn't remember. I look to Del Monte and Mamma for an explanation.

"Montoya, you remember our Michele," Mamma insists.

"Caravaggio," I say.

Montoya shakes his head. This has-been diva is faking dumb on me.

"He painted you," Del Monte says, pointing to my *Lute Player* hanging adjacent to *Musicians*.

"Who the fuck is he? Does he know who the fuck I am? If so, he'd know I hate being fucking interrupted. God brought me here to sing, not talk small."

He's the same temperamental bitch, the vain diva, but now his ginormous Adam's apple is entombed in a double chin. He flounces over to my *Lute Player* as if it's not there. Standing beside the picture, he aligns his posture and unknowingly provides a ghastly before-and-after that illustrates his tragic fall from grace. He takes a deep breath and signals to Del Monte, who plucks his way into another madrigal. If I closed my eyes, the voice would still choke me up.

"*I was yours and shall be whilst I still live.*"

How can I not think of Lena?

"What were you saying about my Virgin's hair?" I ask the gopher.

"Her red streaks. All the ladies of Rome are combing paprika into their hair."

Montoya amplifies his voice in annoyance.

"*Believe me, I have never forgotten you*
And I will never forget you."

How can I not think of Mario? After I painted my first *Lute Player*, the one next door at Palace Giustiniani, every femme-fop in Rome was styling their hair in Mario's bouffant.

"They're not just highlighting their hair, they're teasing it too, blowing it out all slutty. They've dubbed the style The Lena."

The pride gets to my face. I let the gopher see. He smirks back. Montoya bites the bait and throws a mercurial hissy, stomping and shrieking. Our chitchat has disrespected his voice. I laugh in his face and encourage the gopher to do the same. Naturally, he obeys. Mamma tries to stop herself from laughing but it only makes her laugh harder. Del Monte can't pry himself from the chair fast enough. He approaches the rampaging diva with the intention of consoling him, but it's too late. Montoya collapses and convulses, eyes screwed, seizing and foaming at the mouth.

"What's all this?" I ask with a scientific curiosity.

"It's common amongst castrati when they age," Mamma answers.

"Why was he here?" I follow up.

"To tutor the new Sistine Chapel castratos," Mamma answers again.

Del Monte beckons the gopher to help. More servants enter, helping to pin Montoya's flailing parts to the floor. Once subdued, the servants transport the fallen star from the music room. The silence is brisk. Del Monte closes the door and returns to his chair. Mamma sits up. I endure Caravaggio a tear or two before grabbing Del Monte's lute and taking the seat next to him. I finger the chords. It's been a while.

"Your Virgin has Papa worried. He wants to grant you commissions, but he doesn't want any more wretches or pros." Mamma glances at my *St. Catherine* on the wall, Fillide running her finger down the length of my sword.

"I've always casted my subjects from the street," I reply.

"Don't bite the hand," Del Monte says. "Paint street people but tone it down. Papa liked the Christ child finger wag. I thought it was too kitschy."

Del Monte leans over and places my fingers on the correct chords. I pick. He sings.

"But do you know, yet, I am dying for you..."

I fuck up the chords and start again.

"I just want to paint her as I see her. I've never been so happy in my life."

"Would you like some wine?" Mamma asks.

"No. I want a charger."

"What on Earth would you do with a charger?" she asks.

"He wants to bounce around Rome on a high horse. Like his friend," Del Monte says.

"Yes. I want to trick a beast out. Teach it to capriole and courbette. Ballotade and croupade. I'll train it to kick, strike, and bite like the horses of Attila. Sword raised, I'll gallop about the city waging war on the egos of doubters, posers, and slanderers. On Sunday mornings, I'll park my charger in the middle of a crowded square, sitting high and mighty, eating donuts, getting eye-fucked, looking bored."

"I've heard that rant before," says Mamma.

"Can I borrow your coach?"

"Why?" she asks.

"I want to take Lena for a spin. I want to treat her."

"Treat her like what?" Mamma asks.

"The Farnese let the Tomassoni brothers drive theirs," I say.

"That shit-box? The Farnese spent all their money warring protestants. They can't afford a new luxury coach," she says.

"Lena doesn't know the difference. I want to spoil her."

"You've made her plenty famous. Do *not* paint her for your other Virgins," Del Monte says.

"Why not?"

"Your Virgin has offended important people. They'd gladly expend political capital for your head. You've fulfilled your wish. Powerful people want you dead," Del Monte says.

"Name them." I strike the right chords, but Del Monte doesn't sing.

"The usual suspects. Cops. Captains. Cardinals. Definitely God," he says.

"Reinstate my license to carry."

"Ask Giustiniani," Mamma says.

"For my license?"

"His coach. He'll let you borrow it," she replies.

"If the Tomassoni come after you. Go to Malaspina," Del Monte says.

"I want to please Lena. She deserves it. She deserves everything."

"You love her too much. You can't paint that way. The picture proves it. That Virgin is flat with idealization," Del Monte says.

"Flat minus those breasts. Have some wine," Mamma insists.

"She's better than me. I can't satisfy her. It feels so purposeful to try. I'm so happy. Have I told you how happy she makes me?"

"I thought we lived a happy life in Caravaggio before and after the plague. Your riding lessons. Your fencing instructors. The art apprenticeships."

Mamma relapses into her reposed ennui. It's not so voluptuous, mostly downhearted and dejected. I've offended her. Maybe I meant to. It feels worse than I thought.

"Caravaggio doesn't function on happy. He thrives on guilt and contrition," Del Monte says.

"Who wants me dead? Farnese? Baglione? Masetti? Corporal Malanno? The Knights of Malta? My landlord? Has Galileo written you? What's his theory on the star? Why does it only shine at night now?"

In lieu of an answer, Del Monte sings to me. He's the mother of all fathers. He hasn't wanted to fuck me in five years.

"How this ardent fire is reducing me,
You will see me consumed, little by little."

Mamma weeps at his mordant bass. I turn to Mario's disinterested glamour. I look to Fillide. She still reigns as the woman who fucked my genius best.

XV.

I've never seen Lena this happy. Dare I say delighted, enraptured. She's so fucking into this. Her Mona Lisa smile is history, her cryptic visage along with it. There's nothing ambiguous about this blank expression. It's one of exorbitant stupor. Her mightiest johns haven't done this for her. Not Cardinal Montalto. Not Monsignor Crescenzi. Not Ranuccio Tomassoni and his aberrant schlong. Not even the superstar sexuality of Caravaggio. Yours truly has become the first man to give Maddalena Antognetti a deluxe coach ride in the shimmering veracity of day. The chargers amble at a clip faster than our chasing fans. Their goony enthusiasm is killing the rush of six-horsepower luxury transport. This ride isn't about celebrity optics. It's about bridling bestial velocity with human engineering. Lena draws the curtains so we can enjoy the experience in private. Her hand slides between my thighs. She wants to giddy-up. I'm rock-hard and rearing. I could pull this coach on my hands and knees.

Yesterday was raw with ranting rain. January in April. Some Barberini or Pamphili had the imperious whim of flooding Navona. They ordered the storm drains and fountains plugged. They diverted and sprung the nearest aqueduct. The resulting deluge washed away the dealings of vendors, whores, and pimps. The rain continued through the night and past dawn. Shortly after the sacristans jerked the ropes of morning prayer, the sun finally won its billionth comeback victory. Sensing we've been doubting its invincibility, the sun is now hulking over a world-weary Rome, browbeating us with a summer fierceness in early spring. Lena is dressed for it, a flowing red satin bodice with an austere reticella collar. Her hair is huge and whorish, combed with beetroot. The Lena. Every other female head is sporting the coif. Unfortunately for them, they're decked in black velvet, inspired by Lena's chichi dress. The bored housewives of Rome are sweating their fucking balls off. I am too. My velvet outfit is designer but faded. I've doused my family jewels in the last of Del Monte's civet anus.

The square is oval. The square is a lake, a flooded quarry with travertine facades carved into its cliffs. It resembles the Grand Canal, reminding Caravaggio of the time he let an old chicken-plucker suck him off so he could enter the Great School of San Marco and behold their Tintoretto. For Michelangelo it conjures the crepitations of the card-cheating Spanish soldier whose throat he gashed. I rolled his twitching corpse into the Rio di Noale. This so-called lake reminds me of neither episode. Those are their ghosts, not mine. How could I think of those ghosts when I'm zeroed in on Lena, regarding her with particular artfulness? I'm learning to see beyond my infatuation. Prospero and Del Monte are not wrong. My Virgin is a statue, the worst woman I've painted. I never worshipped Fillide. Certainly not my Martha. My next two Virgins will throb. Papa prefers lads, but my Virgin will make him love women. If I can save my own soul, I can save his too.

We enter Lake Navona at the northern shoreline. Every coach I know is here, rounding the flooded square counterclockwise, axel-deep, rainbows strewing from wheels. The whirring and sloshing of rapids provide a lush and dozy accompaniment. Beneath the lake, below the pavers, is the ancient trackway of Circus Agonalis, where, fifteen hundred years ago, gladiators and charioteers lost heads and broke necks. Today, Lake Navona is a play bath for socialites. Today's event is a gentleman's race between patricians, none of whom have bought my work. They handle each turn at riskless speeds, dousing bystanders by the dozens. Hundreds more spectate from the storied windows of Pamphili Palace and surrounding tenements. Along the shore, it's a who's who festival of public gorging and boozing. Families camp under decorative canopies, their personal chefs barbecuing tuna, mackerel, red mullet, and eel. Servants refill cups and carafes. Pamphili men are slurping oysters on the steps of the palace, skipping the empty shells across the lake. It's a hammy scene, something Carracci might paint.

I ask Giustiniani's driver to speed up. He whips the chargers. Lena cringes, but accelerates her rubbing of my cock. Our followers chant some jumbled words as we pass.

"What were they saying?" I ask.

"They've married our names. *Lenavaggio*. We've become a single entity."

"I like it. *Lenavaggio*. It sounds rich."

"If we ever have a son, we should name him Livio. Livio Lenavaggio."

I've been a staunch opponent of procreation since the deaths of my father and grandfathers, but the thought of my Virgin carrying my actual son drops a stone in my throat. I feel ashamed for having ever doubted her love, not that it stops me.

"I'm a horrible father. I'm selfish. Abusive. Destructive. Irresponsible. Plus, I'll be dead soon."

"I'll be dead in three years. Five tops," she says.

Our melancholia is wonderfully romantic. I kiss her neck. In doing so, I spot the Farnese coach pull in behind us. Lena doesn't see it. I say nothing. I can't identify the passengers. I clear my throat. The driver snaps his whip.

"Please make him stop that," she says loud enough for the driver to hear.

I remove her hand from my cock and place it on my cheek.

"Shortened lifeline or no lifeline, you don't get to die. I've already immortalized you."

"I don't want Caravaggio. I want you. I would also love another son. Your son."

"Stop making me cry."

"I love extravagance. I love riding in this coach. I love this dress. I want nice things, but I don't want to live forever. I've done some lousy things in my life, but I don't deserve immortality. I'm not Fillide. I don't want women dressing like me. I don't want them wearing my hair. I don't want men getting off on me unless they're dropping coins in my purse. Celebrity is unkind to men and barbaric to women. St. Catherine. Beatrice Cenci. Joan of Arc. Fame will be the death of me. My sister read it in my palm."

Mamma's coach pulls behind the Farnese coach. I can't see him, but I know that Malaspina is at the reins with another knight sitting passenger. The coach of Francesco Borghese, Duke of Rignano, gains on Malaspina. I saw Baglione boarding the Borghese coach earlier. He's been bad-mouthing my Virgin and Christ child. I wouldn't be upset if the coach cracked a wheel and flipped, cartwheeling and splintering into a thousand pieces, snapping the necks of its passengers. Lord Mattei passes us on the southwest apex, drenching our horses with the spindrift of his iron wheels. Lady Mattei hangs her head out the window. She wolf-whistles and then howls a congratulatory *Lenavaggio*, her red streaks streaming in the wind.

"Imitation is the sincerest form of hostility," says Lena.

"Two more Virgins. After that, you'll own more homes than Fiammetta, and a vineyard with twice her acreage. You'll never need another scudo from the bookworm."

"I already earn more than him. The Virgin has boosted my clien-tele. I'm making fistfuls. More dick than I can shake a stick at. I'm moving out of Gaspare's. I'm leaving him. I want you. I want your son. I don't want to be immortal. I want to die someday. I want to be forgotten."

She returns her hand to my wokeness.

"Papa is commissioning a John the Baptist for Lateran Palace. Del Monte told me. After that, we'll build a house in Caravaggio. I inher-ited a vineyard there. We'll drink and fuck all day while Livio and Ovidio stomp our grapes."

She pushes her laughter into my mouth. Our front teeth clink, smiling into each other's smiles. She slides her tongue inside. I can't breathe. My nose is pressed into her cheek. I finger aside a fold of satin and then a fold of silk and then two folds of hot wet her.

"I love you."

"I love you."

"You don't believe me. Tell me you believe me when I say it."

"I believe you when you say it," I say.

"No. Swear on my life that you believe me when I say it."

"I swear on your life that I believe you when you say it."

"Say what?"

"That you love me."

"Believe it."

"I believe it."

I don't believe it, but I believe myself when I tell Michelangelo and Caravaggio that I'll kill both of them if they ever fuck this up for me.

I open one eye while we grope and French. Onorio intersects Lake Navona, his charger at a full gallop, rainbows spitting from hooves. Onorio enters the race, a nose behind Malaspina. The *Lenavaggio* chants soar into anthem.

"We've gone viral." She sounds only a little displeased.

"It's time to exit this race while we're ahead."

We're high on life, but when is that ever high enough? I want Lena, fame, and fun in that order. Not wanting to heinously murder the moment, I ask the driver to take us home the long way. I tell him to lay down his whip. Let the beasts walk. Let our truest followers behold Lenavaggio. Those who can't afford a coach. Those who can't afford a donkey, let alone a charger. Those whose filthy soles were not permitted the splish-splashy frills of Lake Navona. Let them see their starlet. They love her because she is their own. I lean across Lena and open the curtain.

We arrive at my stoop, rosy and sexed from all the fussing over us. There's nothing like working-class adulation. Masetti and Signora Bruni stand out front waiting. The driver escorts us from the coach like we're royals. Signora Bruni is starstruck by Lena and galled by my audacity. Masetti squints, envisioning Lena as the Duke of Modena's Madonna of the Rosary. Signora Bruni watches in disbelief as the coach departs. She turns to come at me hard, but I beat her to the punch.

"Ambassador Masetti, could you please pay this woman a month's rent?"

"I just paid her two," Masetti says.

"Pope Leo wants a John the Baptist," I reply.

The news pleases and annoys Masetti. The value of his boss' Madonna has increased, along with the wait time.

"You still owe three months. Shall I go to Pope Leo for it?" Bruni asks.

"Is that a threat?" I ask.

Lena reaches into her cleavage. Masetti gnaws his lower lip. Lena withdraws a small purse. Signora Bruni licks her lips. I stop Lena's hand from digging out the coins.

"Please put that away. I'm not worth it," I say.

"Classy move. There's hope for you yet," Signora Bruni says to Michelangelo.

"Can you start the Duke's Madonna before summer?" Masetti asks.

"He can start it tomorrow," Lena says.

My Virgin is back on board.

"I don't deserve that either," I say to her.

"You deserve the hype," Signora Bruni says to Lena. "You're even more sublime in person."

I receive the insult with distinction. Lena takes the compliment poorly, responding to Bruni with the sphinx treatment, which makes her wow on Lena all the more.

"Let's leave Lenavaggio to their Catullus," says Masetti.

He clears his throat and politely nods Signora Bruni away. She accepts his authority. The two of them make off in run-of-the-mill footwear.

"I'd rather die young and walk barefoot than wear shoes like that," Lena says.

Inside the house, Cecco sits at the table reading the afternoon newspaper. He's distressed about something. John the laborer has been spending his time at Prospero's studio, modeling his battered face as a vulgar. I invited Cecco to the lake. He turned me down hard. Michelangelo even tried insisting.

"How was the lake?" he asks.

"Serene. Surreal," Lena says.

"We invited you," I say.

"Third wheels," he replies.

Lena kisses Cecco on the head. "Never think that."

"Papa is sick," Cecco says.

He hands me the newspaper.

"He was out in yesterday's rain, attending the ceremony at the Archbasilica of St. John Lateran. He caught a fever. It's not good. They're saying he might not survive."

I'm not sweating it. God didn't deliver me a pope to kill him three weeks later. There's also the reality of modern medicine. Papa has access to the best drugs and doctors. Speaking of drugs, I hit the pantry for a handful of poppy seeds. Then a swig of wine. I pour some seeds into Lena's palm. She smacks them into her mouth. I hand her the flask. She swigs and passes it back to me. I swig. Cecco heads upstairs to the studio. Lena and I go to my bedroom. She lifts her satin dress. I pull my velvet britches. Halfway to Lena almost fading, my Cupid starts stroking his violin. It's not an actual song. He's just riffing, putting his best pain into it.

"You're a better fuck than Jove," Lena says, quoting Catullus.

XVI.

Boy was I wrong. Papa has died. The Great Bells of St. Peter announce as much. Throughout the week, his condition deteriorated. God the Indian giver. My Lateran John the Baptist dies as nothing more than hearsay. Leo was *my* Papa. He was going to get me into St. Peter's. God won't replace him with another who publicly sponsors homoerotica, or maybe that's why he assassinated Pope Leo with a deadly cold, to cock-block me with that omnipotent dong of his. I'm in the studio prepping a canvas for my *Death of the Virgin*. I drop everything and sit on the floor. I call almighty God the rottenest words. I pray he hears most of them. It's almost dusk. At any moment, he'll be visible in the sky. His wannabe star doesn't come out during the day anymore. Cecco enters looking harrowed, but not enough for my liking.

"All hell's about to break loose," he says.

I stand. There is a small knife on top of the desk across the studio. I go to it. I take it in my hand and hack the canvas to shreds.

"Why do that?" Cecco asks.

"You all but dared me. You invoked hell."

"All hell would break loose in *Rome*, I meant. Farnese soldiers are rioting for a Spanish pope. A perfect opportunity to murder Ranuccio."

I hadn't thought of that. I was too busy thinking of myself. Cecco was also taking Papa's death personally, holding me to my promise of avenging John the laborer's beating. I bend over to clean my own mess.

"When the rioting starts, we'll round the posse and take to the streets. In the meantime, let's finish my Virgin's death. I want to make it an ensemble cast. Go fetch my Peter, my Paul, my Matthews, and whoever else."

"That was our last stretch of canvas."

"Buy more while you're out. Buy enough canvas to sail the entire papal fleet. I want to make *Death of the Virgin* my largest piece of filth yet."

"Where's your better half?" he asks.

"I don't know. Here one night, gone the next six days. A few weeks ago, she said she was ready to model her death scene. I haven't seen or heard since."

"She's too precious for your kind of fame."

"As much as me, you wanted her to be our Virgin." I point the knife at him.

"You can't paint her again. You love her too much. You care too much. It alters your sensibilities. That last picture was tacky. You're only a third of the artist. You have to give the brush back to Caravaggio."

I fling the dagger down into the floor.

"I'm not painting *her* this time. I'm painting death."

"She loves you."

"Is she fucking Ranuccio? What have you heard?" I ask.

"I don't think she's fucking Ranuccio. She's not fucking anyone in your immediate circle. Some friends of friends. Traders and bankers. Maybe a lawyer or two. A furrier. She's all the rave amongst the merchant class."

"Go get the fucking canvas. Round the saints. Dig up John the laborer. I'll throw him in the picture too."

Cecco sucks hard on a comeback. I deserve to hear it. I want to hear it. He refuses me the satisfaction, heading downstairs, leaving the house. I'm proud of him, and remarkably sad for myself. Feels like old times.

While Cecco retrieves my models and supplies, I kill time by feeling sorry for myself. I punch a few walls. Kick over a trolley of paints. I lift my halberd, a weapon that didn't fit into the composition of *Christ Taken*, and hurl it into the ceiling, affixing it along the perimeter of the makeshift skylight. After a few minutes, punishing my own possessions gets old. I aim my hostility toward God again. He's the one. Why dangle Leo before me only to yank him up to heaven? Why gift me genius I can't use? Why curse me love I can't fuck? He wants me to self-combust and disappear so He can have His tongue next to Caravaggio's ear.

Someone knocks on my front door. I ignore it. Lena still has a key.

God is trying to break me. He's still positioning yours truly to fail. He wants my fall to make a splat heard around the world. He builds me up to tear me down, limb by limb, starting at the neck. Just like John the Baptist. Just like St. Catherine. Just like Beatrice Cenci. He doesn't like me perfecting His woman. I've made His Virgin mine. God has never been more jealous of my omnipotence. He could never beatify the mother of His child the way I have. Instead of being proud, he wants to retaliate. Eliminate me so He can get inside this head and paint His own vision of Lena as the Virgin. I stole His woman so now he's trying to steal mine. Fine. Try it. Do with me what you will so long as I have a brief but lasting moment. Is this how my models think of me? My lovers? There is another, more plausible possibility. Someone poisoned Papa. Someone who knew he was my likeminded ass-fucker. Del Monte said my Virgin picture had earned powerful enemies. I'm easier to kill without a pope patronizing my genius. Mamma and Del Monte have already made me close to untouchable.

I pull the knife from the floor. There's a small canvas leaning against the wall, a study I painted after the idea of Malaspina's zucchini. It's all but dry. I carry it and the dagger down to the pantry. I cut an onion and some cos lettuce. I pile the salad onto the canvas' underside. I drizzle olive oil on it and season it with salt. I sit at the kitchen table and eat, chewing over the possibility of Papa's assassination.

Another knock comes at the door. Prospero's knuckles. He's come to mourn the loss of my pope with me. I don't budge. He tries again and leaves.

Why would Ranuccio Farnese, the Duke of Parma, let some eponymic ninny ride his coach? Does his brother Cardinal Farnese find my barefoot Virgin a crime punishable by death? Ranuccio Farnese is married to Margherita Aldobrandini, niece of Pope Clement. Does her brother Cardinal Aldobrandini want me decollated? He loves smut. He and the Duke of Parma own Carracci porn. Maybe the sensual inelegance of my Virgin has offended them. Married out of financial necessity, the Farnese and Aldobrandini hate each other, but sometimes a common enemy is the best peacemaker.

I finish my salad, leaving the oily canvas on the table, not for Cecco to scrub, but for self-preservation. I need to put myself in a safe place. I lick the knife clean and carry it to the bedroom. I close the shutters. I don my armor and bring the knife and my dagger to bed. I'm painfully sober so it takes time to fall asleep, an hour or three, no more than six. Lena wants my son. I would rather make her fade. I bring her fading to mind. I imagine what sounds she might make. I imagine the trembling she might cause. I imagine her blood turning so cold my cock goes numb inside of her. I can't pull out. I die alongside her in my armor.

I awake to Cecco sobbing in his bedroom. It's only the second time I've heard him grieve. The first was in Mattei Palace shortly after his ascent from apprentice to lover. I'd fallen remarkably ill, my premier bout of headache, fatigue, and stomach cramps. I was in bed, sallower than my *Sick Bacchus*. The poor lad thought I was dying. Four years later, I'm nothing to cry over. I'm probably the last person he wants comforting him, so I ride away with Lena in Mamma's coach.

I awake to unrest. I awake to gunshots, clanging swords, and guttural outcries. Men are fighting in the streets. Michelangelo wants to enlist in the violence. Caravaggio wants to wake up and paint the death of our Virgin. I try falling back to sleep, but Mario's knock comes loud and weighty at the front door. Cecco beats me to him. I approach Cecco from behind as he opens the door, placing a fatherly hand on his shoulder. He shirks it off. Mario poses in his armor, his glamor varnished with bloodlust. He's surprised to see me in my armor with messy morning hair.

"Are you sober?" he asks.

"As a judge," I reply.

"The Farnese are capitalizing on the vacant Holy See. They've unleashed their bodyguards, soldiers, and mercs onto the city," he says.

"Rome is our city. We're the only ones who get to terrorize it," I say.

"The Tomassoni brothers attacked the governor's police at Borghese Square. The police had arrested the Rugieri brothers for instigating a brawl. The Tomassoni arrived and claimed the square as their jurisdiction, ordering the police to hand the brothers over. The police refused so the Tomassoni thrashed them. Now they're hiding out in the Garden of Oranges."

"Garden of Oranges? Why there?" Cecco asks.

He's right to scratch his head. There are only oranges and knights near the Basilica of Saint Sabina. The Order of St. John is headquartered there. Sacred knights don't fraternize with venal mercs.

"The Tomassoni brothers really think they're something," I say.

"Onorio and the others are on their way to the Garden of Oranges. We want to slay the Tomassoni before the Knights of Malta have at them. If anyone gets to annihilate that family, it should be us."

Cecco couldn't agree more. He makes off like Mercury to his bedroom.

"Fetch my dagger and that knife," I shout.

"I have a sword you can borrow. There's a hackney waiting around the corner for us. It'll drive us to Sant'Anastasia Square. We'll hike Aventine Hill from there," Mario says.

"No hope. No fear," I reply.

The ride through Rome is congested with human and architectural debris. Governor's police fighting cops. Cops fighting mercs. Onlookers raining bricks, tiles, and toilet water upon them from windows. Soldiers robbing peasants. A wretched young man with a mutilated nose wanders Via Arenula cradling a severed hand with bejeweled fingers. It's said that the four seasons of Rome are riot, orgy, feast, and prayer. Riot is Michelangelo's favorite time of year.

Mario and I disembark at decidedly tumultuous intersections, drawing our weapons, marching alongside the hackney, causing marauders to think twice. We arrive at the foot of Aventine Hill unscathed, and hike to the Garden of Oranges in humid silence. Enthralled with the lawlessness of the streets, I hadn't observed the late-spring perfection of the sun until this particular bead of sweat tickled my neck. So here it is. Rome. Almost all of it. In full view from the Garden of Oranges. It would be asinine to say how pretty it looks, but there are no signs or sounds of violence from this vista. Most notably, there's no Giovan. No Luca. No Alessandro. No Ranuccio. Nothing but tiny green oranges. Nothing but cranes, scaffolding, and belfries shadowed by a murmuration of starlings.

Before I can ask Mario what's up, Malaspina arrives atop a coffee-colored charger. Onorio rides wide flank. Without a hello or goodbye, Mario mounts Onorio's charger and canters away with him. My two best friends, too guilt-ridden to explain or justify their actions. Malaspina and the knights dismount. Malaspina offers his flask. I accept. It's only water. I spit it out. The two knights peruse the trees, smelling the leaves and germinal fruit. I finger the hilt of Mario's backup rapier, readying myself for anything.

"With all this rioting, I thought it'd be a good time to get you up here and talk about St. Jerome," Malaspina says.

"I started some studies," I reply.

"Pardon my French, Sir Malaspina, but what the fuck? Are the Tomassoni coming or not?" Cecco asks.

"They never were. Del Monte and the marchioness don't want me partaking in riots. They want me painting Virgins."

"And Jerome." Malaspina smiles.

Cecco is incensed. I'm not. I smelled fish the entire ride here, and not because of our proximity to the Tiber. Nobody brawls or duels at the Garden of Oranges. People come here to picnic and fuck. I wish Lena were here with a flask of claret and jar of poppy seeds. Michelangelo doesn't want to hear this, nor does Cecco, so I act mad for both of them.

"This is bullshit. No one can stop me from punishing Ranuccio Tomassoni. He pummeled my John the Baptist. He insulted my manhood on the street."

"He's not worth the grace that God gifted you," Malaspina says.

Caravaggio loves hearing this, but I've heard enough of it.

"People keep saying that. Leo was my Papa. Who will God appoint next? Cardinal Toschi?"

"That's the plan," Malaspina answers.

I look to the sky. Remus and Romulus held a contest of augury atop two hills of Rome. Romulus prepared a sacred place at Palatine. Remus here at Aventine. The winner would choose the location and name of their new city while also attaining the right to lead it. The two brothers sat under the sky taking auspices from bird sightings. Remus spotted six birds. Romulus saw twice that. The Garden of Oranges is for losers. I point to the morphing cloud of starlings.

"I see a black heart. What do you see?" I ask Cecco.

"The decollated head of Goliath dangling from the fist of David," he answers.

XVII.

Heads cool within days. Riot season has ended. It's orgy time. Rome has kissed and made up. The College elected Cardinal Camillo Borghese as the new Papa. Most of Rome couldn't be happier. Farnese didn't get his pope. Nor Aldobrandini his. Nobody got their man, which makes this Papa the ideal deal. He's pro-French, pro-Spanish, and pro-scudi. He's a monocrat at heart and lawyer in soul. This Papa is a self-proclaimed Roman from Siena. The coronation is this weekend. Whatever. Papa Borghese means nothing for me. Aesthetically, he's a Guido Reni guy, Carracci's up-and-coming apprentice. Papa won't be blessing me with shit, but that's okay. If not championed by the despot, be thoroughly unknown to him. That's what Bruno always told me.

I feel safe enough, but I've brought Mario's backup rapier to the tavern despite my revoked license. My posse is not here. They've been AWOL since exiling me to the Garden of Oranges. My Virgin and saints are here. My Peter sips grappa. The rest of us swill claret. My two inspired Matthews. My John and Mary Magdalene of *Christ Buried*. Laerzio Cherubini, nouveau riche lawyer and proud owner of *Death of the Virgin*. We're hosting the cast party at the tavern so Cecco doesn't have to clean up after us. Michelangelo's idea. His double-broken heart deserves some downtime.

"The picture is monumental. I waited three years for it. I'd wait six more," Laerzio says.

"Don't give him any ideas. We have another Virgin to finish for the Duke of Modena. He won't wait another month, nor will our land-lord," Cecco says.

He's sitting next to John the laborer. As promised, I put him in the picture, kneeling before the cadaverous Mother, face buried in palms to hide the damage Ranuccio caused his face. The disfigurement is hardly noticeable in the darkness of the tavern, but his dumb loud voice is permanently impaired from getting throat punched.

"Never thought I'd find my way back into a Caravaggio," he rasps. "A blockbuster at that. It so beats humping dirt."

"What did I tell you about returning to work after spending your celebrity?" Peter lives for I-told-you-so's.

"That the foreman would assign me easy tasks," John the laborer replies.

"And?"

"He's been breaking my balls like a Turkish slave."

Everyone spews a little booze in laughter. Lena keeps hers in her mouth, swallowing the claret along with her mirth. She has absolute control over herself. She broke it off with the bookworm and rented herself a bohemian apartment on the Corso.

"Why has the foreman been breaking your balls?" *Burial* John asks John the laborer.

John the laborer looks to Cecco for permission. Cecco looks to me. I nod in approval. I don't want to hear it, but I'm trying to impress Lena. Cecco passes my okay to his lover.

"Because my celebrity attracted the hate of my creator's enemies. They wrecked my face to punish Caravaggio. I'm not so handsome anymore. Not so strong either. They knocked my brain loose. I can't hump like I used to. The foreman lets me hear it, but I prefer toiling to fame. I'd rather any foreman over that pimp."

"Amen," Lena says, gargling wine.

Hilarity ensues, mine almost genuine. Did she mean amen as in she was happy to be done with Ranuccio? Or did she mean amen as in modeling for Caravaggio has brought her pain? I'm afraid to know so I don't ask. One more Virgin picture and then I'll kill him. One of the Matthews raises a glass.

"To our divine creator!" he cheers.

"Hear, hear," the other Matthew toasts.

I take a seated bow. I deserve it. *Death of the Virgin* is a secular coup. It's death's newest and most decisive showpiece. I've repented for the kitsch of *Pilgrim's Madonna*. The new picture is real, its Virgin so dead the Son Himself might not recognize her. She's here on the bench, hipped against me, and I already miss her. She's long gone, thinking of God knows what. I drink the rest of my claret, intuiting an unhappiness with me.

Laerzio signals for another round. He burns money like it's falling out of style, like a self-made man should. I spent his commission two years ago. I slam his libationary bonus and announce my departure. Lena suggests a final moment of silence to our fallen cast member, her body double, the pregnant pro whose corpse I doctored into the picture. Lena's face. Dead pregnant pro's body. Another one of Ranuccio's. A noble john dumped her and his unborn child into the Tiber. We fished her out and painted her bloated corpse as the dead Virgin. I did it as a fuck you to my mortal enemy. We returned her downstream with a garland of bluebells, poppies, and magnolia. We came to the tavern straight from the river. My pant legs are about dry.

We pay the pro a quiet prayer and leave the tavern like priest and server exiting the nave. The night air replenishes. I look God in the eye. His luminosity has faded some. He's also shrunk. Maybe he's less angry at me. Maybe he's relatively happy that I'm loving a woman and not a lad.

A gathering herd of paparazzi follow us down the Corso with carols of *Lenavaggio*. One voice has a severely gay inflection. I steer my eyes toward it. A young man with a chevron mustache. He's a Duke Dildo dressed in sheep's clothing; violet cashmere worth more than a Carracci altarpiece. He's a real deal cocksucker. I stop to catch his name.

"Scipione Borghese," he answers.

"I know lots of Borghese, but I've never heard your name," Lena says.

"He's Pope Paul's nephew," someone shouts from the crowd.

Hearing that, the crowd of pros, pimps, and wretches turn and flee from potential incarceration.

"I'm a huge fan of your work," says Papa's nephew.

"What have you seen?" Lena asks quizzically.

"Everything. I've been binging since my uncle was elected.

Noblemen open their galleries to me to get on his good side. *Sick Bacchus. Boy with Basket of Fruit. Boy Bitten by a Lizard*. All your John the Baptists. Of course, I've seen all your public pictures too. *Peter Killed* is my favorite of those. I've seen it seven times. That Peter. I'm a sucker for the grizzled."

"Are you a priest?" Lena asks.

"A law student. Just graduated from Perugia. My mother is Pope Paul's sister. He's going to appoint me cardinal-nephew. My first order of business will be lengthening the nave at St. Peter's. I want a Caravaggio for it. Every church in Rome should have a Caravaggio. That many more souls would attend Mass."

"I want my shine. I'm tired of promises. I'm tired of lesser artists getting the best commissions."

"I told my uncle about you. I told him to commission a portrait."

"He doesn't paint portraits," Lena replies.

"I love *Pilgrim's Madonna*. Your bosom is the Second Coming," he answers.

"Get me into St. Peter's, and I'll paint Papa. I'll paint your mother. I'll paint the family dog. I just finished *Death of the Virgin*. Come by my studio this weekend after the coronation. The picture will floor you. It's my largest yet."

"I look forward to seeing it."

Scipione turns and walks away with his ass way up in the air.

"Seems like a nice guy," I say.

"Him? He's a creep. Take me home. I need a bath to wash away the sleaze."

Lena's apartment is above a greengrocer. Signora Della Vecchia owns the store and building. She lives in the adjacent house with her daughter, who's young with a pleasant face. I've considered immortalizing her, but it would embolden the mother's snobbery. She's snooty and bitter, but her onions are sweet and her lettuce earthy. Her rental property isn't the dreamiest place to impregnate the love of my life, but I throw Lena down on the bed and love her just the same.

I fade so hard my calf cramps. I jump from bed and skip across the floor trying to ride it out. Lena tremors in a series of sputtering fits. As for planting a life inside of her, how can you know a thing like that? My claret-soaked gut tells me yes.

"Did I do it?" I ask.

She is unresponsive. Another seizure jolts through her.

I rephrase the question. "Did it finally work? Are you still here? Have you left the building?"

"Stop asking stupid questions. Get back here and snuggle me to sleep."

I go to her. Her body is cool but not chilled. I'll take it.

It's not against Church laws for men to sleep at Lena's house, but Della Vecchia prohibits it. When the morning birds sing, I inch out of bed and tiptoe out of the apartment. Rome is poorly lit. I raise my hood and scurry down the Corso. I make it a block before hearing the click of a wheellock at my back. If it was Ranuccio, I'd be dead already.

Three cops angle toward me. The one with the wheellock orders me to lift my cloak.

"You have a license to carry that rapier?" he asks.

"No, but the governor ordered the police chief to let me slide if pulled over."

"We'll see about that," says one of the other cocksuckers, pulling my hands behind my back, and cuffing my wrists.

I bite my tongue. I bite it for Lena. I bite it for the life inside of her and the dead life inside of her body double. I bite my tongue for Cecco. I bite it for Mamma. I bite it for Scipione Borghese and everyone else who needs me in their life.

As the cops perp walk me to the precinct, I spy a man standing in the shadows of Della Vecchia's grocery store. He looks like my thuggish bureaucrat, only stonier. I make a mental note of him. Is he the one who called these cocksuckers on me?

XVIII.

Solitary confinement for a man like Michelangelo? He relishes the exclusivity, that his sins mean so much to the authorities. Caravaggio also welcomes the isolation. He spends the peace, quiet, and continual darkness brainstorming for shadowy compositions. It's me who minds being here. I'd rather be giving Lena's womb another go. I find prison redundant. I'm the only one who can punish me. No one does it better. It's always been my principal function as Michelangelo Merisi da Caravaggio. I use prison as an opportunity to berate the other two-thirds of myself, directing the majority of my anger and disappointment at Michelangelo. It's his fuckery that lands us here. I exaggerate my frustrations with Caravaggio, that way Michelangelo doesn't feel ganged up on. They clap back at me. I shout back at them. It does no good, accomplishing little more than driving the guards crazy, which is the beauty of it, the foolproof method to our madness. Get in their heads to keep ours from battering itself against the dank walls. We rarely argue publicly. I want God and any other eavesdropping adversaries to hear my supremacy over the maniacal genius.

I'm in the blackest, dampest, coldest cell that Tor di Nona has to offer. They call it *the pit*. For men like Michelangelo, it's the Pantheon, a crypt for antiheroes and apostates. Beatrice Cenci spent her remaining days here. Bruno calculated his final cosmological summations lying on this very floor. Benvenuto Cellini, the most pornographic mannerist known to God, goldsmith and court sculptor to Cosimo de 'Medici, the ass-fucker extraordinaire who silenced enemies with a sword, that motherfucking scamp. He spent four years in the pit for treating his apprentice like a wife. My sins will be inhumed with those of my trespassing soul mates. My being here will monumentalize Tor di Nona. Scipione Borghese will rename it the Mausoleum of Michelangelo Merisi da Caravaggio.

"Like I told Scipione, I'm tired of unfulfilled vows. I want my shine," says Caravaggio.

"You're tired? I'm bored out of my skull. I haven't rearranged anyone's face since Fallacci," Michelangelo replies.

"I'm tired of fathering you both. I want a Christ child of my own. One who obeys me," I say.

The guard tosses a bucket of water over us. I laugh. I recite some random Bruno. I fence Ranuccio. I passata sotto and castrate him with a diagonal slash. I catch my breath. I place a hand against the wall and commune with it. I cross the cell and commune with the wall opposite. We hold a silent and lengthy conversation. I fall asleep. I awake and model the poses of each figure from every picture. I model some new ones—pedestrian movements—crouching, squatting, and slouching. I sit in what I think is the center of the darkness. I reach my arm all the way out. I can't see my hand. I bring it halfway home. I still can't see it. I hold my hand in front of my face. I've lost total sight of myself. I don't know how many days. I have eaten nine bowls of rice. I've taken ten pisses and three shits. My love handles are gone. My abs are back. I'm so sober I can no longer daydream, and that's when the creativity erupts. I generate enough brilliance behind the eyes to light my remaining days. I see my next Virgin, my superfine buxom fox stepping on the head of a serpent.

They release me from prison, refunding my house key, but not the rapier. They say that Cardinal Del Monte has confiscated it. I wait until I'm outside to smirk, but the sun sears the hubris from my face, disorienting me like Plato's allegorical prisoner first stepping outside the cave. I look to the ground and open my eyes. The coffee globules return but no headache. I feel my way home like a blind man. I could have made it the entire way, but after a block or two, Del Monte's new but modest coach pulls alongside me. The door opens. I squinch through the light to see Scipione sitting across from him.

"Get in," Del Monte says.

The coach's interior smells like brandy and leather-bound smut from Gabrielli's bookstore. Both men are pink. They're also blurry, but that comes from my end.

"You wreak," Scipione says.

"Tor di Nona is a prison, not a spa," I reply.

"I heard you were talking to yourself in the pit," Del Monte says.

"Is that a crime?" I take the space next to Del Monte.

"The guard said you were making too much sense."

"Reason is a crime?" I ask.

"Depends on who's rationalizing what," Del Monte answers.

"Galileo no. Bruno no. Caravaggio hell yes," says Scipione.

Del Monte has always believed that Michelangelo Merisi da Caravaggio is a two-man operation, a synthesis of hostility and genius. He believes this because he very much fathered our original success. I've never taken his blindness personally. He wouldn't appreciate yours truly. In fact, Del Monte thinks he is me. He fancies himself Caravaggio's idea guy and the libertine's inner voice. If I could only fool God into thinking He holds that station.

Del Monte reaches under his seat for the brandy. He fills his glass and then hands the flask to Scipione. I clear my throat and cough, holding out my hand.

"Stay sober. You have a big day tomorrow," Del Monte says.

"Will I be needing my sword and dagger?"

"You'll get those after you paint Papa," Scipione says.

I cough for real on the idea of me painting Papa.

"I told you last month. I made you a promise."

Scipione is drunk on himself. I should be that confident when it comes to Lena. I look to Del Monte. His smile is meek. Maybe he's jealous. Ten years under his guardianship, and I never received a commission outside his immediate circle of family and friends. I hope he doesn't feel too bad for himself.

The coach stops outside my house. I look around for Masetti or Signora Bruni. No sign of them. I sigh. Del Monte reaches under his cassock and removes a blank sheet of paper. He hands it to me. Scipione passes me a writing board.

"Write a contract," he says.

"To who?"

"Massimo Massimi wants another Christ picture," Del Monte says.

"I pressured him," Scipione follows.

He tosses me a sack of coins. It's heavy. Three hundred scudi if I had to guess.

"There's one hundred and twenty scudi in there. He's paying up front. I told him you would finish in five weeks," says Scipione.

I write a contract promising to paint Massimo Massimi a picture similar to the one I've already made him. I hand the contract to Del Monte. He passes it to Scipione. He's not a cardinal yet. He's never been a priest. He's wearing the glazed linen and sheered collar of a flaming poet.

"Next time triple the price," I say.

"Go inside. Take a bath. Remain sober through the night. My driver will pick you up in the morning and take you to Quirinal Palace. Papa is expecting you," Del Monte says.

"Stop sabotaging yourself. I'm going to get you into St. Peter's," says Scipione.

"Only I can get myself into St. Peter's," Caravaggio replies.

"Gentlemen, we can all wash each other's feet," Del Monte says.

"That sounds ticklish." Scipione slaps our knees. "Let the fun begin."

I turn to Del Monte for confirmation. I've never seen him like this, passive and unsure. The driver opens the door. I step out. I wait for the coach to trot off before hurrying into the house. I've got drinking to catch up with.

The place is stifling and spotless. I can't hear or apprehend any evidence of Cecco. I don't expect Lena to be here, but I'm disheartened when I don't find her in my bed. I drop the sack of coins on the kitchen table and peel out of my rank clothes. Naked, I open every shutter in the house, saving Cecco's room for last. I put my nose to his sheets. They smell of his sweat, like ripe quince. I go to the pantry for claret. The shelves are stocked with fruits and vegetables, oils and grains. No claret. No poppy seeds. Someone has put me on the wagon. Someone wants me healthy and productive. I don't want to trust Scipione. I don't want to know him. What choice do I have? A cardinal-nephew is the closest I'll ever come to having a Papa.

I head up to the studio. It's tidy and swept, too much for my liking. My Virgin is gone. The halberd in the ceiling is missing. The hole in the roof has been enlarged, the only way of maneuvering a picture of that size out of the room. I return downstairs and wander about, communing with various areas and corners of the house. It has nothing left to say to me. I go to Cecco's room and lie prone in his bed. I haven't seen Lena in a month. I'm frenzied over it. Tomorrow, after I've painted Papa as he is, I'll run over to Lena and plant something of my own inside of her. Michelangelo and Caravaggio have their own thoughts on procreating. I gave them too much say in Tor di Nona. Now they think they can voice themselves whenever.

"You're not fit for fatherhood," says Michelangelo.

"You're not my father," says Caravaggio. "More like an older brother who's in the way of acceding our father's throne. If you fuck up St. Peter's for me, I'll kill you."

"In your dreams. Without me, you two would have killed each other two Papas ago," I reply.

"Let me paint this Papa."

"He's all yours. I'm not interested in painting anyone but the Virgin of my child."

XIX.

The ride up Quirinal Hill to Papa's summer palace grates Caravaggio's skin. The landscape is littered with the finest family homes in Rome. The city's loftiest hill in meters and scudi, its ecclesiastical majesty is sliding. The femme-fops are moving in. Lawyers. Bankers. Industrialists. Men with inferior forms of genius mightily rewarded by Rome's modern economy. They're buying up Quirinal real estate and erecting magnificent villas. Caravaggio feels cheated. Michelangelo wants to burn them all down for him. The only time they feed off each other is when lesser men receive undue remunerations, lesser men like yours truly.

Caravaggio finds solace in the transit of peddlers slogging the hill on foot, some humping wares on their backs, others shambling beside a loaded donkey cart. None of them stop to envy Del Monte's coach. Not a single double take. They look once before returning their chins to the road, a coincidental bow directed at the business afoot, not the upward mobility of a mediocre luxury vehicle.

I lean out the window to see if my celebrity can enrich the coach's personality.

"What are you doing?" Malaspina asks.

He's chaperoning me to Quirinal Palace, ensuring my safety from myself. He's been talking nonstop about his Jerome. I haven't broken the zucchini to him, but he and his Jerome are growing on me. The man is cutthroat and cultivated, a perfect Christian soldier. He's slaughtered more Arabs than my virtual Colonna grandfather. Malaspina and I are practically related. He's cousin to Giovani Andrea Doria, Prince of Genoa, who is married to Mamma's cousin. He's also uncle to the wife of Ottavio Costa, the patron who owns my five best pictures. I'm circumstantially bound to Malaspina. Rome distanced itself from me while I was going mental in the pit. In regard to my posse, I understand why. They want Caravaggio to boom, so they're ghosting Michelangelo. I miss them, but the Knights of Malta are the next best thing. I would still bet on my posse against any of their five in a brawl.

"Are you nervous?" Malaspina asks.

"Of not getting Papa's face right?"

"Be generous is all I'll say. Actually, it's what Cardinal Del Monte told me to tell you."

"I paint dirty feet, crooked teeth, and holy terror. I paint reality. Pain is real. Human imperfection is real. Suffering is most real."

"You speak my language. I've caused immeasurable suffering. God shepherds my hand through a battlefield as he guides yours across a canvas."

"Pretty much," Michelangelo replies in genuine agreement.

Quirinal Palace appears at the end of the road. For the past twenty years, it's been under a constant state of renovation since Pope Gregory made it the papal summer home. Papa Gout also dumped considerable coin on its expansion. It's still under construction, but has already formed the appearance of a heavenly kingdom as conceived by a bombastic tyrant.

We stop at the palace checkpoint. The Swiss guards salute Malaspina and stare me over like the murderous weirdo I am. Michelangelo snarls at them. Caravaggio gives them airs. My face probably looks like a deranged consolidation of the two.

"This is Master Caravaggio, the best painter in Rome. He's here to paint a portrait of His Holiness," Malaspina says.

Hearing him tout me feels better than some of the commonplace sex I've had.

The guard signals to the gatekeeper. My left leg trembles. Why? I don't know. Malaspina doesn't notice. He's appreciating the hilltop view of Rome.

"I won't miss this place. It's too far from the sea." He takes a disappointing huff of air.

"You've retired from commanding the Papal fleet?"

He nods. "Be yourself in there."

"Did Del Monte tell you to say that?"

"No. Not at all."

I honor Malaspina with a high and stiff Roman salute. He bows his head in return. The trembling in my leg stops. Three Swiss guards usher me toward the palace in hostile silence.

A lumpy attendant in wrinkled linen greets me in the vestibule and walks me to an anteroom with one of the guards accompanying us. The palace interior is flashier than its exterior—gilded, vaulted, marbleized, and gaudy. It has nothing to do with Jesus or his apostles. I don't look around. I won't give Papa Gout the satisfaction. I keep my eyes on myself. There's a rustic pine chair beside an elaborate oak door.

"Please sit. His Holiness will be with you momentarily," says the secretary.

The attendant leaves. The guard stays. Someone doesn't trust the Lombard hick in me. I remain on my feet out of self-respect and to keep the guard on edge. This is the reception Caravaggio gets? No complimentary breakfast. No private tour of the art collection. None of the passing staff members stop to notice me. Everyone who works here is fucking miserable. I'd rather my chicken-plucker's spattered studio than this prim drudgery.

I stand like bronze for an hour. The guard budges first, a shifting of weight from one hip to the other. I win, but within minutes, my leg resumes trembling. I shouldn't be this close to Papa. To Bruno's advice, I've always maintained a purposive distance from His Holiness, the closest being his Beatrice's executions. Papa Gout attended neither, but his hands struck the flint and swung the axe. This Papa isn't that Papa per se, but they're all terribly similar. By day's end, this Papa will know me all too well. Maybe that's why God has brought me here, to be sentenced by his chief justice.

The oak door opens. A heftier, wrinklier attendant appears.

"His Holiness will see you. The easel and paints are arranged as the cardinal-nephew specified. His Holiness is seated in his preferred pose. This will be the only sitting."

The attendant backsteps through the doorway. The guard waves me in and follows. It's a windowed library with adequate natural lighting, but the uptight mountain of bureaucracy sitting on an undersized throne is unpaintable, his horridness too real, his dissymmetry too cumbersome. This Papa is unsightly. This Papa is him, the man who will have my head. Pope Paul V is the enemy I've been surmising. No more paranoia. My worry has been legitimized. I finally see it, the selfie I've been vowing to myself. The decollated head of Goliath dangling from the fist of David.

The attendant announces my name in full. I approach Papa. The two guards standing a defendable distance from him do not kill me. The guard at my back lines up next to them. I genuflect so deep both knees crack. Papa does not offer the Piscatory Ring for a kiss. He fixes a hasty glare on Michelangelo Merisi da Caravaggio. He squints his eyes trying to catch a glimpse of the genius, but all he sees is the heretic, the libertine who curses him. I can see it in his grimace, lips tighter than a clam.

I approach the easel and mix paint while his narrow eyes hate on Michelangelo. Caravaggio doesn't care if this man castigates Michelangelo. He's better than both men. Caravaggio looks beyond Papa's egghead. He sees past his triple chin. He can make beauty of the wrinkles, pleats, and frills of his attire. The white cassock aproned by a lace rochet. The red mozzetta buttoned. No insignia. No regalia other than the Piscatory Ring. I leave his face a smudge and paint the fabrics. After two hours of the silent treatment, Papa breaks.

"Cardinal Del Monte speaks of you like a son."

"Your Holiness is just saying that."

"I don't *just* say anything."

"I was poor, naked, and starving when I arrived in Rome. My feet were dirty as the pilgrims in my Virgin picture. Del Monte saved me, Your Holiness."

"*Saves* you."

"My job as an artist is to fulfill almighty God's grace, Your Holiness."

"What geniuses don't say or discover can be deadly."

"If it ever happens, I want to be decollated. Can you please do that for me, Your Holiness?"

"My nephew has big plans for you."

"God has big plans for me. What does His Holiness think of God's new superstar?"

He doesn't answer. He's artless. He's not much for science either.

His face regains its hate. Hours pass. He leaves once to urinate, or maybe shit, how do I know? His inertia impresses me. I can't think of a model who rivals it. The man is physically impossible. Eventually, he slides a foot. The toes of a Papal slipper protrude from the hem of his cassock. He's unaware. I paint the slipper before it disappears. Not painting it as a naked foot betrays Caravaggio's one and only belief, but he does it for St. Peter's.

"What is that putrid smell? I was told that this palace was beyond the stench of the river, even on the hottest days of summer, but that rot, what is it?"

"Tor di Nona, Your Holiness. I just got out yesterday."

"I heard you were delivering sermons in the pit, talking to yourself like a kook. You should listen to your genius and not the hick in you. God might favor you more."

"His star follows me at night. It would also follow me during the day when it shined beside the sun."

"Is the portrait finished? I think it's finished."

I raise my brush in surrender. Papa stands from his chair. I genuflect. Papa leaves the room without checking my work. The guards follow him. The portrait is flattering. It makes Papa look like a sadistic bureaucrat, and not the impenitent chicken-plucker that he is. The portrait won't get me killed, but it won't win me another commission, not with Camillo Borghese.

———

I arrive at Lena's sometime after the curfew bells. She's not home. I go home. She's not there either. Neither is Cecco. I go to San Luigi Square. My posse is not there. They're not at Navona. The food vendors have snuffed their fires. Some wretches eat dripping off the pavers. I'm starving too. The only thing I've had all day is crow.

"You fucked us. You provoked Papa on purpose," Caravaggio says to me.

"Me? You did the painting," I reply.

"Yeah, but you had to rub that superstar in his face." Caravaggio points up at the sky.

Its brightness has dulled. A minor star at best.

"I agree. Papa hated us. It was all you," Michelangelo says to me.

"Nothing is all me. Not when it comes to us," I say.

Three femme-fops instigate a chant of *Lenavaggio*. I ask them to stop. They continue in hushed voices, tailing me to Lena's. Once there, they chant from the curb as I climb the staircase and pound the door. Signora Della Vecchia appears from the downstairs storefront. I plunge the staircase in three leaps. She's sporting a Lena hairdo, but her snotty puss is all her.

"Where have you been?" she asks.

"Painting His Holiness," I reply.

"Lena's boyfriend. He slashed her face. She's at her sister's."

"What do you mean her boyfriend? Ranuccio?"

"Not her pimp. Her boyfriend."

"I'm her boyfriend. She doesn't have a pimp."

"I thought you were her pimp. The other boyfriend then. The nerd. Albertini. He found out she's been with you. He thought she was only modeling."

"She left Albertini. She moved out of his house. I'm going to cut his entire face off."

"Cut the other man too."

"What other man?"

"That man. He's been snooping around. He's the one who told Albertini about you."

Della Vecchia points across the street. The fanboys and groupies fall silent. It's the functionary, the stonier Masetti from the night of my perp walk. He's slinking down the Corso. He sees that I've spotted him and darts off. There is a hatchet buried in a stump. Della Vecchia uses it to make kindling of vegetable crates. I yank it free and sprint after him, my fans cheering for blood. I turn into an alley and head him off at the palace of the Spanish ambassador. I back into a doorway and listen for his scudding footsteps. He passes without seeing me. I chase him down, striking the back of his head with the hatchet. He makes an infernal grunt and flops to the pavers, his forward momentum creating a spectacular whirligig of limp parts. He's dead to the world, but I leave him a parting message in case his soul is listening.

"Snitches get stitches, cocksucker."

I catch my breath and look around for witnesses. There are many. All of them scared stiff. I hide inside my cloak and take flight down the alley toward Madama Palace.

XX.

I fucked up. I sabotaged myself. Papa hated the portrait. Worse, the head I axed belonged to one of his bureaucrats. Mariano Pasqualone is not dead. He's heavily stitched and concussed. Serves him right. He was the deputy lawyer who interviewed Beatrice Cenci upon her arrest. Pasqualone is a civil servant, a secretary of oppression and malice. An anonymous source has also informed me of his penchant for biting pros, but Mamma doesn't want to hear this. Neither does Lord or Lady Mattei. Nor Del Monte or Giustiniani. Ottaviano Costa is somewhat amused by Pasqualone's sexual proclivities, but Mamma shoots him a look. This is an emergency intervention. My patrons stand over me in silk pajamas and robes. I'm sitting on the daybed in Del Monte's music room. Mario strums his lute above my head. Mamma does the talking.

"His Holiness is not a fan. A newly elected pope of middle-class origins must prove his supremacy with an excessive display of force. He needs a head to roll. Don't give him yours."

"I did his egg of a head a miraculous favor."

"You cleaved a Papal functionary in the fucking skull!" Del Monte throws his hands in the air.

I haven't heard him curse since my Baglione arrest for slander.

"Pasqualone ratted out my Virgin to her boyfriend. The boyfriend cut her face."

"Her landlady. The greengrocer. She's the one who told Albertini," Mamma says.

"Why was he creeping around Lena's apartment?" I ask.

"Doing his job. The landlady told the police that she had a tenant whoring herself on the property while living with her pimp. Pasqualone was investigating. He was going to clear you of wrongdoing. I arranged it," says Del Monte.

"Is Lena still fucking Albertini?" I ask.

"I don't know. Probably. The landlady probably called him too."

"Who let you borrow my coach when I was out of town?" Giustiniani asks.

"I finally did it. I finally managed to get myself killed. Can I have my rapier back? I'd love to go down swinging, not tied to a burning stake or bent over a block."

"Why are you hell-bent on wasting your genius? Why are you hell-bent on jamming images of the starving down the Church's throat? Do you resent God? Do you resent me? I've loved and treated you like a son," Mamma says.

"You don't have one Caravaggio hanging in your palace."

Mamma excuses the others from the room. I drop to my knees. I bring the hand of each patron to my eye and butterfly kiss it. They bid me their fond and cost-effective adieus.

"Take care of my John," I say to Lord Mattei.

"Your ram John is taking care of your newest John," Lady Mattei scolds.

"Then take care of my Cupid," I say to Lord Giustiniani.

They promise to feed my pictures the proper love before leaving me and Mamma to our unresolved affections. She's pale as plaster. She came straight from bed to Madama in the middle of the night. I walk to her on my knees.

"You kill me," she says.

"You killed me first. You sent me to art school instead of military school."

"I've invested more emotion and care into you than my own sons."

She throws guilt like bricks. I've learned to catch them with my teeth.

"I'm vanishing you to Genoa. You'll stay with the prince and my niece until I fix this."

"I'm not losing my head? I haven't run out of favors?"

"Not yet. Almost."

"Are you my mother? Am I a Colonna?"

"Be a Caravaggio. Be the star child, the one I comforted in my arms."

I tear up. I hug her left leg. I remember. I'm thirty-four years old. I'm six.

My father's father fell ill shortly after supper and died the next morning. That night, my father died in little more than an instant. His brother died two mornings later in no time at all. The Plague had returned. The governor of Milan prohibited citizens from fleeing. Two days later, he fled with half the city's army bulwarking him through the countryside. That same day, my maternal grandfather's nose and fingers turned black. My mother was left to remedy the material losses of two patriarchies while feeding four children. The marchioness took me and my brother to Caravaggio along with her own sons. The marquis was staying in Milan to assist Archbishop Borromeo in his efforts to temper panic. My mother kept my two sisters in Milan with her while settling both estates. The triple patricide happened so fast the men didn't have time to write wills.

We left Milan in the marchioness' coach, twenty soldiers riding alongside us, protection from bandits, wolves, and dragons. The soldiers might have been overkill. Half a day behind the governor, we slipstreamed in the safety of his immensely weaponized convoy.

After an hour, the monotonous jiggling of the road rocked the other six children to sleep. I was too distraught to doze. At four, my brother was too young to fret the voidance of losing all the men in our family. My virtual brother Fabrizio Sforza-Colonna, six months my elder, hadn't lost anyone or anything. I sat between my two brothers, habitually peering out the back window, expecting to see Plague himself galloping after us. The marchioness sat opposite with sleeping heads on her lap, a statue of maternal comfort, the pacific confidence of someone who wholeheartedly believes in heaven, the tranquil fortitude of a woman rich enough to buy her family from harm's way. This was not her everyday demeanor. More often than not, she was dark and broody. Sardonic in gesture. Outspokenly cynical. Her superhero father had forced her into marriage at twelve. She threatened to kill herself and her soul. She eventually warmed to her husband, but never lost her edge. It's like she was born to be my Mamma.

The marchioness sat in the coach, staring out at the roadside

Armageddon while calmly drinking tea. I was traumatized. Whenever the coach slowed to maneuver around a ransacked carriage, I closed my eyes and sniveled. The marchioness would whisper consolation across the coach, lying to me, telling me we were almost home when we weren't. I knew the road well. Milan to Caravaggio. Our lives were divided between town and country. Spires and mulberry trees. Violence and peace. Michelangelo and Caravaggio. I knew the bends of the road. I knew every bump. I knew the mile that smelled of warm focaccia. I knew the mile that smelled like milled wood. The two miles that reeked of sewer. That smell had finally left my nose when I turned to see if the Plague had gained on us. What I saw was the raw and glossy entrails of a slaughtered horse. I convulsed with silent terror. My fear was inconsolable. The marchioness lifted the sleeping head from her lap and waved me over. I brought my muted wailing to her, pushing my face into her belly. She rubbed my back, but I couldn't stop. My artistic temperament was getting the best of me. Finally, perhaps wanting to serve that genius, perhaps wanting to share the beauty of darkness and despair, the marchioness offered me a sip of tea. It worked like a charm. The high went right to my head.

We passed a brown and blighted melon pasture. Birds skirred the heavy afternoon sky feeding off the seeds of famine.

"Let's play a game of augury," said the marchioness, counting a squadron of starlings.

"I count seventy-five hundred thousand million," I blurted out, trying to beat her to whatever punch.

She laughed and tousled my curls.

"That formation looks like a letter V," she said.

"That one looks like a mouth singing *whoa*," I replied.

We laughed like mad. She squeezed my head in her armpit. Even in the shade of the coach, my face felt hilariously sunny. I was smiling so hard it hurt, my eyes squinty and wet.

"The mind on you," said the marchioness.

When I reopened my eyes, I saw a large white star just below the sun. Its light was sharper, more effusive.

"I spy a star," I shouted.

The marchioness batted her eyelashes and gazed deep.

"I don't see it. Where? What are you talking about?"

"It's saying something," I said.

I reached for the teacup, but she pulled it back. I measured two fingers parallel to the sun.

"It's there just below it."

I looked up at her face. Her giggle wrinkles had flattened into iron wonder.

"Are you sure it's there? I don't see it. What's it saying?"

"I can't understand. I think it's speaking Greek."

The marchioness placed a hand over my forehead as if checking my temperature.

"My genius boy. Mamma will see to it that you understand."

XXI.

Monday morning traffic has slowed this holy donkey cart to a two-beat scuffle. A phantom of stone dust rises from our wheels and journeys onward. One mile outside the People's Gate after a fifteen-day ride from Genoa. My coccyx prays for mercy.

"Let's get out. It'd be faster to walk," says Michelangelo.

"The Lombard hick doesn't want to be seen carting across the People's Square?" Caravaggio needles.

"It wouldn't be the first time we entered Rome broke, tattered, and culpable," I say.

"Forget buying a coach, I'll never afford a charger," Michelangelo gripes.

"Coaches are pimps. Carts are saints, vessels of the sick, the old, and the dead," says Caravaggio.

"The criminal too," I interject.

"Carts transport all the best people and all the best things. Bricks. Marble. Vegetables. Wine," says Caravaggio.

Michelangelo raps Mario's secret knock against the oak barrel cinched behind us. The Prince of Genoa has forwarded a keg of his favorite claret to Mamma, a gift for loaning him yours truly. Prince Doria porked me up on pesto ravioli, salami, and honey cakes. His Colonna princess packed a seven-day feast for my journey home. I immortalized Prince Giovani Andrea Doria in my Christ picture for

Massimi. The prince is now my Pontius Pilate displaying Jesus to a crowd of maddened Jews like a trader proffering a slave on the auction block.

"Carting the wretched to and from places of rest, prison, and enslavement. It's the ultimate Caravaggio vehicle if you think about it," I say.

"No. A studly charger pulling a rustic cart." Caravaggio always has to one-up me.

"No cart. No charger. It's the waft of donkey farts forever. Am I getting off or what?" Michelangelo asks.

The driver clears his throat. "I'm bringing you to Colonna Palace. The prince ordered it."

He has a wheellock and lethal biceps veins. He's bodyguard to the prince but currently serves as my babysitter. Michelangelo thinks we could overtake him. I'm dead either way. Mamma sent word of a pardon. I'm to sign an affidavit of apology and peace to Papa's lawyer. I'm to meet Pasqualone at Quirinal Palace, shake his hand, kiss his cheek, and embrace him. I trust Mamma with my life. I also trust Papa with my death. Immortalizing his hateful little face certified it. His Holiness will make me pay for that portrait double the malice he'd already intended me. If Mamma and Del Monte have wrangled a pardon, then why the secrecy of my return? Why send me home disguised as a peasant carting a donkey? Why send me down the road swordless in possession of invaluable pictures in the care of a Genovese hitman? Someone has gone great lengths to organize my homegoing in the most thoughtless way possible.

"Shoot me," Michelangelo says, hopping off the cart.

"I have your pictures," my babysitter threatens.

"You wouldn't know what to do with them. I'll be at Colonna Palace finishing my cacio e pepe by the time you cart there."

His wheellock reels and clicks, sounding eerily similar to Lena unlocking my front door. I'm not falling for it. I skip off toward the People's Gate like a homo, diminishing myself into the army of seekers. We approach the entrance, a cavalcade of big dreams and living nightmares. As per usual, I'm somewhere in between. Centered and embossed above the archway is the papal coat of arms winged by two abounding cornucopias. The empty promise of Rome's prosperity. The archway swallows us whole, a great snake ingesting a greater prey.

I'm halfway to the square's obelisk when a stargazer finally sees through my insolvent disguise. A man of ageless poverty dressed in sacks. He points to Santa Maria of the People and poses as the laborer hoisting my Peter's upside-down cross. He might be Rome's most wretched art fan, meaning he spends too much time in church. I wish there was a better way.

"I'm with you," I say to the stargazer.

My pity hits him between the eyes, sending him stumbling toward Santa Maria where he'll stare at my Peter and Paul for hereafter. More stargazers flock to me. A femme-fop charades my Matthew's assassin. An off-duty pro tiptoes as my Virgin. Neither brings me pleasure. If anything, I'm irked. All this fame. All this adoration. And what? Poor and condemned as ever. Thirteen years ago, I arrived at the gates of Colonna Palace naked, emaciated, and guilty of ass-fucking, cocksucking, and murder. Today, I'll appear before Mamma ragged, pudgy, and hard up for Lena's pussy. What will Mamma spare me? What great favor will Del Monte and the cardinal-nephew pay me? One hundred and twenty scudi for resurrecting Christ? My early still lifes earned more than my recent blockbusters. Why? Del Monte blames the pugnacity of Michelangelo. Mamma blames Caravaggio's undying fixation on the imperfect. God blames the former ass-fuckery of yours truly, which I gave up. I sacrificed Cecco. I'm not asking for reward. I'm fine with persecution, but put some respect on it. Give it to me atop a charger. Give it to me in a bed of silk wrapped with Lena. Get me into St. Peter's and then have at me. These masters of mine put the cart before the ass when it comes to driving slaves.

A horse-faced flagellant crosscuts my path. He's all business, lashing himself with the same Monday morning earnest as the vendors, couriers, and beggars hustling about the square. His blind faith moves me. I hoof it home for a kitchen knife. I'll take the blade to Lena's. If john, or the bookworm, or Ranuccio are in her bed, I'll kiss their face with it. If she's alone, I'll pare us some breakfast fruit.

I pass Firenze Palace in full character, hood up, head down, and hunched, limping like a lamed and spiritless veteran. Del Monte never enters work this early, but it's time for my devilry to smarten up. Stop making it easy for my masters and enemies. Shield myself from God's eye. Scarecrow the stool pigeons and the finky little birdies.

Turning my alleyway, I'm stopped by the endeavoring tempo of hammers on nails. I raise my head but augment my gimp. Two men are standing on the roof of my house. They're repairing my hole, blinding my shine. My heart barfs as if finding all four Tomassoni brothers in bed with Lena. I race to the rescue of my light source, the speed of which uncloaks my hood. My front door is wide open. I bull inside like a fool, into an overawing vacancy. Everything is gone. My three-legged table from *Matthew Called*. My *Supper at Emmaus* dinnerware. My *Death of the Virgin* copper basin. My Cupid's *Love Conquers* stool. Signora Bruni has evicted me. I've lost count of the months I owe. The rooftop hammering rattles the walls, resounding through my vertebrae. My angel wings. Has that dickwad confiscated my Cupid's feathers?

I run upstairs. Everything is missing. My studio has been erased. My canvas and paints gone. The walls and floor repainted. All signs of Caravaggio nullified. I gaze up at my hole. It's been sawed square. A wooden face glares down at me.

"What are you looking at, cocksucker?"

The face turns reverent.

"Master Caravaggio? Sorry. I thought you were a beggar scrounging around the house."

"Where's my shit?"

"Signora Bruni took it. Please don't hurt us. We're only here to work."

Another face bumps his face from the frame, this one leathery and twice as awed.

"Master Caravaggio! I'm your hugest fan! I sit at Sant'Agostino morning and night worshipping your Virgin. Her beauty kills me."

"It kills me more," cries the other roofer.

"That's why I made her, to kill all men, leaving only me."

I turn for the door. This studio is dead to me.

"Should we tell Signora Bruni you were here?" one asks.

"No. I'll leave her a message," I shout from the stairwell.

I stop and squat in the front doorway, paying Signora Bruni three feasts worth of Princess Doria's generosity.

XXII.

Colonna Palace footholds the upper crusty development of Quirinal Hill. My ass itches so good by the time I hike there. Every couple of breaths I catch a whiff of myself. The donkey cart is out front. A guard escorts me to Mamma's chamber, taking me the long way through the gallery, rubbing my nose in the absence of Caravaggio amongst the Tintoretto, Pietro da Cortona, and Palma Vecchio. I don't hate the Tintoretto portrait of Willaert the composer. I like it enough to have stolen from it: the gravitational stare irradiating from blackness. Dragging my eye away, I'm blindsided by something blunt. Some mother-fucker has hung a Carracci on the wall. The peasant eating beans. A fart joke that looks worse than it smells. It used to hang at Farnese Palace.

"Is that a prank?" Caravaggio asks.

"Someone is trying to provoke me," Michelangelo answers.

"Is it a copy?" I ask.

The guard doesn't answer. He doesn't know and he knows better. Michelangelo wants his job of playing dumb and standing strong for Mamma, the original plan for her Michele.

Mamma lolls in bed, gloomy as a teen. Noon in a silk peignoir. The room is muggy from the dissipating humidity of a recently poured bath. The chambermaid from my *Judith Beheading Holofernes* collects towels from the floor.

"I can smell you from here," Mamma says.

"The road was long and hot."

"Where have you been? Your babysitter said you jumped cart."

"I attended morning mass at Santa Maria of the People."

"You smell like shit. Take a bath. I just got out. The water was still warm."

I lean over the oak washtub like my Narcissus, the water offering no reflection. Cursive strands of hair float on the surface. I get naked and sink into a kneel.

"How was Genoa?"

"Stellar. I drank like Bacchus and ate like Pope Clement."

"Did you work?"

"I finished Massimi's *Ecce Homo* and a *Jerome Writing*. A still life of fruit and veggies too. I left them with the hitman. He didn't give them to you?"

"Del Monte and Borghese took them. They were waiting for you."

"They're cashing in before I self-destruct, before my Michele gets my Caravaggio killed."

My chambermaid hands me Mamma's dirty washcloth. I lash my back with it.

"Do you know that wannabe author Piccinardi?"

I know of him and I know what she's about to tell me. The news traveled to Genoa. I bow, submerge my face, and recite an amphibious Our Father. I can hold my breath forever. When I come up for air, Mamma continues.

"Piccinardi wrote a tedious biography about Pope Clement. Compared him to Tiberius. Pope Paul had him decollated on Sant'Angelo bridge. The book wasn't even published. I told you Papa needed to flaunt power. He found a sacrificial lamb, but don't give him another excuse. Beheading people is addicting, and as your portrait illustrated, our new Papa is a sociopath. He really doesn't like you."

"His nephew likes me."

"His nephew likes your pictures."

"And you don't."

"Stop fishing for flattery. I love you like a son. How many times must I say it?"

"All the time. Is that the original Carracci in the gallery?"

"My cardinal brother bought it from Cardinal Farnese. I told you, the Farnese are short cash. All that warmongering. The Carracci is an investment. His paintings will be worth thousands someday."

"And my pictures won't?"

"Not at your rate of behavior."

"Do you really love me?"

"I really love you."

"Like *really* really love me?"

She releases a girlish sigh, and rolls onto her stomach. Her bare legs fork at my face. I look away.

"Why won't you buy a picture?"

"Pictures do nothing for me. Sculptures less. I love madrigals. I love operas. And I love you. I haven't bought a picture, but I've bought you inestimable second chances. Why isn't that enough? Why do you take them for granted? Your sins betray my care and affection."

I bow my face into her scum and bubble a Hail Mary. When I'm finished, I stand.

"Are you my mother?" I ask.

She sits up as if all the bells in Rome have rung an alarm.

"Your mother? How would that even be possible?"

"I don't know, but I've heard crazier dramas. Palace intrigue tales of house stewards and baronesses. My father spent more time in the Sforza palaces than our home."

The maid pours Mamma tea. She wraps a towel around my waist and pours a cup for me.

"No thanks. I want to be lucid for this."

The maid takes the cup for herself and leaves. Mamma sips in silence. When the cup is empty, she lies back and gazes into the ceiling coffers.

"I was madly in love with your father for about five weeks," she says.

"So, you are my mother?"

"You know that's impossible."

"So, you and my father had a brief fling."

She closes her eyes. "You might be brother to my Fabrizio."

"Might? How do you know?"

"How does anyone know? There's no science to knowing that. Want me to hire Galileo to look into it? Fabrizio looks like a Colonna. I had sex with my husband twice that month. I had sex with your father at least ten times. I also fooled around with your mother once."

"All in the same month?"

"People were dying by the minute those days."

"Uckingfay utslay."

"What?" she asks.

"Nothing. What am I supposed to do with this information?"

"Know that I love you like family and stop destroying yourself."

"Your Michele dies lest he has someone's face on his fist."

"Don't make my Michele your whipping boy. His temper isn't the whole problem. Your Caravaggio and his love of whores and peasants. Papa deems your Virgin whore as blasphemous as Bruno's heliocentrism. He'll have your head. No more Virgin whores. No more slave saints. Fuck who you love. Paint everyone else."

"I love Lena. I can't paint her for shit. *Pilgrim's Madonna* is my weakest picture. It's too caught up in her cleavage. I glorified her face but neglected her soul."

"The miserable can't get enough of it. Sant'Agostino is the busiest church in Rome. The Virgin death scene you painted was foul. It reminded me of those Plague days. All those tumid corpses. Your father. Your grandfathers. Your uncles. Why'd you make the picture so large? To offend Papa all the more? The Carmelites at Santa Maria della Scala will never hang it. The death is too real. The Virgin too whorish."

"She was pregnant. A client of Ranuccio Tomassoni killed her and his bastard fetus."

"Stop saying his name. You don't know anyone by that name."

"*Death of the Virgin* is nearly a masterpiece, but it's only Lena's face. The one she makes sleeping after sex, after I've failed to make her fade. She's always on the threshold. I can't deliver her. Not on canvas. Not in bed."

"You should have kept Cecco in your bed. Why did you move him to the guest room?"

"For fear of God."

"Michelangelo Merisi da Caravaggio is afraid of God?"

"I was afraid of what he might do to Cecco for lying with me."

"The Divine One had young lovers. Da Vinci too. God made you this way. Genius must be served."

"I'm not the Divine One. I'm not da Vinci. They were decent men. I'm a terror. I axed an unarmed man in the skull. I killed a cop in Milan. I murdered a Spanish soldier in Venice."

"That's a bathtub, not the Jordan. My chamber isn't a confessional."

"Can I have my rapier back?"

"No."

"Can I call you Mamma?"

"Absolutely not."

"Can I call you Mamma when no one's around?"

"Fine."

I wipe myself with her washcloth and step out of the tub. I approach her bed, dripping all over the floor. "Can I just lay with you?"

She doesn't answer. I help myself to her satin sheets. She rolls to the far side of the bed and puts her back to me.

"I'll make Lena the Virgin every chance I get. No more wistfully chaste Virgins. I've smashed that mold. It's Mothers with untouchable sensuality from here on. Bored housewives of Rome."

The maid enters with an armful of folded clothes.

"My prince brother's linens. Put them on. Shave. You're going to Quirinal Palace. Del Monte, Borghese, and Pasqualone await your apology."

"I'm going to make a child with Lena."

"If she has a child, you'll never know who the father is."

"I'll take that tea now," I say to my maid.

Mamma reaches back for my hand, squeezing it in apology. Fuck her. She doesn't even know Lena.

"Does Fabrizio know about his father?"

"He was my husband's favorite. He cherished Fabrizio's malice and bigotry. Fabrizio takes being a Sforza-Colonna very seriously. Since he was a toddler."

"He has the Merisi eyes, the hooded eyelids."

The marchioness throws my hand at me. I sit up on the edge of the bed. My chambermaid has brought my tea.

"Put my brother's clothes on and go to Quirinal Palace before I change my mind about everything."

I obey my stepmom, but not before finishing my tea, getting good and geeked so I can make peace with my enemies.

XXIII.

Nightfall. The house bakes in daytime heat. It's darker outside than inside. Lena closes the shutters and disappears. I'm still here, listening to her undress. I picture her breasts. I picture Rome picturing them. Dames and maids trying them on for size. Lonely men wanking to them. Numb men pounding their bored wives, Lena's bust on both their minds. Me and some exclusive johns are the only ones. Consigning her baby to a wet nurse was a wise career move. Saving her breasts for the Virgin. My Christ child snores in the next room, sleeping in his aunt's bed. She's out making ordinary gents feel godlike. Lena shuts the door and arrives in bed. Her dry heat greets my stickiness. We feel around for the reunion. It's been six weeks. Her stomach is flatter than Papa's view of the Earth. Something has changed for the worse. I'm soft. I'm unwanting.

"We can't have a son like this," she says.

"I'm still motion sick from the road."

"Says the genius who wants a coach."

"I rode a donkey cart."

"The prince couldn't lend one of his thirty coaches? Did he at least share his women?"

"No courtesans. Lots of salami."

She stings my soft belly with a slap. Michelangelo gets a teeny hard.

The first time a woman has ever turned him on. I fit my eyes into her cleavage and open them.

"I want to see you. It's been six weeks."

"I'm right here," she answers.

"It's not the same. Light something. The eye is the lamp of the body. Has your wound healed?"

"It was never a wound. A nick on the cheek. He was heartbroken, but he has no vengeance in him. He was more nervous than angry. I had to hold his hand steady while he pricked me. It was his bookish way of saying goodbye. He's read too many books, seen too many plays. It's only a tiny red dot, but I don't want you to see it. You'll slaughter him."

"I can't. I promised the cardinal-nephew. I signed an agreement. Light the lamp or a candle. I want to see it."

"My sister is low on oil and wax. We need to go to the store. We've been too busy."

"But you have the money? You're doing okay financially?"

"I could buy enough olive oil to light a palace. I'm saving for a house on Capitol Hill. That neighborhood is on the rise."

"Campidoglio? Nothing up there but politicians and the laborers who build their villas. You'd be out of the public eye. No fandom. Wolf whistles at best."

"I'd rather wolf-whistling ditchdiggers than copycats chanting my name."

"Lenavaggio has been fun."

"It's not worth the headache of getting kicked out of my apartment. It's not worth ladies hating on my face. We've gotten too big. Another Virgin picture will push the bored housewives over the edge. They already resent my celebrity. They'll topple it. They're more dangerous than johns and jealous boyfriends. They're like Papa yearning for a reason to torch you. He beheaded a poor author for treason. The bored housewives are stealing my head, painting their faces and hair like mine. It cheapens me. We can be together without being Lenavaggio. We can love each other without another Virgin."

I'm relieved to hear her say it. I'm afraid to paint her. Terrified of having sex with her. She's my one and only failure, but I'm more than happy to die trying.

"Don't let a jealous landlady cloud your shine. You're the Virgin to end all Virgins."

Her hand dies on my chest and withdraws. She slides off the bed and crawls on the floor to the far wall, or maybe that's the shadow of an open trunk.

"Come back."

"Ranuccio is at it again." Her voice is strange and disquiet.

"At what again?"

"At me again."

"At you for what?"

"My celebrity. He says it's his doing. His clients and connections. He's been taxing me."

I stand. I'm wanting. I feel around for her. It's just a trunk.

"He's hassling you because of me," I say.

"I've been sleeping with his Farnese cohorts," she says somewhere.

I grovel there. She's unfeeling and cold.

"He doesn't own you. My Virgin belongs to everyone."

"I don't want her. I told you from the beginning. Men fuck different now, like they're trying to get something out of me. It's demeaning. I've never felt debased in my work until posing as the Blessed Mother of fucking Christ."

"I'm sorry. I tried doing you right. I've never come close. You're too much for me."

"I love you. I love us. We didn't need the Virgin. I told you she'd be our death."

I scoop her up and place her on the bed. She slithers off the other side. I slither over the bed after her. She climbs onto me like flotsam. I stand and roll us back onto the bed.

"Death changes nothing for us. They already love Lenavaggio a thousand years from now." I hold her breast as if swearing on a bible.

"Immortality doesn't mean not dying. I want to die. I want to die like your dead Virgin, but without the great beyond of superstardom. I want to die for real. I want to die in the final thoughts of my children, not in the wet dreams of fans. Ranuccio visits Sant'Agostino daily. Spends hours in front of your picture. He already loved me. You made him idealize me. His new bride is pregnant. He blames you because his wife is not me. He kills what he can't have."

She exorcised my ghosts but is now rearing her own. Maybe she'd be better served and protected by Caravaggio and the violent hick. Maybe I should step aside before I get all four of us killed.

"Ranuccio is nothing," Michelangelo says. "He swings his sword like a limp-wristed fop. He's a nobody. He fetches hand jobs and the morning paper for the Duke of Parma's bum chums."

"Ranuccio isn't the lanky pimp you and Onorio used to slap around. He's filled out. He's ascended. He turned his highborn johns into political equity. He's a Farnese functionary. He's somebody."

Caravaggio stands over the bed. Power-poses bare-assed.

"I'm a bigger somebody. The cardinal-nephew is addicted to me. The Prince of Genoa is now a Pontius Pilate of mine. His cousin offered me six thousand scudi to fresco his gallery. I'm grand stepson to Marcantonio Colonna. I'll have Ranuccio sucking cock for crumbs in the bowels of Tor di Nona. Don't give him another scudo. Has he touched you?"

"What's a grand stepson? Sounds like something Caravaggio would make up. Stop talking like that," she says.

The door opens. The darkness lightens to umber. My Christ child enters rubbing his eyes. I look to Lena for a glimpse of her scar. Her face is stunning as ever, aside from its saying something mournful, but I wouldn't say guilty.

"If someone slaps your right cheek, turn and let them slap your left," my Christ child says.

"Spoken like a peace-loving messiah. Takes after his mother," I say.

"At least he's done quoting Ovid," she responds.

"I'll never paint either of you again."

I mean it. Masetti can kill me. I'm not painting my Virgin for his duke. Every time I paint Lena, I lose her. It breaks her and tortures Caravaggio, not painting someone to perfection. It's not fair to either of them.

My Christ child takes my place at her bosom. I dress and leave my Virgin and Christ child to their peace.

XXIV.

The tavern is blotched with light and shadow. Candles on tables. Lanterns from joists. A space of yellow orbs and inexplicable umbras. For an anxious second, I think another migraine is coming. I pinch the flame at my table and sit in adumbration like my called Matthew. I feel the eyes of femme-fops and fanboys, but I only see Michelangelo fucking everything to hell for me and Caravaggio. It's just the illumination and not a migraine. My impotence toward Lena. Why she believes in Ranuccio. The answer gives me butterflies.

"Would you like your fennel cooked in butter or olive oil?" the waiter asks.

He's joking. He knows me. He knows the artichoke story. The waiter who mocked Michelangelo's hickish appetite for dairy. The waiter who got his skull split open. This waiter knows how to sustain my good graces—a plate of buttered vegetables for Michelangelo, one of olive oil for Caravaggio.

I don't have money for a plate of fennel. I have double the nothing for two plates. I'd starve before asking my Virgin for money. Mamma only offers political charity. I have no pictures. No commissions. I'm in existential debt to Del Monte, subsisting on the sacred words of a hedonistic cardinal-nephew. On the positive, Cecco should be here soon. He comes every Wednesday after his painters' guild meeting. In the interim, femme-fops are good for one thing: philanthropic food and drink. Michelangelo begs in the form of a question.

"Which one of you sluts wants to buy Profane Love some claret and fennel?"

Ten men jockey for three empty chairs. Losers stand. A mug of wine is placed before me. I down it. I let the fanboys tell me that the sullied protagonists of my pictures have rusted the chains of feudalism. I let the femme-fops call me the Columbus of reality. I let them tell me that I've discovered a new way for man to perceive himself. I know all this, but it feels nice to have my proverbial cock sucked after two weeks on the road with an artless bodyguard. I'd enjoy it all the more if the table was missing a leg.

Dead-eyed while they gnaw my ears off, I come to life when Fright and Gabrielli enter with Andrew Ruffetti. He's a sound guy, an intellectual with a vast library of Latin smut. He's got everything Catullus ever wrote and everything written on Catullus. He went to law school with Onorio and lives near Colonna Palace. I thumb the three Dildos out of their seats and stand to salute my friends. Their hugs crush my butterflies. Fright looks hideous under the light.

"I hear a certain Doria offered ten thousand scudi for a picture," he says.

"Six thousand to fresco his gallery," I answer.

"You fresco walls worse than you portray popes," Gabrielli says.

I dare the dildos and fops to laugh. They don't dare. I crack the fuck up and the entire tavern cries along with me. My three friends sit. Everyone else turns and converses amongst themselves, pretending not to listen.

"The superstar has shrunk," Gabrielli says.

"You think I've shrunk?" I drum on my ravioli belly.

"The superstar in the sky," Fright says.

"It already shrunk. It shrank more?" Ruffetti turns to the waiter and orders five mugs of wine. "Two for him," he says, pointing at yours truly.

"Galileo wrote me. He has a theory on its provenance," Gabrielli says.

"It's not God's angry eye?" I ask.

"Not even close. A celestial rainbow. It's sunlight reflecting off clouds."

"It has diminished, but it's also changed and intensified in color. It's been red like Mars. It was gold as Saturn for months," Ruffetti says.

"I don't think it's a star at all. I think it's celestial fire," Fright says.

"Papa won't let it be a star. The heavens have to be fixed. It came from nowhere and altered its properties. Stars aren't born. They can't die. Papa insists," says Gabrielli.

"Superstars are born. We die," says Caravaggio.

The wine arrives. I swill one. Both plates of fennel arrive. I eat the buttered bulbs first.

"It's a star and it proves Copernicus right," says Ruffetti.

"I'll be proven right, but long after I'm dead. Until then, pornographers like Carracci get rich while I live on the street."

"You haven't heard?" Fright asks.

"I don't hear. I see."

"Carracci had a stroke. Then he had a nervous breakdown. Ten years of patronage and the Farnese rewarded him a measly five hundred scudi. The slight destroyed him. He moved out of the palace. Lives in a rented room now. He's gone mute. He has petit mals. He's lost parts of his memory. He's quit painting." Gabrielli sips in waiting for my response.

I've never hated Carracci. I've only hated his work. His colors richer than salami. His content banal, not vulgar. His Virgins and their phony orgasms. But he's a better draughtsman than yours truly. Carracci deserves a convoy of forty coaches for inspiriting the Church's customers. Maybe it's better to have no patrons than ungracious ones.

"Let's go outside and feast our eyes on the dying superstar. In honor of Carracci," Caravaggio says.

I push my chair back to rise. The crowd parts. I'm halfway to my feet when Cecco blows in from nowhere, brandishing that smile, the one I'll never paint. Head outside or stay for another mug? Caravaggio continues upwards as Michelangelo sinks. I stumble with indecision and wine, falling into the chair like the corpse of my *Christ Buried*. I dare the onlookers to laugh. They pretend not to see.

Cecco drags a chair to the table. He salutes and bows before sitting. I stand and open my arms. We embrace. I kiss his head. His hair has grown into a Mario bouffant. My butterflies are resurrected. I slide the plate of oiled fennel into his spot.

"I went to the house," I say.

"She locked us out. The court confiscated everything. Mirrors.

Easel. Halberd. All the furniture and props. Fillide's pearl earrings. My violin."

"The wings?"

He smirks and shakes his head. "But she took the money."

"The money?"

"The sack of coins on the table. The *Ecce Homo* commission. She took it. She took it along with the table."

"What kind of hag steals a three-legged table?" says Gabrielli.

"The *Homo* commission should have covered five months' rent," I say.

"Not the repairs for the roof. She wanted us out. She said she didn't want the trouble of renting to an enemy of the pope."

"Make her pay," Ruffetti says.

"I took a dump on the stoop."

"That's just a down payment," Gabrielli replies.

"Lena's landlady. Della Vecchia. She snitched on us. Told the cops I was her pimp."

"Pay both bitches back," Ruffetti says.

A young fop stands in the corner fumbling over the strings of a pricey lute. He's been there the whole time, butchering the madrigals from my music pictures, waiting for acknowledgment.

"Do you know the chords to any bawdy songs?" I ask.

"Sorry," he says.

"Come with us anyway. You can accompany our ad-libbing with that noise you've been making."

The night is draped in charcoal clouds. The sky eyeless. God has been blindfolded. Only the humpbacked moon burns through. An opportune time to sin. I'll go big and waste my talent on punishing landladies. It's destructive and lazy but that's my creative process.

We hit Della Vecchia's first. Nobody has to shit so we piss on it. Then spit and snot-rockets, whatever excretions our bodies have to offer. The lute player makes a loud mess of the madrigals. The stump is there with the Pasqualone hatchet buried in it. I tip the stump over and deadlift an end. I signal to Ruffetti. He deadlifts the other end.

"On the count of three," I say.

We heave it through the shop window. The destruction conducts us into harmonious laughter, Cecco in falsetto. He'd rather I waste my genius avenging his John or inspiriting Catholics for next to nothing.

Or maybe he just wants me to be good to myself. I suppose that I don't know him these days.

We head to Signora Bruni's, a band of merry fools. We line up on her stoop, clear our throats, and sing. The fop pulls at the strings as if launching arrows.

A rich girl has a coach. A poor girl has a cart.
Bruni takes it in the ass but not when she has to fart.
Oh, Bru-ni. Bru-ni. Bruni, won't you show your twaaat!

Signora Bruni shouts from behind a shuttered window upstairs.

"You ass-fucking heathen! Have you taken your lad back now that Ranuccio is fucking your whore again!"

The *again* modifier cuts me at the knees, but I stand brave for my former lover and friends, hawking the anguish from my throat to start the next verse.

A rich girl uses oil. A poor girl uses lard.
Bruni uses axle grease cuz her cunt's so fucking hard.
Oh, Bru-ni. Bru-ni. Bruni, won't you show your twaaaaat!

Cecco has unearthed a considerable stone. He hurls it at Bruni's shutter with the prodigious oomph of David slinging Goliath. The shutter splinters and drops from its hinges. Ruffetti and Fright high-five him while I slap the shit out of his ass. Gabrielli tucks the shutter under his arms and flees. We stream after him hailing our victory.

We hike to the steps of Santa Maria della Scala. The fathers haven't hung my *Death of the Virgin* yet. Cherubini presented it months ago. They're deliberating. They're worried she looks too dead.

We sit on the steps of the church, putting each other in stitches, drinking from the same flask (Fright's I think). Cecco sits next to me, his elbow on my lap. We take turns stomping the shutter into never-ending halves as Ruffetti does the fop's lute justice. It's a grand moment, a night for the ages, but I can't stop wanting to fall on my own sword. It's not here. Maybe that's why Mamma won't give it back. I lie on the steps and raise the flask intending to toast Carracci. The haze has lifted. God is eye-fucking me.

"Michelangelo Merisi?" a voice asks.

Corporal Malanno and three cops approach, two swords and two wheellocks drawn.

"That's Lenavaggio da Caravaggio to you, you philistine cock-suckers you," Michelangelo replies.

"You're under arrest for two counts of destroying private property," Malanno says.

I offer the law my wrists and turn to Cecco.

"Get money from Masetti and find us another home."

"Move in with me when you get out. Both of you," Ruffetti says.

XXV.

Propsero and Gabrielli pay my bail. Ruffetti pens an affidavit vowing that Michelangelo Merisi will not attack the persons or property of Laura Della Vecchia or Prudenzia Bruni. In total, freeing Caravaggio cost my friends two hundred scudi. Loving Caravaggio is a burden. Believing in him is a liability. I'm more than ashamed. Michelangelo thinks nothing of it. Caravaggio expects it.

I exit the gates of Tor di Nona and cross the street. Cecco is waiting on the riverbank with our Cupid wings on his back. It's all we have left. I look upstream for Lena. The morning aurora floods the Tiber. My thoughts swim in it. Caravaggio visions our dead Virgin floating downstream. Michelangelo does not.

"Stop looking. She's too embarrassed," Cecco says.

"Because of Ranuccio?"

"Donuts?" He sucks at changing the subject.

We move our wings into Ruffetti's newly renovated house, three stories of liberalminded personality translated into inviting space. Each room stocked with books, paintings, and instruments that encourage inhabitants to nurture their best selves. Not the ideal living arrangement for three beings residing in a single body, but again, genius must be served. Ruffetti has converted his attic into a studio, granting us permission to bust a hole in the roof. We spend all of our time there and the rest of our time sleeping. Cecco and I share a large room on the second floor. Two single beds. A nightstand between us. Thinking I'm asleep, he whispers subliminal messages. He tells me to let Cecco give Caravaggio blowjobs. He tells Michelangelo to give Cecco blowjobs. He tells me he loves me. He tells me I love him. He tells me to kill Michelangelo so Caravaggio can satisfy the cardinal nephew. He tells me to paint Masetti's Virgin. Michelangelo loves hearing Cecco conspire against him. It sexes him up. The lad was always too accommodating. Caravaggio and I appreciate Cecco's advocating for my Virgin but there's no reward to painting Lena. Emotionally, it's bankrupting. Financially, The Duke of Modena has already twice paid for the picture, but Cecco always knows what I'm thinking.

"Don't do it for the money," he whispers. "Do it as another chance of getting Lena right."

After a day of painting *Christ on the Mount of Olives* for Giustiniani, Cecco wants donuts for supper.

"Wednesday dinner donuts. Our new ritual," I say.

Our new home is a short walk to the best fried dough in Rome, a donut cart across from the Pantheon. We pass Colona Palace on our way, Mamma's birdies flitting in all directions spying on me. I've done nothing egregious. Superstar geniuses are allowed to shit on their landlady's stoop. There's no sin in breaking her shutters or smearing her in song. No one has summoned me. Not Mamma. Not Del Monte or the cardinal-nephew. They turn a blind eye on misdemeanors. I'm free to promote myself, so I acknowledge the birdies. I force her servants and emissaries to salute and bow. I might be a has-been artist and hypersensitive hothead, but I'm virtually one of their lords.

"She's not the woman you think," Cecco says.

"Fabrizio Sforza is a Merisi. I'm her stepson. She loves me like her own."

"Not the marchioness. Lena. *She's* not the woman you think, but yes, the marchioness is shady too."

"You know about the marchioness and my father?"

"I assumed. He has the Merisi eyelids, and why else would she be so committed to your well-being? She's no art fan."

I calculate the odds of Fabrizio seeing the same math that Cecco has.

"Besides beauty, I don't know what you see in her," Cecco says.

"We're talking Lena and not the marchioness?"

Cecco nods.

"There's nothing to see in her. She is what she is. She wants nothing. She certainly doesn't want fame. She wants nice clothes but only for work."

"She wants you."

"Well, yeah."

"Not Caravaggio. Not Michelangelo. She wants *you*. The force who stands between them."

"Well, like, yeah."

"That's selfish of her. Caravaggio is too important. You and Michelangelo get in his way. She does too."

"You loved Caravaggio more than me?"

"No, I didn't love him more. He just mattered more. More than you. More than me. More than us."

"She wants my son."

"You'd be a terrible father. A sure-handed Abraham."

"At least you didn't say Francesco Cenci."

"I'm no Beatrice."

"I've asked her to move in with me. She always says no."

"Should we go home and snuggle for old times' sake?"

Michelangelo is a yes. Caravaggio is a whatever. I'm a no. I say nothing. My blushing speaks of our inner dissonance. We arrive at Rotonda Square. The entire crowd turns to us as if hearing our entire conversation. I hope they did. The records must show my love for him.

The grandeur of the Pantheon has never rubbed off on the square. It's been ghetto since 609 when the Turk Emperor Constans scrapped the Pantheon of its bronze. After that, the square went to shit, becoming a marketplace of sin and filth, inhabited by miscreants, murderers, scamps, and thieves. When they enshrine my genius here, Michelangelo will preside over the square's unruliness. You can get away with anything at Rotonda Square. You can also buy anything here. Livestock. Birds. Donuts. Ass-fucking. The pavers are slick with feces, rotten vegetables, and lard. Shoppers constantly lose their footing, cracking coccyx and lower vertebrae. Cecco and I grab some donuts and shuffle over to the bird cages. The jangle of chirps, caws, and squawks makes Michelangelo want to kill.

"Smells like a quill dipped in asshole," I say.

"More like a dirty whore's dirty pillow. Buy me one?"

"A whore?"

"No. A bird."

I wiggle my finger inside an owl cage. The predator blinks and looks away.

"How about a parrot? Or a nightingale?" I ask.

Cecco has lost interest. A fracas has blossomed at the northeast corner of the square. The crowd spirals and parts. People tumble to the muck. Michelangelo rushes toward it, Cecco and I sucked into his slipstream.

A regal convoy enters the square. Six silver coaches, each drawn by six horses draped in the finest velvet, manes prettied by ribbons. Pages and grooms dressed in red and gold silk. I don't recognize the coat of arms.

"Probably a French ambassador sightseeing," Cecco says.

The convoy is too wide for the narrow maze of booths and stalls, but that doesn't stop it from trotting onward. The front wheel of the second coach knocks over a cart of melons. The crowd spits on the horses and coaches. The melon vendor smashes one of the fractured cantaloupes off a horse's muzzle. The grooms strike him down with whips and beat him with truncheons. Cecco and I love it, prodding at each other with our elbows.

As the convoy inches by, I catch sight of Ranuccio Tomassoni between horse rumps, smiling sideways at me. He and his brothers are armed and armored. Lena was right. He isn't the same lad I bitch-slapped for stiffing pros. He's taller, thicker, and better looking than yours truly.

The convoy and escalating violence buffer us from the Tomassoni brothers. I've never run from a fight, but this is the fastest I've walked away from one. I swipe a hammer from a cobbler's kiosk and slide it up my sleeve.

We make it back to Ruffetti's, but the brothers are in sight, striding up the alley with every intention of fucking me up. Obviously, Ranuccio Farnese never gave them Del Monte's message of leaving me alone. If I hide in the house, they'll destroy the door and shutters. It's unfair for another home to suffer my drama. I grip the hammer and go on the offensive.

Ranuccio draws and swings for my head. I duck and kneecap him with the hammer. He genuflects in agony. I raise my arm to demolish his skull, but one of the brothers strikes my ear. I fall but tighten my grip on the hammer. Someone takes my arm. Another takes my leg. The other two take turns on me with their feet, stomping as if the

Farnese flag has caught fire. Cecco collapses next to me. He stands. He falls again. I clutch Giovan and kick Alessandro. Ranuccio stabs my heel with his dagger. Does he think I'm Achilles? Luca swings his dagger at my neck. It's not deep enough for decapitation, but it unlocks my teeth from Giovan's jowls.

Ranuccio punctuates my humiliation with a rib punt. He wants to be paid for all the times I've fucked his quote-unquote *prima puttana*, twenty-seven scudi as if he's been tallying the entire time. Flat on my back, I spit at him. My saliva apexes and plummets to my chest like a failed theory. The brothers laugh themselves away. I can't stand. My heel is smoldering with pain. My ear is screaming. The pain in my neck doesn't help.

"I'll get the barber-surgeon," Cecco says.

"Fuck him. Go back to the Pantheon and get those donuts."

I look to God. His eye won't open for another eight hours. I'll just lie here and wait for him.

XXVI.

I've been high in bed for days. My Achilles is stitched up. My neck is collared in bandages. A jarful of poppy seeds every four hours relieves the pain and numbs the remarkable aching of my emasculation. The poppy does nothing for my maimed and ringing ear. I've been virtually castrated. Even with my rapier, I can't fight the Tomassoni solo. My posse has been fully dismembered by domestic obligations. Mario has upstarted a factory producing scriptural pictures in the likeness of Caravaggio minus the dirty feet. Onorio has landed a job managing the construction of some Duke Dildo's urban villa. He's become so committed to work and family that he broke it off with Menicuccia. The cardinal-nephew has hired Orazio to paint figures on the great hall walls of Quirinal Palace. When not deploying paint for the Borghese, Orazio has upped his devotion to tutoring his prodigious daughter Artemisia. She's eleven and already paints better than Baglione. Prospero's around but without Onorio and Orazio's ire, he's prone to coolheadedness. Feeding offspring starves the fiercest egos. Maybe I should be thankful that I only have Cecco. Michelangelo and Caravaggio weren't wrong in doubting my paternal fitness. Still woozy from the brawl, they're in no condition to gloat.

Fra Malaspina, my Mamma-appointed bodyguard, has moved to Malta without the Jerome I painted him. Nephew-cardinal Borghese confiscated it, the fee for his uncle's leniency. When this foot heals, I'll shank Ranuccio and give Papa his reason to kill me.

Cecco pulls me from bed, wraps my arm around his neck, and walks me to the commode.

"Is she worth it?" he asks.

"Am I being honest with myself?" I sit.

"I'm asking you, not Caravaggio or Michelangelo."

"Papa is going to kill me regardless. I'd rather die for her than art."

"Let Ranuccio have her. She's not worth your genius. You still haven't painted a true masterpiece. The last two Virgins don't live up to Caravaggio because you're no Caravaggio. You're too decent for art. You have no business pushing paint. She put that dumb idea in your head. Forfeit the brush to Caravaggio. Unmarry Lenavaggio. The name's too cute. Cute only works in your pictures where you're idealizing men."

"You wanted her as much as me," I say.

"I'm my own man now."

It's the sexiest thing he's ever said to me. Michelangelo groans his way out of the coma with a hard-on. I don't want to give it to Cecco. I don't want him to see me like this, but I need to stand up and pee. In an attempt to soften Michelangelo, I dwell on Ranuccio kicking me to death. It does the trick. I stand and lean on Cecco. He walks me to the bed and returns to the bathroom for my pot. He carries it outside to the cesspit. In his absence, I disprove Cecco's accusations regarding my artlessness by envisioning Masetti's Virgin—Lena in her red dress, stomping the serpent of Eden. Damn she's good. She's in this head like Del Monte and God could only dream.

Cecco returns and opens the curtains. The morning light is smoky. He takes to bed with a book, turning pages with a frustration that could tear lesser paper from its spine.

"Want to snuggle for old time's sake," I say.

He doesn't answer. It's the best thing he's never said to me.

I return to my new Virgin, posing in the spacious blue-blackness of Tor di Nona dungeon, wearing a red dress with the deepest of necks, her breasts proving Galileo's theory of gravitational acceleration, her foot on the voice box of the Satan's snake.

Lena knocks before Cecco finishes his book. He puffs and puts it down to answer. Lena enters the chalky afterlight wearing a new velvet dress. Black or brown. It's too dark to tell. Her sable contemplates me from her shoulder. I haven't seen it in a dog's age. Who's she trying to impress? Cecco strikes a match and lights three candles, not the lamp. What kind of mood is he trying to set?

I can't read her face. It's shadowed like my Christ in *Matthew Called*.

"Here we are. Family reunion. The Lenavaggios. One big happy family."

"I'm going to the tavern," Cecco says.

Michelangelo wants him to stay. I want Lena to join us in bed. If Caravaggio was conscious, he'd want her to join us too. I squirm to make space. Moving hurts everywhere. Cecco grabs his cloak and makes for the door. Lena goes after him for a hug. He turns his back to her and exits.

"He resents me," she says.

"He's only serving my genius. He's worried about it."

"I'm worried about you. Have you eaten?"

"Not really."

She lays her sable at the foot of the bed and leaves for the kitchen. Then I hear her in the bathroom. She re-arrives with a bowl of something and a mug of claret. I sit up.

"What's this?"

"I got my period yesterday. No son, but here's some medicine. I mixed my blood with some sage. It's an ancient pro remedy."

She hands me the bowl and kisses my good ear. I eat. It tastes like steak and herb sauce. Her serum works. I love her all the more madly. I rinse my mouth with claret and kiss her, kicking the vermin off my bed. She tries sexing me back to my feet. With a little effort and considerable pain, I make it to my knees. She backs herself into me. I try for a child knowing it's impossible. She's impossible, but I pull at her hips and reach into her, praying to almighty God that it's far enough. She quivers and splutters. She hasn't faded. She's right there. She wants more. I don't have any more in me, not without Caravaggio. I flatten out, face-up, facing nothing. She remains on all fours unlaxing. I wait for the bad news. She bends back onto me, reckless and ungraceful. Her toe jabs my heel. Her head butts my neck. Belly to back, she doesn't want me to see her say it.

"I paid Ranuccio," she says.

"Paid him what?"

"The money we owed."

"We owed him shit."

"It's worth the peace."

"He and his brothers shake me down, and my lover pays their extortion. I haven't a dick left."

She grabs hold of my cock.

"You got enough."

"You're just saying that."

"Stopping fishing for compliments. You just like hearing that you're the best."

"You really don't know me, do you?"

"I know *you*. I don't care to know the artist or brawler."

"You have twenty-seven scudi to give Ranuccio?"

"Chump change."

"What about the dress? Who bought it?"

"Me. I just wanted to make a living. You made me a superstar. You insisted."

"Did you just come from his house?"

"Am I being honest?"

"Move in with me. You and my Christ child."

"No."

"Then let me paint you. One more commission."

"No."

"Then where's this going? What are we doing?"

"This is how we love each other to death."

"*To* death? Or *until* death?"

"Will you ever believe in my love?"

"When I finally paint you right."

She pillows her head on my sore ribs. I take shallow breaths or else. I push my neck bandage against the curve of her skull. I push past the pain into something deeper. Her body cools on me. She twitches and slackens, muttering on her way to dreamland.

"In the room, women fuck and blow, moaning of Caravaggio."

She chuckles and dozes off. I wait an hour before getting out of bed. I go to the window to check in with God. He's gone. I map the sky. It's bright and lucent. His eye is nowhere. I look down at the street. People pace and wander the square in search of him, panicked and delighted by his sudden departure. After months of His omniscience, what happens next? Everything and anything. Free to perfect myself. Free to fail. I for one am thrilled. Michelangelo seconds the feeling.

Caravaggio leans out the window to be seen, to reassure the panicked. Their superstar is right here. I'll be my own star witness until Papa kills me. A star has died. The heavens are not fixed. Galileo has won. Bruno has won, and like him, my victory will come after death.

I return to Lena. I stare into her sleeping face until Cecco comes home, and then I close my eyes. Heavy-footed with wine, he undresses and crashes into bed and whispers some Bruno.

"When the end comes, you will be esteemed by the world and rewarded by God, not because you have won the respect of princes and popes, but rather for having loved, defended, and cherished one such as I."

I think about that until the morning Ave Maria bell chimes. Lena signs a lazy cross and rises. As I open my eyes, Caravaggio regains consciousness. He's in a world of hurt, a world constructed by yours truly.

"How are you feeling?" Lena asks.

"My neck and head kill."

"More seeds?"

"And a slice of bread?" I make prayer hands.

She kisses me and exits. I spread out on the bed and close my eyes, listening to her and Ruffetti exchange morning small talk. Ruffetti tells her about the dead superstar, explaining the scientific implications.

"Everything changes. Nothing perishes," she replies, quoting Ovid.

Ruffetti's retort is interrupted by a ceremonious knock at the door. Cecco opens his eyes. The authorities identify themselves and ask to see yours truly. Cecco sits up to leave.

"Stay," I say.

"Yes, master."

"Speaking of masters, you've got to see my *Ecce Homo*. I put Christ on an auction block."

"Have they come to arrest you?"

"There's no crime in getting publicly unmanned by four cunts."

Lena and Ruffetti enter. They're followed by six men. Two police investigators and four grooms dressed in Papa's colors, labeled by his insignia. The space is absurdly crowded. Lena sits on the edge of my bed to make room. It somehow makes the room more crowded. The investigators do the asking, the short round one with a stick up his ass goes first.

"We're here to investigate an altercation that took place two days ago in front of the Pantheon."

"I haven't been over there in years. Too sketchy," I say while trying to make sense of the grooms.

"What happened to your neck and head?" asks the shorter, rounder cop with donut crumbs in the corners of his mouth.

"I fell down the stairs. Landed on my sword."

The cop pulls the stick from his ass and hands it to his partner. He strikes my bad ear with it.

"We're placing you under house arrest. One month. No leaving this domicile. The papers will be served to you this afternoon."

The sentence confounds but not more than the presence of papal grooms. The cops drool over Lena for a never-ending second and leave. The grooms spread out. The oldest approaches with the benevolence of a nursing nun.

"We represent the Archconfraternity of Papal Grooms. As I'm sure you know, His Holiness is renovating St. Peter's to remove its remaining Constantinian effects. Our chapel has been relocated toward the transept. We'd like it to remain there. A Lenavaggio altarpiece would all but ensure it."

Now it makes sense. The cardinal-nephew places me on house arrest to paint the papal grooms' commission in peace, protecting me from the Tomassoni brothers, protecting Caravaggio from Michelangelo. He's guarding my genius so he can feed it to his uncle at a later date. With God's disappearance, Papa is my remaining executioner. He can't have my head yet. After I phlebotomize Ranuccio.

"How much is the commission?" Cecco asks.

"Fifty scudi," the groom answers with sorry eyes.

"That's offensive. I have dresses that cost more," Lena says.

The groom undresses her with his eyes.

"Our patron saint is Anne. We'd like a portrait of her and the Virgin, like the one at Sant'Agostino. We want our chapel to be the main attraction at St. Peter's."

"Fifty scudi and a ride in the papal coach for me and mine." I motion to Cecco and Lena.

He doesn't respond to the joke, which I admire, but if he doesn't stop fucking Lena in his head, I'm going to throw him out the window.

"How about this? A picture of Anne, Mary, and the Christ child. Grandmother, mother, and Messiah." I snap my fingers in his face.

He flinches, shifting his focus from Lena's cleavage to my bandages.

"Perfect," he says.

"Now you can leave," I say.

"We'll deliver a contract by week's end."

Ruffetti sees the grooms out.

"We've made it. We're in. The House that the Divine One Built," I say.

Cecco kneels from bed, wailing the mattress with his fists. Lena stands and paces. She isn't having it.

"I told you. I don't want this. Ranuccio will demand a brokerage fee. He'll punish us."

"The cardinal-nephew arranged this. Ranuccio can't touch it."

Lena grabs my wounded heel. The pain bolts to my groin.

"What about this? Your marchioness and cardinal-nephew couldn't stop this from happening?"

"St. Peter's is worth everything."

She turns to Cecco for support. He makes prayer hands. "Let Caravaggio paint it."

"I don't care who paints it. It'll be my last picture. Then I'm retiring," she says.

"From men?" I ask.

"From modeling," she says.

I place a hand on her breast. "Genius must be served."

Lena kisses me goodbye. Ovidio needs mothering. She wraps the sable around her neck and leaves. That rodent is her cross to bear. I've never seen a woman wear her foible with such grace.

I close my eyes and Caravaggio dies in elation. "I feel so blissful. I think I'm going to puke," he says.

Cecco comes to me and holds Caravaggio like the angel comforting my Francis in ecstasy.

XXVII.

A new aperture in a new roof. My eye recurs, as always, for always, looking inward and outward. Mario and Onorio scale a stepladder, trimming a hole in Ruffetti's ceiling. Cecco prepares the canvas. Caravaggio and I prepare the paints. The genius and I have agreed to collaborate for the sake of St. Peter's, for the sake of a masterpiece. We've painted blockbuster pictures. We've painted monumental treasures, but we've never stroked a masterpiece. Cecco was speaking a cold truth when he said as much. I'm neither man nor artist enough for Lena, and if I can share her with Ranuccio Tomassoni, I can share her with my genius, albeit vying self. Quoting Machiavelli, keep your friends close, your enemies closer. And God extracts His eye from heaven while this superstar prepares to enter St. Peter's? How suspect. How transparent.

My two best friends want to explain themselves. Why they ghosted me. Why they duped me at the Garden of Oranges. Their reasoning is the same old song, to serve and protect Caravaggio. I don't need to hear it, not from them. I've been putting Lena before my posse, and I too was subserviating myself. I'm learning that it takes more than a village to raise a genius. It takes a city of mothers, lovers, stepfathers, sidekicks, frenemies, rivals, and foes.

"We didn't know you'd been released from Tor di Nona. Then we hear that the Tomassoni had jumped you. It's no excuse. We suck for not being there." Mario raises a handsaw to Onorio.

"When you take your rightful place at St. Peter's, we'll fuck the Tomassoni beyond repair." Onorio takes a practice chop with the saw.

"Luca Tomassoni just became district colonel. Now he's extorting vendors and pros. He fleeced five scudi from my mistress last week. I'm going to carve him a second asshole."

"Care for your families, not my pride. Don't hazard your livelihoods," I say.

Onorio pokes his head through my aperture to threaten Rome. "No hope! No fear!"

In the week since God's eye disappeared, Rome has gone mad. Beatings. Thieving. Stabbings. The violence is indifferent to class. Poor on poor. Rich on rich. The most condonable of all bloodshed, poor on rich. And the most loathsome of all cruelty, rich on poor. The cops can't keep up with the chaos, and in many cases uphold the holy mess by hunting the ghetto for Jews to trounce, clobbering unemployed wretches because they have Papa's consent. Papa's domestic and international policies have stoked the unrest. Serving Spanish interests, he has threatened war on the Republic of Venice for being too independent, powerful, and liberal. He interdicted them for not selling the Holy See its waterfront real estate. Protestants and the French have sided with Venice. Last week, the cardinal-nephew's staff was cudgeled by a Francophile street gang. A gang of Spanish soldiers retaliated, ear-dragging Cardinal Bellarmine from his coach and pistol-whipped his grooms. The Tomassoni are having a field day in the chaos, breaking bones and crushing egos for Cardinal Farnese. Michelangelo is sorely missing out. He wants this Virgin knocked off asap so his shine can flare like a detonating sun.

My new studio is a haven from the rioting. It's all brotherly love in here. We've waited twelve years for this. My success is their success. I'll leverage construction jobs for Onorio. Mario's workshop will supply the rising demand for Caravaggio copies. I'm as happy for them as I am for Caravaggio. Orazio and Prospero bring wine and groceries. Onorio jokes about the cos lettuce coming from Della Vecchia's shop. Gabrielli brings books. Cecco reads them aloud. Fright brings news. Ruffetti is never around. He works all day most days, serving his own genius for making coin. At the end of every day, I toast him in absentia for providing walls and a roof. Soon after, Lena brings the sexy, rocking her red velvet dress with a neckline all the way down to Sicily. Her hair up. Her cleavage high and protuberant. The ambit of each breast twice that of her head. What are we to make of this? Something artful, human, and undying. Otherwise Caravaggio and I have failed her all over. Caravaggio has perfected women before, but Fillide coxswained much of that success by fucking Caravaggio silly and modeling that patent aphrodisia. Maybe that's the point of Lena's dress, to deter me from laying brush on her again.

She has brought my Christ boy and his nanny to portray my Anne. Unlike Lena, the nanny makes for an ideal Caravaggio subject, an old southerner with a neckful of baroque wrinkles. I position my subjects: Lena leaning forward, her heavy breasts sheltering her naked Messiah as he stands on her foot, their combined weight crushing the head of a snake that I will paint into the picture post-diem. The holy grand-mother Anne stands over her sacred descendants from a respectful distance, accepting the relation of her wrinkled face to the silken white-ness of her daughter's skin. Cecco situates a lantern near the feet of my Virgin and Christ boy that purifies their complexion. The skylight overhead achieves my desired dungeon effect. I paint it all like God's not watching—a barefoot pro and her bastard. A buxom but bored housewife and her spoiled son. Anne, the tall battle axe with a neck more wrinkled than her shawl. Papa will hate it. Cardinal Borghese will love it. Del Monte loathes breasts, especially in his art. Mamma will never see it. It'll charm Masetti into loaning me ten scudi while he waits for his boss' Virgin. The papal grooms will drool over the picture, but hanging it isn't their call. The cardinal brass at St. Peter's sit on the yays and nays. The board is headed by cardinals Del Monte, Giustiniani, and Colonna. Two former Caravaggio patrons and a Michelangelo guardian. My Virgin is in the bag.

My studio becomes the most popular venue in Rome, but it's an exclusive viewing. My posse takes turns standing at the door. Friends and former models only. They come and go as I try to get Lena right. All my Christs. My Matthews. My first John. My Peter and Pauls. My Thomas. My Abraham. None of my heroines. They hate seeing one of their own getting some of mine. The men in my life are well-wishers. They fist-bump and pass flasks, oohing and ahhing over my creative process. I hear it. I appreciate it. I love them for it, but I don't acknowl-edge it. I'm too honed, too centered on my subjects, not unlike a duel. Whenever I paint a picture, it always feels like I have everything to lose, but I was already at a loss when starting this picture, and it feels like painting in reverse.

My Christ boy wants to make it particularly difficult with constant whining and fidgeting. When not punching my Virgin's stomach, he's flipping me the bird and quoting raunchy Ovid passages.

"*When Zeus saw the Virgin nymph Callisto, a flame erupted in his bone.*"

Anne shushes him. I promise donuts, but the laughter of spectating saints eggs him on.

"*I love to hear her rapturous gasps imploring, 'take your time, keep boring!'*"

I'm the only one not finding the humor. My Christ boy thinks he's the absolute funniest, grinning like an imp. My Virgin waltzes him on her feet and reiterates my donut bribe. Cecco offers to make a run for some. My Christ boy agrees to shut up and pose until the donuts arrive. This family of mine operating like a finely lubed machine.

Some poet friends show up. One says, "We're witnessing the ineffable spirit of light." I think he could do better than that, but I'm not a word guy. Ruffetti strolls in with his ninety scudi lute. A singalong breaks out. Cecco returns with donuts and a live snake he bought at Rotonda Square. He releases the serpent. It slithers straight to my Virgin and naked Christ boy, coiling into a defensive spiral at their feet. Someone makes a joke about reversing the contagion of original sin. Someone adds to the joke at the expense of my Christ boy's peen. I encourage my Virgin to squash the snake for the sake of art. I say it in complete sarcasm of her pacifism. For the first time in hours, my hottie Virgin breaks into Lena, the owlish unblinking and amorphous Mona Lisa smile, which causes me to break from Caravaggio. Yours truly is a little horrified. The object is looking to render the artist. She tightens her grip on Ovidio's wrist and commands him to remain standing on her feet. He resists. She overpowers him, two-stepping around the satanic symbol until there's an opportune angle at which time she stomps and mashes the serpent's head as it unfurls and writhes in a slow death.

"Behold, baby Hercules," she proclaims.

Everyone cheers except for Ovidio. My Christ child is disgusted. Michelangelo loves the baby Hercules allusion. I stamp the scene onto my brain speculum. This has to be the picture. The mind-boggling breasts. The tiny dick. The serpentine superscription. The so-called genius who paints the woman he can't fuck. Lena Antognetti. The supreme beauty. The worst model. I paint her for another hour while fanboys, followers, models, and patrons overindulge in my process. The ultimate painter rendering his pro lover as the Blessed Virgin. It's the event of a lifetime. Not for my Christ toddler. A hard nope for my Virgin. She wants it over with. She's putting on a good face. Our viewers can't see it. They're fooled. All they see is her beauty. She's so goddamn good at this, posing motionless, looking obscure. The worst model in the business.

It's too much. My Christ boy needs food and sleep. I was hoping Lena might send him home with his nanny, but it appears she's leaving with them. She's hungry. Her legs hurt. She needs time and space away from Caravaggio. She doesn't say as much, but I sense it. It's humanly impossible, being under his scrutiny six hours straight. A model has to want it. Her goodbye kiss is quick and thin. Our fans hail it with an uproarious *Lenavaggio*.

My posse escorts them home. I stay and work. A few fanboys leave. A few followers arrive. The studio smells of wine and sweat. I paint until dark and then descend to my bedroom. Cecco stays put. He likes to examine my progress without me around. I don't sleep much. Nothing to do with the upstairs partying. Everything to do with conceiving Lena in the right light. I hate beginnings. Too much tracing. Not enough values. She's little more than a likeness sketched in white lead, but I worry that I've already made too much of her. An unmoving deity. Not a mortal phenomenon. Caravaggio painted Fillide to perfection. What's the difference? We never idolized our Judith. We never idolized our Catherine. Fillide wanted fame. Fillide wanted to fade. Lena only wants me. I don't trust myself with her.

I rise the next morning to empty and clean the studio. Regardless of where he sleeps, Cecco always takes his work home with him. I'm fortunate. Michelangelo won't let me forget it. Ruffetti is the day's first visitor, Masetti stalking in behind him. He looks grayer than I remember. Hounding an artist can age a man.

"He came to the door claiming to be an ambassador for the Duke of Modena," says Ruffetti.

"This was supposed to be his Virgin," I reply.

"The duke was bumped for a St. Peter's altarpiece?" Masetti takes a deep breath through his eyes.

"Making my next Virgin more valuable," Caravaggio answers.

"You mean more expensive?"

"How's Carracci?" I ask.

"You've won by forfeit, but don't let that stop you from competing."

"Prince Marcantonio Doria offered me six thousand scudi to fresco his gallery."

"You don't paint fresco. How much do you need?"

I blush. It's the right thing to do. "Twenty scudi."

Masetti hands the coins to Ruffetti.

"Should I have this Ranuccio Tomassoni snuffed?" he asks.

"No. I'll do it myself after I finish this Virgin."

"Not after you finish *this* Virgin. After you finish *my* Virgin."

"They're all *my* Virgins," Caravaggio says.

Masetti massages his neck and sighs. He closes his eyes and has a private conversation. He opens his eyes and turns for the door, exhibiting extraordinary poise in not throwing a fist at yours truly.

"There are already people lined up outside. Do you want spectators?" Ruffetti asks.

"Is Papa Catholic?"

The making of the picture proceeds as celebration and ceremony. I've always hosted fans during my creative process. At Madama Palace. At Mattei Palace. At Signora Bruni's house. *The Madonna of the Grooms* is an observation unlike past previews. My career has suffered countless failed launches. Cock-blocked by popes. Shot in the foot by Michelangelo. Me with my collective heads up my ass. This painting preview is a festival celebrating the shine of Michelangelo Merisi da Caravaggio. Day to day, it feels like all seven sacraments. Most days are rejoiceful like a wedding. Others end with the restorative rapture of contrition. This past Sunday was uplifting like a baptism. But every day has an hour or three that feels like extreme unction. My headaches and remarkable sadness are long gone. A new sickness plagues me. Artistic impotence. This has never happened to me before. I can't stop obsessing over my model. I can't stop deifying her. She's too much for me. She's too much for Caravaggio. Even he is second-guessing every stroke, committing the same mistakes as my *Pilgrim's Madonna*. Too much flat adoration. Not enough vitalizing. Caravaggio has lost all confidence in himself. Her reluctance isn't helping. Every morning, she drags herself into the studio, my Christ boy kicking and screaming behind her as if being led to the chopping block. Neither of them has any interest. If not for the optimism of our viewers, I might have given up by now.

Lena always leaves shortly after the Ave Maria lunch bells. She doesn't return in the evenings. Ovidio is her excuse. I assume she's working nights. I suppose she has to. I can't pay her. I try giving her Masetti's money. She graciously declines.

"You're paying me in advance of eternity," she says.

She's right about that, but I hustle to finish the picture and keep her home, preferably pregnant with my child. I paint day and night, only stopping for a few leaves of cos and to piss. I have a mouthful of wine before bed but sleep without losing consciousness. When the picture is mostly there, I tell Lena that she can stop coming. She's relieved. I don't see her for two weeks, during which time, I kick everyone out of the studio, Cecco included. I race toward Lena's face with a blind faith in Caravaggio's genius. In the end, he creates Lena in our own image. Michelangelo is wild about the buxom results. He almost forgets about Ranuccio. The picture is not a failure. We might be able to live with ourselves.

Cecco enters with a bag of oranges. We sit across from each other on short stools, devouring the fruit over a bucket, their juices pattering against the tin.

"What do you think?"

"You fell into the same trap as *Pilgrim's Madonna*."

"What trap?"

"Her beauty. It's all you painted."

"Caravaggio painted most of it."

"He can't paint her either. I told you she's not worth it."

"What about the snake?"

"Counter-reformation propaganda. It wasn't like that when you painted me and Mario."

"No. There's nothing Catholic about the homoerotic."

"Are you serious? Catholicism is all wine, cock, and incense."

"What's this picture then?"

"Tits and kitsch."

"Loving Lena is just as destructive as loving you and Mario. God punished me for loving men. Now he's punishing me for loving a woman I don't deserve. A woman I can't paint to save my life. Caravaggio is giving up women. Saints and martyrs only. This was my last Virgin."

"What about the Duke of Modena's picture?"

"I'm not painting that. Cardinal Borghese has bigger plans for us."

"You believe in the cardinal-nephew's love but not Lena's? You're impossibly fucked."

"What do you know about love?"

Cecco wipes the nectar from his chin and stands, leaving Caravaggio, Michelangelo, and myself to point fingers while counting blessings.

XXVIII.

After the last day of creation, I rest for seven days, staying in or around bed, catching up on sleep and wine, praying for my Virgin to return. We never had our cast party. I wouldn't take it personally if my Christ boy and Anne stayed home, leaving Lenavaggio to our glory.

On the eighth day, I'm tempted to bring the cast party to her house, but the first rainstorm of spring is douching Rome. I'm above getting soaked. With all my loafing around, a peaty bouquet has festered between the legs. I'm not ready to water it, but I am sappy enough to stand by the window romanticizing the silver-wet square. It's deserted, too torrential for commerce or prayer. There's no sky, only limitless breadths of rain falling in steep slants. The fountain reiterates the quenching in feeble squirts. The bronze St. Paul standing atop the Column of Marcus Aurelius can't drink any of it, nor can he read the band of relief that spirals the column, detailing one hundred feet of pagan war triumphs, which Michelangelo has committed to memory.

The weather has a taker. A lone figure crosses the square at a leisurely clip as if it's a sunshiny Saturday, as if they want to catch cold. The figure is a woman. The figure is wearing my cloak.

Cecco is reading the Bible in bed. I turn to him. "Lena is coming. Meet her at the door with a towel and send her up."

"Anyone with two tunics should share with him who has none," he replies, quoting John the Baptist.

I hit the bathroom to soap and splash my crotch. I sneak into Ruffetti's chamber to borrow his perfume. I douse my undercarriage and return to bed, tenting the covers with my excitement. Caravaggio also has some skin in the excitement. He wants to prove his celebrity to Lena after painting her a less-than-perfect Virgin. He's never been in the position of owing a model and blames me for it. He knows that it's his own fault for trusting me.

Lena carries a cool moisture into the room. She smells of clouds and wet pavers. The red Madonna dress is pasted to her skin, dripping on the floor. Her teeth are chattering. Her Lena coif has been bobbed and the color is back to her natural tar.

"I'm freezing. Heat me up," she says.

If I can't make her fade to the sound of a downpour on roof tiles then damn.

She climbs out of her dress through the neck. Her shimmering nakedness turns me inside out. Four purple fingerprints on her ribs. I pretend not to see them. She pretends to not see me seeing them.

She falls back onto the bed pulling my cock along with her. I plunge in slowly. She squeezes and pulls my ass, locking me in, grinding my angle. I kiss her neck. She slides her hands around my hips. I limpen and give her reign. The flimsy bed screeches. With the operation in her hands, I inflate with confidence, my average cock mounting to new heights. Sweat and rain puddle her stomach, our wet heat humidifying the room. She moans. I moan. This is going to happen. Our rhythm crests. A crest has to crash. The laws of science demand it. Unlike the undulations of celebrity, a wave can't overturn its own momentum. Lena bucks and free-falls. I dive after her. She spasms in my arms. I wait for her to catch her breath before asking.

"Did it happen?"

"Yes."

"I don't believe you."

"Of course you don't."

"My fucking has much to be desired."

"Don't start."

"I don't do it for you. I know."

The peacenik loses her shit, pouncing on yours truly with both fists. I cover my head, but only out of habit. I let most of the punches through. She's speaking my language.

"Every time you doubt my love, it's a slap in the face. You're more disrespectful than a john."

"Where have you been the past three weeks?"

"Where do you think?"

"I'm going to kill him."

"It's business. I don't love him."

I stare at the fingerprints on her ribs.

"They're not his."

She puts her head on my chest. Her cheek is hot but the rest of her is ice.

"It's not always about you," she says.

"What isn't?"

"Everything."

"I want you to be about me. I want us to be about each other. A family."

"How can I belong to someone who doubts my love? Why would I subject myself to that?"

"Okay. I believe you! I believe you! I made you fade. You love me. Does that mean you liked the new Virgin picture?"

"They hung it at St. Peter's yesterday. It's a sensation. The pilgrims and tourists were out of their minds."

"Did *you* like it?"

"It's a miracle, like everything Caravaggio paints."

I don't know how to interpret that. Why Caravaggio and not yours truly? She's the one who encouraged me to paint alone. I don't want to bring it up. Her fists hurt too much, and it's gotten Caravaggio off my back.

"I want you to quit working. We're in St. Peter's now. Big commissions are coming. I'll support you."

"When the first few commissions come, I'll quit, but I'm not modeling."

We gaze into each other's eyes. She sphinxes on me. I try sphinxing back. I don't have the power. I don't know what's true. Michelangelo has a hunch. Caravaggio thinks himself omniscient. The wind and rain have their own opinion. We accept it for the remaining hours of this Saturday. I have more in me, and she always has twice that.

XXIX.

Bright Mondays. Modern Rome obeys them, its squares blistering back to business. Only the wretched question the perpetuity of commerce. Two cops chase down a beggar and knock his remaining teeth out for standing outside the bakery with his palms up.

"This city is losing its soul," Cecco says.

"At least we're not the problem," says Michelangelo.

"Not yet," Cecco replies.

We cross Colonna Square eastward, stealing the eyes of shoppers, merchants, and grandstanders. Lenavaggio is all the rage again. *Madonna of the Grooms* all the talk. We're bound for St. Peter's to be witnessed and to witness the power of my work on damn near anyone. Yesterday, people waited hours outside the Divine One's House to see my Virgin, a woman of everyman with a womb lusty enough to carry God's seed and breasts hearty enough to feed his Son. If my ascendency continues, I might have to reclaim the name Michelangelo.

When we reach the intersection of Via della Missione, Del Monte's coach turns the corner and brakes in front of us, causing a donkey cart to veer into a street stall. The victims blame everyone but the fat cat responsible. Cecco bows before the door even opens. I pick up three artichokes and hand them to the maligned vendor. Del Monte opens the door. I look past him to his passenger. Cardinal Borghese sits with his legs spread so far apart I can almost see up his cassock.

"Get in." Del Monte isn't asking.

"You, wait here," the cardinal-nephew says to Cecco. "We'll be right back. We're just taking your Abraham for a spin around the block."

Cecco eats the cardinal-nephew's crow with tight lips. Michelangelo has a good mind to gauge his eyes out, but I think twice on behalf of Lena and Caravaggio. My armor, rapier, and dagger lie at Del Monte's feet. Michelangelo wants them as much as I want Lena. He takes a seat next to the cardinal-nephew, so we don't have to look at his beady Borghese eyes. Del Monte closes the door. The coach rolls onto the square.

"Do I get all that back?" I point at my plate and steel with my foot.

"Are you going to stay away from the Tomassoni?" Borghese asks.

"The Toma-who?" I say.

I wink at Del Monte. He is unamused, his face bloated with worry. The old bear has been muzzled and declawed like a circus pet. This isn't the man who saved me from the streets. This isn't the man whose ass I couldn't remember not fucking.

"I got you an altar at St. Peter's and you painted a whore on it," Borghese says.

"Not a whore. A pro. The dearest in Rome."

"Yes. I hear the Farnese have been spending a fortune on her," he answers.

I bite my tongue and sit on Michelangelo's fists. He really wants that steel back. God help us.

"She's worth every scudo," I say.

"You're a fucking wild animal." Del Monte has been calling me that for twelve years, but today he means it as an insult.

"I'm the antagonist of my own story," I say.

"You're truly suicidal," says Borghese. "I didn't believe it. I couldn't believe that a man so blessed by God could spit up at His eye like this. Your guardian here told me you hated yourself. He told me you'd self-sabotage any opportunity I gifted you. I didn't believe him, yet here you are desecrating the Mother of God with a humongous pair of knockers."

"The people love her," I say.

"I love her too, but my uncle will hate it."

"How do you like my Jerome?"

"I'm crazy about it, but paint another whore and I won't be able to stop my uncle from decollating you."

"His Holiness," Del Monte says, correcting the cardinal-nephew's informality.

"We can skip the decorum. The eye of God is no longer watching over us," says Borghese.

He spreads his legs wider, knocking a knee against mine. He grabs a handful of his balls and squeezes, establishing their size, laughing like a psycho. Scipione Borghese is not a pious man. He's not even halfway decent. He's a heathen, an uncouth hillbilly from Artena. Michelangelo almost admires him.

"How's your staff? I heard they were attacked by some Francophiles. Rome has become a war zone. Is that why you're returning my blades?"

"The assailants wore masks, but we'll catch them. I'll have them flogged. Maybe cut their hands off. Do you know who it was? Mario Minniti maybe? Onorio Longhi? Orazio Gentileschi? Michelangelo Merisi?"

"My posse doesn't fight working people. And why would I bite the hand that feeds?"

"You bite God's hand. You spit in His eye."

"God never fed me. I was starving and naked when I came to Rome," Caravaggio says.

"I wish I'd been around to see that."

"We're giving back your blades so you can kill yourself, if that's what your heart desires, but the cardinal-nephew has three commissions with your name on them," says Del Monte.

"Do they pay more than fifty scudi?" I ask.

The coach turns up the alley behind the high wall of Chigi Palace. I've crashed in the fleabag hotel across the street and stabbed a Spanish soldier outside the tavern next door. I've never gone to the barber-surgeon two doors down. He's legally blind and cuts hair crooked. His stitches leave jagged scars. The handful of drunks hanging outside the tavern spot the cardinal pennons of the coach. They go running, hands disguising their faces, my killed Matthew leading the pack. Borghese points my attention to the Chigi wall. It's been graffitied.

THE POPE LIKES DICK.

"Care to comment?" Borghese asks.

"That's not me. I don't do fresco or graffiti. I insult a man to his face," I say.

"It's not his handwriting," Del Monte says.

"I wouldn't know. He hasn't signed my Jerome yet. For your next picture, I'd love to see another David and Goliath," Borghese says.

"He wants *my* David and Goliath," Del Monte says.

"Has he been in your chamber to see it?" Michelangelo asks.

"Take your plate and steel. Retire them. They're props now," he says.

"I'm a lover not a fighter," I say.

"Since when?" Borghese asks.

"Since I fell in love with my Virgin."

"She's no peacemaker, more like a Helen of Troy," he says.

Del Monte kicks my steel across the floor of the coach. Michelangelo gathers it up like a starving beggar gathering crumbs.

"Go. Be safe. Eat poppy and paint. Live a long life," Del Monte says.

"Is Carracci staying in that hole?" I point at the boarding house.

"Your career started there. His has ended there. He chose the wrong patron." Borghese places a soft hand on my knee, the same one that clutched his junk.

I gather my armor and exit the coach. Del Monte draws the curtain behind me. The driver snaps his whip. The horses snort and clonk off. I don my armor on the spot, looking over my shoulder for Swiss guards, or Tomassoni, or whoever. For all Michelangelo knows, Borghese dropped us here to be dry-gulched.

"No more talking about Ranuccio," he says.

I listen for Caravaggio's response. Nothing. He's not here. He never got out of the coach.

I return to the intersection of Via della Missione. Mamma's coach is parked incognito, stripped of its Colonna flag and matching red pennons. Her six chargers are also unadorned. Her standing is clogging traffic. Detoured and inconvenienced by the unmarked vehicle, a thick-necked butcher walking an ox strikes its front wheel with his rod. Mamma's driver steps out to scold him. The butcher jabs his chest with the rod. Cecco appears from the other side of the coach, pleading with the butcher. The chargers anxiously neigh. Mamma finally needs my saving, and Michelangelo has really missed his steel.

I smash the pommel of my sword over the butcher's head. He wilts to the pavers. Civility has been repaired. Mamma opens the door.

"What are you doing with that rapier?"

"Saving you."

"Get in. You need more saving than you'll ever know."

I kick the squirming butcher in the head until he's asleep.

"Wait here," I tell Cecco. "When the cops come, tell them he was attacking the marchioness."

"I don't like where any of this is going," Cecco replies.

"When Rome burns, be the one with the lute, not the suckers with swords," says Mamma.

An interesting take from the daughter of a Catholic war hero. I take my inaugural seat in her coach. It smells like civet anus and tobacco. The coach rolls in the same direction as the previous joyride.

"Was someone just sitting here?" I ask.

"My brother. He's back from Flanders. His Holiness has elected him cardinal priest of Santa Croce. I'm moving back to Milan at the end of the month. Rome isn't fun anymore. Too many country bump-kins getting rich and amassing power."

"Hey, I resemble that remark."

"You're no hick. You spent too much time on our property."

"And I'm not rich. My power is only cultural. It doesn't generate money."

"You'd be terrible with money. You're loveable when you're suffer-ing. It's why we've underpaid you all these years, to save you from spoiling yourself."

She's too sober. Without the sheen of coffee or poppy, her world-view is darkened by privilege. She's too old to be looking like a rich little brat.

"Why aren't you high on something?" I ask.

She looks me over, sizing me up for some real talk.

"You're not hearing me. Rome is burning. Get out. They're going to make a Bruno of you."

"Papa?"

"He and the cardinal-nephew. He's obsessed with your work. Not in a good way. In a Judas loves Jesus way. He's going to build you up, buy you up, and then topple you."

"St. Peter's Square is crowded with Caravaggio fans."

"The cardinal priests will label your new picture obscene by the end of the week. They've already hired the workers to take it down."

"Did Cardinal Colonna tell you this?"

"The cardinal-nephew has already arranged to buy it from the grooms."

"He stole my Jerome. I painted that for Malaspina."

"He's a greedy little rube. Leave Rome. You're dead here. Genoa. Milan. Napoli. We'll find you a place."

"*We*? Who else? Your brother?"

"All of us. Me. My brother. My cousins. Del Monte too."

"Del Monte isn't himself. I think he's with Cardinal Borghese."

"He's fronting. Keeping the cardinal-nephew close. He's a useful idiot. Del Monte talked him into releasing my Fabrizio from prison. He's joining the Knights of St. John. Malaspina helped coordinate. Del Monte broached it to the cardinal-nephew who sold it to the pope."

"What did it cost Del Monte? What will it cost you?"

"I'm not sticking around to find out. You should talk to Del Monte about enlisting in the Knights of St. John. Malaspina is a Caravaggio fan. Live on Malta and paint. Go kill Muslims when your genius bores you. Live your three best selves."

"Why do the Tomassoni keep attacking me? Didn't the cardinal-nephew arrange a truce with Cardinal Farnese?"

"No truce. The cardinal-nephew likes your street brawling. It appreciates your legacy. Why do you think he gave your sword back?"

"Jesus Christ. Don't rich people have anything better to do than sit around playing God with the talents and interests of poor people?"

"No. Not really. That's sort of the whole point of power."

"Not artistic power."

"No, which is why you need to leave Rome. Go paint in peace. Be supernatural. Your father was a gifted mason. He could have developed that talent and became an architect. The marquis made things too easy for him. Paid him a handsome salary to oversee our properties. Your father undersold himself to be our steward, my right-hand man. He chose family over talent. God punished him with the Plague for it."

"I thought my father was an architect. Why are you telling me this?"

"So you'll understand the pain you're in."

"So I can make beauty out of it?"

"So you can make beauty out of it."

"Master my own soul? Play God with myself?"

"I wouldn't know, but I think that's the point of artistic power."

The coach rounds the corner of Via della Missione, the back wheel clipping the curb. My teeth absorb the jolt as I'm tossed from the bench onto the floor. Mamma remains perched, having made a miniscule adjustment mid-bump. The coach brakes hard, and I slide on my back into her shins. I turtle over and push myself to my knees. She's way too sober to be smiling but does so anyway, against the best interests of her face. She looks like Fillide. If I placed my sword in her hands, she'd be a spitting image of my Judith with marionette lines and crow's feet. Fucking gingers are crazy. I'm done riding in coaches. My next ride will be in a box on a cart.

"Pack your things. Pack Cecco too. We'll relocate Caravaggio so he can master himself," Mamma says.

"I'll think about it."

I step out of the coach appreciating the full value of Michelangelo Merisi and his father Fermo. Fuck Milan. Fuck Napoli. Fuck Scipione's churches, I need to get myself inside of Lena. I don't see Cecco. The butcher and his ox are gone. I search Colonna Square for Cecco's face, looking just below the tallest heads for him. He's had a growth spurt. He's average height, a hair shorter than yours truly. Most of the faces watch my searching. I hear their thoughts. *Who's he looking for? What's he after? What's he seeing? Why did God choose him and not me?* The short answers are on God. The long answers belong to them.

Cecco's brown curls surface from a tiding of white Dildo plumes. The face of my ravaged Isaac next to the face of Mario wearing the distress of my *Boy Bitten by a Lizard*. Onorio, Orazio, and Prospero walk behind them, booted, suited, and armed. They approach as if I'm a Christmas pig in a pen, but I can run. There are only femme-fops and pencil-pushers behind me. I step back from my posse. I don't want to hear the bad news they're carrying. I turn and march away from it, but within a few strides I'm seized, manacled at the arms by the four of them. Something has happened to Lena. My posse wouldn't cause such a spectacle for anything less. Cecco tries shouting my fury down with common sense.

"You can't kill Ranuccio in public. No witnesses. Let's make a plan."

I pry my right arm from Onorio and Prospero. Ranuccio lives

blocks from here. I could be at his doorstep in minutes. I grab for my rapier. Cecco blocks my hand. Onorio and Prospero reassure their grip.

"She's not dead. She's not dead," Mario shouts.

"Otnay erehay. Ebay ilentsay," Prospero says.

Caravaggio is still riding in the coach with the cardinal-nephew. Michelangelo can't control my anger unassisted. My posse carries me back to Ruffetti's like my taken Christ, but I'm wearing the scowl of my Matthew's assassin.

They hold me up in my bedroom, the door locked and manned by Fright, Gabrielli, Ruffetti, and Onorio's old war buddy, Captain Troppa, an alpine brute with tree trunk thighs. I stab and jag the wall with my dagger as Mario gives me the details of Lena's rape.

The beauty and popularity of my new Virgin picture infuriated Ranuccio. He forced Lena into having sex with him and then told her to never see me again. She refused. He punched her nose in. After that, Ranuccio consoled her, as pimps do to their pros after abusing them. While Ranuccio kissed her head for forgiveness, Lena grabbed his dagger and sliced his face with it. Ranuccio wrestled the blade away. First, he marked up her face. Then, he dissected her womanhood. She has no more use of it. She can't work with it. She can't have children with it. She can't enjoy it. There's nothing left of her. That's the way Lena saw herself. She left my Christ boy with her sister and fled somewhere. Her sister wouldn't tell Mario where. Lena doesn't want to be seen. She doesn't blame me. She blames Caravaggio. Mario doesn't say so, but I know. I hear her cursing him in pain somewhere.

I have to get even with Ranuccio. I've been threatening it for two years. I've heard enough reasoning and justification about serving my genius. I've heard enough talk from others and myself. Caravaggio is not afraid of death. Michelangelo is not afraid of being murdered. I'm afraid of losing Lena. I'm not afraid of dying. I'm afraid of being defeated. I'm afraid of looking weak. I want Lena back. I can't die for that. I have to live. If I kill Ranuccio, Papa will have me decollated. The only way to punish Ranuccio and keep my head is to cut the pimp's dick off. It'd be perfectly legal. A man has every right to defend his honor when his woman is raped. A man can't flex power and strength without a cock. The only plus of your sexual adversary having a big cock is that it's an easy target.

I turn from the stab wounds in the wall and face my posse.

"I'm going to castrate him."

"Tomorrow evening at the tennis courts. I'll arrange a duel," Mario says.

"Tomorrow is Papa's one-year anniversary," Prospero says.

"Perfect. The city will be occupied," says Onorio.

Cecco and my posse seem happy with the plan. It awards me justice and keeps Caravaggio's head on my neck. Michelangelo gets to neuter a bitch. I can continue loving Lena if she comes back. If she'll even look at me again. If she doesn't curse the day that we bumped into each other at Market Square. Why would she love me? Why would she do that to herself? I'll teach her to do better than that if she ever haves me again.

My posse guards the door while I sleep. They know Michelangelo too well. They don't know me at all, but if they did, they'd see me failing at my duties, botching my fool's errand. The genius is on the brink of getting his shine, but here's Michelangelo sleeping in his armor. In hearing that, Caravaggio finally returns from Del Monte's coach, foaming over the cardinal-nephew's promised commissions. I focus on Lena's devastation. Caravaggio won't see to it. He wants her out of the picture, no more complicating his vision.

"That beady-eyed weasel is making good on his promise. We'll be more famous than the Divine One," he says.

"A king's favor is no inheritance, and almighty God is the biggest shylock of all," I whisper.

"What did you say?" Cecco asks from his bed.

"I'm sorry for everything I've ever given you."

XXX.

Come morning, I've managed to quiet Michelangelo's fury. I feel nothing but nauseating sorrow and guilt for Lena. I place myself in the room during her assault. It's not enough. I place myself in her body. I feel the steel cutting into me. It's not enough. I should be the one dissevered. I pushed Lena into it. I pushed the blade. I destroyed my Virgin with this mega ego of mine. I had no business holding the brush. I didn't know my place. Michelangelo Merisi da Caravaggio is a three-man operation for a reason, and now everything relies on the hick. Michelangelo must save our reputation without snuffing Caravaggio's orbit. Avenge Lena's honor without earning us a murder sentence. Our best bet is for yours truly to stay in my corner, this dark cavity with despairing claw marks on the far wall. Caravaggio has never thought less of me. Michelangelo can't thank me enough.

He and Mario spend the morning practicing in the studio. The mood is professional, humorless. Michelangelo hasn't swung his rapier since the tennis court melee. Ranuccio is better with fists than steel, but Michelangelo needs practice if we're going to unsex him. Ending a man is easy-peasy, severing his cock takes dexterity. Michelangelo would rather puncture the pimp's throat, but Mario and Caravaggio have talked him into castration as a crueler punishment. Michelangelo seems to accept it.

Mario has the quickest hands of our posse, but he's got rust of his own. Too much wheeling and dealing for his family, not enough split-ting skulls. Michelangelo beats him on the down parry for three straight thrusts. After five more goes, they're sweaty and winded, Mario's bouffant frizzled. They take off their shirts and continue. Mario finds his hands and sorts out his patterns. He catches Michelan-gelo in the throat with a riposte. Michelangelo takes it out on Cecco by ordering him out of the studio. The lad's been in the corner, busying his nervous energy by cleaning brushes. He leaves, his ears scrunched in sadness.

"Be delicate. He loves you like you love Lena," Mario says.

"Be honest. I love him like you loved me," Michelangelo says.

Mario stomps and swats Michelangelo's blade. I bind him and elbow his chest. He coughs and backpedals. Onorio enters with the lowdown.

"Tonight. The tennis courts. A duel. No interference. Each man can only have three men by his side. If someone jumps in, everyone jumps in. Regardless of the outcome, each gang must swear to a full omerta. No testimonies. No witnesses."

"He'll beg you to finish him after you've amputated his cock," Mario says.

"Who do you want there? What three?" Onorio asks.

"You two and Captain Troppa," Michelangelo replies.

Raniccio's brothers Giovan and Alessandro are killers. They've done it professionally. They've done it for sport. Ranuccio has never killed anyone. He's a glorified femme fop with a kid brother complex. He's never sent a man to the barber-surgeon for anything more than a few stitches. His most damaged victims have been pros. He doesn't worry me. I owned him with a hammer. Michelangelo could own him with a spatula. When he gets the best of Ranuccio, when Michelangelo puts him on his ass and lunges for his dick, I worry about Giovan and Alessandro safeguarding their little brother's manhood. Our friend Captain Troppa is an indestructible monster. He's been stabbed, shot, and pitchforked. During the Battle of Guruslau, he slew Turks and Transylvanians with a yatagan in his back. He'll gladly jump on Giovan's sword while running his own through him, saving my two best friends from a murder wrap or casket, ensuring that their families retain a provider. Captain Troppa's death wish is more palpable than even mine. I'd only die for Lena, Cecco, and now Caravaggio.

Mario leaves to spend the next, and potentially final hours with his children. Onorio too. I lie on the floor of my studio taking long breaths, thinking of anything but Lena. I can't let that grief get the best of me. The Spanish poets are wrong. The British playwrights too. Don't get me started on the French singers. Sword fighting is not about passion. Swords are not dick metaphors. They're not extensions of manliness. They don't hum of a man's love for pussy, ass, or blood. Men who fight with passion die beautifully. Sword fighting is methodical, cold, and ugly like science. It's ugly as reality, like crooked teeth, dirty teeth, and fingerprints on a pro's ribs. Swords don't lie. They don't even exaggerate. Swords are deadpan. Clang. That just happened. You're dickless.

I spend the next few hours in my lightless cavity, replaying various moments of Lena. Lena under the moonlight in the backyard garden. Lena under the lamplight in my arms. Lena lighting up Rome with her sphinx gaze. I catch Michelangelo daydreaming of Ranuccio, of pushing a dagger through his throat, driving it down his neck, up into his armpits, across his mouth. I stand to walk Michelangelo off, pacing the room until I hear Papa's anniversary festivities begin. Drums and horns. Fireworks. Cannon blasts. People hailing. People heckling. The cops will be busy keeping order, protecting Papa from his haters. It's been a year since I saved one of his necks and two of his chins. I did make his eyes beadier. Someday, when he finally cuts off this head, I'll still have gotten the best of him. My picture will be his face through the millennia.

Cecco knocks. I open the door. His ears are scared red.

"Can I just say one thing?" he asks.

"No."

"Be careful. You've been underestimating him for two years."

"Underestimating who? Michelangelo or Ranuccio?"

Caravaggio closes the door in his face. Michelangelo straps into his armor. He pulls his cloak over the armor. I pull the hood up over our head and disappear.

We cross town in a loose V formation, my full posse plus Captain Troppa. We're all cloaked, hoods up, heads down. We walk casually, a jaunt inspired by the festive atmosphere, not the tromping of a squad on a mission. I look to the evening sky only once, just in case. He's not there. God doesn't want to witness this. I wanted to be sure.

Orazio and Prospero wait outside the tennis court, guarding from a Tomassoni ambush. The court is empty except for two teens lighting fireworks. Captain Toppa scares them off. We remove our cloaks and wait. We're the first ones here. Does that mean I'm the nervous one? My shaking knee says yes.

Within minutes, Ranuccio arrives with Giovan and his two brothers-in-law. They're expensive armor tells me they're supposed to be something. They look strong, strong enough to each lift an end of Ranuccio's huge cock and carry it home to their sister.

Ranuccio is only wearing a plackart. He wants to kill me in high style, showing off the silk ruffles of his blouse and the pleats of his velvet trousers. Giovan is wearing heavy armor and carrying a dragon sword. Captain Troppa positions next to him.

Ranuccio starts right in with the verbal assault, how I still owe him money for fucking his pro, how he was fucking her the whole time, how she loved him and not me, how she said that he fucked her best. Blah blah blah blah blah. I nod my head in agreement.

Ranuccio doesn't like that. He comes swinging in a blitz of anger. It's too directed and obvious. It's easy to parry and sidestep, but his intensity surprises me. Where did he get it? At the end of the day, we don't really know each other. Our contact has come through Lena. Maybe he knows how much she loves me. It's the only accounting for his energetic hatred.

Giovan barks instructions to his little brother. It's good coaching, but Ranuccio isn't deft enough to perform it. Michelangelo pounds back at his sword, knocking Ranuccio back until he trips over his own feet, spilling onto his ass. His eyes grow with panic. His brother yells. I panic too and lunge at Ranuccio's cock. Michelangelo commandeers my aim, thrusting the rapier with more force than I intended. The blade pierces Ranuccio's groin. Michelangelo twists and flicks. Ranuccio's panic crystalizes. He's about to die. It'll be painless compared to Lena's suffering. At least he'll be buried with his cock. I lunge for his stomach. I want him to agonize while he bleeds out. Giovan blocks my rapier and counters across my head. I've never felt anything like it—death. I kneel and pray to it, clutching the wound to keep my head from halving. Captain Troppa swings for Giovan. I rise to assist but Michelangelo is empty and slow. I watch as Giovan cuts Captain Troppa at every opening, high and low. I hear steel on bone. I hear the others clashing. Splayed like my converted Paul, Ranuccio reaches for me. He wants me to stop his bleeding. Caravaggio wants to help him. If Ranuccio dies, he can kiss St. Peter's goodbye. But Michelangelo meant to kill him. He still means to. I turn from Ranuccio toward Giovan as he punctures the Captain full of holes. I rise and strike Giovan's shoulder, but it only achieves his attention. Giovan buries his blade in my neck and then runs to his kid brother. I run off the court. Within the first block, my legs miscarry me to the pavers. Prospero and Orazio lift yours truly, dragging me through the gaiety of Papa's feast toward Firenze Palace, our blood staining a slipstream onto the pavers.

XXXI.

They've buried me in the bowels of Firenze Palace, in the darkest dinge of the servants' quarters. Tor di Nona would be an improvement. The cops are hunting for me. Farnese soldiers are prowling the alleys outside the palace walls. Cecco is literally holding my head together, cupping the fracture with amorous pressure. Del Monte orders him out of the room. He refuses. This is Cecco's big moment and mine. He won't let go of me. We probably resemble my ecstatic St. Francis in the arms of an oversized angel. My cavity has cracked open. If ever there was an opportunity to escape. I could ooze my way out of here without notice, but I no longer want that. Maybe I'm having a change of heart. Getting brained by a sword is a life-altering experience, up there with being nailed to a cross. The pain is out of this world.

Caravaggio is comatose. I'm almost gone. Michelangelo is the one fighting to keep us alive.

Del Monte won't stop chastising me. He paces at my bed. I've never seen the big bear so fleet of foot. I've never witnessed him this nervous. Then again, I'm only seeing things through one eye, the other crusted shut.

"No one can save you from this. Not even God," Del Monte says.

Talking kills so I signal for Cecco to do it for me.

"Is Ranuccio dead?" he asks.

"As a doornail," Del Monte answers.

"I hope he got the message before his light went out," Cecco says.

"What message is that?" Del Monte asks.

"Michelangelo Merisi da Caravaggio is all that and more," he says.

"The Tomassoni have friends near and dear to Papa, and Papa holds Michelangelo Merisi da Caravaggio to be an irredeemable atheist, sodomite, and now murderer."

"And the cardinal-nephew? Which of those three sins does he condemn?" Cecco asks.

"He cares about pictures, and that grisly skull in your hands couldn't paint a Caravaggio to save its life."

Is he talking about yours truly? Can he see me? Am I showing? Has a portion of me oozed out? The consummate apprentice, Cecco covers for me.

"This is the kind of folly that triggers genius. Caravaggio will make it right. His best work is now ahead of him."

Caravaggio couldn't have said it better myself, and I actually believe it coming from Cecco, the young man whose love and devotion we abused. The pain is bad. The guilt worse. If I don't make something redemptive out of it, my remorse could annul Caravaggio's immortality.

"You've failed God. You've failed yourself. Your marchioness too. Your lovers. The prostitute and this lad. You've failed them all," Del Monte says.

"Any word on Lena?" I ask from the gash in my neck, the pain roiling into my eyes and ears.

"She's been shredded. Not a single piece of her is ever coming back."

"We'll find her. We'll go to her," Cecco says.

"She's not long for this world. A woman can't heal such injuries. It might take a few years, but Ranuccio's dagger will murder her, which makes your crime all the more tragic. Ranuccio kills her so you kill yourself to kill him? I thought you were more narcissistic than that."

"I'm not dead. I'll survive this," Michelangelo says.

"Your soul is dead. Your body next. Ready yourself. Prepare for it. Start repenting. Even if you survive, someone from the Farnese militia will eventually assassinate you. Papa also has your death in his head."

"It was an accident. He was trying to cut off his dick," Cecco says.

"You believe in him too much. Stop before he ruins you. Have too much faith, and he'll pound you into a crucifix and mount himself to you. Don't make the same mistake I did," Del Monte says.

"You're more alive than ever, and you only have Caravaggio to thank," Cecco says.

He's wrong. The cardinal-nephew is also responsible for Del Monte's renewed vigor. Their burgeoning friendship is my only hope for survival. Del Monte is right. I've wasted myself. I've been going about myself all wrong. Caravaggio is the only one worth a damn. His genius must be served, even by yours truly. If I had it in me, I'd crawl out of this cot to kneel and swear my deference.

Someone takes my hand. Mario. He's obscured by my crusty eye, but I know the crushing of his grip. I didn't even know he was in the room.

"Oinggay otay Icilysay," he says.

"I know how to speak hog Latin. I'm the one who taught you boys. See how you've disregarded me, like I never existed, like I never cared for you," Del Monte says.

"Giovan is holding the Captain's dying corpse hostage at the Tomassoni compound. The cops are looking for me and Onorio. He's going to Milan. When you mend, and you will fucking mend, come to Siracusa. The Kingdom of Sicily is outside Papa's jurisdiction. If not for the asylum, come for the entertainment of watching me juggle two wives."

I laugh so hard I cry. Cecco coalescing my skull. Mario moistening my palm.

"You're not going to Sicily. You're going to the Zagarolo territory while Cardinal Borghese and I try to broker a pardon. Cardinal Colonna is on board. He was just made Bishop of Palestrina. You'll hide in the various fortresses of the Colonna family fiefdom under the care of the marchioness' cousin Don Marzio, the Duke of Zagarolo. You won't be wining and dining there. You'll be holed up as you are now, staying out of sight, counting your lucky stars and praying to God for mercy."

"Cardinal Colonna? Where's Mamma? Why isn't she here in case I die?" I ask.

"Mamma? Mamma who? Lucia? You're closer to death than I thought. Your mother Lucia died nearly ten years ago. You didn't visit her deathbed."

Cecco covers for me again.

"What about the marchioness? Does she know how bad he is?"

"The marchioness has returned to Caravaggio. She's done with Rome. She's done wiping her Michele's shit. Myself, Cardinals Colonna and Borghese, we're all have you left."

"Why can't I go back to Genoa?" I ask. "The Dorias love me. They want more pictures. Why Zagarolo? I can't believe you're banishing me to the sticks."

"I'm not banishing you. I'm saving your neck."

"Can I go with him?" Cecco asks.

Del Monte stares him down. I cough violently. Closing my one good eye, I pretend to die.

"If you survive the next few nights, we'll smuggle you to Zagarolo in an ox cart," Del Monte says.

"I think he's dead," Mario says.

When I open my eye, Del Monte is gone. Mario has walked around to my good eye.

"You know I love you and adore you. I was yours," he says, quoting my lute player. "Meet me in Siracusa. God can't scare me away from you. Not again."

"Can I go to Siracusa too?" Cecco asks.

Mario kisses my cheek and leaves without answering him. Maybe he's giving Cecco tough love. Maybe he's looking out for the young man, protecting him from Caravaggio. Either way, our sudden privacy feels awkward. I don't know what to say, so I make something up.

"I killed Ranuccio for you and your John."

"You didn't kill him. Michelangelo killed him, and he killed him for his own pleasure."

"I had a hand in it. The finishing flick of the wrist, the one that cut his artery, that was for you. I did it. Not Michelangelo."

"Thank you."

"I love you."

"You're only saying that because you're dying somewhat."

"You said I was all that and more. That's not true. I've exploited you."

"What was it like? Killing him."

"Way better than sex."

"With a woman or man?"

"Either."

Cecco puts his hand on my cock. I barely feel it. I barely feel anything.

"Relax. Close your eye," he says.

Cecco lets go of my head. I don't come oozing out. Wasted as I am, I make a conscious decision to stay, to see Cecco through, our mutual adoration for Caravaggio. What if Giovan's sword knocked the genius out of us? What if he never wakes up? Cecco deserves a little hope.

"I'm rowing my way back on the great black ocean." I say it in my best Caravaggio impression.

"If that's the best you got, you'll never be a god, man," Cecco says to yours truly.

XXXII.

My gashes are scabbing well in the muggy cellars of the Colonna family fortress at Paliano. Weeks of Cecco nursing me in desolation and obscurity. He's been callous about it. No singing. No reading. No coddling. Essentials only. Clean sheets. Clean water. Clean pot. Change bandages and feed, like he's pet-sitting the Duke of Zagarolo's prized mastiff. Cecco cooled on me two weeks ago when it became clear that I wasn't going to die from Giovan's cheap shot. The trauma of the violence has worn off for Cecco, the frenzied emotions lulled. Now there's just bruising, swelling, and a slight misshapenness to the right side of my face, but I'm healing, which means Cecco is free to treat me like a disastrous nobody. I welcome his detachment. It enhances my guilt, which is great. I need to own this. I want someone to lash my back with it. I want someone to stick this guilt up my ass sideways. It's my only hope of Caravaggio making masterpieces with it. I'm back to accepting my forsaken role, but let me be clear. I don't regret killing Ranuccio. Hell no. I've never felt better about ending a man, and God doesn't blame me for it. He blames me for wasting His blessing. Caravaggio remains vegetative. The migraines have seceded, but my head space is still askew. I ache for Caravaggio. I regret sacrificing him to avenge Lena, but I'd do it again. I don't care if He hears me think it. I'd swap Caravaggio for Lena every time, but for now I've forfeited both, which is why Cecco and God are ghosting me.

I'm determined to find Lena and throw myself at her. Maybe she'll reject me. Maybe she's cursing me for inspiring Ranuccio's mutilation. She deserves reprisal. She deserves the gratification of blaming me to my face. I'm a horrible being, a toxic mega ego, but I'm man enough to fulfill my lover's grievance. Nothing will keep me from finding her, except for maybe Papa's capital ban. He damned me the morning after killing Ranuccio, placing a bounty of five hundred scudi on my head. Anyone within the Holy See can decollate me for the prize. My head is now worth twice that of a Caravaggio picture. Until Cardinals Del Monte, Borghese, and Colonna can negotiate a pardon, I'm stuck out here in the sticks. It should only be another week or two. The cardinal-nephew is still set on monetizing me. Now that he owns two Caravaggio pictures, my continuing fame is in his best interest. I'll paint my way out of this. I'll paint my way to Lena, but first I have to pull a Lazarus with Caravaggio. It'll take the three of us to resurrect him—Cecco, Michelangelo, and yours truly.

There are no Colonnas here. Prince Filippo is in Spain. Don Marzio spends summers at the Napoli palace. Here in the dilapidating fortress of Paliano, it's essential staff only. A steward, two housemaids, and the gardener. They keep the place from crumbling and growing jungly. For their own safety, they've been ordered to steer clear of me. For our safety, Cardinal Colonna put me and Cecco under arrest during daylight hours. Some disgruntled serf might try cashing in on my head. Most of Rome thinks I've fled to Genoa again. Some believe I'm hiding with Mamma in Milan. There are rumors that I killed Ranuccio over a tennis match. There are whispers that I killed him over a debt. The staff doesn't want to know anything. They can't bring themselves to look at me. When people think you're a murderer, they're intrigued. When they know you're a murderer, they're repulsed. It's not moral, more of a gag reflex.

I only see the staff while praying in the palace chapel. There is a priest and altar server on duty. My cardinals have commanded that I attend mass at dawn and dusk to atone for the murder I've committed. I owe them at least that, so I'm here at Mass praying for Lena. The priest mumbles in Latin, stomaching the presence of a murderous libertine. I've heard of this geezer, an infamous chicken-plucker and third-cousin Colonna. Papa Gout reassigned him to the sticks after he was caught bedding two generations of acolytes. His new altar server has the oblong malformations of a defunct castrato. Father Chicken-

Plucker drops the Latin and speaks a few phrases of Greek. He could scream in Arabic without a single jeer from our six-person congregation because nobody is listening. Save for Cecco, everyone else is trying to eavesdrop on my repenting.

We sit. We stand. We sit. Father Chicken-Plucker makes wine. He makes a sign of the cross. I shiver, but only because of my profuse sweating. The nave is an oven. The daylong, inland sun heat cooks the palace stones and our collective sins. I elbow-nudge Cecco's ribs for old times' sake. He shakes his head in denunciation, wobbling away on his buttocks. Cecco is finally man enough to withstand me. Hallelujah to him! Father Chicken-Plucker returns to the altar and prays, mumbling an inaudible secret. We stand and sing *Amen*. He reads the Preface. We chant some shit. Father Chicken-Plucker knocks on his chest, declares his disreputableness, and chaws on Christ like a swine. He drinks His blood. We draw crosses on our heads. The sanctus bells ring. I walk my butt cheeks toward Cecco, just to be irritating, and because I'm a little hurt. He sighs and accepts my nearness.

After Mass, Cecco and I stroll the grounds. We walk until the void of Caravaggio unsteadies my balance. We rest on the patio, a promontory overlooking all of Latium. Rome shimmers in the deep distance, the sun crowning it. I can see the glint of domes. I can see glimmering belfries and the spangle of superstructing palaces. I see the progress. Our city is growing without Caravaggio. I feel excommunicated, in a bad way. Michelangelo diverts our sights to the alluvial plains. The patches of vineyard and evergreen. It's nothing but monotonous strata to me, nothing but the rectilinear diagrams of land barons. The Lombard hick loves it here. He loves being in the boonies. He loves the oceanic pines. He loves the midday blues and clean air. It makes me sick. Where the hick sees alluvial plains, I see swampy flatlands. I see mosquitos and malaria. I see the jaundiced face of my sick Bacchus. I remember the vomiting and diarrhea. The high fever and stomachache. I remember convulsing as if being exorcised of my demons. I remember the disease so well that the nausea resuscitates Caravaggio. He's blurred and fagged but alive. He squints over the flatlands and up toward the purple Apennini range.

"Am I in hell?" he asks.

"Worse. We're stuck in a Carracci landscape," I answer.

"God's country," Michelangelo says.

"You're all over the map," Cecco replies.

We're closer to hell than we are to Lena. I don't need a map to tell me that. Michelangelo doesn't care. He's already over her. She's faded once and for all. My map to Lena in heaven will be drawn by Caravaggio. Cecco ain't seeing any of it. He's looking lower and closer. He's taking in the feudal towns splotched about Latium, Etruria, and south toward the Kingdom of Sicily. The boxy tenements and gothic arches. The ovate walls. The archaism of the Middle Ages, of Lucia and Fermo Merisi. This is the landscape of our Caravaggio origins. Cecco and Michelangelo are hicks at heart, but Cecco doesn't miss it. He's not contemptuous either. He's sitting proud, stroking the scruffy pubes on his face. Cecco del Caravaggio has sacrificed everything to get where he is, sitting high as Jove, deep in the heart of God's favorite creator. I don't tell him that Caravaggio is back. I don't want him to be nice to me, not yet.

Beyond the nearest hamlet, a billowing string of dust approaches. A convoy of ten coaches.

"Do you see that?" Cecco asks.

"If I had to bet Caravaggio's life, I'd say it's Cardinal Colonna. They look about thirty minutes away."

"Can you see a flag or pennants?"

"No, but I recognize the coaches."

"Should we hide in the crypt to play it safe?"

"If it's the Farnese militia or Swiss guard or Ambassador Masetti coming for the duke's money, save yourself. Run and hide. Don't get yourself killed trying to protect me."

"Trust me. I won't."

"The beard looks good."

"Thanks."

"Be careful though. Summer beards get soily. The humidity and sweat. Food from the corners of your mouth. You have to wash them every other day or so."

"Is that why you've never grown one? Because you hate bathing?"

"What's your deal? Two weeks ago, you had your hand on my jock while I was dying."

"Go to the crypt. I'll fetch a flask and bring it down. Why not catch a buzz while we're down there waiting for your new collectors?"

He's really giving me the business. I love it. I can't help but slap his ass like a charger as he walks past. Not a spank, but a love-tap, a giddy-up swat to let him know that I recognize his invaluable contributions to the corporation and encourage him to continue.

Cecco and I hand the flask back and forth in the quantum darkness of the family crypt. Some, not all, of the Colonnas are buried down here. The most important one is: Marcantonio II Colonna, the catholic superhero and step-grandfather to the great prodigious scoundrel of our modern era. The Viceroy of Sicily is the only Colonna whose immortality is not dependent on yours truly. As the protagonist in Christianity's greatest victory over Islam, Admiral Colonna captured the Ottoman fleet's flagship, handing that unhallowed empire their first naval defeat in more than a century, halting Satan's expansion across the Mediterranean. As the records show, I was born days prior to said victory. I approach my step-grandfather's tomb and thank him. I thank him for his valor and strength. I thank him for his daughter's love. I understand why Mamma distanced herself from the murder I committed. It's not permanent. She'll return. I have faith that she's pulling every string within her grasp. Her inheritance depends on it. If not the Pantheon, I can see myself entombed here. I'm as deserving as my brother.

"The entire fortress is a shithole. It's totally falling apart. And the furniture. My parents had nicer furniture. I thought the Colonnas had money growing out their ass," Cecco says.

"War is expensive. Military families spend money faster than they pillage. The Farnese. The Colonna. The Dorias. They're palace-rich but purse-poor. They're not diversifying. Banking and trading. That's the only way to increase wealth."

"And collecting masterpieces at discount prices."

He drives the truth into my self-deceit like a spike through the palm. I dwell on the realness of my trouble. Death is the least of it. God has nothing on me. Papa has nothing over me. My pictures of them will remain the be-all-end-all. Decollating my head will martyrize Caravaggio. I'm not worried about the chopping block. I'm worried about reckoning with Cecco and Lena. I never believed in her love. I never did her justice on canvas. How could she ever forgive me? Cecco forgives Caravaggio's selfishness every second of the day, but the Cupid in him is dead. I, Michelangelo Merisi da Caravaggio killed Sacred Love. That's on me. That's hanging over me. Who will I enrich? How will I enrich them? That's what I dwell on in this lightless Colonna crypt. Cecco is here with me, but he feels distant as Lena. I dwell on them both until the door creaks open. I sense Cecco's nerves jumping through the ceiling.

A lantern is lit. It illuminates Cardinal Colonna's face like a David I've been meaning to paint, although he looks like a bald Mamma with a goatee. They share the same eyebrows too (crazy high arches).

"I like that you obeyed my orders to hide down here. It makes me hopeful," Cardinal Colonna says.

"Is there reason for hopelessness?" I ask.

"Yes. The pope refuses to pardon you despite our best efforts. The police are scouring the Holy See for you. The Farnese too. That Masetti is searching high and low, hounding Cardinal Del Monte about your whereabouts. We might send you to Napoli. It's outside Papa's authority. My cousin, the duke, is there until winter. He's happy to provide refuge."

"He's happy to have Caravaggio make pictures for him," Cecco says.

"Does your master want to keep his head on his neck? We're all risking ours to save his genius. Painting some gifts is the least he can do. Offerings of gratitude for Cardinals Del Monte and Borghese. My sister too. It's going to take every favor. Papa thinks you're evil."

"Ranuccio raped my lover with a knife and I'm evil?"

"The Farnese were extremely fond of him. Ranuccio Farnese and Papa share Spanish interests, and now they're extremely interested in collecting your head. You may have to leave the Holy See forever."

"He destroyed my lover's body and soul."

"My lover's body and soul too," Cecco says.

"This isn't a courtroom. If you want forgiveness, start mixing paint. Get your lad stretching canvases. I brought you supplies. Paint something for the cardinal-nephew. Atone for that blasphemous portrait of Pope Paul."

"We're getting low on wine," I say.

"Have you been attending Mass?" he asks back.

"How much did you pay for the Carracci? His bean eater?"

"More than the Farnese paid him, and I never had to save his life."

"That's because the Farnese sucked all the life out of him," Cecco says.

"Tell the cardinal-nephew my head is all his. He can come get it by summer's end."

"Cardinal Del Monte wants another Francis," Cardinal Colonna says.

"How are my new Virgin pictures? Drawing mega crowds?"

"Papa had them taken down. They were profane and crude. You eroticized the Holy Mother's bosom. You vulgarized her assumption. You had men masturbating to the Holy Mother. If Papa doesn't decollate you for murder, he'll burn you at the stake for blasphemy. The cardinal-nephew is straining his familial graces arguing for your pardon."

"Well, at least the cardinal-nephew owns a Jerome, and now he owns a Virgin. Which one did he buy? The grooms' picture, if I had to guess."

My clairvoyance crumbles the cardinal's eyebrows. He wants to know how I knew, but he's a professional sociopath. He doesn't ask. He rebuilds his eyebrows and provides an inverse answer.

"The Duke of Mantua bought the assumption Virgin," he says.

"I'm happy to help the noble class diversify, and like you said, it's the least I can do."

"Speaking of nobility, please allow me a private moment with my father," he replies.

He turns for Marcantonio's tomb, taking the lamplight with him. I can feel Cecco's anxiety in the darkness. It's nothing compared to mine. Caravaggio takes his hand.

"Help me turn one of these shithole rooms into a studio," Caravaggio says.

"Master? Are you all there? Are you right in the head?" Cecco asks.

I bring his hand to my heart.

"The cardinal-nephew wants a David. I need you to shave that beard. Pretty please."

XXXIII.

Caravaggio gets to work. Cecco busts a hole in the wall, hammer in one hand, iron crow in the other, boring through centuries-old plaster and brick. His swings are festive. It's a crummy room with copious sun. The cracked walls are covered with tapestries depicting a high dame consorting with a lion, monkey, and unicorn. Cecco contemplates the one of her playing an organ, the monkey standing upright, the unicorn and lion on their haunches.

"It's worth ten of your pictures," he says, tracing the golden thread woven into the foliated vine boxing the picture.

"Or a swanky coach and ten horses."

"When we're done, I'll unstitch the thread," Cecco says.

"Flee to Spain. Buy yourself a castle."

The bedroom has not fielded a dream since Mamma and her younger sister Giovana slept in it. Mamma moved out at twelve after marrying my father's sexual rival and boss. The green duvet and matching tuffet are the girliest things about the room. Cecco pushes the bed into the far corner. He pulls one tapestry from the wall and nails it face-out over the nearest window. He unhooks another tapestry and nails it over the second window. The room falls dark, a sun shaft blasting through the hole. Cecco steps into it, posing with an imaginary sword held low.

"How's that?" he asks.

"If Isaac could see you now," I say.

"That swollen head of yours, scarred and bruised. It's ripe for decollation. You've finally perfected your gory selfie. You're the perfect Goliath."

He raises my decapitated head and drops it to the floor. He turns for the windows and pulls the tapestries aside. The same light returns, but it's a new day. The sun has evaporated his worship. Cecco hasn't reappeared. My David remains. My reluctant conqueror. His shoulders budding with manhood. Barely an ounce of baby fat to his bald cheeks. Caravaggio never saw him coming. Isaac has the knife.

A deteriorating fortress is the perfect place to paint my demise, the perfect setting for Isaac to shank Abraham, for Sacred Love to commandeer the cock-munching. I'll paint my wanted poster staring into the childhood mirror of my stepmom. Papa can have my head. The Farnese and whoever else too. First come, first serve. Here I am at Paliano Palace. Here I am at the decrepit stronghold of my foster family. Come and cash in on my head!

I get this underdog picture off on the right foot by stretching Caravaggio's canvas. I prime it too. Cecco watches over me, the sunset in his eyes. He goes to the window for a view of Rome. The twilight strikes his ear, glistening like Lena's clit.

"I need a sword. David needs a sword," he says.

I shrug. Del Monte took my blades and armor. Cecco leaves. I sit on the bed and study the umbral reflection in Mamma's girlhood mirror. Big bad Goliath is mortified by what he sees. Yours truly. The face of a beaten man. Is this what I look like without Michelangelo's confidence, without Caravaggio's eminence? The genius will have a field day with this face of mine.

"You deserve to be infinitely shamed," I say to the mirror, but it comes out sounding like Caravaggio.

My David returns carrying a sword with a decorative knuckle bow. It's a sword for hanging on walls, not gutting Turks.

"Did you get that from Marcantonio's study?" I ask.

Cecco nods.

"Good. I want the Colonnas to get high on my David."

"*Your* David? Try again. *My* David. My visage is my own from here on out," he says.

I can't argue with that. I don't have the energy or self-esteem, and I appreciate his iconoclasm. Someone has finally stood up to Caravaggio.

Cecco has more balls than God. I go to the window. He chases me down and places an overbearing arm around my waist. Rome burns in flashes of orange and pink. A nimbus of starlings rises from a stand of stone pine, their flight helixing into the most awesome forms.

"I see a bereaved Mary Magdalene. What do you see?" I ask.

"Sometimes birds are just fucking birds."

We shake the dust from Mamma's duvet and take to bed. I'm too anxious for sleep. The gesso can't dry fast enough. I have all the angsty causations of a masterpiece inside of me. Loss. Guilt. Madness. Cecco falls asleep with his prick in the curve of my back. I let it be. It's nothing. Lena let Ranuccio do worse. I'm up all night with it, keeping her face from fading.

Come morning, we're after it, Cecco's ambition rivaling mine. Caravaggio paints his David first. He paints the sheer darkness surrounding him. It's the truest black of his career—soft, textured, and inescapable. Its perfection deepens as it nears the glow of David's historic win. The pure white light on his arm as he holds the gruesome trophy by the hair. His fist and cheek are blushing. David takes no pleasure in the head of Goliath. He presents it as a burden. He aims the superhero's sword at his own thigh, the point at Ranuccio's kill spot. The twerp has a long sheath to fill. Now he has to play hero every time some monstrous Philistine comes around. He's surrendered his free will for mythology. His life no longer belongs to him. David is a loser. Caravaggio paints Lena's vulva as his ear. Is it an homage to our Virgin, or is he merely throwing my guilt a bone?

Cecco can't get over his David. Caravaggio has recreated him again. Cecco wanted to do it for himself, but Caravaggio beat him to the punch. He wanted to rule over Caravaggio's genius. Now he's a self-made king of the Jews. Thanks to Caravaggio, he's more human than the Divine One's anatomically sublime David. Cecco's David ain't heavenly. He's no Achilles, juiced up on supernatural powers, slashing through fleshly opponents like butter. Cecco's David toppled his supervillain fair and square, with lean arms and unformed pecs. The colossal Philistine has been beheaded by a shepherd. Rome's evil genius has been decollated by his own boy. Now Cecco must make something of his David. A hero is only as good as his last kill. Caravaggio has painted Cecco an epic. He's painted him an apology, but that has everything to do with my guilt. I have had a hand in this blockbuster. I played my role. I served the genius, providing him my essential consciousness. That's my guilt in that picture. That's my pathos. Cecco can't help but see it. He can't help but worship me again. Cecco walks out on me.

I prop Mamma's mirror next to the picture and sit Caravaggio on her tuffet. I watch the genius execute my portrait. I sit for him over an indefinite period of days, marked only by Cecco entering to feed us and empty our pot. We're too invested to acknowledge him. We paint fast. We paint thin, conserving pigments. Cardinal Colonna skimped out on materials. That miserly boor knows shit about making pictures. The cardinal-nephew has some idea, so we paint every bit of my suffering into this Goliath. We paint my shitty teeth. We paint the swelling of Giovan's sword. We paint the scab as David's slingshot wound. We paint the giant. We paint the giant asshole. The mega ego. I'm not talking sick Bacchus or my boy musician. I'm not talking Michelangelo or Caravaggio. This Goliath is me, yours truly. The first time Caravaggio has painted me, I can barely stand the sight of myself. I can barely sit here while Caravaggio applies the finishing touches of my wanted poster. Here I am. The tortured consciousness. The lambent superego. The defeated bandit. No hope. No fear. But enough sado-masochism for the cardinal-nephew to fall in love.

Cecco returns a week later, whiskers sprouting, nose sunburnt. He beholds my gory selfie with a sapphic bob of the head, resigning himself to the return of my existential prominence.

"It's how I always pictured you," he says.

"Profane Love after getting kicked in the teeth?"

"Dreadful and ugly doesn't mean evil."

"Forgive me for everything?" I stand from the tuffet to rub the tingle from my buttocks.

"This picture is a game-changer. You've revolutionized painting, again. You're the Galileo of the human psyche. I'm astounded, but it's not enough. I don't want your head. I want your body."

"I can't."

"Because you still love her?"

"I want to be the Lenavaggios again. You were part of us. Cecco del Lenavaggio."

"Don't call me Cecco anymore. It's a lad's name. Call me Francesco, the name my parents gave me."

"I'm proud of the man you've become. Bold. Handsome. A decent painter."

"So, do me."

"I can't. It's wrong. God will punish you."

"That's just an excuse. He never punishes men like Del Monte or the cardinal-nephew. If anything, he rewards them. Give me your body. Whip it out."

"I can't. I love her."

"Why? What did you actually have with her? You shared nothing. You did nothing but wait around in bed for her. She wanted fame. She wanted money. You gave her all that. Then she didn't want it. She lied. She fucked your head."

"We had great sex."

"That's not what I heard. I heard your grunts and gasps, but I never heard a peep from her. Not a moan. Not a breathy *yes* or *oh my god*. She took you for a ride."

I could kill him. I consider the superhero's sword on the floor. I consider smothering him with a tapestry. I consider ramming his head against the wall until it turns to ragu, but he's right. Lena lied. She screwed my mind. She gave me nothing but unconditional love and I fucked it all to hell. I didn't deserve her satiety. I don't deserve her forgiveness. I don't deserve Mamma's mothering or Del Monte's patronage. I don't deserve Papa's pardon. I have no business painting for absolution, but I'm going to anyway. I'll paint Lena a weeping Mary Magdalene, a picture of the holy pro's pain and suffering. I'll gift it to Mamma. I'll paint it to hurt Cecco for his words against Lena. He's already softening on me. The David I gave him was too kind.

We carry our picture downstairs to the great hall. It's wide as some piazzas but dingy and unfurnished. The cornice is Greek. The echo is Ovidian. There is a maritime mural consisting of asymmetrical gulls and disproportionate galleys. It's said that my step-grandfather adored the fresco. Judging from the shoddy brushwork, I believe it. One of the housemaids enters, the younger one with a unibrow and hairy arms. She's pushing the broom ironically. The dusty floor merits a shovel. The cobwebs need a sword. She stops for an incurious look at my picture. She drops the broom and covers her eyes, screaming at the viscera pouring from my Goliath's neck.

"I'll make your body eternal. Would you like that?" Caravaggio asks her.

She's too scared to say no. She spreads her fingers apart, acknowledging me through the cracks.

"Come up to my studio after tomorrow morning's prayer. All you'll have to do is sit in a chair. Wear what you have on."

Cecco and I return upstairs. I take to bed naked, rolling onto my side facing the wall, daring Cecco to make a move. He makes a move. He strips and spoons me. He's full of himself. Good on him. He's earned this right. He was always on the receiving end of my vanity. He sticks it to me. I take it. It's the least I can do for his growing confidence. Mario was the last man I let in. This pain is just enough. Cecco kisses my back. I lean away from his mouth. I don't want the comfort. I want him to be selfish and inconsiderate. He's not very good at it. It feels like someone is rummaging through my soul. He won't find my love there. I shattered that and buried the pieces in his portraits.

"Tomorrow, when I start my weeping Magdalene, make yourself absent. I don't want you around for it."

"You're really going to paint the housemaid as the penitent pro?"

I don't answer. I brace the wall and push back against his shaky hips.

XXXIV.

The housemaid knocks and enters. Cecco doesn't wake up. I've been up all night envisioning Lena, her contours and surfaces. Her posture and hues. Her immutable sorrow. The housemaid doesn't blink at our David and Goliath bed fellowship. She's alright. She's wearing the same white blouse, but her shoulders are wrapped in a red shawl on loan from the duchess' wardrobe. Her unibrow is plucked. The blotchy irritation matches her shawl. The dawn chorus has progressed through blackbirds, robins, and wrens. Warblers now call the morning. The prayer bell hasn't chimed.

"Are we skipping Mass?" I ask.

Cecco digs his arm from my stomach and untangles his legs from mine.

"I'll fetch my own food and dump my own pot. Don't come back until I call for you," I tell him.

The housemaid throws him his pants. He sits up but doesn't put them on.

"Should I assume her house duties?" Cecco asks, sounding rather bitchy.

"Let this Tor di Nona crumble to dust. Your new burden is having my back. Keep a lookout for Swiss guards, cops, mercs, and everyone else with a poster of my head."

David bends for his sword and exits, pants wish-boned around his neck. I get dressed. I push an oak scissor chair across the room, adding extra muscle, ensuring scratches on the pine floor. I butt the chair against the foot of the bed. The housemaid sits and reclines, resting an elbow on the mattress. I open the neck of her blouse, baring the pitched shoulder. I tilt her head back, nose straight up like a keel.

"Can you hold that position?"

"For as long as forever takes," she says.

"Probably five, six-hour days."

"That's all? I was hoping for a longer holiday."

I spread the shawl over her legs. I mix my colors. I cover the windows. Light enters from the punched hole, a translucent beam uppercutting her jaw. I vanish the housemaid and conjure Lena, the dark side of her dead Mary face. I paint it in complete light, a picture of Lena's grieving. I picture her deprivation. This woman has lost her messiah. She's lost herself. A woman devastated. A woman foiled. A woman dissatisfied and deceived. A knifed woman. A total breakdown. Rome has hammered her to pieces. Trampled by coaches, gossip, and machismo. The johns of Magdala. Wretched and rich. Bald and lion maned. Bookworms and dolts. Some with hard abs. Others with moobs. Donkey cocks and wee peens. Men are all the same. They all think they had her. She bested all of them. It cost her everything, the power to love herself. She's pregnant with misery. She's carrying it to term. Her eyes closed. Her sockets welled with tears. The ecstasy of a pro's suffering. A portrait of Lena fading. I paint her body from memory. I paint her emotions from fantasy. She loved her sorrow. She was most loyal to it. She didn't need anything else. She didn't need Caravaggio, Michelangelo, or yours truly. She wanted us. That was too much for Michelangelo. It wasn't enough for Caravaggio. I took it for granted. I dragged my ass on her. We should have killed Ranuccio the night of the rock-fight. I let her pacifism get the best of Michelangelo. I let her beauty get the best of Caravaggio. She got the worst of me. My compulsion to please. My aversion to decision-making. I should have painted her a Magdalene all along. I forced the Virgin upon her. I forced her upon the Virgin. It was too much for God, Ranuccio, and yours truly.

I've gone psycho to psychic. We've never imagined a picture into existence. Carvaggio has always painted reality. Every bruised apple. Every moldy grape. Every leaf of ivy. Every rotten tooth and fungal nail. It all preceded the genius. God made all of it. We just did its justice.

We've never forged a person or thing. But here's Lena's exquisite throat. Here are her fingers, clasped with blessedness. Her tangy lips. The rainy balm of her skin. She's all here but the bosom. I left her breasts out of it. A mastectomy for Lenavaggio to reconcile Ranuccio's botched castration. It's my most personal picture since *Love Conquers*. In painting it, Caravaggio has learned something about me. I'm not here to serve his genius. I'm here to guilt him into perfection. I'm here to better his humanity. We've bettered our art. Not that it's mended Lena. Ranuccio undid her body. I coopted her soul. A picture can't heal the mutilation, and immortality will only prolong the pain in perpetuity. I'm hapless. I'm contrite. Caravaggio has expressed me to perfection, filling Lena's corpse with my penitence. She'll never see it hanging in the cardinal-nephew's gallery. She'll never dwell in the queendom that she created in my head. She owns the real estate of my mind. It's her fiefdom. She has occupied us. The victor. The spoils.

"You grew out her Lena coif," the housemaid says.

She's a fan. She wants to talk about it. I'm not feeling worthy. I roll the tapestries open. I go to my hole and piss out of it. Finished, I wipe my fingers through my hair.

"She's crying like she doesn't believe in heaven, like it's the end. No eternal bliss. No reunion. Her love is gone," she says.

The first throb of a remarkable headache gongs my skull. My arms and legs turn molten lead. Maybe it's what she said. I haven't slept in six sunsets. I collapse onto the green duvet. Cecco in my nose. Lena in my eyes. The housemaid's words in my ears.

It takes days to fall asleep, and another two for the headache to fuck off. I lie in bed empty, draining Caravaggio and Michelangelo, letting the guilt and dysphoria putrefy. I play invalid for Cecco. He feeds me lettuce by the leaf. He brings the wine to my lips.

"Montepulciano? What happened to the claret?" I ask.

"No more luxuries. You called this place Tor di Nona. So, drink like it."

He's minding me like a guard, not a lover.

"I told you to never take me back."

"I warned you about stardom," he says.

"You talk from both sides of your mouth."

He kisses my forehead. He kisses my cheek. I open my mouth on his neck. I hear God retch, spying on us through my aperture. Cecco pulls my hair. I relax my neck, granting him the weight of my head.

"My David is groundbreaking. Your Magdalene is mental. She's a reincarnation. I thought Lena had scaled the fortress wall. I thought maybe she's been hiding here all summer. I thought maybe she teleported here in the Virgin's flying house of Loreto. I actually entertained the idea. You painted her that real. Her grief. My wistfulness. You're still idealizing her, but you've redeemed yourself. You're flirting with perfection," he says to Caravaggio.

"I love you," I say.

"No, you don't," he says.

"Don't do that."

"Don't do what?" he asks.

"Doubt a lover's sincerity."

"You're no Lena, and I'm no you."

He drops my head into his lap. I eat his words, the ecstasy burning my eyes.

I paint two more pictures, re-imaginings of older works—a rehabbed Francis and renovated *Meal at Emmaus*. Summer peaks. No headhunters storming the fortress. No word or visits from cardinals. Cecco and I capitalize. Every night I let him do whatever. Sometimes I cry over Lena, but not all the time. This isn't Shakespeare. I can live without her. I never stopped loving Cecco. Michelangelo loves him too, but he loves getting hammered and wrenched more. He loves the reaming. He dies when Cecco fists our hair, when David upholds his trophy. Cecco is adopting the role. He dies with silent contemplation, knees locked, hands strangling my ears. He loves us heart, soul, and mind, but that won't save him from God's wrath.

Finished with Del Monte's Francis, Cecco and I now have the mornings too. We lie as a cross, Cecco the transom, the back of his thighs perspiring on my stomach. The tapestries mask the windows to prevent the late-August sun from making the room hell. I've stuffed the aperture with Magdalene's red shawl, obstructing God's omniscience. I can't fix Lena, but I can save Cecco. We share a flask and daydrink in the quiet grey. When the lunch bell rings, he says what's been on his mind since dying.

"Paint me and Lena only from now on. Don't waste your genius on anyone else."

I agree with him in principle, but I seldom have a say in who we paint. Most patrons stipulate a specific saint or martyr. Cecco ain't no Jesus or wizen Francis, but I want him to feel essential. I want him to live as heroically in life as his David will in death. I'll continue painting him to perfection, overwhelming God's animosity toward ass-fuckers. Maybe I'm overreaching, but I nod at Cecco's proposition.

The housemaid barges in and goes straight for my hole, unplugging the duchess' red shawl from it. The beam highlights Cecco's shins and knees. He lifts his hand and makes a barking dog shadow puppet against the wall.

"They're coming to kill you," she says.

We roll off the bed in opposite directions. Cecco goes for his pants. I go for Marcantonio's sword.

"Who's coming to kill me?"

"The coaches are nondescript. No flags or pennants."

"It's probably Cardinal Colonna," Cecco says.

"Why would he ride here in an unmarked coach?" the housemaid says.

She removes the tapestries from the windows and rehangs them in their original places.

"Your last chance to steal the thread," I say to Cecco.

"Don't. They'll think it was me," says the housemaid.

She folds the shawl into sixteenths, slides it up her skirt, and leaves.

"Should we go to the crypt?" Cecco asks.

"My executioner won't arrive in a stately convoy. He'll lunge from a shadow, stabbing me in the liver."

"Nah. Michelangelo will kill you when he's good and ready."

"Help me carry Magdalene to the great hall. It smells like ass and sweat in here."

"The cologne of cardinals."

"Cardinal Colonna isn't a chicken-plucker."

"You suddenly care what cardinals think?"

"I care about you. Papa will torch your ass to please God."

"Perhaps those who pronounce my sentence are in greater fear than I who receive it," he says, quoting me quoting Bruno.

The great hall smells sneezy. Both housemaids are sweeping like devils. A universe of motes expands beyond the sunlight projecting through the lone window. It's the perfect cosmos for my work. We stand our four pictures side by side against Marcantonio's mural. It has no business fortifying my pictures. I can only blame myself for putting them in such a position. Cecco and I find some folding curule chairs and place them by Lena. We don't talk. We sit with our backs to her, waiting for my killers, acting like we haven't been boning for weeks.

My killers don't come in wooden stomps. They arrive in the nonchalant patter of leather sandals—Del Monte and the cardinal-nephew. They're dressed in sacramental vestments, the scarlet cassock and mozzetta. Del Monte's dome is covered by a standard biretta. Borghese wears a broad galero and splashy ferraiolo. He looks like a femme-fop pimp. Del Monte's face has grown. His neck has absconded. He's had a summer for himself, cooking the cardinal-nephew's appetites. They toddle across the great hall, the earliest clump of gout to their gait. They traverse the piles of dust like fat-cat generals stepping over enemy corpses.

The housemaids ride away on their brooms. I kneel and kiss Del Monte's ring like a beholden son. I pucker up to Borghese's band because my genius depends on it. I can't die now. Caravaggio is painting his best work. Cecco kneels one begrudging knee at a time and gives each gold ring an affected peck.

"They're coming to kill you," Del Monte says.

"Is that why you've come dressed in fancy work clothes?" I say.

"Is this masterpiece for me?" The cardinal-nephew goes nose to nose with David.

Del Monte regards the four pictures, skimming past his Francis, landing on Lena. He leans into the blackness surrounding her. His beard absorbs the tears, hers and his.

"Who's coming to kill me?" I ask.

"How on earth? Did she come to you? Is she here?" He looks around the hall for Lena.

"She came to me, but not in person. Who's coming to kill me?"

"This picture. It's a Renaissance, better than the first," the cardinal-nephew says.

"Who's coming to kill him?" Cecco asks.

"All of them," Del Monte answers.

"One of your young followers attacked Baglione. Almost killed him." The cardinal-nephew lowers his gaze to Goliath.

"I had nothing to do with that."

"Tell that to His Holiness."

"Does Papa know we're here?" asks Cecco.

"He knows everything. He knows that Cecco del Caravaggio sucks his master's cock."

"My name is Francesco Buoneri."

The cardinal turns from Goliath and slings a limp-wristed back-hand, his ring chipping my Cupid's one good tooth. Cecco takes it like a messiah. He grins the sting away and offers his abuser a chair. Borghese accepts. Del Monte assumes my seat. They wow over my pictures for the time it takes paint to dry. Cecco and I stand there like attendants. I could snap the cardinal-nephew's neck and be done with myself, but these pictures. They're worth more than Cecco's pride. Even he agrees.

"These pictures. They're an embarrassment of riches," says Borghese.

"I'm ashamed. Please take them off my hands. Except the Magdalene. She's for the duke, and she's not finished."

"Your Magdalene? I don't want that whore."

I make a fist and imagine my next picture. A Christ child. The one I never gave Lena.

"I want to go home," I say.

"Keep painting like this, and I'll persuade my uncle."

"Has the marchioness asked about me? Is she worried?"

"You're going to Napoli," says Borghese. "We've arranged commissions there. A Croatian trader wants a Madonna and child accompanied by a choir of angels. Don Marzio owns tenements there. We'll hole you up in one. You can knock holes in every wall."

Del Monte stands, pinching back more tears. After a sorry smile, he rests his heavy paws on my shoulders.

"Your genius has fully matured, finally. The David and Magdalene. I saw them in you back when."

"You saw them before I did. I didn't see them until Ash Wednesday sixteen hundred. My first glimpse came in the eye of Bruno's blaze."

"You'll be back at Campo de' Fiori casting beggars and pros by next summer," Borghese says. "Until then, go to Napoli and paint more of these. Your salvation depends on it."

He's talking out his ass. Almighty God is the sole executor of my salvation. Borghese wants to monopolize Caravaggio before his uncle decollates me. He's afraid of blowing this investment opportunity. He's in love with his David, but he can't sit still, tapping a foot and drumming ten fingers on both knees. Something is up. Papa's hitmen must be close.

Borghese stands, sneezes twice in one breath, and slithers off.

"I'm not spending the night in this derelict dungeon. My coach is plusher. We'll load our pictures and drive back to Rome," he says to Del Monte. "I apologize for your tooth," he shouts to Cecco from the other side of the hall.

Del Monte bear-hugs me farewell, nuzzling his whiskers against my neck. He's afraid to let go. The blood might pour from his hands.

"You've finally transcended. It's just you and the Divine One now. Don't crash."

"Why should I give my genius to him? Why should he profit off it?"

"Your pictures will belong to him for a few decades. After he dies, they'll belong to the world."

He thinks I was talking about the cardinal-nephew.

"Who's coming to kill him?" Cecco asks.

"Farnese mercs. The knights from the Supreme Order of Christ. The knights of St. Gregory the Great and the knights of the Golden Spur."

"Don't forget the Knights of the Round Table," Michelangelo jokes.

He loves Del Monte more than any of us. Del Monte nursed Caravaggio's genius, but he fathered Michelangelo's aggression. He gave it carte blanche. Michelangelo should have gotten us decollated years ago. Del Monte glamorized his wildness. He explained it to popes, cops, and prospective buyers. He sold Michelangelo and Caravaggio as inverse functions. I'm the resultant nothing. He covets that power, being Michelangelo Merisi da Caravaggio's summation, his final say. Del Monte has always wanted the job. It's why he's been waging a clandestine war against yours truly, enabling Michelangelo's violence, advocating Caravaggio's brilliance, hoping to snuff me out. It's why he insisted on hearing my confession weekly while residing in Madama. I haven't repented since the artichoke assault. I take his paw. I kiss the ring and kneel. A confession for old times' sake. I owe my foster father that much.

"I dishonored Maddalena Antognetti. I lied to Costanza Colona Sforza the marchioness of Caravaggio. I lied to you, Cardinal Francesco Maria Bourbon Del Monte. I slandered Pope Clement VIII by calling him Papa Gout. I slandered Pope Paul V by exaggerating his beady eyes and chins. I bludgeoned a man named Alfonso, or maybe it was

Alonso. I axed Mariano Pasqualone in the skull. I murdered Ranuccio Tomassoni."

Del Monte coughs a tickle from his throat.

"And...what else?" he asks.

"Cecco and I have been lying together the past month. I let him serve. I also gave him a mouth hug."

He pulls me to my feet and kisses a cross upon my face, forehead and cheeks.

"You're a paranormal talent. You're not human," he says.

The cardinal-nephew's servants enter the hall, able-bodied lads in pink linen. They carry the pictures away. Del Monte parades alongside his Francis. The housemaids return with shovels and buckets to excavate the dust. Cecco and I stand before Lena with bowed heads.

"Will he tell Papa about us?" he asks.

"Let's go starve in Napoli," Caravaggio answers.

XXXV.

In November, it rained every few days. It has rained a few days more in December. Today is the solstice. The morning prayer bells have coerced the day, but I'm still in bed, covered in Cecco. I'm declaring it a personal holiday. The Messiah won't mind sharing his name day with me. I spent my thirty-fifth on the craggy coastal road to Napoli, stowed in a farm wagon full of onions, pumpkins, and mice. I have some glory coming to me.

Caravaggio has painted four pictures in as many months—a Madonna and child, an *Andrew Killed*, a portrait of a boy twiddling an orange blossom, and *The Seven Works of Mercy*. He painted the Madonna for a wealthy Croatian trader who paid two hundred ducats. *Andrew Killed* earned another two hundred ducats, paid by the King of Spain and disbursed by Juan Alonso Pimentel de Herrera, Viceroy of Napoli. The picture will hang in the saint's Amalfi tomb when the current renovations are completed. The tomb is King Felipe's pet project du jour. *Andrew Killed* blew the viceroy's mind. Caravaggio painted the boy with the orange blossom as a thank you to the viceroy for heavying our purse and shielding our neck. Don Marzio Colonna is the former mayor of Napoli. He and the viceroy are amigos, but I can't entrust my life to their shared love of brandy and African pros. I take some comfort in having a thousand ducats to our name. That's a lot of money. I don't know how much in terms of scudi. Cecco knows the exchange rate. I've put him in charge of all earnings. I've surrendered my value to him. We're rolling in it. I've instructed Cecco to keep our bounty for himself. He'll need funds after the knights kill me.

Napoli outranks Rome in crime, poverty, and prosperity. A century ago, the Spanish renovated the city's palaces and fortified its infrastructure. The walls and roads are glossy and sheer, but the populace wan and gaunt. Napoli's poor out-wretch the most wretched of Rome with three times the population residing in tenements twice as tall, equaling seven stories of neglect and ruination. The narrow streets below are perennially sunless. In the short winter hours, noon is only bright as dusk and the pavers more frigid than the icy lake grounding Dante's hell. The shadows are long and unremitting. It's the perfect darkness, intensifying the mercies of my latest work. If ever a city hungered for a Caravaggio.

A confraternity of young aristocrats, well-heeled social justice warriors, commissioned my new blockbuster *Mercy*. They wanted the seven works of mercy on a single canvas. *Feed the hungry. Refresh the thirsty. Clothe the naked. Shelter the stranger. Visit the sick. Visit the imprisoned. Bury the dead.* I'm the poster boy for those commandments. I was born, suckled, and condemned to paint this picture. The bleeding-heart oligarchs paid four hundred ducats for it. I'm on top again, hiding at the bottom of the peninsula, painting in the shadows of a somber metropolis.

Don Marzio has stashed us on the top floor of a crumbling tenement. He owns it. He and the viceroy own much of the city's decay. Our hideaway is tall and dark as Tor di Nona. I feel very much at home at Mamma's brother's house. We boarded some of the windows from the inside and converted two of the chambers into dark rooms, punching appropriate holes into respective ceilings. The first half of the workday is spent in the eastside chamber, the latter half of the day within westside lighting. The two smaller chambers in our apartment have been modified into painting studios. We've remodeled the place into a veritable factory. I have followers. Maybe a dozen. They inhabit the floors below. Cecco is training them to paint copies. We can't keep up with sales. Local collectors are buying up said copies. My pictures preceded me to Napoli. I already had a name here. Lena and her voluptuous Virgin too. Copies of *Pilgrim's Madonna* were made by two Dutch painters who immigrated to Napoli. They were traveling through Rome when the picture premiered. They're my most zealous followers since Cecco. Finson and Vinck are their Christian names. I seldom look at them. I barely speak to them. I haven't said much of anything in Napoli. Exile. Silence. Industry. My best defense at keeping Caravaggio's head on my shoulders.

Mercy is a few strokes from completion. Caravaggio rushed the other pictures, reserving his genius for the ensemble cast of *Mercy*. It's my largest canvas yet, inching out *Mary Dead*. It's inhabited by sixteen figures. Two gravediggers entombing a corpse. St. Martin of Tours slicing his robe in two, donating the halves to a pathetic cripple and buck-naked beggar. Samson drinks from the jawbone of an ass. An imprisoned Cimon drinks from his daughter's breast. An innkeeper welcomes two pilgrims. Hovering above, two teen angels broadcast God's grace, arms entwined, wings outspread. They're wrapped in bedsheets. Cecco posed for one. I conjured a young Mario as his angel lover. The Virgin and Christ Child apex the picture. I haven't finished their faces. Their features are figurative strokes reminiscent of Bruno's melting skin. I will conjure another Lena for this Virgin. Like my weeping Magdalene, I will summon her from guilt. Caravaggio is eager to paint my next vision. He's grateful for the Magdalene and pleased with the Mario angel, but it's not as easy as closing my eyes. Lena's not coming to me like she did in Paliano. She's been fading. Her memory dims every time Cecco does me. The guilt of fucking him outweighs the murder of Lena's other lover.

I leave bed careful not to wake Cecco. His beard is back, thick as a grieving pope. I leave our chamber and enter the large studio where my followers have been copying *Weeping Magdalene*. Finson and Vinck are at her early. I bow to Lena and smile at them. I go to the window. Daybreak kisses the rooftops. Seven stories down, dappled street shadows morph into silhouettes. There's an inn across the street owned by my innkeeper who welcomes the two pilgrims of *Mercy*. He's German but speaks better Italian than most Neapolitans. Dozens of pros live and work in his four-storied establishment. The German pimps them. He pimps them well. My Cimon's daughter Pero is his top earner. I watch a john baby-step his way out of the tavern, the blood returning to his legs after a long night of acrobatic screwing.

"Should we go to the sea?" Vinck asks.

I turn from the window and nod. Finson retrieves my scabbard. I've bought myself a dagger and capable rapier. Napoli is a coliseum of three hundred thousand gladiators. Without a blade you're robbed, sliced, or dead. Some Napoli thugs go robbing with a hammer. Some are more formidable than the mercs, cops, assassins, bounty hunters, and Spanish soldiers who want to bag my head. We don't go out much, but not because we're scared. We keep indoors because we know how much bloody fun Michelangelo would have out there.

Finson and Vinck strap their scabbards as I cinch my belt. My new Mario and Orazio. They're a downgrade, but Michelangelo is lucky to have anyone. As we descend the shadowy staircase, inhabitants of the lower floors join our brigade. Some aspiring artists. Some aspiring ruffians. Most of the models from my Napoli pictures. They all squat in this slum. They're all wretched. Young and old, they're skin and bones, starved of stomach and mercy. They're all high as fuck, their bleak reality tempered by coarse poppy bread and homebrewed Tears of Christ. Someone offers me a flask. I drink. Someone else passes me a heel of bread. I gnaw at it and pass it back. We reach the ground. Some Noah-looking fossil opens the door for me.

"Nothing great was ever achieved without danger," he says, mouthing Machiavelli.

Or maybe he didn't say it. Maybe Michelangelo was thinking it. Who am I to care? These morning walks are for him. They're the only way to keep Michelangelo entertained. If his aggression isn't amused, Caravaggio's art turns soppy. That's what I learned from painting Lena's breasts while swallowing Michelangelo's bile—the idealized lust of the pilgrims' and the grooms' Madonnas. Caravaggio can't be left to his own devices. Michelangelo and I must have some hand in the process. Our best pictures are painted with Michelangelo's sword, which is why I've been giving him a taste of the street while Caravaggio ruminates. We three have struck a deal to stay out of each other's way. I've kept Michelangelo from getting bored, and Caravaggio has taken flight. It leaves me feeling excommunicated, but that's the entire point of yours truly.

We rove narrow limestone canyons, kicking litter, eyeing every mark of graffiti, my army of wraiths eddying in my slipstream. My new posse, a significant upgrade in size and desperation. No hope. No fear. To the umpteenth power. I don't know where we're going. I never do, but we always find our way to the sea. The sea is everything the poet says, but I never hurry there. I take my time forgetting the way until Lena comes to me from the shadows of urban decay, the dilapidation so tall it blocks the sky. God's eye can't reach me down here. I'm screened from His supervision. In Napoli, Cecco is safe to love me. In Napoli, God can't take credit for Caravaggio. It's this city's lack of mercy and light that inspires the genius. My *Mercy* will save Napoli in kind. I need to summon Lena so it can hang in the church of Pio Monte della Misericordia to be worshipped by the city's miserable. So far, only the rich have seen my pictures. The miserable have been revering me on hearsay and copies. That's bad faith. That's fraudulent art.

We pass Santa Anna dei Lombardi, a church built by my hick countrymen. There's a small community of Lombards here. They were the first to herald my arrival in Napoli. A few tattered souls leaving morning mass join my army, marching alongside us with a fidelity that warms their bare blue feet. Three soldiers clop by on horseback, decapitating me with greedy looks. The viceroy has forbidden them from collecting on my head. Caravaggio is too important. King Felipe loves what the viceroy has told him about my *Andrew Killed*. If those Spanish ass-sucking Farnese brothers could see me now. The cardinal and duke would shit themselves and die. Thinking on that brings me great joy. It makes me homesick. I'm misperceiving faces at every block. For every antagonistic cop glare, I see ten friendly likenesses from Rome, the facsimiles of groupies and fanboys, models and patrons. I double-take a Vincenzo Giustiniani. I double-take a Lady Mattei. I avoid a Masetti. I mistake my Peter. I mistake my Paul. Napoli is crawling with my haggard *Pilgrim's* maid, but pilgrims don't tour Napoli. Why would they? Napoli is the anti-Rome. There are thousands of priests here but no Church. There are hundreds of churches but no salvation. There's shit, piss, and blood, but not the fun kind as stained on the pavers of Navona. Michelangelo isn't homesick. He loves Napoli. He wants to die here. The sooner the better in Caravaggio's mind.

There are Lena hairdos everywhere, worn by pros and ladies alike, inspired by the Virgin copies of Finson and Vinck. I always turn away from them. I don't want my conjuring of Lena to be influenced. A Lena summoned from a simulacrum would be personal blasphemy. When we're reunited, she'll know that I've been aesthetically unfaithful. She'll know just by looking at me looking at her.

Lena finally comes to me as I arrive at the corner of rape and murder, two alleyways joining the northwest corner of Napoli's most lawless square, which is hardly wider than the average Roman avenue.

The viceroy has erected a temporary monument of severed hands and heads, the butchering of insurrectionists who challenged his taxation of fruits and veggies. He's profiteering from the current famine. He wants everyone's subsistence to depend on pasta made from his wheat shares. I'd kill for a head of cos about now. I approach the martyred parts to pay my respects. My army collapses around me, whispering in their benighted dialect. One of the martyred decollations reminds me of a Roman grocer who sold the zestiest greens. One of the severed hands brings a certain castrato to mind, a particular tug he gave me in Del Monte's music chamber. Or maybe I don't see Montoya's hand. Maybe I don't see the pale white face of my greengrocer. Maybe the poppy bread is working its magic. Maybe it's my homesickness, but the Lena I've conjured is realer than this mound of death. It's purer than my hate for Ranuccio Tomassoni. This Virgin's beauty is unembellished. No makeup. No hair dye. It's the face she entrusted to me on her days off. It's the ambiguous visage that unmanned me, Lena's Mona Lisa stare. I had exclusive rights to it, and then I somehow stumbled over my own tiny dick. This Virgin belongs to a world more deserving than my self-destructive interior. The streets of Napoli need this Virgin watching over them, inspiring merciful acts with her unblinking placidity. I see her atop my *Seven Works of Mercy*. I see her seeing me here. She places my face in the viceroy's monument. There I am, more putrefied than my Goliath, the priciest head in the Holy See rotting like squash. The Virgin blesses my decollated head as it continues dreaming of her, long after my executioner has disembodied it. Whoa, I'm so high.

Somehow, someway, we twist and turn ourselves to the sea, to a rocky spit a few blocks shy of the docks. The sea is green, and the sky is blue like the cloak of Raphael's Madonna. A gang of naked children kneel in the foam sucking rocks. Having known such hunger in Venice, I climb down to them. Finson and Vinck follow. The rest of my army stays to secure the bluff.

I can't tell the boys and girls apart. Poverty has emaciated their gender. They're just ribs and clavicles with purple lips. They balk at my presence before returning to their meals. There's this one, a green-eyed skeleton cradling a ceramic amphora. It pulls a rock from its mouth and sidearms it at me. I'm too high to dodge. The stone stings my chest, causing me to note my assailant's bitsy penis. He's got a good arm. Michelangelo would love to put a racquet in that hand. I rub the hurt from my sternum and grin. The boy smiles. The others laugh. He passes me the amphora. It's antique. There's an expiration date stamped on the neck: Oct 1520. I take a swig. It tastes like fermented piss. I dump the rancid wine into the Mediterranean and hand the amphora to Vinck. He empties his flask into it and passes the amphora back to the boy, who drinks and passes it to the nearest girl. She sips.

"Tears of Christ," she says. "I was praying for claret."

Finson points at the amphora. "Where'd you get that?"

The boy points to the horizon. It's dotted with galleons, or maybe they're carracks. I don't know my ships. I only know coaches. I unfasten my scabbard and hand it to the boy. He unsheathes my sword and lobs the viceroy's imaginary head. He's a natural. I wade out toward the cargo ships. The cold sea swamps my pants. I yodel like Montoya, raising my arms into a V. I want God to see me. I want Him to see me without Cecco. I want Him to see these miserable kids of His. I can't hear His ovation. Maybe I'm not high enough. I return to Vinck for the amphora. It's already light. Finson empties his flask into it.

"Jetsam and flotsam. It's how they feed themselves when not sucking the nutrients from rocks," he says.

"This has been the worst Nativity Feast ever," says the green-eyed boy.

He's a piss-poor brat. Ovidio comes to mind, my *Pilgrim's* Christ child without the finger wag. What does he look like now? His rapist cop father? I conjure a Christ imp clinging to our Holy Mother, his chubby hand on her boob. That shall be the boy Christ of my *Mercy*.

We sit in a crystal tide pool sucking rocks and sipping Tears of Christ. The children take turns playing with my sword. The rest of the children ask Finson and Vinck questions in their salty dialect. Something about me being the savior of Napoli. Something about me murdering a Spanish cop. The lore of Caravaggio and Michelangelo has preceded me once again. We continue drinking in mutual incomprehension.

The sun intensifies, warming my shoulders and returning some pigmentation to the children's faces. I shield my eyes and look to the bluff. A spry silhouette hops, steps, and jumps down the rocks. I'd know Cecco from anywhere. He's not bearing wine, but he has a hunk of poppy bread. He offers it to Vinck. He offers it to Finson. He offers me nothing but shade. He has a hair across his ass and a pimple in the corner of his mouth under his whiskers.

"You never wake me for your walks? I open my eyes and you're gone. I worry."

"Exactly," I say.

"Exactly what?" he asks.

"I won't be around much longer. You should get used to my absence."

"Did you see that one face in the martyr monument? He looked like Giuseppe the greengrocer."

I turn my back to him and make for the bluff. My green-eyed boy chases after me.

"Your sword," he says.

"You carry it. Kill the first knight who breaks our defense."

He rests my sword across his shoulders like a hunter with a pheasant in hand, like a David I should try to paint.

It's almost dusk when we return home. We wrap the children in blankets and seat them at the table. We bought sardines, anchovies, caciocavallo, and three bottles of claret for my girl. All that, and it only cost Cecco five lire.

After dinner, we sit on the roof, high as fuck, watching the sun bomb Napoli. I teach the children to sing my favorite madrigal. One of the boys has a pleasant voice. If only he had a lute.

The evening prayer bell rings over our belching and singing. Cecco stands and walks to the edge of the roof. He looks yonder until the sun disappears. He returns to the table. He chats up Finson. He chats up Vinck. Some models from my *Mercy* show up. Cecco makes a meta-joke about chugging wine with my Samson. He talks exile with my St. Martin while sliding resentful glances my way.

"I miss going to Mass. In Rome, we went every Sunday. In Paliano, we attended daily," he laments.

All the attention I've bestowed upon him, and now he yearns for God's superintendence? It's reckless and dumb to trust Him, the dictator who gave Abraham the knife. After months of having his sexual way with me, Cecco's conscience has ulcerated. He's not cut out for topping. He cares too much for his soul, proffering it to God, praying for mercy like every other weakling. I've been trying to save him from this since our beginning. Standing before God isn't for the faint of heart. I've always loved Cecco more than myself, but apparently God is the only one who believes it. Cecco is now certain that he's going to hell, and maybe he is, if God is half the punisher the Old Testament claims. Maybe his fear is justified. Maybe he's right to blame me. Maybe he'd inform Papa of my whereabouts to win God's mercy. Maybe I see it in my Cupid's eyes. Abraham's resolve fixed on the face of my Isaac. I've never been so afraid. I'm losing Cecco. Caravaggio urges me to steal his thunder, to woo our Cupid back by confessing our cocksucking before God. Michelangelo, of all people, thinks we should just shove his hallowed Cupid off the roof, but ethics and aesthetics prevail. Yours truly and Caravaggio out-vote the hick two to one. Playing martyr is excruciating. Jesus makes it look so easy. I stand and raise my cup.

"Listen up, everyone! I have important news. I, Michelangelo Merisi da Caravaggio confess my undying love for Francesco Buoneri. He's my primer and varnish. He's my pedestal. This young bearded stud makes my veins tremble."

"Gross," my girl says.

My models laugh it off, busting into the chorus of a Neapolitan love song that I've now heard a million and one times since arriving in Napoli. Cecco dresses a piece of bread with anchovies and bites. He chews thrice, regurgitates the mush into his palm, and lobs it off the roof. I told him he wouldn't love anchovies.

XXXVI.

Cecco poses inside the dark room, sword on shoulder, holding a sheaf of spring onions by their stalks. I'm painting him a new David. My Cupid is all man now. There's nothing left of my Isaac or my juvie John in the Wild. Unlike his predecessor, this David owns his heroic sex appeal. He exudes the sporty murder of Hercules, of Michelangelo slaying Ranuccio. Cecco as gratified killer. It would have been a stretch had I not witnessed the hunter pose my green-eyed boy struck on the beach. I know a killer when I see one. Cecco won't gut me until I put the blade in his hand and fall on it.

The workday light is dulling. Today is our anniversary. Francesco Buoneri came to me at Mattei Palace on this day in February 1601 and took my name thereafter. We celebrate the date as a combination anniversary/name day. Historically, the feast day of Cecco del Caravaggio consists of sex and donuts, but we haven't observed it since Lena, and Napoli has zero fucking donut stands. I'm up for partying, but Cecco is still ghosting me. Without Lena fending off my ghosts of murders past, they've returned to their rightful places, at the anterior of this conscience, but haunting remorse comes with the territory of yours truly. I'm here to redress Michelangelo's sins, and this Francesco Buoneri is here to declare my failure. He speaks to me in the form of yes or no questions. *Roasted pigeon for dinner? Are you running out of carbon black? Do you need more gesso? Is your pot full?* He's strictly about the business of Caravaggio, managing the studio, tutoring Finson, Vinck, and the rest of my followers. He has my green-eyed boy sweeping and emptying pots. His sister primes canvases. The other children monitor the streets for bounty hunters. Our pasta and cheese have put meat on their bones. Our poppy bread heightens their outlook.

Young and old, the city's wretched can now hold their chins high while begging. They've finally witnessed my *Mercy*. Mirrors are the best rhetoric in riling the wretched. Now they see what's owed them. Now they know what Christian charity looks like. I made them see themselves being denied. No uprising yet, but there's been underground rumors and grumblings. The viceroy has enhanced his security and canceled public appearances. I've yet to meet him in person, but he keeps throwing business my way despite the seditious reverberations of my pictures. He heard about the cardinal-nephew's *David and Goliath*, and now wants one for himself. His gopher arrived with a contract and advance of two hundred ducats. Another two hundred ducats will be delivered upon completion. At this rate, Cecco's savings are approaching swanky new coach territory. At this rate, the cardinal-nephew will grow envious and raise the viceroy's hand of one-upmanship by pardoning my sin and recalling me to Rome. His Caravaggio obsession is my best bet of rejoining Lena. Caravaggio loves being worshipped and I love Lena, our current working relationship in a nutshell.

Cecco leans my sword against the wall and drops the onions. I'll paint Goliath's head later. I'm undecided on his face. This one can't be my own. One wanted poster is enough for yours truly. My little orphaned birdies have spied a ragtag gang of mercs showing people a secondhand sketch of my gory Goliath selfie. My Tomassoni scar is a dead giveaway. These mercs are nothing more than poppy-eating desperados, but word is out on my whereabouts. Michelangelo suspects Cecco of leaking our location. Caravaggio suspects Michelangelo of wanting our location outed so he can die in inglorious battle. I predict the three of us dying, each in our own worst way.

Cecco lights a candle, his face kindled by the small flame. He goes to his new David and holds the candle to himself.

"My God. There's no end to your genius," he says to the genius.

He stands the candle on the floor and comes to me in umbrage. I kiss him. His lips are tight as Lena's Mona Lisa smile. I try prying it open with my tongue. He has morning breath at sunset. He grabs Goliath by the curls. My mouth toils against his. I open his shirt. I pull it down around his waist. I untie the drawstring of his pants, and with my knee, force them down around his knees. Someone in the studio sneezes.

Finson says, "God bless you."

Cecco exhales and limpens into standing dead weight. He's trying to overpower my passion with softness. I genuflect upon his effort, overwhelming his inertia with kisses across his chest. I suck his nipples with the diehard slobbering of an attritional master. It makes him very hard. He tightens his grip on my curls. I kneel. A name day isn't a name day without fellatio. Cecco croaks, gnarrs, and pulls my ears. I stand. We kiss.

"You don't love me. You never did," he says.

"That's something to say after a blowjob."

"It's true. You don't."

"I killed Ranuccio for you. I killed him for your John."

"Still telling yourself that?"

"You begged me. You wanted it."

"You don't know what I want."

"No. I don't, but at least I didn't wish Cecco del Caravaggio a happy name day. I've been a good boy about calling you Francesco."

"You have."

"I know your actual name day, Francesco."

"Bravo, Master Caravaggio."

"Don't say it like that. I love you."

"Still nope."

"I love you more than Mario. I love you more than Fillide. I love you more than Lena. You were right. I only worshipped her. She was a fixation. Do you want me to worship you? Do you want to be idealized? I've done you better than that. Your Cupid. Your Isaac. Your John. And now your David. They're better than her Virgins. They'll outshine all of my Lena pictures. You'll always be my leading star."

"And now you deprecate your Virgin because your Cupid feels unloved. You're loyal to no one. You love no one, not even yourself."

"I love empowering you. When we get back to Rome, we'll build a villa on Quirinal Hill. We'll buy a coach and cruise Navona."

"What about Lena?"

"We'll find her. We'll support her. At first, you'll be the one to deliver her money. She wouldn't take a bucket of water from me if she was on fire."

"How much will you give her?"

"Enough. She never wanted much. Nice clothes. Food for Ovidio. I wanted to buy her a coach. She loved riding in Vincenzo's the day they flooded Navona."

"I wasn't there. I was home taking care of my wounded lover."

"I don't miss the Rome traffic. I haven't seen a single coach in Napoli. It's nice to see men riding horseback again. That's how God intended it."

"Coaches are for chicks," he says.

"Blowjobs too."

We have a great laugh, catch our breaths, and kiss. He lowers himself to return the favor. I pull him up by the shoulders, cup the back of his head, and pull his face into my neck.

"It's your day. It's all about you," I say.

"I'm hungry," he says into my throat.

"Me too."

"We've been eating well."

"Like cardinals on my feast day," I say.

Cecco rubs my soft belly like a proud husband.

"They're calling Napoli the center of the art world," he says.

"Because you're here with me."

"The world revolves around you. You could be back in Caravaggio and they'd call that backwater the capital of mankind."

"You're my capital." The three of us say it together, but I mean it most.

I blow out the candle and let Cecco have at me in the darkness. On the floor. On my back. My knees pegged to my shoulders. He squats and piledrives me. God can't see him, not here in the shadows of my ingenuity. As Cecco hastens his thrusts, a terrifying hypothetical spikes my thoughts. What if God has similar technology? Is our reality his camera obscura? What if our actions are projected onto the walls of heaven and printed for eternity? What if that's the basis for God's omniscience? God sits down to read our sins like the morning news. God is the nosiest, creepiest ghost of all ghosts. He has godding all backwards. God should be the one inside the camera obscura, scoped by His followers, day and night.

Out in the studio, they're having a loud conversation about natural disasters.

"One good earthquake and this building would crumble to hell."

"The Big One is coming. Fucking boom."

XXXVII.

Caravaggio watches ankle-shackled slaves shamble down the gangplank, a lumbering centipede of Turks and Moors with the torsos of hardened laborers and faces more Christlike than da Vinci's dining Messiah. Behold the men! My *Ecce Homo* is the closest Christ on canvas, but these chained martyrs are the real deal. The only thing missing is their crowns of thorns. The halos are there. I see them clear as nimbus clouds against another Raphaelite sky.

Grand Port is an industrial clash of wills fenced into an L-shaped pier, no bigger than Navona Square. The congestion is what I've been trying to achieve in my compositions dating back to *Doubting Thomas*: two saints watching a third saint finger the stigmata of Christ. Four holy beings stuffed in a cramped cell. Infinite moments occurring in finite quarters. Massive anxieties inhabiting choked spaces. People bending and reaching around the stretching and lifting of others. While Rome is happy to loaf about clutching its balls, Napoli works its ass off. Crates and baskets being humped. Overloaded carts drawn by beasts and mortals. Begging and bartering. Bumping and grinding. Of the pier's entire bustle, the slave trader is the only one standing still, tapping the butt of a whip into his palm. He's the first Duke Dildo I've seen since killing Ranuccio on the tennis court. His cocked cavalier hat could use a brick upside of it. Michelangelo begs me to do it. I could almost let him, but I'm feeling these slaves, studying them for a *Christ*

Whipped picture. I want Caravaggio to feel them too. I want him to sensualize the Martyr's sadism the way Neapolitans cope with the viceroy's ruthless governing, by living all sexy in his filthy streets. Caravaggio has finally come to trust my judgment. He has finally admitted to my ability. I can spot a fellow martyr. I can see our nearing death.

One of the huskier specimens refuses to step onto the auction block. A sailor grabs his hair as another kicks his leg. The slave stands soft, slackening his considerable girth, forcing the onus on them. They handle him with elbows and knees. The slave drifts back and forth, sinking his deadened weight onto them. They struggle to keep him up, punching all the while. It's a cruel tarantella. The trader finally whips the smirk from the slave's face, but a stony satisfaction remains in the eyes. Behold my Christ! That's the martyrdom I'll paint for Tomasso de Franchis, father to one of the social justice warriors. He wants a *Christ Whipped* for the family altar in San Domenico Maggiore, the church where Bruno earned his novitiate, the church that exiled him for preaching Arian heresy and reading the banned books of Erasmus. It's ironic that I've risen amongst the violent destitution of my martyred friend's hometown. Maybe Michelangelo is on to something. Maybe we should crash and burn in Napoli. If not reunited with Lena, my preference is anywhere but inside this infinitely crowded head, caged between a genius and brute.

The port drops everything to stargaze at Caravaggio. Long-shoremen stand on crates. Vendors climb atop carts. Naked waifs scale each other's shoulders. The slave trader steps onto the auction block. Others hop in place, clearing the shoulders of my army for a glimpse of the genius. I'm the city's biggest celebrity since Peter and Paul came to evangelize. My pictures are better than their stories. More nudity. More violence. More justice. Unlike gospel, I don't glorify the passive resistance of martyrs. I lionize underdogs. In Napoli, *David Beheading Goliath* is more than a blockbuster. It's a manifesto. Some in the crowd cheer and ask for my David. He's home in bed. I woke him before leaving for our walk. I invited him. He said that he had a remarkable headache.

In Rome, I shaded my fans, acknowledging their love from the slimmest periphery. Too many femme-fops in the mix. Too many cut-throaters. Too many backstabbers. Too many conspiring cardinal-nephews. Not enough wretches. In Napoli, the wretches know my pictures. In Napoli, I feed the admirers my eyes. I sign every face with Caravaggio's best smile. His only smile. It's conceited. They love him anyway. They're better than Caravaggio, but I'm the only one who believes that.

My boy pulls me to the fishmongers. He wants anchovies. The fish queue stretches half the length of the pier, lawyers standing behind laborers standing behind servants. In Napoli, everyone waits their turn. Everyone cohabits its teeming adversity with zero personal space. There's no hiding in coaches. There's no discretion. Rich? Flaunt it. Poor? Flaunt it. Virile? Flex it. Sickly? Rub it in their face. Napoli is a mile-wide Caravaggio picture co-starring three hundred thousand models.

A cute priest standing toward the front of the line shouts something to Vinck, who relays the message to Finson, who poses the question to yours truly.

"He wants Caravaggio to jump his place in line."

"Tell him thanks, but I wouldn't dream of it. I'm happy to wait with my adopted homies. I'm browsing faces for an upcoming picture," Caravaggio answers.

Finson shouts my response to Vinck, who repeats it to the priest. The crowd whistles and applauds. I wave and look around for assassins. In doing so, I misperceive some Roman faces amongst the fishermen. I spot my supper Jesus selling mackerel. I watch my *Taken* Jesus sans beard as he murders a fantastic tuna. I see Onorio in police garb chasing a gang of thieving runts. Man, I'm not high enough. I ask Finson for poppy bread. He says we're fresh out. By the time we get to the monger, he's out of anchovies. I buy my boy two eels. The monger transfers them from his barrel to our bucket. They splash about like holy hell. I suggest killing them. My boy says something about grilling them alive. Something about the blood. I can only understand his dialect when paying close attention to his mouth, and I'm presently distracted by a lookalike Masetti, a wool merchant with the same thuggish mug and stark black doublet. He eyes me from the bow of his ship. I eye him back waiting for his face to vary from Masetti's, but it does the opposite. It reaffirms his features. Masetti is here. He's come to collect. How much do I owe him? Sixty scudi? Is that a debt worthy of murder? Probably not, but maybe it's the starting price for the Duke of Modena's pride. I take a deeper look. It's not Masetti. He folds his arms and nods at some realization. It's totally Masetti. He sailed here to get paid. No. Modena is a landlocked city five days from the sea. He's in Modena eating fatty sausage. I turn home to feed my family eel.

I carry the bucket up the seven flights of stairs. My boy stomps ahead to the roof. He's a master at lighting the grill. My followers disband to their respective floors. Finson and Vinck remain, plodding each step with heavy hesitation. They're quiet. I look back at them. They bury their heads. Have they betrayed me? Are the Knights of the Supreme Order of Christ waiting upstairs? My boy would have screamed a warning.

The apartment is too quiet. My girl sits on the floor at the far end of the main studio viewing my *Weeping Magdalene*. I present her the bucket of eels. She's too mesmerized. I go to my chamber to check on Cecco's remarkable headache. He's not there. His cloak is not there. His boots are not there. His sword is gone. There's a letter on the bed. I ignore it and go to the dark room. No Cecco. I go to the other dark room. He's not there either. Finson and Vinck have taken to the sofa, fidgeting with their hands. I return to my chamber and go through Cecco's drawers. They're empty. The nine hundred ducats are gone. My Judith's pearl earrings are all that he's left. What a boss move. Michelangelo is disappointed. He was hoping for an Isaac versus Abraham knife fight ending. He was leaning toward letting Isaac win. I wasn't opposed to the idea either. We deserve such an offing, a surprise gutting from a misemployed lover. Caravaggio is relieved. No more living with the guilt of Cecco. I'm devastated, nauseated by panic. I fall into bed facedown and try enacting my best weeping Magdalene. I'm no good at it because I'm no good. Cecco did a fabulous job of letting me know it. I tear the letter into confetti without reading it. I snowfall the pieces into my pot and return to the studio. Finson and Vinck are still picking at their hands.

"Did he tell you he was leaving?" I ask.

They nod in fear of my reaction. My boy's amphora is on the table. I suck down some Tears of Christ while thinking over Cecco's escape. When it's empty, I drop the amphora with the intention of it smashing to pieces. It bounces and rolls across the floor instead.

"I'm putting both of you in charge of the factory. The copies. New commissions. Materials. I need you to take the reins."

Finson and Vinck stand to shake my hand in appreciation, curbing their excitement out of respect for my loss. Vinck retrieves the amphora and refills it in the kitchen. He returns and hands it to me. I drink and pass it back to him. He drinks and passes it to Finson.

"I assume he left you specific instructions."

"He gave us the name," Finson says.

"What name?"

"*His* name," Vinck replies.

"Francesco?"

"Cecco del Caravaggio. He told us to sign the name onto our pictures," Finson says.

"If that's okay with you," Vinck adds.

"He's not going to use the name? He quit painting?"

They don't want to say.

"He said he was going to leave you a letter," Vinck says.

"I didn't see any letter," Caravaggio answers.

Cupid has pulled his arrow from my throat. Isaac has rejected his inheritance. No loss has ever felt so grim, so meritorious. I could almost try weeping again, but I know better. Not wanting to give Francesco Buoneri the satisfaction, I dam it up and walk my shit over to my girl. I sit next to her as she regards *Weeping Magdalene*. I've always wanted Caravaggio's genius to drive people crazy, so crazy with awe and envy that they mob and tear us apart. I finally know how awesome that feels. My followers should be able to witness this. They should have unlimited access to my suffering. I want to show God how to god.

"Do you know how to prepare eel?" I ask her.

"Are you asking me or talking to yourself again?" she answers.

She flexes her biceps. I squeeze it. There's something in there. It's walnut-size. She deserves some wine. I pass her the flask. She drinks and passes it back to me. I raise the flask to my lips, but it's empty. I stand and head to the kitchen for more. The kitchen has a small ocular window just large enough for a swollen head to fit through. I stand on a crate of potatoes and poke mine out. In a rare moment of mercy, the sun is extending a wealthy slice of luxuriousness to the pavers. The bony plebs and gouty aristocrats standing outside the German's tavern aren't seeing it. They're elbow-deep in conversation, talking with their hands about sex. One of them looks up and sees me. He looks away. He looks back up at me. He looks to his friends. He says nothing to them. He returns his gaze upward. I wave to him like a totally reachable superstar.

XXXVIII.

The morning prayer bell dongs. The air smells of sea and spoiled wine. Sunrise is in full media res through the open window. Crazy-bored, Michelangelo got up in the middle of the night to watch a street fight in front of the tavern. Seven naked orphans armed with bricks tried robbing two shit-faced sailors. The sailors won handily, sparing the children no lenience. Michelangelo returned to bed disappointed, forgetting to close the shutters. It took me forever to fall back asleep. I'm exhausted and remarkably sad over Cecco. I don't want to wake up, but Caravaggio makes me. I'd rather thrust my arms into my pant legs, pull the crotch of my trousers over my face, and toss myself seven stories, but I don't because I'm Caravaggio's bitch. Tying my trousers is also a bitch, my waist now haloed with flab. Too much caciocavallo and bread. I've stopped caring. I don't wash or shave. I don't brush my hair. I don't wipe my ass. This is the god I want my followers to witness, the histrionic spectacle of a dying superstar. I'm not even trying anymore. I'm letting them run the show. If Michelangelo wants to maim some loudmouth dildo, fine. If Caravaggio wants to indulge his genius as a way of forgetting Lena and Cecco, so be it, as long he paints my visions. He's been painting my martyrdom like a man possessed, like a genius passing the halfway mark toward his spectacularly cataclysmal climax. This is the end that I see. Our death won't come at the hands of mercs. It will occur in the psychological theater of our warring selves. I'm picking a side. Caravaggio is my best bet to Lena.

Like me, Caravaggio also thinks we'll be dead soon, but he's thinking we can govern Michelangelo. He's more concerned with the mercs and knights. Our latest pictures have put Napoli at the end of Galileo's telescope, if Papa actually allowed Galileo to build said telescope. Everyone in the world knows that Caravaggio is here in Napoli revolutionizing art. Grateful that I've ennobled his city, the viceroy continues to ordain my safety, but it's not like he's staking guards outside our building. My army of followers and fans can protect me from bounty-hunting yahoos, but a trained merc or knight would cut through them like butter. Last week, my little street birds spotted two Farnese mercs lodged in a Spanish Quarter tavern. My orphans have been spying on them day and night, sleeping in an alley behind the tavern. I pay them in blankets and poppy bread. They don't need the blankets. Come nightfall, the pavers are warmer than the air. It's mid-May. I expect to be dead by my name day.

Caravaggio has been busting his ass in the interim, confronting our pending assassination with the tenacious work ethic of a Mezzogiorno laborer. Southern laborers slave like champs for next to nothing, and unlike their Northern comrades, they're damn proud to do so. They march to work like knights advancing upon Antioch, but these heroes don't win any honors. They hump valiantly, knowing that a bankrupt death is forthwith. This fortitude proves something to God and Caravaggio. He finds their backbone incredibly sexy and fashions it after yours truly, bronzing the sadism of his three labors in *Christ Whipped*, vindicating their deltoids and triceps in an august light as they lash and kick God's son. The picture has been giving the entire city erotic nightmares. The noble. The miserable. They're infatuated with its ambivalence, especially those who haven't seen it.

I sleepwalk into the studio shirtless. Finson is scraping palettes. Vinck is drying brushes, spinning the handles between his palms. My boy enters carrying a basket of fruit, looking nothing like my early portrait of Mario, but their fruit is almost akin. No grapes, apples, pears, figs, or apricots, but my boy has three pomegranates. The season is all wrong. His is a spring cornucopia. Strawberries. Rhubarb. The oranges look blemished enough to paint.

My boy unloads his basket and sets the breakfast table, arranging the plates and bowls under Cecco's exact blueprint. He's adopted his mannerisms too, counting each setting with the same wheellock-firing finger motion. It's a little much for Michelangelo and myself. I'd like to get stoned, but we're not allowed. No wine or poppy until dinner. The policy belongs to Finson and Vinck. It's sensible and productive. They run a fair and efficient workshop. We all work hard. We all eat well. We rest whenever for however long. We function like the citizens of Christ's first Jerusalem commune—from each according to his ability, to each according to his needs, and all I'm asking for is Lena. The hick is sick of hearing it.

There are two copies of *Andrew Killed* and two copies of *Weeping Magdalene* on the four studio easels. I approach the lesser Magdalene and pray for Lena before taking my seat at the head of the table. My boy and his sister share the bench to my right. Finson and Vinck take seats at the opposite end. They find my body odor unappetizing. I peel an orange and wipe the pith off my fingers into my chest hair.

"Thank God the viceroy lifted his fruit tax," Finson says.

"Your pictures have softened him." Vinck squeezes each of the pomegranates for ripeness. He settles on one and pares it.

He and Finson are my finest administrators to date. Lucky for me, I find neither man attractive. They're free to manage and promote Caravaggio without Michelangelo or myself dicking it up. I give them a once-over in case I've overlooked some vague appeal. Nah. They're too Dutch to fuck. Vinck eats the halved pomegranate like a man who very much likes women. I yawn and catch a whiff of my own breath. It's revolting but not enough. I bow my head into my lap and sniff.

"We used to smell like civet anus. Now we just smell like anus," Michelangelo says.

My boy leans over his plate and spits up strawberry. His sister laughs against his shoulder. Half a child himself, Michelangelo is encouraged by their laughter.

"Keep foregoing the hygiene. I think it enhances your genius. Your new Judith is next level," says Finson.

I suppose that's a compliment if you're not the one bored out of Caravaggio's skull. If Michelangelo has to hear one more Caravaggio ovation.

"Any news on those mercs? They still at the tavern?" Michelangelo asks my boy.

"The tall mustached one caught a gangster cheating at cards and challenged him to a duel. They all went outside to pull blades. The gangster's crew jumped both mercs. The tall one lost an ear. The fat one got curb stomped. His teeth are still all over the street."

The boy reaches into his pocket and reveals a chipped incisor.

"Broken jaw. No teeth. At least he'll be skinny soon," my girl says.

I squeeze a roll of fat and slap my belly. Michelangelo is ashamed of us. He's also envious of the gangsters. He's never made a man eat curb. He'd like to curb-stomp the remaining Tomassoni brothers. It's hard for him to sit on his hands while Caravaggio fulfills his genius, while I get some long overdue shine. He could be perfecting his violence on the mean streets of Napoli. Instead, he's cooped up here in the studio with yours truly, more dissatisfied than a chicken-plucker in a brothel. He's jealous of Caravaggio. Envy is a cardinal sin. Self-envy is a malignant disease. Ours is metastasizing. Wars are seldom started between poor and unhappy nations. They're waged between powerhouses. They're fought between happy, rich sovereignties who want more. We're getting too much of what we want. Michelangelo wants us to die his way. He wants to blast off. He wants to be fired from an eight-ton Austrian cannon, exploding headfirst into the side of St. Peter's Basilica. I remind him that we are indeed dying by his hand, that our capital ban came courtesy of his dissecting Ranuccio's artery. Caravaggio and I were happy with castration. I blame Michelangelo for losing Lena and Cecco. I blame him for engendering my pain. I accuse him of getting off on it.

"You've got us reversed," Michelangelo says to yours truly. "I'm the sadist. *You're* the masochist. *You're* the one who gets off on punishment. The guilt. The contrition. The self-loathing. That's all you. I love myself. Caravaggio loves himself. You're the defeatist."

"He's right. You're also a control freak. You've got a real god complex," says Caravaggio of all people.

"Someone has to be the adult in the room. The adult in this body. I'm the true self, and the true self is but a shadow of the divine perfection," I answer, paraphrasing the Divine One.

"My perfection is the only divine perfection around here," Caravaggio says.

"There is one God but God, and his true name is Michelangelo Merisi," says Michelangelo.

"We'll leave you to your conversation," says Vinck.

He and Finson flee to their easels. They're both painting the Magdalenes. Now that I care to look, Finson has the better hand. His rendering of her ear and lips could almost pass for my hand, but the rest of his Lena is shit. How could she not be? He isn't the one who ruined her.

My boy excuses himself. He'd rather fetch my pot than listen to us quibble. My girl piles the leftovers onto my plate and clears the table. I thank her. She thanks me back and sallies off for a broom. Caravaggio wants to get painting. He pesters me to hurry and finish eating. I take my sweet time, gnawing the pith from orange peels, licking every last crumb from the plate. I untie my waistband and marvel at my halo of fat. I do so to get under Michelangelo's skin.

"Sure. Go ahead. Throw salt in my wound," he says.

"You have no wounds. You're the one who does the wounding," I reply.

"You want to talk pain? Try painting reality. Try painting it with God breathing down your neck," says Caravaggio.

We go on like this, blaming each other for Tomassoni and for Cecco's departure, until my followers and models arrive for work. Some are assistants to Finson and Vinck, local artisans who left well-established bottegas to retrain under Caravaggio. Most live on the floor below. The models live on the floor below them. Most of my models are too old or too wretched to fuck. My breastfeeding Pero from *Mercy* greets me with a brownnosing smooch to the side of the mouth. She's my new Judith. She wants to be my new Virgin. She thinks she has a chance now that my Cupid is out of the picture. She has little of what it takes. She's a bedeviled pro with hooded eyelids and sacrilegious breasts. That's about it. She's too chatty to be sensual. She's too blunt to sphinx. Her lips are puffy and posh but it's impossible to see them due to their constant state of motion. She loves to gossip and talk shit. She won't amount to Fillide's Judith, and I'm not over Cupid. I'm not over Lena. I want them both back, in no particular order.

"If only this Virgin had some Judith in her. I might have painted a Holofernes selfie," Caravaggio says to me.

"I'd make you a damn-fine Virgin. I regret every man I've ever fucked," my Judith replies.

I go to my room and slip into my velvet work coat. It used to be a fine item. Paint smears and drips have made it an invaluable artifact. I wear it unbuttoned, baring my gut and fledgling breasts. Judith, her maid, and Holofernes are waiting for me in the eastside dark room, discussing last night's street melee that woke Michelangelo. The neck of Judith's maid is lumpy with goiter, her cheeks more wrinkled than Noah's nutsack.

Caravaggio puts the sword in Judith's hand and positions her chin. Holofernes lies across the bed and cranes his neck. The maid puts herself in Judith's ear. Caravaggio gets to it. I check out. I pay no attention to his genius. This one ain't mine. Until he paints our way back to Rome, his success is not happening to me. Until then, I distance myself from his virtuosity. I walk myself to Navona with Lena on one arm and Cecco on the other. Rome burns in our slipstream.

Halfway through the day and Michelangelo doesn't know what to do with himself. He has no flights of fancy. He's grounded in discontent.

"Want to know what I think?" he whispers.

"Not really," I whisper back.

"I think Cecco never left Napoli. Think about it. Why would he? Do you really think he'd ditch Caravaggio? He finally has Caravaggio to himself. No Mario. No Lena. No Mamma."

"No, but there's still us. He found us revolting," I say.

"Let's revolt against Caravaggio. Fuck this guy. Look at him. He's so into himself he can't even hear us conspiring."

"I'm not conspiring. You're conspiring. You're our murderer. It's been you all along. Not Ranuccio. Not mercs. Not the cardinal-nephew. Not Papa. Not God. It's you. Michelangelo Merisi. The Lombard hick. You killed everything I ever loved, you butter-eating philistine."

"Cecco is out there. He never left Napoli. He opened a studio on the other side of the city selling Caravaggio knockoffs. He spends his downtime at the docks looking for a new John, a strapping long-shoreman."

I know what Michelangelo is trying to do. I know he knows I know, but maybe I'd rather play into his mind game than continue spectating Caravaggio's genius. I excuse our models. I tell them I've run out of lead white paint. Caravaggio objects. Michelangelo objects to his tyranny. While they bicker, I pry my rapier from Judith's moist hand. I promise to make her a Virgin. I say it to get rid of her. She kisses the corner of my mouth and rollicks away. I sneak off to my room to collect my dagger. I start toward my cloak hanging on the back of a chair, but Michelangelo pulls the brakes on me.

"No cloak. No hood. Let our foes spy us. Let's confront our killers once and for all."

"Don't listen to him. He'll get us killed. I can paint us back to Rome. I can paint you back to Lena and Cecco. My stardom has tremendous magnitude. Have faith in me," Caravaggio says.

Caravaggio has always been Caravaggio's biggest fan, but cardinal nepotism, backstabbing, cut-throating, and double-dealing have invigorated his narcissism. His egomania could keep us alive for decades. Narcissism as self-preservation. A martyrdom fit for a king. Jesus, eat your heart out! No thanks. I'd rather be my own Judas and Pontius Pilate.

I leave my cloak on the chair and walk straight out of the apartment, sword and dagger on both hips. No one notices my exit. They're too busy shining Caravaggio's stardom. My weeping Magdalene is the only one who tries stopping me.

XXXIX.

The sun graces the cornices and upper quoins in the yellow of old masters. See Titian's adulteress. See the Madonna of Aldobrandini. See Lena's halo in *Pilgrim's Madonna*. See the jaundiced horror of my decapitated Medusa. But down here, down here in the cool neutral white, the crowded avenue is all hot and bothered by my unguarded presence. Those bothered are followers and idolaters, jittered by the sight of Caravaggio promenading solo. They want their cultural savior protected. They want Caravaggio wrapped inside his posse at all times. The hot ones, those excited by my wide-open aloneness, are groupies and fanboys. They want to witness this Lombard hick's expert violence. They want the full Michelangelo Merisi da Caravaggio experience. Napoli has only experienced half my mythology. They've only seen the genius, his empowering of the wretched, his immortalization of slaves, laborers, and pros. They hail Caravaggio for bringing art off the canvas and into the streets, but they haven't seen Michelangelo cut a man. They haven't seen me bust a dildo's jaw. They haven't witnessed the demonic irrationality. Without Michelangelo's punchy fists, Caravaggio is just a run-of-the-muck genius, inert and innocuous, spineless and dismissible like Carracci.

And for all my demonstrable guilt and stinky sadness, not a single fan has witnessed yours truly.

A Caravaggio cavalcade trails me as I get myself good and lost. I turn a couple of corners. I walk in circles, bisecting the same square twice, passing the viceroy's newest heap of martyrs. The street widens, the sun painting one side into a Tintoretto cityscape. I cross over to it where the sidewalk is choked by a ruck of nuns standing by a food vendor. They're eating folded slabs of dough, oil running down their wrists, soaking the cuffs of their ratty tunics.

"Behind every great artist is a greater psychosis." Michelangelo bows to them.

"I don't need your delusions of grandeur," Caravaggio replies. "I don't need blind persistence. My genius is the very opposite of psychosis."

Michelangelo keeps at the nuns. "I'm Cain to his Abel. Romulus to his Remus."

The nuns cross themselves and genuflect. They stare past the genius and hick into the subliminal eyes of yours truly, imploring me with prayer hands. They see me! My first witnesses! My first fans! Inspired by their abysmal faces, I confess to everything, loud enough for my convening cavalcade to hear.

"I murdered a cop. I also murdered a chicken-plucker. Two months later, I murdered a Spanish soldier. Last spring in Rome, I murdered a pimp, bled him at the loin."

The nuns chorus, "The glory of love will see you through."

"The pimp raped my lover, mutilated her with a knife, but it was my doing. I defiled her with fame. I did so against her will. She wanted material comforts. I placed her on the thorny throne of celebrity. The pimp cashed in on her stardom. Bled her soul dry. It was my fault. I couldn't make her fade, so I made her larger than life. I made her every man's Virgin. They desecrated her. I painted their lechery into being. And I didn't even paint her all that well."

"And now you want to end yourself, walking the streets alone, exposing yourself to your enemies," says the wrinkliest nun.

"I'm in a deep dark wilderness," I reply.

"Shut up," Michelangelo says to me. "Don't you worry about us," he says to the nuns.

The nuns reiterate their chorus. "The glory of love will see you through."

"He's trying to assassinate my genius. Save me," Caravaggio pleads.

"Come to our church. Confess to Father Salvetti," says a barefoot nun, the only one who looks like an actual Virgin.

"What church?" I ask.

Those not chewing dough answer in unison. "San Domenico Maggiore."

"Bruno studied there. He was a good friend," I say.

"And a better Dominican," says Mother Wrinkles.

"Help me find my way back to my studio. I'll paint you. I'll canonize all of you. Please. Take me there."

Caravaggio doesn't sound like himself. He sounds desperate. He never sounds desperate. He doesn't want to fight mercs. He's not fearing death. He knows Michelangelo can't lose when his rage has been corked this long. He's afraid of snapping his current spell of genius.

"After everything you just said about defiling your lover with fame, why would I star in a picture?" asks Sister Priggy No-Shoes.

"What are you eating?" I ask.

"Poor people food," she says like I'm not worthy.

"It's *pizza*," says Mother Wrinkles.

"What's in it?" I ask.

She reveals the pizza as if hoisting the Eucharist at Mass. "Anchovies, olive oil, and cheese."

"My new favorite foods. Buy me a slice?" I pat at my absence of a purse.

"You're the peninsula's most acclaimed artist. You should be buying us slices," says Sister Prig.

"My lover left me and took all my money with him."

"*Him*? The Virgin?" Mother Wrinkles asks.

"No. My other lover. My Cupid. My Isaac. My David."

"So, you're not *just* a murderer?" At least Sister Prig is kind enough to lower her voice.

I place a hand over my cock and look to heaven. The white of God's eye is there, blighting Raphael's ultramarine sky. The superstar has returned. My faith hurtles toward it, but my nerves plummet. This is it. We're finished. God has come to collect. He's here to brush the final coat of lacquer on my wanted poster. I blink in preparation for staring into eternity. I blink twice and He's gone. I feel like He was there long enough to doom me.

"Did you see that?" I ask.

"I've always seen it. I didn't want to share it with you," Caravaggio replies.

"I didn't see a thing," says Michelangelo.

"Let's find our way to my studio. I'll beatify you for real." Caravaggio takes Mother Wrinkles by the hand.

"I wouldn't live that life if you paid me," says Sister Prig.

"You don't smell very nice," says some nun with a face shaped like a saggy heart.

"That's the god in me. I'm foul by design. Inside and out."

Mother Wrinkles kisses my hand and offers her pizza. I take it. I eat it with some shame. It's the happiest thing I've ever tasted.

"I'll never eat donuts again," I say.

"You don't deserve pizza or donuts. God blessed you with miraculous talent. You can't have everything. It's only fair that you make sacrifices," says Sister Prig.

"Today, I left the studio with the aim of sacrificing myself," says Michelangelo. "I'm heading to the Spanish Quarter. I'm going to find my would-be assassins and swing my sword until one of them strikes me down."

"But I don't want to. I want to stay home and fulfill God's blessing," Caravaggio interjects.

"I can see the cross within yourself. I see violence intersecting compassion." Sister Prig wipes her greasy hands on my coat. "It must be brutal living like that, like driving a coach drawn by two diametric beasts, but I guess that's the modus of your greatness. Like the torment of Christ, I'm grateful for your suffering. I'm grateful for your pictures."

"Me too, but don't sacrifice yourself yet," says Sister Wrinkles. "Each picture brings us closer to the truth."

"What *us*? What *truth*?" I know the answer but want to hear an actual virgin say it.

"The truth of our economic and spiritual oppression. We need more pictures. Each one brings us closer to liberation. *David*, *Seven Works of Mercy*, and *Christ Whipped* are just the beginning. We'll rock Napoli. Its palaces will crumble."

"Imagine if Bruno had paced his martyrdom. Imagine how much more we'd know about the heavens. Imagine what we could do with that knowing." Sister Prig does a little dance with her eyebrows.

"I love men. I don't care who knows," I say.

"I love them too, but I'd never let one kill me," Sister Prig says back.

I look around. An audience of college fanboys has gathered across the street. They're staging living pictures of mine. Two mime my David and Goliath. The other twelve are recreating *Seven Works of* Mercy, every character in the picture except for Lena and Ovidio.

"I don't want to die either," I say to Sister Prig.

"Coward," Michelangelo replies.

The fussing of the avenue goes dumb as if someone has sliced its throat. I watch a shadow of worry eclipse the prudent faces of my nuns. A percussion of iron footsteps come clomping upon my ass. The jingle-jangle of heavy armor makes Michelangelo smile. He's getting his wish. I grip the hilt of my sword. It feels good, and you know I hate giving it to Michelangelo.

"I see you're still dressing like a vagabond," my killer says.

Michelangelo recognizes his voice. I turn to face it. Caravaggio recalls his features in an instant. Why am I always the last to know everything?

My beautiful bastard brother Fabrizio Colonna Sforza suited in vintage Milanese steel. The bright white cross of Malta branded on the chest of his sleeveless tabard. My murderous brother has been released from prison. My Merisi half-brother is now a member of the Knights Hospitaller in the Order of St. John of Jerusalem. He looks like Mamma decked in armor. I interpret his arrival as a gift from God. The brief reappearance of His eye wasn't damning me. It was guiding my highborn half-brother to this pizza cart. My blood has come to save us. I for one feel blessed. I can already smell Lena's skin.

Michelangelo turns to Sister Prig. "Guy's like a brother to me."

Fabrizio stands before a small cadre of ironclad knights. My silver fox, Fra Ippolito Malaspina stands to his left, and a youngish, velvet-clad aristocrat flanks his right. He's got the oval Colonna face and pointy chin. He's a dead ringer for Admiral Marcantonio, their super-hero paterfamilias, but he doesn't have his male pattern baldness. This up-and-coming patrician has a staunch hairline. I recognize him. He's poked his nose around my studio, escorted by the viceroy's gopher. I was too busy and concentrated to care. He ogles at me as he did then, with the acquisitiveness of a wanting collector.

The nuns genuflect, and then pinken over their monastic brothers. I step away from them to salute Fabrizio. I salute Malaspina. They bow and approach, the aristocrat on their heels.

"You let a Tomassoni brand you like that?" Fabrizio points at my Goliath scar.

"I allowed the blow to land. I wanted to see how sharp he kept his blade."

Fabrizio hugs me with the intensity of a truth.

"You smell worse than you look," he says.

"I can't stop eating anchovies. They're tastier here. Everything is gamier in the Mezzogiorno."

"You've rejuvenated the entire region," Malaspina says.

"I painted you a Jerome. The cardinal-nephew stole it."

"He also expropriated three pictures from Cesari. Your *Boy with Fruit*, *Boy Peeling Fruit*, and *Sick Bacchus*. He imprisoned your old master for possession of illegal firearms and sentenced him to death."

The news is slightly shocking and mostly flattering. "He executed Cesari for collecting old rifles? Just so he could confiscate my pictures?"

"The execution was repealed when Cesari surrendered your pictures to the cardinal-nephew," Fabrizio says.

"Now he owns five Caravaggios," says Caravaggio.

"There are Farnese mercs lodging down the street. They're here to collect your head."

"I know. I was on my way there."

"Why?" Malaspina asks.

"Why not? I've spent a year in purgatory. Last week marked the pimp's death. Our anniversary. I wanted to celebrate."

"We need to be expeditious. Let's walk and talk." Fabrizio waves me on.

I turn to my nuns and blow them kisses.

"Thank you for hearing my confession. Thank you for the pizza."

"The glory of love will see you through," they sing, Sister Prig's voice sounding the most heavenly.

I follow Fabrizio. My followers and fanboys hitch their fanaticism along, but the other knights scare them away.

We walk in a huddle, Fabrizio and Malaspina at my shoulders, the aristocrat and other three knights coiled around us. I miss my old posse. I'm tempted to speak in hog Latin. I think we're headed toward the pier.

"The Duke of Mantua bought your *Mary Dead*," Fabrizio says.

"Your uncle told me."

"It infuriated the cardinal-nephew. He had his heart on it," Malaspina says.

"His heart?" I ask.

"He's investigating anyone who owns a Caravaggio, dragnetting for an excuse to confiscate it," Fabrizio says.

"I'm toxic. I should give Papa my head before his nephew destroys everyone dear to me."

"Papa knows you're here. Everyone knows. The entire peninsula is raving about Napoli, which is why everyone in Rome wants you back, including the cardinal-nephew. Rome is just another city without you."

"What about Papa? My portrait of him?"

"He no longer accepts the title of *Papa*. He prefers *Vice-God Upon Earth* or *Monarch of Christendom*," Malaspina says.

"Holy shit."

"The Vice-God Upon Earth pardoned my murder sentence when the Order of St. John knighted me," Fabrizio says. "Grand Master Wignacourt appointed me general of the Malta galleys and prior of Venice. He holds me in high esteem. I'm just back from battle. We blew a fleet of Turks out of the water. I'm returning to Malta with a shit-ton of gold and two hundred slaves. I'll launch another incursion this winter. Michele, I could use that wicked sword of yours aboard my galley."

"The Order could use your skills." Malaspina slaps my shoulder with the heavy paw of Del Monte.

I stop to unbutton my coat, advertising my flab to them.

"I'm not knight material."

The other knights agree with silence. Malaspina fingers the neck of his armor and fishes out his gold Maltese cross.

"You told me you wanted one," he says.

"Me? A knight? And then what? No more capital ban? No more wanted posters? Papa pardons murder in exchange for pictures? Since when? He's no art fan. It's the cardinal-nephew. He wants my pictures. He has that much pull with his uncle?"

"The cardinal-nephew wants you back in Rome," Fabrizio says.

"He doesn't want *me* in Rome. The Grand Master doesn't want *me* joining the Order. They want Caravaggio."

"That's the bitter Lombard talking. You haven't been a Lombard since the day you sold your mother's vineyard and bolted to Venice. You're a Roman idol. Let that persona reign your decision-making."

His advice prompts some mixed emotions. I look to the other three knights for some perspective. They're feigning alertness on the wide amiable street. They don't like what they're hearing. The nasty cock-sucking son of a mason who smells like asshole joining their gentry. Michelangelo loves the sound of it. Caravaggio thinks it has an invigorating ring: himself painting in peace while Michelangelo fights under the legality of knighthood. Another win-win for them and a monolithic question mark for yours truly.

"I was hoping to hear from my marchioness while in purgatory. A letter. A message from your uncle's gopher. I never heard a word. I'm worried. Is she okay?"

"Bored and macabre as ever, but healthy," Fabrizio answers. "You're her only worry. She's in Milan. I'm still not allowed to travel there without the Vice-God's approval. You joining the Order is her idea. She, Del Monte, and Fra Malaspina have already spoken it into the Grand Master's ear. The Grand Master wants Michelangelo Merisi da Caravaggio on Malta."

The aristocrat fake coughs. I button up my coat. Fabrizio dope slaps himself.

"Forgive my manners. Michele, this is my older cousin Luigi Carafa Colonna. Do you remember him? He used to visit Caravaggio every summer. Our mothers are sisters."

Luigi cuts Fabrizio off from further explaining their noble lineage. I have a hazy memory of him. He's the Duke of Mondragone's son, for whatever that's worth. He's an earl or baron, but handsome enough to be a second or third prince. He's shy and demure. I like that.

"I've been to your studio. I watched you work. You're a world wonder," he says.

"Thank you. I remember seeing you there. I'm consumed when Caravaggio paints."

There's a deliberating silence. He wants to commission a picture. He's processing all the times I've been solicited. He doesn't want to put it on me. I hate seeing him like this. A Colonna baron deserves better.

"I'm going to paint you a picture. A gift to the Colonnas for fostering me."

"I'll pay twice the going rate," he says.

"You'll pay nothing," I say.

Fabrizio turns to the other knights. "This guy's a virtual brother. His father was my father's steward. You should see him with a sword."

The knights act like they're impressed, but only out of respect for my brother's grandfather.

"I should have thrashed the Tomassoni that day at Navona. It would have deterred them. They would have left you alone thereafter. You never would have left Rome." Malaspina sounds like he's broken a pledge.

"For whatever it's worth, I've painted my best pictures while in purgatory."

"Your weeping Magdalene. Who commissioned her?" the baron asks.

"Ranuccio Tomassoni," I answer.

"But really, in all seriousness, who owns the weeping Magdalene?" the baron asks.

"Nobody owns her," I say, trying my best to sound like myself, but mostly sounding like an irked Michelangelo.

"That's the moxie we need," Fabrizio says, trying to distract the incivility of a hick saying no to an aristocrat.

The knights escort me to the pier. Fabrizio's galley is docked there, the gangplank guarded by four more knights. They all salute each other. I get nothing. Fabrizio introduces me to his galley as if it's his new bride. It's a fine galley, if you're at all interested in galleys. I am not, but I give the boat my best applause.

"How many people have you killed since joining the Order?" Michelangelo asks.

"We don't just kill Turks. We also heal the sick," says the knight with a Socratic pug nose.

I pretend not to hear him, but my cold-shouldering is turned by the sound of dinked armor. Malaspina has been assaulted by a rock. My boy stands in plain sight, cocking his arm for another hurl. Fra Socrates goes for his dagger. I seize his wrist.

"The boy's with me. He's my bodyguard."

Fra Socrates doesn't care. We tug-of-war his wrist until Malaspina yells at us. I release his wrist. Fra Socrates draws a kerchief and wipes his wrist like there's black plague on it. Fabrizio beckons my boy. He's too smart to obey. I wave him over.

"Your master is joining the Knights of Malta. What do you think of that?" Fabrizio asks.

"Knights of Malta? Isn't their motto 'sleep, pray, sodomy'?"

The knights make stormy faces. They reject cursing and all things wretched. They look to Malaspina. Malaspina looks to Fabrizio. Fabrizio and I resume the laughter of our youth. We yuck it the fuck up. My boy joins in. I search the contortions of my brother's laugh mask for some semblance of our father. I can't remember Fermo so much as smiling.

XL.

In the room, the Colonnas come and go, cooing over Caravaggio. Every Colonna in Napoli is here partying in my eastside studio, watching me paint a family portrait. I've got Mamma throned atop a human power pyramid of Colonnas. I've got Colonnas stacked on Colonnas stacked on Colonnas. It's only a virtual family portrait. Mamma is not here. She remains in Milan, but I'm modeling a rosary Madonna after her and her family. My birth prophesized Admiral Colonna's Lepanto victory, and the Madonna of the rosary blessed it. That's what Mamma always said. I'm painting the Colonnas a Virgin as gratuity for their love. I'd prefer Lena portray that love, but I couldn't conjure her for the role. She has stopped coming to me. I walked the extra-long way to the sea. I walked across the sea to Sicily and back. She's ghosting me. I hate to think why. Worst case scenario? She's finally died of her wounds. Ranuccio's dagger. My brush. What's the difference? And the best-case scenario of her ghosting me? She's finally cut me from her intuition.

Now that I can't generate apparitions, Caravaggio has reduced my role in the picture-making process. I've been demoted to symbolism consultant. Mostly, I'm back to being Michelangelo's keeper, a titular position now that he's on the fast track to becoming an ordained killer with the Knights Hospitaller. Caravaggio is even allowing Michelangelo to have a swipe or two at our pictures. They've awarded our new

Judith her dream role of Caravaggio Virgin. She's chaired above the Colonnas on an unseeable throne, and standing on her lap is our newest boy Christ, the youngest son of Don Marzio Colonna. He wanted his child immortalized. The boy ginger is dumb and affectionate, but he'll grow into those fat fists. He'll grow into the family militance, but his name won't bring him eternal life. A Colonna can't champion every Catholic war. Future battles will spawn higher-caliber superheroes. Marcantonio will become a lesser Argonaut. The Colonna name will degenerate into empty appellations chiseled onto the name stones of atrophied palaces. The Colonnas need my genius. Proof? Don Marzio is allowing a pro to hold his noble son. Christ Himself didn't have that kind of currency. Don Marzio wants a Caravaggio miracle. His cousin wants one too, Filippo Colonna, Prince of Paliano. He's seated next to Don Marzio. Both men are younger than yours truly. Don Marzio is bald with an ashen face. His nose is purple. Drinking, whoring, and gobbling lard has cost him. Like Baron Luigi, the prince has escaped Colonna baldness. He's got hair efflorescing from his scalp and nostrils. Suave and handsome, he couldn't look more princely. He's the desired effect of every Duke Dildo. Fabrizio stands before the duke and prince recounting blow-by-blow details of his recent Turkish bloodbath. Baron Luigi eats it up and washes it down with Tears of Christ, swilled from my boy's amphora. Every couple of swigs, he passes it to his mother Giovanna. She's alternating between Tears of Christ and coffee. She has Mamma's mouth, chin, and ennui. The prince's pregnant wife Lucrezia is on her fifth child and third cup of coffee. Her three-year-old son Federico is also being immortalized in the picture. He's the kneeling boy at the base of the human pyramid, clenching his model mother's wrist for dear life. His wretched shoes belong to my boy, as I belong to the Colonnas. They've never asked me for anything, not a single picture, until now. Now they want compensation. Now they want answers. Is Caravaggio's head worth the political capital we've spent on him?

Lesser Colonnas are also present. Second cousins and third cousins. Some wanted inside the picture. I positioned them on their knees, filthy soles facing outward, begging in the dirt for rosaries. St. Dominic dangles the beads before their eyes like a butcher vaunting sausage links to customers. The Virgin and Dominic are the only non-Colonnas. Dominic is my wine-chugging Samson of *Mercy*. His beard belongs to Cecco. Michelangelo paid Cecco's barber-surgeon to trim a replica onto Dominic's face. The axe wound on St. Peter of Verona's skull is an amalgamation of the one Michelangelo bashed into Papa's lawyer and the one Giovan Tomassoni bashed upon me. Peter's streaming blood is some parts Colonna. He's a cousin twice removed. His bald brother is the kowtowing gent in a ruffled collar, clinging to the sleeve of Dominic's habit, gazing back at the viewer. This second cousin twice removed is a spitting image of the Catholic superhero. Sometimes greatness skips and shuffles a generation, but usually it just dies infecund.

My Lena. My Mamma. My Virgin. My Madonna. This time, it's Caravaggio who has done our woman wrong. The brushwork is superb and the composition remarkable, but the picture is far from genius. It's not even great. It's hokier than Lena's first Virgin. It's a pile of dogma inspired by the viceroy's martyr heap. He's idealized our father's lover. We can only hope that Baron Luigi will hang it in the family church. It was my idea to frame the left side of the picture with an imposing column, the Colonna totem. A little insurance just in case.

The spectating Colonnas are wowed by the picture. I'm actively ignoring their praise because how hard is it to paint a column? Michelangelo doesn't want to hear their praise either. He doesn't want Caravaggio breaking focus. He wants the picture finished so he can set sail for Malta, and start his new life as a righteous murderer. He smiles when the topic of conversation shifts to him.

"He has his father's hands," says Giovanna.

"Fermo Merisi. My father treasured that man," Fabrizio says.

"He managed the Milan and Caravaggio households like a lieutenant," says Mamma's youngest sister Vittoria.

"I hear he and his brothers did masterful stonework," says the prince.

"They built the Temple of Santa Maria del Fonte. It's a mini St. Peter's," Fabrizio says.

"They could have built the Duomo," Giovanna replies.

"Where are they now? I'll hire them to renovate this building," Don Marzio jokes.

"I have some failing tenements that could use their mastery too," says the viceroy from behind a rack of boar's ribs.

Finson refills Giovanna's wine glass. Vinck tops off her coffee.

"When are we going to have the Paliano fortress refurbished?" she asks. "It's ruined. I spent a night on my way here. The place is decimated. There was a hole in my bedroom wall. I almost went outside to sleep in my coach."

"We don't have the money. The admiral spent half a fortune funding his fleet during the war. He spent the other half restoring the streets of Paliano," Don Marzio says.

"I'm having the fortress remodeled into a palace," says the prince.

"How are we going to afford that?" Vittoria asks.

"My financial advisors have formulated a strategy. I'm consolidating our assets. We're also getting out of the war racket and getting into the art game."

The prince approaches my models. He stands just outside the frame, pissing distance from the lookalike Marcantonio.

"I can never remember. How are we related again?" the prince asks him.

The doppelganger looks to me for permission to speak. I nod. He's nonessential at the moment. Caravaggio is dying our Madonna's hair a red closer to Mamma's.

"My grandfather and your grandfather were cousins," the doppelganger answers.

The prince accepts the answer and returns to his chair.

"No. Your grandfathers were second cousins," says Vittoria.

"No. They weren't cousins. My father was his grandfather's nephew," Giovanna says.

"That doesn't even make sense," Don Marzio says.

They're all wrong. Odoardo Colonna and Agapito Colonna were cousins; therefore, Filippo and the doppelganger are third cousins once removed. But I keep quiet. It's not my business. My business is painting my way back to Cecco and/or Lena.

"I don't know how we're related, but we're both Colonna men. Our features document it. Long noses, round eyes, and egg-shaped heads. All Colonna men have them," says the prince.

"But some Colonna men get to hide their egg under a head of hair." Giovanna's acrimony makes me miss Mamma.

"Fabrizio has the hair, but none of those other features," says the princess.

"I've got the head of a Sforza, and the heart of a Colonna." He believes it. He hasn't the faintest that we're brothers.

"I still don't know how we're related. Second cousins? How can that be? You're my grandfather's twin. My father, his son, didn't have the same likeness," says the prince.

The chitchat is starting to annoy Caravaggio. Caravaggio's loss of focus irritates Michelangelo. He selfishly takes it upon himself to educate the Colonnas on their lineage.

"Lorenzo Colonna was the brother of the original Fabrizio Colonna, your great grandfather," he says, pointing to the prince. "Lorenzo Colonna was the father of Anna Colonna Fortebraccio. That's the great-grandmother of this here Marcantonio doppelganger."

The Colonnas are dumbstruck and a little creeped out by Michelangelo's expertise. They set down their booze, coffee, and meats. Everyone stands but the viceroy. He remains seated, gnawing gristle off the ribs with his incisors.

"I don't know if I've heard of Lorenzo Colonna," the prince says.

"How do you know all that?" Don Marzio asks Michelangelo.

"A little birdie told me," he replies.

They all get the Mamma reference. They all laugh, like it's their first time in centuries.

"I've been telling you. This guy's like a brother to me," Fabrizio says to the viceroy.

"I have an idea," Giovanna says. "Michele, why don't you paint yourself into the picture?"

"Yes! What an idea! Like in *Christ Taken*," Malaspina says.

"Or *Matthew Killed*, only in this picture, you're wearing pants!" Fabrizio slaps my back.

God bless him. God bless God for delivering Fabrizio to me at that pizza cart. God bless pizza. God bless the Knights of Malta. God bless the Colonnas for charting me a map back to Lena. God bless them for saving us from Michelangelo's evil, but there's no fucking way I'm painting myself inside this picture. Caravaggio agrees. It's not good enough for us.

When the light melts to the floor, I relieve my Colonna models of their duties. They break pose in a collective exhalation. The spectating Colonnas deliver a standing ovation. Caravaggio bows. Michelangelo blows a kiss. I genuflect.

"Keep painting like this, and you'll have a palace of your own," says the viceroy stumbling out the door.

"I wouldn't live that way if you paid me," I reply.

He stops under the rotted transom. "I have paid you."

"And I spent it all on love."

He scoffs because he can't understand. The man is married to his cousin.

Fabrizio and Baron Luigi encourage everyone to leave. They have business with me. I strip the amphora from Baron Luigi, paint from my hands staining his. He defeats the urge to wipe them on a nearby rag. He knows I'd judge him. My Virgin and her puffy lips exit without a word. I'm relieved. I was afraid of her big mouth deterring the Colonnas from buying the picture.

"*Mercy* has tripled attendance at Pio Monte della Misercordia. When *Rosary Madonna* is hung at San Domenico Maggiore, you'll have to widen the walls and install more pews," I say.

"You didn't have to paint this for us." Fabrizio sounds overly appreciative.

"I want to honor my marchioness. I want her to feel venerated."

"That's extremely respectful, but you shouldn't have," Baron Luigi says.

"This is the fifth or sixth time that the Colonnas have saved my head. For as long as it remains on my shoulders, I'll be indebted to them."

"We're awed by the picture. It's magnificent, but it's not what my mother and aunt want," Baron Luigi says.

I know that the Madonna failed Mamma, as my Virgins failed Lena, but I'm surprised that a family of philistines would notice its aesthetic failings and conceptual heavy-handedness.

"I'm not entirely finished. I could make some alterations. I could recompose some of it. I'll paint that selfie in the background."

"It's perfect, brother. It's just not what my aunts want thematically," Fabrizio says.

"What theme do they want?"

"They want the weeping Magdalene," Baron Luigi says.

"Finson and Vinck just finished two copies. You can have one of those and keep the rosary Madonna."

"They just want the Magdalene," Fabrizio says to the floor.

"The original," Baron Luigi says.

The Colonnas built their naval dynasty on hate. They don't want my idolization. They want the disappointment and grief that comes after it. Lena has left me in body, and now in mind. Weeping Magdalene is all I have left. I don't deserve her or the one suffering in Rome.

It's time to let go of the dissatisfied women in my life. I slap Fabrizio on the shoulder.

"She's all yours, Brother Superior."

After finishing *Rosary Madonna*, I sleep for three days. It would have been four, but I awake in a brine of July heat, the sheets wetter than sex. Despite the oppressive atmosphere, I'm feeling annoyingly breezy and carefree. The Knights Hospitaller have secured Napoli. They've chased away the assassins and mercs. For the first time since failing to castrate Ranuccio, I can take a piss without looking over my shoulder. I get out of bed and piss in my pot, sniffing each armpit in the process. Uncharacteristically, there's no scent. I have no more stink to spread. My godliness is over. It's back to the business of being tertiary for yours truly. Michelangelo leads us to the window to survey the climate. Down on the street, three Hospitaller brothers march into the German's tavern, booted, suited, and armed. I go to the mirror and style my hair using my piss fingers. I make a *Boy Bitten by a Lizard* face. I make an Isaac face. Michelangelo punches it. Not hard enough to crack the glass, but hard enough to harness power.

I dress in my grimiest clothes and cinch my belt. I attach my dagger and carry my sword into the studio. My boy and girl are preparing supper. Fennel and eel. Finson and Vinck tinker with their Magdalenes. Their Magdalenes look prettier without my weeping Lena around to cheapen them. Her absence has gutted the room. Our emotions have already sailed for Malta.

"I'm leaving the day after tomorrow," I say.

"We know. We're almost finished. These are the last copies," Finck says.

"Good. No more copies. Start painting for Cecco. Spread his name far and wide."

"We'll paint as he trained us, but we don't feel right signing his name. If Caravaggio doesn't put his name on pictures, why would Cecco del Caravaggio?" Finson asks.

I'm happy to hear it. I never liked the idea of them adopting my Cecco's name, even if they are better painters than him.

"I'd be a hypocrite to disagree with that," I say.

"We're relieved. Thanks for understanding," Finson says.

"I'm sorry for not saying much to you for the past year. It wasn't personal. It was a matter of productivity and self-preservation."

"You talked plenty," Vinck says.

"I did?"

"After work. After a few bites of poppy bread. You'd go on craft tangents. They taught us a lot."

"I would? Me?"

"Yes, you, or you know, the other you."

"I'm leaving my Judith to the both of you. I'm also leaving you *Rosary Madonna*."

"We don't deserve them. You've paid us well for our work," Finson says.

"They're yours. I'm leaving them here. Take them or they'll be confiscated by Don Marzio."

I turn to my boy and tap his head with the flat of my sword as if knighting him. I then turn the blade on myself and offer him the grip.

"Take it. Use it to castrate Don Marzio if he tries confiscating the pictures. He's a slimeball. He was involved in the arrest and persecution of Beatrice Cenci. I couldn't bring myself to remember that about him while he was saving my neck."

My boy snatches the sword from my hand with thankless speed. He doesn't say thank you. He's not sentimental. He's nothing, just as I found him. He runs it up to the roof to practice swinging.

"What about me? What do I get?" my girl asks.

"There's a half a keg of wine left over from the *Rosary Madonna* party. Tears of Christ. It's all yours."

"That's it?" she asks.

I throw her over my shoulder and walk her into my room. I drop her on the bed and open Cecco's drawer. Fillide's pearl earrings. I call my girl over.

"Take them," I say.

She holds the pearls to her ears. Her ears are freaky. It's a shame I'll never paint them.

"Did your weeping Magdalene wear them?" she asks.

"No. Another model. The only woman I ever got right."

She squeezes the pearls in her fist and flexes her biceps. I feel them. Her muscles have grown. I'd like to think that *Weeping Magdalene* had something to do with it.

. . .

The tavern disappoints Michelangelo. It's bright. It's clean. It's orderly. There's no shouting. There's no physical contention. Customers are earnestly engaged in academic discussions, even the table of Spanish soldiers drinking on their captain's purse. Half of my social justice warriors sit at the bar talking to a painter named Caracciolo. The Croat Radolovich is here, the buyer of my Neapolitan Madonna and child. He's talking to the Hospitallers about the crusade poetry of Torquato Tasso. Everyone else looks like an artist or literati. Everyone is ecstatic about seeing yours truly, except for the three Hospitallers. Two of them accompanied Fabrizio the day of the pizza cart. The alpha's name is Fra De Varayz. He faces me from his stool, but as he scans the tavern, I'm the only thing he doesn't see. Michelangelo already wants to put some hurt on him.

"You've been here a year. It's about time you came," cries the German.

He offers me cognac. Uninspired by the dispassion of the place, Michelangelo seeks to fulfill another urge.

"I'd love a tour of the upstairs," he says.

At last, Fra De Varayz acknowledges my presence with a commending nod. He's happy to learn that I fuck women.

"I have an idea of who you might be wanting." The German points his finger, mimicking my rosary Madonna.

"I prefer the strong, silent types."

"A silent woman is a gift from God. I think you'll find luck on the third floor. Head on up. Shop around."

The German keeps a better building than Don Marzio. The stairways and halls are shipshape. The rooms tidy. His women hygienic. Most of them are almost attractive. They all recognize me. Most have spent time in my studio. I try not to make prolonged eye contact. I don't want them thinking that I'm casting a new Judith or Virgin. I don't want to disappoint yet another woman.

In the rooms, women fuck and blow, moaning of Caravaggio. I should have believed Lena when she said it.

I pace the third floor looking for the pro with the oldest face. When I find the one, I pay twice her rate to pillow my head on her squashy breast. Michelangelo's hard up for some Mamma affection. She's a ginger. She smells like a bucket of apples.

"I'm nervous about sailing. I've never stepped foot on a boat. I'm more of a coach guy."

"I rode in a coach once. Hated it. It was like getting badly fucked by a guy with no dick."

"They're going to make me a knight, but I don't think they'll be letting me kill anyone. I think I'll be stuck there painting the whole time."

"As you should be. *Mercy* and *Rosary Madonna* changed my life. I'm done being a pro. I'm going to join the convent at the end of summer, once the busy season is over."

"I met some nuns a few weeks ago. They gave me love. They gave me pizza."

"Love God unconditionally. He gave you so much. He gave you your own star."

Michelangelo sucks her breast for a time. Then we eat some poppy bread and drink wine. We talk all night. I make her tell me her life story. It rings of my girl's origins and future. I pay more money and fall asleep on her tits. At dawn, I climb up to the roof and watch the sky turn into a Raphael. Cecco is somewhere in that painting, sharing his bed with a sailor. They're talking about my shittiness, laughing at my failures as a man.

XLI.

I sit next to Brother Superior on the edge of his berth. Fra Malaspina, Fra De Varayz, and Fra Valette sit atop two chests. I don't know what's in them. Amputated souls if I had to guess. The lighting is ideal, single-sourced from the starboard porthole, an amber sunray transmitting warmth across their wayward faces. My new brothers are either wicked or truly fucking wicked, not that it matters. We're on the same team, the four of us dressed in matching black linens. The chest of my surplice is missing the white Maltese cross.

The sails have been shortened. The ship surges south, powered by the unfathomable respiration of thirty slaves.

Fra De Varayz is reminiscing over the Great Siege of Malta. He wasn't alive in 1565. He's only three years older than Brother Superior and yours truly. He has a triangular face with a scimitar scar down his cheek. His ire began long before he was born. In this way, he has me missing Onorio.

"Mustafa took the fort of St. Elmo and captured nine knights. He beheaded them and floated their corpses across the bay on floating crucifixes."

"Grandmaster Valette's response? He decapitated his Turkish prisoners, loaded their heads into our cannons, and bombarded Mustafa's camp with them." Brother Superior presses his thumb and index finger together and draws a horizontal line in the air. "Perfecto!"

"Wish I'd been at St. Elmo," says Michelangelo. "On land, I'm my namesake, the Satan-slaying archangel. But by sea? Not so much. I suck at everything having to do with boats."

"They're not *boats*. They're *ships*. Boats are for netting tuna." Fra De Varayz drops his head in frustration.

I know the proper terminology, but Michelangelo enjoys goading his evil, this fucking Fra Diavolo character. I should probably reel Michelangelo in, but I don't feel like it's my responsibility anymore. His unruliness now belongs to the Knights Hospitaller. Let Malaspina and Fabrizio mitigate his feistiness.

"You won't have to navigate. You'll be a marine," Malaspina says to him.

"What does a marine do?"

"Once we've latched onto a ship, you jump aboard and start slaying. Turks. Tunisians. Whoever else is on board," Fra Valette says.

"I can do that. When do I start?" Michelangelo asks.

"We've already started. There's gold in those chests and slaves in the hold. It's summer. This is our killing season. When the sea is calm. We have three months to prosper and clear the peninsula of non-Italians." Brother Superior makes the decrescendo whistle of a cannonball.

Fra Diavolo makes the sound of bursting timber.

"I should probably learn to swim," I say, knowing Michelangelo hasn't even considered that snafu.

"A marine who can't swim." Fra Valette looks to Malaspina for an explanation.

Malaspina doesn't see him because he's eye-fucking me for a Jerome.

"Maybe I can wear a life jacket over my armor." Michelangelo catapults the joke right over Fra Diavolo's bow.

"Maybe you should stick to painting. Stay inside Magisterial Palace and make pretty pictures for the grandmaster," he replies.

"I'm not a painter," Caravaggio says.

"He's an artist, the greatest since the Divine One," says Malaspina.

"I'm not an artist."

"What are you?" asks Fra Diavolo.

"I'm a discoverer."

"Oh really? Okay, Columbus. What have you discovered?"

"I'm a cartographer of human consciousness."

"Human what?" Fra Valette asks.

"Consciousness. Man's inner testimony."

Fra Diavolo and Fra Valette sandwich Malaspina with incredulous stares.

"You'll see," he tells them.

Brother Superior starts talking Grandpa Colonna and the Battle of Lepanto. He hardly ever mentions Francesco Sforza, Marquis of Caravaggio. He only eulogizes his mother's father. After recounting Marcantonio's decimation of Ali Pasha's flagship, he requests a moment of privacy with yours truly. We all stand. Everyone gets a salute but me, but Malaspina gives my chest an exalting rap, stirring the sleeping Jerome in my heart.

Brother Superior watches them go topside through the hatch. He turns to me and makes a paternal expression that I imagine on our father. He grabs the flask from his desk and returns to his berth. I take a seat on one of the chests.

"Del Monte wrote to me. Your fame keeps skyrocketing in Rome. You're in higher demand than coffee. Everyone wants you back. Cardinals. Nobles. The working-class and wretched."

"Everyone but the Vice-God Upon Earth."

"Del Monte, my uncle, and the cardinal-nephew are still working on the Vice-God. Rubens is obsessed with *Mary Dead*. He thinks it's a masterpiece. He's advising the Duke of Mantua to buy it. The Duke of Modena still wants his Virgin. Masetti is canvassing every cardinal in Rome for a Caravaggio pardon, so you've got two dukes greasing the Vice-God on your behalf. Once you become a Hospitaller, the Vice-God will have to annul the capital ban."

"Any word from my marchioness?" I ask.

"She sends much love. She's finally feeling optimistic. She's happy we found you."

"She's happy, but she still thinks her Michele will self-sabotage," I say.

"She'll never stop worrying about our tempers blowing up in our faces."

"Blasting our own heads from a Hungarian cannon?"

He's not at liberty to laugh, not at the expense of the Order. He tries submersing his humor with wine, but some gurgles up on him, dribbling from the corner of his mouth.

"Fra De Varayz is the best kind of grim. His austerity will grow on you."

"Can I go below and see the rowers? I want to observe them."

"It reeks of piss and shit down there. Why do you think you can smell a galley two miles upwind?"

"I smell like piss and shit," I say, testing his ability to see my godliness.

"You'll bathe when we dock. The Grandmaster doesn't tolerate uncleanliness, not even from a genius. When we were kids, you washed religiously. You bathed twice a week."

"I was going through a phase. It had something to do with the Plague killing all the men in my family." I look around his cabin. None of my ghosts are aboard, not even Fermo.

"We spent a month quarantined in Caravaggio palace during the Plague, cosplaying the Battle of Lepanto and playing Paladins. Our mothers wouldn't even let the servants handle our food. They prepared our meals and practically spoon-fed us themselves. Your mother cooked us the most delicious meals. I can still taste her artichokes! And her gnocchi! We practically puked whenever my mother cooked. Once the Plague ended, she never prepared another crumb. Thank-fucking-God!"

"I want to see them," says Caravaggio.

"Our mothers?"

"The rowers. I want to study their muscles for a picture."

"Alright, but only because I'm on strict orders from the grandmaster. Don't deny Caravaggio if his request pertains to art. He's eager to abet your genius. Some knights will resent your..."

He can't bring himself to say it.

"Knighting the son of a bricklayer?" Michelangelo beats me to the punch.

"Malaspina was right. They'll see. You'll win them over."

"I want to see the rowers," says the genius.

The inhumanity doesn't disappoint. The slave deck is the fetid battlefield of a lopsided war. The war is age-old and endless. The good guys are losing. They're chained. They're naked save for scars, sores, and welts. Their heads are shaved, their bare feet cankered. The stench of ulcerated flesh suppresses the rank of piss and shit. The slave driver whips them, French and Italian convicts turned oarsmen. Brother Superior identifies them as murderers, adulterers, thieves, and one donkey fucker. I'd almost fit right in. I hear myself humming along to their irreligious chanting. I'd love to see their beastly traps, triceps, and deltoids swing a sword. Some of the newly captured Muslim slaves are fumbling at their new vocation. The slave driver whips the ever-living Christ out of them. The rowers behind them spit on their necks. It's too much reality, even for Caravaggio.

Brother Superior's galley is not a ship. It's not even a boat. It's a floating prison. A sailing Tor di Nona. Brother Superior is not an admiral. He's a prison warden. The Knights Hospitaller are not caregivers. They are maritime mercs.

"We can row eight knots for twenty minutes," Brother Superior says.

"Feed them pizza. You could reach ten knots."

"They don't need pizza. They need adrenaline. Hence, the whip."

"I've been painting with adrenaline for the past year. I've been painting for redemption. Before that I painted for fame. I'm looking forward to painting for the sake of my genius."

"That's what we want for you. We want to help you help yourself. You're home, brother. You can have the best of both worlds in Malta. Paint and joust to your heart's content."

My heart will be content when I rescue Lena dressed in knight's armor, bearing a Maltese cross. I'm already favoring galleys over coaches. I see myself riding waves, sharing a berth with Lena and Cecco. Papa Clement, Papa Borghese, Cardinal Farnese, Baglione, and the remaining Tomassoni brothers suffer on the slave deck, Mamma obliterating their flesh with a whip as we cruise toward Kingdom Cum.

XLII.

I stink of fancy olive oil soap, my balls evoking a Provencal wildflower field, not that I've ever been to Provence. Soap is a good lubricant. I'll give it that. I've taken another vow of chastity. The Order is crawling with teenybopper pages and silver foxes. Both are forbidden. The Knights Hospitaller in the Order of St. John of Jerusalem don't fuck each other. It's unwritten rule number two. Knights Hospitaller only bed pros and sex slaves. The newfangled city of Valletta has a cohabitation ratio of seven pros for every fra. The lodges are stocked with male and female sex slaves abducted from various corners of the Mediterranean. Wanting nothing to do with that evil, I make love to myself. Lena is still boycotting my intellection, but Cecco has yet to excommunicate himself. He's down here in St. John's crypt with me. The grandmasters of yore aren't raising much of a stink.

Grandmaster Wignacourt has housed me down the hall from his chamber. His stated reason for accommodating me in Magisterial Palace is to better serve my genius, but I think it has more to do with monitoring Michelangelo's impulses, to keep him from destroying Caravaggio. Personally, I'm insulted. I've never been so overlooked. The grandmaster thinks it's just Michelangelo and Caravaggio in here, and he thinks he can do my job. His method is hackneyed: pamper Caravaggio while tantalizing Michelangelo with a knighthood. Maybe it would have worked had Michelangelo been knighted by now, but the grandmaster accelerated our martial training and skipped convent training altogether. Michelangelo has done little more than thwack a few wrists sparring brothers with a wooden sword. The grandmaster delays Michelangelo's dubbing every time a picture is commissioned. The hick is wise to the empty bribe, resenting the grandmaster's manipulation but adoring his silver foxiness.

Caravaggio adores being adored by Grandmaster Wignacourt, Fra Malaspina, and other senior knights. The fanfare has neutered his ambition. He's only made three pictures in nine months. He painted Malaspina as a shirtless Jerome scribing his war memoir. He also painted another portrait for the grandmaster's most allegiant elector, Fra Antonio Martelli, prior of Messina. Caravaggio's portrait of the grandmaster and his page is laudatory. Unlike his portrait of the Vice-God, he paid the grandmaster every compliment. There will be hundreds of other grandmasters, but Grandmaster Wignacourt has been recorded by Caravaggio. I've gifted him immortality, but my capital ban remains. Many of the haughtier knights begrudge the hick's presence in their exclusive fraternity. My head could buy a string of steeds or harem of sex slaves. I need to be knighted and pardoned pronto, but Brother Superior has commissioned a supersized dramatization of John the Baptist's decollation, which will further postpone Michelangelo's dubbing. The picture will hang in the oratory of St. John's Conventual Church. Knights will pray under it. Pages will be dubbed before it. I've been dragging ass on it. It's the only way to negotiate being dubbed. I'm also trying to muster some nerve. Five times I've painted my John with more love than I've tendered any man. Can I possibly draw the sword across his neck? It remains to be seen.

Cecco spreads his Cupid wings and flaps away from my intellection. I wipe my hands on the hem of my tunic, and step from the darkest corner of the crypt. I light three candles and cough up some heartache. It echoes off the vaulted ceiling. Montoya's voice would sound godly down here. I'm sure the dead grandmasters could use some serenading while they await Judgment Day. I belt the refrain from my favorite madrigal and approach the sarcophagus of Grandmaster Jean Parisot de la Valette, the absolute savage who cannonballed the heads of his Turkish prisoners. He's great-uncle to Fra Valette, who's currently nursing a sprained wrist thanks to Michelangelo. Grandmaster Valette lies bronzed atop his tomb, palms facing heavenward. I dab him up and continue to the tomb of Grandmaster

Jean de la Cassiere. Two embossed angels preside over his sarcophagus, reminding me of a young and not-so-young Cecco. Below them it reads *Hoc Omnis Caro*.

"I want to be buried down here," Michelangelo says.

"What happened to dying in Napoli?" Caravaggio asks.

"Napoli can fuck itself," answers Michelangelo.

"What about pizza," I say, trying to keep things light.

"Malta is purgatory. Nothing but rock. The people are drier than the landscape. These knights are fucking empty suits. Name-brand noblemen with no extraordinary traits other than the family sadism. They think they're better than us. Most of them don't want us here."

"The important ones want us here." Getting them to buy in has become increasingly difficult.

"John the Baptist is my favorite subject but Jesus Christ everything in Malta is John this and John that," Caravaggio says. "They pray to St. John about St. John at St. John. They pray half the day and spend the other half fucking slaves. At night, they drink and count gold. Order of St. John my ass. More like pestilent frat. The wilderness of my decollated John will scare them straight."

"You've painted three portraits and they still haven't knighted me," says Michelangelo. "You painted the grandmaster better than you painted Papa."

"Vice-God," I say.

"And they're all fucking related. Malaspina. Costa. Carafa. Colonna. They're all here. We know their genealogy better than they know it, but they'll never accept us."

"The important ones accept us." I'm getting so sick of hearing myself talk.

"The death yelp of my John will pop their fucking ears," Caravaggio assures Michelangelo.

"I want to die in Rome," I say.

"Every fucking dude in Valletta is named John, Jean, or Juan," Michelangelo says to Caravaggio.

They're not ignoring me. My voice has lost its tenor over them. Caravaggio has Grandmaster Wignacourt. Michelangelo has Fra Malaspina. I've become the nonself. This, that, and I'm the other.

"Echo!" I shout.

"Ecco!" Michelangelo shouts back.

"Ecco the homo!" Caravaggio echoes above us.

"I'm tired of these frat boys throwing their dicks around," Michelangelo says.

The two-beat clacking of Brother Superior's heel iron jackboots canters across the crypt. He emerges from the darkness like my Paliano David. Under said lighting, I can see him as a Merisi. He has the earlobes, but not the bushy eyebrows.

"When did you start talking to yourself?" he asks.

"Maybe five minutes ago."

"No. How *long* have you been talking to yourself? When did it start?"

"The Lombard hick started talking to me in Milan after I killed that cop. The genius first voiced himself while painting *Doubting Thomas.*"

"You were always an alpha, fiery and free. You'd snap on someone, cut them open, and recompose yourself before the blood flowed. You're conflicted now. You're carrying some heavy guilt. You seem more likely to snap on yourself."

"I have no guilt about bleeding the pimp."

"No. I know. Your guilt is more theoretical than that. You're censuring yourself on principle, to make a point."

"What is my point?"

"That you'll make a point of annihilating yourself."

"That is precisely my point. No one has the balls to punish me. Cardinals excuse my perversities and enable my violence. For what? To see me record God's dirty realism? To see me dignify the jobless wretches who Papa expels from Rome? They play a double-dealing morality with my art. Even my critics, holy rollers like Baglione, they're quicker to judge my aesthetics than ethics. I'm the only one who holds the hick accountable."

"How many voices are talking in that head of yours?"

I'd like to introduce myself to my brother, but I know he'd think less of Michelangelo if he knew there was a shred of decency in here, so I give him the torn artist.

"I disgraced my Cupid. I wronged my Virgin."

"I dishonored the Sforza-Colonna name. I dishonored my gentry by murdering a lesser gent over a card game. My brother almost renounced me. I nearly turned my mother into an alcoholic. Killing Muslims is the only way to redeem myself. It'll be your exculpation too."

"I disappointed Mamma."

Brother Superior catches my slip of tongue but spoons the word back into my mouth like a nun feeding a convalescent.

"You're a luminary. There's no chance you disappointed Lucia. She was proud of you. She advocated for your talent. She did the same for your brother's priestly predilections. How is Giovan? I hear he's a rising Jesuit."

"You're the brother I never had," I say.

"We'll be actual brothers by the end of the month."

"That's what you said last month. The hick is getting restless. He wants to be dubbed."

"Start the John picture. Let Wignacourt see the enormity of it. I'm cruising for Turkey in a few weeks. Another crusade. Talk about impoverished? We're almost broke."

"The Order is almost broke? This city is sky-high with new construction. There are more cranes in Valletta than Rome."

"The Sforzas and Colonnas are going broke. My uncle is sick. He's written his will. When he's gone, we'll lose significant clout in the Vatican. Don Marzio bleeds money, and I'm not waiting around for Prince Filippo's financial schemes. My brother has depleted our inheritance building his university, teaching poets how to fucking terza rima. I need my own money, and I'll make it like a Colonna. Fighting and heisting."

"Terza rima is so Renaissance. Everyone's writing ottava rima these days," Caravaggio says.

"This poetry talk is making me irate. Let's go to the armory and spar some German brothers."

"I smell too nice to fight."

The Knights Hospitaller in the Order of St. John of Jerusalem don't fuck each other, but they love to spar and wrestle in their breeches. There are no less than one hundred oniony armpits in the armory. I smell each one like a sow hunting truffles. Brother cranking headlock onto brother. Brother hip-tossing brother. Brother riposting brother. Their bawdy grunts are muzzled by the ceiling coffers and further quelled by the chinking of rebated swords and the knock-knocking of oak batons striking oak pells. The armory runs the entire rear end of Magisterial Palace. It's the largest armory in the Mediterranean, housing enough pikes, maces, and swords to weaponize two thousand men. I'd love to get my boy in here, give him the run of the place.

Every naked chest has a gold Maltese cross dancing upon it. I have no necklace. My tunic has no cross, but my abs are back. I strip down to my undies and follow my nose to Fra Diavolo, smelling his lilac taint through a forest of BO.

Fra Valette and a dozen other brothers encircle Fra Diavolo, who's squared against the tallest length of flesh I've ever seen. This goliath is a Turk. It's been ten years since I've seen the Divine One's David, but Fra Diavolo's opponent appears as tall. Someone has wrapped the Ottoman flag between his crotch and up and around his waist. He's standing southpaw, his right arm fully extended, keeping Fra Diavolo at an insurmountable distance. Fra Diavolo stutter-steps and jukes vying for an angle, his motions lithe and nearly quick as my eyes. I see that I've underestimated him. He's as muscular as my Matthew assassin. If Goliath were at all human, I'd put all Cecco's ducats on Fra Diavolo, but these biblical disproportions don't fit the story. Malta is hardly Israel. My brothers are the Philistines, and this here Goliath is the underdog.

"The behemoth is stoned," Brother Superior whispers. "Fra De Varayz drugged him."

Before I can process the implication, Fra Diavolo slips past Goliath's arm, and hugs him chest to groin. Goliath overreacts and totters. Fra Diavolo thrusts his pelvis into Goliath's thighs and hoists him off the ground. Our brothers hoot and haw, Brother Superior along with them. Fra Diavolo twists his torso and throws Goliath backwards, slamming him to the mosaiced floor. The monster's lungs jump out of his chest. Fra Diavolo rear chokes the remaining air until Goliath falls asleep. My brothers bump and pound each other's chests. Their alpha felled the tallest Muslim in the world. From the looks of things, myself, Brother Superior, and Fra Diavolo are the only ones who know better.

Two brothers drag the unconscious slave from the armory by his legs. I pick a wooden sword from the rack and ask the six closest brothers if they want to spar. No takers. In nine months, I haven't lost. Fra Diavolo has yet to accept my challenges, but his staged David victory has him in a mood.

Michelangelo shouts over the ovations. "You owe me a dance."

Brother Superior hands Fra Diavolo a stick. He gladly accepts, a chump to his own sham.

"It's past noon. Are you just waking up?" he asks.

"I am. Your dinking swords woke me. I could hear my brothers training from the second floor."

"You're not a brother yet," Fra Valette chimes in.

"The brother who used to live in your chamber was a lieutenant-general. He was also a Pamphili," Fra Diavolo says.

He has wicked long nipples. Usually, I can't look at them without laughing, but today they're grossing me out.

"I'm sober as a judge. I'm not going to swoon for you," I say.

"You should be sleeping in the stables," Fra Diavolo says.

"This hick has slept in more palaces than a royal pro," Michelangelo replies.

"Where else have you slept?" Fra Valette points to his ass.

There've been whispers about my cock-gobbling. Now it has become public inquiry.

"Your alpha brother is the one with steel-tipped nipples," Michelangelo says.

I point my stick at Fra Diavolo's left tit. He appels with a boisterous stomp, but I don't flinch. Then come the lunges. His feet are fast, but his shoulder slow. I riposte and poke his right tit. I step back and reset. Dogged, Fra Diavolo advances, extending a series of rapid thrusts that are forceful, rhythmic, and predictable. I parry and slide my stick down the length of his, pinning his hilt against his thigh. I seize his sword hand with my free hand and step behind his legs. Twisting his wrist and arm backwards, I toss him over my hip. I land on top of him, knee in his chest, the forte of my stick on his throat. I ease off, and Fra Valette suckers me with a blow to the ribs. I spin to my feet and down block Fra Valette's second thrust. Someone else jabs the small of my back. Back on his feet, Fra Diavolo lunges from my right. Valette lunges from my left. I slip and block both advances, but my anonymous third opponent jabs my ribs again.

"Now you're dead twice," he says.

Michelangelo loses it. He spins and confronts the coward. He's a young Fra Someone from a noble Spanish family. Michelangelo drops him in a fury of slashes and thrusts, but his belligerence leaves us unguarded. Fra Diavolo and Fra Valette strike us down with blows to the spine and legs. Then there is a final one to the head. I curl into a ball and cover up as the three of them club my forearms. A fourth brother paddles my ass.

"I think he likes that," Fra Valette says.

I welcome their hatred. I'm loving their abuse. I'll ram it back up their asses when an opportunity presents itself. Until then, I'm left wondering. Why is Brother Superior standing by, biting a fingernail?

My demoralization is stopped by Fra Malaspina. He enters the armory wanting an explanation. My brothers disentangle themselves from yours truly. Fra Diavolo offers me his hand. I smile it away and stand on my own throbbing legs.

"We were putting this marine through a new training simulation," Fra Diavolo says to Malaspina.

"It recreates the outnumbered chaos of boarding the enemy's deck," Fra Valette says.

The German blueblood says something in a thick accent that I don't care to decipher.

"Readying myself for the next Battle of Lepanto," Michelangelo says.

"Go clean yourself up. The grandmaster wants to lunch with you," Malaspina replies.

Everyone grumbles at my preferential lunch invitation and disperses. Diavolo's ropy-armed page lingers, holding me in the fuzzy corner of a Lena-like Mona Lisa gaze. The youngster has a sophic profile. He wants me to see him musing over something. He's unsure of the thing. He's hoping I'll know. I salute him. He turns a blind eye and falls into his master's slipstream.

"Our decollated John. Share your vision with the grandmaster," Brother Superior says in my ear.

The grandmaster and I are seated in the courtyard, the sun banging above us. It's the worst light for discussing a Caravaggio, but that's not stopping the grandmaster. He's all genius genius genius in my face. As he charms Caravaggio, the hurt of my brothers' sticks starts shouting— the back of my head, my shoulders, my lower back. Thank heaven this chair is decadently padded in velvet, or my buttocks would be crying. Michelangelo is about to gripe on behalf of our buttocks when a well-groomed boy servant delivers two large pizzas, one anchovy, the other plain. This is the fiftieth time I've lunched with the grandmaster. It's always chickpeas, chicory, and fish pie. I look around for an explanation, but there's only the boy and a row of potted lemon trees, their green fruit just starting to nipple.

"A little birdie told me that you fell in love with pizza." The grandmaster's gooey French accent is a knee-slapper, but it has ceased to entertain Michelangelo. He'll resume laughter after he's been dubbed.

"Pizza made me fall out of love with donuts," I say.

"I had these pies shipped from Napoli on our fastest galleon."

The grandmaster is crowned by a severe crew-cut, the highest and tightest in the Mediterranean, but his sarcasm is even more vicious. I play along with the pizza delivery joke. I need those Maltese crosses, the white one on the grandmaster's black tunic and the gold one around his neck, sparkling in my eye like a migraine aura.

"A galleon? Those are the boats with six sheets and a high round stern?" I ask.

Grandmaster Wignacourt laughs hard, but it's all in his chest. He can afford a joke at any expense. He has kingly autonomy. He has Papa kind of money. He's commanded and suffered an affluence of absurd evils. He's a Columbus of finding humor. He'll laugh at death, his enemy's or his own. He'll laugh at malfeasance, his doing or a Turk's. He'll laugh off his own success, dismissing it as, in his own words, undeservingly divine intervention. His chivalry doesn't operate on righteous delusions. It operates on steely pragmatism. He eats his plain pizza with a knife and fork. I imagine him slaying Muslims during the Siege of '65 with the same insanely practical dissections. His chivalry is a man's man's straightforwardness highlighted by a silver foxiness. Brothers joke that he was born with gray stubble on his chin. The icky mole on his nose does not depreciate his magisterial kisser. I left the mole out of the portrait. I painted Grandmaster Wignacourt in his own likeness. He chose the pose. He chose to have his page included. He also chose the wardrobe, his designer armor by Spacini. I painted him with such steely decorum that he's yet to notice his stubby bow-legged-ness. He's yet to see his page stealing the show. Caravaggio could watch him eat pizza all day while Michelangelo eats his heart out.

The pizza is good, not great. The dough is thicker than in Napoli. The olive oil is a lesser quality. The anchovies are not as plump.

"Delicious," I say.

"It's not as good as Napoli. It's the dough. Dough is all about the water. Their water has more minerals. It's why I'm building the aqueducts. They carry water from the plateau above Rabat. My dough won't be so soft."

"You made this yourself?"

"I made the dough. My cooks assembled and fired the pizza. It's my new hobby."

"Almighty God did not sire Grandmaster Wignacourt so he could alchemize yeast and flour." Michelangelo cringes at my pandering but recognizes its necessity.

"Almighty God hatched me to punish infidels and train other Catholics to punish infidels, but great men, the chosen ones, we must filch a little self-determination for ourselves when possible. God won't respect us if we're too loyal. How do you exercise your independence? How do you defect from God's grace, aside from being a constant hazard to yourself?"

"Are you saying I'm a great man?" the hick asks.

"You're a great talent. The man part is TBD."

"I want to be great. I want to execute the full potential of everything God has gifted me. The Order will help. You can train me. Please, put a cross on this tunic."

"The Vice-God has granted me permission to knight you and lift your capital ban."

The news comes like a double ear slap, my head ringing with the joy of returning to Lena. I can barely hear myself asking the grandmaster when.

"Before dubbing you, I need to know something," he says.

"I'm done hazarding myself. I'm done causing trouble. I'm done murdering pimps."

"I don't care about that. The Order is a fraternity of firebrands and cutthroats. We're not those dildo knights from the Supreme Order of Christ. We don't curtsy and jive. We're real knights. We kill. Then we steal from those we've killed. Then we enslave the families of those we've killed."

Caravaggio and I are morally opposed to slavery, but the hick wants to be dubbed.

"I can kill. I can kill better than any brother in this Order. It took three of them to knock me down, and I was seconds from getting to my feet before Fra Malaspina intervened."

"Your marchioness says you could disarm her best guards at the age of fifteen. She wasn't exaggerating. I've seen you in the armory. You would have skinned me in my heyday."

"Then dub me. What is your hesitation?"

"The same little birdy who told me about the pizza also told me that you suck cock. The little birdy told me that you take it in the ass. I need to know that you're over all that. I need to know that you've put the assfuckery behind you."

"I have."

"The Vice-God has no love for you. He thinks your pictures are vulgar. He also loathes your assfuckery. I'm putting my reputation on the line. I'm cashing in on favors owed. I need to hear you say it. I need to hear you say, *I've put the assfuckery behind me.*"

Caravaggio and the hick try biting my tongue, but I utter it from the depths of our throat.

"I've put the assfuckery behind me."

The grandmaster probes me with a Doubting Thomas gaze.

"I need you to stand up and say it. I need you to stand up, place your right hand over your heart, and say, *I've put all the assfuckery behind me.*"

I take a slow bite of pizza. When finished chewing, I dab the corners of my mouth with the linen. I go to stand up, but Caravaggio pushes me down. Michelangelo and I each occupy a leg and force our way through the genius to our feet. We place our hand over our heart, repeat the pledge, and return our crying ass to the decadently padded chair. I fold the final slice of anchovy in half and bite.

"*Assfuckery behind me*, that's quite the double entendre," says the grandmaster.

Alas, Michelangelo laughs at the candied pretension of the Frenchman's accent. The grandmaster, the hick, and yours truly, we all laugh at my acquittal and the loosey-goosey morality that allowed it.

"Prince Francois of Lorraine is coming in two months. He's an ardent admirer of yours. I wrote to him about my portrait. He wants to commission a picture."

"Then you will dub me?"

"Start Fra Sforza's decollated John. I'll dub you when it's finished."

"*Whose* decollated John?" Caravaggio asks.

"Your brother is paying for it. Not the Order. It will belong to the Sforza-Colonna family."

"My pictures are my world. Everyone else just lives in them."

"Your marchioness has resurrected you ten times over. You owe her family a picture. Humility and obligation. Those are a knight's most shining attributes. You think too highly of yourself. You self-destroy, but you don't self-deprecate. There is an ocean between the two.

The Order will teach you to sail that breadth. Your brothers will shame the lesson into you."

The grandmaster coughs up a chuckle. When he says *shame the lesson into you*, he's referring to Michelangelo and Caravaggio, but it only speaks to yours truly. His chuckling grows wicked. He's on Caravaggio's team, but Michelangelo and I are personae non grata. He wants us shipped off on the next boat to hell.

His page approaches our table from across the courtyard, bearing some favorable message in his glossy eyes. Smiling straight out of my portrait, he has one eye on his master and the other on his creator. He was born from so much stupid money that he'll believe in just about any noble injustice. I'd show him otherwise, but Knights Hospitaller in the Order of St. John of Jerusalem don't fuck each other's pages. That's unwritten rule number one.

XLIII.

I'm in the oratory about to kill my new John. The Caravaggio haters
have congregated on one side of the long, narrow hall—Fra Diavolo,
Fra Valette, Fra Someone, and every other highborn elitist in the Order.
They're hissing about the hick's indecorous bloodline, trying to cut the
towering silence of my mega picture at the knees. My collectors,
fanboys, and brothers are camped on the other side of the oratory.
Many are the bastards and second-born hellions of royal houses. The
grandmaster and Fra Malaspina sit with the Prince of Lorraine, one of
the most aristocratic Knight Hospitallers. They're eating pizza,
washing the doughy crust down with vintage claret. Lorraines, Gonzagas, Medicis, Carafas, and Colonnas. There's a brother Del Monte
nephew and brother Borromeo nephew too. The fuckup nephews and
sons of my favorite noblemen, dubbed and scrubbed by the grandmaster's authority. Caravaggio's coalition of black sheep. Brother Superior
stands tallest, his heel iron jackboots adding surplus inches. He's just
back from a conquest, returning with seventy-five Turkish slaves and
enough coin to overpay for this John picture. I'll use the money for
down payment on a galley. The grandmaster has ordered the cross for
my neck, but I'm still waiting on official authorization from Papa
Bureaucratic Beady Eyes. Grandmaster Wignacourt says it looks
promising. My cross is currently being melted by the Order's goldsmith. Michelangelo has a theory. He thinks that our capital ban has

already been lifted. He thinks that his cross is contingent on us completing our John. With that in mind, he's muscled his way into the process, hurrying Caravaggio's hand down the triceps of John's executioner, impelling the muscles with a pressing streak of evening gold.

"The hick can't be dubbed. He's got no pedigree," Valette says.

"Caravaggio is a progeny of God. Look at that picture and tell me otherwise!" Malaspina chomps back.

Have I been here before? You're damn right I've been here before. Painting for my life in front of an ambivalent audience. We have but one solution. Get to it. Michelangelo kills our John. His executioner has struck an amateur death blow, the head still attached to the neck. The executioner drops his sword and bends over the Baptist, pulling his hair, situating the throat, fixing to cut through ligaments, tendons, and bone, a knife readied behind his back. Michelangelo paints John's face a ghoulish-blue. He paints two scarlet strings splurting from the unfinished slit. The dusky glint of the executioner's arms and back mismatches the warden's silky Turkish duds. He's supervising the task, pointing a menial finger toward the gold platter held by Salome. There's a hoary maid standing next to her. She blocks her ears, anticipating the nauseating rends and cracks of decapitation. Hers is the same pose Lena struck before passing out during the decollation of Beatrice Cenci. Caravaggio thought of that, not yours truly. Two prisoners watch the cruel banality from a barred window, waiting for the money moment. But there's nothing redeeming here. No one will be saved. The picture lacks a hero. The picture lacks a martyr. It is void of angels. Not the scantest halo above any of these wretched heads. The male models are brothers with crewcuts in the vein of Wignacourt. Salome and her maid are the grandmaster's laundresses. They modeled for weeks but are now spectating among my fanboys. They forget to breathe as the blood of their immortal selves hardens on canvas.

I walk away from the picture backwards, gaining perspective, rubbing the side of my neck. Caravaggio has outdone himself again. He's bettered the former perfection of *Mary Dead*. *John Killed* is our ultimate blockbuster. It's Michelangelo's new favorite. He's never had a larger hand in the process. Pining for his Maltese cross, he quickened and economized Caravaggio's brushstrokes. I dare say that Caravaggio learned something from him. I can't imagine painting a better picture. Another masterpiece, and my head might burst from our skull. I contemplate its thirty thousand square inches and deduce this—I have nothing left for Caravaggio. He's officially outgrown me. He's learned to make pictures without my dreary axiological guidance. He's learned to paint without our ghosts. I've become the ghost, the Holy Ghost of this artistic synthesis, and like the Church's Holy Ghost, I can't even provide a decent explanation or definition of what the fuck I actually am. What have I done? What are my greatest accomplishments or contributions? I can't cite a specific one, but I know this, yours truly had nothing to do with *John Killed*. If so, the Baptist's head would have mercifully rolled on the first blow. Caravaggio tortured John. He did to John what he did to Mary. He stripped him of sanctity. He painted Mary into a swollen corpse. He painted John as a carcass. Our favorite subject and this is how Caravaggio retires him? Beheaded, not decollated. My four Johns glow eternal with love. The big dick energy of Cecco's John will burn for millennia. Even Lena's johns enjoyed more stamina than this life-sized stiff.

Michelangelo walks us back to the picture. Caravaggio globs his brush with red ochre and extends the scarlet bloodstreams into an asymmetrical pool under the cadaver's nose. I don't have to watch this. I close my eyes to commune with my other Johns. Cecco voices something from 1602, but I can't hear him over the oohs, ahhs, and sniffles underscoring the wowed silence swamping my side of the hall. The pages respond to John's butchering with choked panic and trembling chins. They've only heard the stories of Mustafa decollating brothers during the Great Siege. My picture is a graphic allusion to those murders, pictorializing an inglorious, poorly executed execution of the Order's namesake. I want the pages to know. I want these squiring Isaacs to see what they've signed up for: a potential beheading at the hands of infidels. In a few years, they'll be dubbed in the oratory before my botched John. Over the course of centuries, every page in the Order will be dubbed before him. Diavolo's page (his name is Juan Angel) thanks me in advance, his face stealthily moored abaft his master's shoulder, the admiration unblinking.

The servants delivering pizzas and pouring wine stall in dereliction of their duties. It is not a revolt. They're not being defiant. They've never seen a war picture like this. They've only seen histrionic maritime battles. They've only seen the cartoony frescoes of infantrymen modeled in silly death throes. These wretches who slaughter the Order's hogs and sheep, they know God when they see Him.

My divinity stuns my haters into silence. It brings palsy to the legs

...lemen. I've partied with
...sert coins into the orifices
...ats in my asshole right now,

...Diavolo's arm-drag attempt,
...at brothers. They scream and
...e charges Malaspina, ramming a
...na absorbs the force, hooking an
...y unhook and unlock limbs in an
...aspina is the better technician. He
...ength by tying it up with his superior
...ter-hug. They slap each other's wrists.
...o one gets the upper hand. No one sets a
...er in counteracting inches. It's boring to
...cheer the stalemate, but countering Diavo-
...es Malaspina. He sluggishly mishandles an
...self torqued to the floor. It's an honorable fall.
...my greatness.
...so sees it that way. He uses the defeat as an oppor-
... Among the cheers and whistles, he removes a
...from his pocket and stretches it around my neck,
...aspina steps behind me to clasp it.

...one for all our brothers," the prince replies. "Our
...our prince," he says.
...a knight of supernatural merit. I'd be honored to sponsor
...g."

...enius is worth losing a fight over," says a winded Malaspina.
...langelo bows to all of them. He genuflects like a mother-
...Brother Superior, to the firstborn son of a mason. He and
...a have saved the hick from himself. One thousand ducats to kill
...n. It took them my whole life to buy a picture, but they've made
...ait worth it.

..."Should we go into the city and celebrate?" Michelangelo asks.
...The prince looks to the grandmaster. The grandmaster looks to my
...ead John. He then looks to Fra dell'Antella and nods. He holds his
...heart and breaks the news.

..."You've behaved exceptionally since arriving, but it's wise to keep
...you from the taverns for a few more months. The Vice-God suggested
...it when granting your pardon. We don't want you falling into old

gut any...
seasoned killers,... They...
military careers. They...
from the nullity I've painted wi...
the retreat. He turns his back to their d...
aging his frat brothers into some bathhouse ban...
new batch of slaves. Their brazen apathy and artlessness ga...
He crosses the hall to accost them with his veteran length and sta...
militancy.

"I told you. I told you in General Sforza's galley on the way from
Napoli. I told you to wait and see. So, turn around and see it. See our
Caravaggio. He is a phenom."

Diavolo doesn't turn around to respond. "The son of a mason, and
what did he paint? The extrados of an archway. The jambs and sills of a
window."

"He painted our courtyard as background. He's immortalized this
palace. He's glorified the Order. Go stand before it and see." Malaspina
points to my sixth, maybe eighth masterpiece.

"The martyrs buried below this very floor glorified the Order, and I
think they might have a different interpretation of this image of our
John being unceremoniously killed by Turks. No offense to General
Sforza, but the picture he's purchased for the Order doesn't appeal to
me. I prefer the work of Carracci."

"No offense taken. Everyone has their tastes," Brother Superior
answers.

Fra Malaspina blocks his ears, unconsciously modeling my hoary
maid.

"Don't compare our Caravaggio with Carracci. Ours is a stand-
alone artist. Da Vinci. The Divine One. Our brother Caravaggio.
Italy's new trinity. They are peerless."

Diavolo turns around. Juan Angel steps aside, unlocking our corresponding poker gaze. Diavolo pays my picture sarcastic consideration,
wrist clasped behind his back like a pretentious academic. Halfway
across the canvas, his ego gets snagged on my genius, his face curdling
with indignity. This firstborn son of a mason has it all over him, the
second-born son of a count. Diavolo hates me for it. He looks as I
might have looked had I ever walked in on Ranuccio making Lena
fade.

"Now you see," Malaspina rasps, pleasure welling from the back of his throat.

He grins over Diavolo as he grinned over the Tomassoni that day in Navona from atop his charger. Is Diavolo my newest Tomassoni brother? I should kill him now for the Carracci comment, nip our rivalry in the bud. Michelangelo is thinking the same thing. The Prince of Lorraine and the grandmaster approach before I can bury the tip of my brush into Diavolo's eye. I can't picture the brother prince killing a bumble bee. He's too pretty and lithe. He starts on me about a picture. He wants an annunciated Virgin. The grandmaster says something about his page posing as Gabriel.

"I have a model in mind for the Virgin," Caravaggio replies.

The prince kisses Caravaggio's ass. The grandmaster and his secretary of Italian affairs, Fra Francesco dell'Antella, join the chorus. They pitch more picture ideas to Caravaggio, all of them Johns.

"How about a sleeping Cupid?" I ask, staring across the hall, into the dark brown curls cresting across Juan Angel's head.

"The Vice-God has approved your knighthood," Fra dell'Antella says. "The official document arrived this morning."

Caravaggio and Michelangelo are free. After two years of foreboding exile, they've been rewarded. Michelangelo's violence has been ratified. Caravaggio's prodigy preserved and bankrolled by the roughest, richest Christian capitalist mercs in the Mediterranean. The worst two years of my life have resulted in Michelangelo and Caravaggio self-improving. They're better than ever. Their diaspora pays dividends. It cost me Cecco and Lena. What do I have? Nothing. Where am I? Hundreds of miles from Rome. What's left of me? Divinations of Cecco and Lena. Caravaggio now thinks he can conjure them without me. In his dreams. I'm the one who generates that light. I'm his camera obscura. I'm the Galileo of ghosts.

Michelangelo and Caravaggio gloat while the grandmaster and his inner circle stroke us.

"The world's greatest genius is one of us now," Wignacourt says.

"I was in England for that three-year family envoy. They have a playwright there. That Shakespeare. His genius is also immense, but I prefer pictures to words," dell'Antella says.

"Apples and pomegranates," Malaspina says.

"Our genius describes more in a picture than Shakespeare does in the lookalike fuckups of rich and famous noblemen. I've partied with some of their patriarchs. I've watched them insert coins into the orifices of pros. I feel like there's one thousand ducats in my asshole right now, but Caravaggio doesn't feel a thing.

Malaspina unravels and reverses Diavolo's arm-drag attempt, slinging him into the front row of frat brothers. They scream and boost Diavolo back into the circle. He charges Malaspina, ramming a shoulder into his sternum. Malaspina absorbs the force, hooking an arm under Diavolo's armpit. They unhook and unlock limbs in an attempt to leverage power. Malaspina is the better technician. He neutralizes Diavolo's superior strength by tying it up with his superior length. The men hug and counter-hug. They slap each other's wrists. They nestle chin into neck. No one gets the upper hand. No one sets a hinge. They budge each other in counteracting inches. It's boring to watch. My fanboys wildly cheer the stalemate, but countering Diavolo's fleet maneuvering tires Malaspina. He sluggishly mishandles an elbow grip and finds himself torqued to the floor. It's an honorable fall. He took it on behalf of my greatness.

Prince Francois also sees it that way. He uses the defeat as an opportunity to adorn me. Among the cheers and whistles, he removes a chunky gold chain from his pocket and stretches it around my neck. Grandmaster Malaspina steps behind me to clasp it.

"A gift from our prince," he says.

"I bought one for all our brothers," the prince replies. "Our Caravaggio is a knight of supernatural merit. I'd be honored to sponsor your dubbing."

"Your genius is worth losing a fight over," says a winded Malaspina.

Michelangelo bows to all of them. He genuflects like a motherfucker to Brother Superior, to the firstborn son of a mason. He and Mamma have saved the hick from himself. One thousand ducats to kill my John. It took them my whole life to buy a picture, but they've made the wait worth it.

"Should we go into the city and celebrate?" Michelangelo asks.

The prince looks to the grandmaster. The grandmaster looks to my dead John. He then looks to Fra dell'Antella and nods. He holds his heart and breaks the news.

"You've behaved exceptionally since arriving, but it's wise to keep you from the taverns for a few more months. The Vice-God suggested it when granting your pardon. We don't want you falling into old an entire play. Besides, he's stolen all his characters and plots from Italian tales. Romeo and Juliet? Fucking please," says the prince.

I'm happy for Caravaggio, but I don't have to stand here listening to this. While they cite the plagiarisms of Shakespeare, I cruise across a flooded Navona Square, standing on the spar deck of Michelangelo's galley. Cecco and Lena lounge on a silk-cushioned sofa, the breeze of our speed caressing their hair. Bobbing topsy-turvy coaches festoon the lake like buoys. I surf over them, the resulting flotsam skimming in my slipstream. I cruise southwards across the floodwaters of Campo de' Fiore, docking my galley alongside the second-story windows of Farnese Palace. I bend for my drum and stick, banging the Christ out of it until Farnese soldiers and mercs come climbing through the windows. They're sitting ducks. I hack their necks as they twist their shoulders through jambs and over the sills. Cecco joins the fun, burying his Cupid arrows into their chests point-blank. I pace the spar deck, bludgeoning heads like garden marmots peeking from their hole. The slapstick gore of it all breaks Lena's smile. Violence no longer sickens her. I swing away until there's no one left to protect Ranuccio Farnese, Duke of Parma Ham, and when he pokes his head from a window, begging for mercy, bribing for his life, I pull him onto the deck by his hair, placing him on his knees. Cecco nails him in place, two arrows in the backs of his calves. Lena rises. I hand her my sword. She decapitates the witch-fucking, Carracci-loving philanderer with a thousand tiny whacks.

Malaspina's battle cry returns me to Malta. He's got his cassock off, standing in his undies, pressing his aging chest into Diavolo's face. Diavolo shoves him off and strips down to his undies. The frat brothers break into a chant of *fight* and semi-circle around them. My noble fanboys complete the circle. They're quietly worried about the contest Malaspina has picked. My Jerome's wrestling days are behind him. He's now a man of the quill. His lean, mean musculature is loosening at the joints. He looks superannuated poised against Diavolo's brawny luster. I scan the expressions of Lorraine, Gonzaga, Medici, and Carafa. They're already watching him lose. Teethy conceding smiles all around. It's like they can't even see Diavolo's ridiculous nipples. Those nipples will never prevail in a contested battle.

"Five ducats on Fra Malaspina," Brother Superior calls out.

My brother sees the odds on those nipples. His wager initiates a melody of counter bets. I watch them throw their old money around, of those knights who've yet to slay a formidable enemy, who've yet to gut anything more than a poorly armed Turkish peasant. Even for the seasoned killers, my ghoulish John presents the biggest evil of their military careers. They don't have the stones to confront it. They flee from the nullity I've painted with oceanic cowardice, Diavolo leading the retreat. He turns his back to their debauched namesake, encouraging his frat brothers into some bathhouse banter about fucking the new batch of slaves. Their brazen apathy and artlessness gall Malaspina. He crosses the hall to accost them with his veteran length and staid militancy.

"I told you. I told you in General Sforza's galley on the way from Napoli. I told you to wait and see. So, turn around and see it. See our Caravaggio. He is a phenom."

Diavolo doesn't turn around to respond. "The son of a mason, and what did he paint? The extrados of an archway. The jambs and sills of a window."

"He painted our courtyard as background. He's immortalized this palace. He's glorified the Order. Go stand before it and see." Malaspina points to my sixth, maybe eighth masterpiece.

"The martyrs buried below this very floor glorified the Order, and I think they might have a different interpretation of this image of our John being unceremoniously killed by Turks. No offense to General Sforza, but the picture he's purchased for the Order doesn't appeal to me. I prefer the work of Carracci."

"No offense taken. Everyone has their tastes," Brother Superior answers.

Fra Malaspina blocks his ears, unconsciously modeling my hoary maid.

"Don't compare our Caravaggio with Carracci. Ours is a stand-alone artist. Da Vinci. The Divine One. Our brother Caravaggio. Italy's new trinity. They are peerless."

Diavolo turns around. Juan Angel steps aside, unlocking our corresponding poker gaze. Diavolo pays my picture sarcastic consideration, wrist clasped behind his back like a pretentious academic. Halfway across the canvas, his ego gets snagged on my genius, his face curdling with indignity. This firstborn son of a mason has it all over him, the second-born son of a count. Diavolo hates me for it. He looks as I might have looked had I ever walked in on Ranuccio making Lena fade.

"Now you see," Malaspina rasps, pleasure welling from the back of his throat.

He grins over Diavolo as he grinned over the Tomassoni that day in Navona from atop his charger. Is Diavolo my newest Tomassoni brother? I should kill him now for the Carracci comment, nip our rivalry in the bud. Michelangelo is thinking the same thing. The Prince of Lorraine and the grandmaster approach before I can bury the tip of my brush into Diavolo's eye. I can't picture the brother prince killing a bumble bee. He's too pretty and lithe. He starts on me about a picture. He wants an annunciated Virgin. The grandmaster says something about his page posing as Gabriel.

"I have a model in mind for the Virgin," Caravaggio replies.

The prince kisses Caravaggio's ass. The grandmaster and his secretary of Italian affairs, Fra Francesco dell'Antella, join the chorus. They pitch more picture ideas to Caravaggio, all of them Johns.

"How about a sleeping Cupid?" I ask, staring across the hall, into the dark brown curls cresting across Juan Angel's head.

"The Vice-God has approved your knighthood," Fra dell'Antella says. "The official document arrived this morning."

Caravaggio and Michelangelo are free. After two years of foreboding exile, they've been rewarded. Michelangelo's violence has been ratified. Caravaggio's prodigy preserved and bankrolled by the roughest, richest Christian capitalist mercs in the Mediterranean. The worst two years of my life have resulted in Michelangelo and Caravaggio self-improving. They're better than ever. Their diaspora pays dividends. It cost me Cecco and Lena. What do I have? Nothing. Where am I? Hundreds of miles from Rome. What's left of me? Divinations of Cecco and Lena. Caravaggio now thinks he can conjure them without me. In his dreams. I'm the one who generates that light. I'm his camera obscura. I'm the Galileo of ghosts.

Michelangelo and Caravaggio gloat while the grandmaster and his inner circle stroke us.

"The world's greatest genius is one of us now," Wignacourt says.

"I was in England for that three-year family envoy. They have a playwright there. That Shakespeare. His genius is also immense, but I prefer pictures to words," dell'Antella says.

"Apples and pomegranates," Malaspina says.

"Our genius describes more in a picture than Shakespeare does in habits. You've been dedicated to your art. We don't want to disrupt your genius."

Brother Superior whistles to Fra Carafa, cousin to Baron Luigi. Fra Carafa leaves the hall but returns within seconds leading two middle-aged Turkish slaves. They're chained at the neck. He hands the leash to Brother Superior who hands the leash to me. I don't take it.

"They're yours. A gift for being pardoned and dubbed," he says.

Fra Michelangelo Merisi da Caravaggio. Artistic prisoner to the Knights Hospitaller in the Order of St. John of Jerusalem. We're free from Farnese mercs. We're free from yahoo bounty hunters. We're free from Papa Beady Eyes. We're free to stay on Malta forever, painting portraits of admirals, painting pictures of how many more fucking Johns? No more Johns. That's what I say, but Michelangelo and Caravaggio are still not hearing me. They walk past the two slaves to their John. I look beyond the courtyard wall. I look eastward toward Rome. I can see the skyline. The cranes are gone. All the city construction is complete. Rome is perfect. God agrees. I see His eye watching over Cecco and Lena.

Michelangelo asks Caravaggio if he can sign their dead John. We've never signed a picture. What name would we record? Michele? Michelangelo? Caravaggio? Ecce Homo? Yours Truly? Before Caravaggio can answer, Michelangelo gobs the brush in red ochre and signs his own abbreviation from the blood of John the Baptist's neck.

f Michel A.

Fra Michelangelo. Caravaggio isn't happy about it, but what can he do? He's the death of us, but genius never dies. This life of ours. Michelangelo perpetually killing us. Caravaggio resurrecting us ad infinitum. I wouldn't live that way if you paid me. From here on out, I'll pursue my own ends. Time for this ghost to ghost himself.

XLIV.

I've named my slaves Ippolito and Camillo, the Christian names of Papa Gout and Papa Beady Eyes. I'm teaching them to read, so they can eventually read me to sleep. We're in my quarters sounding the alphabet. Their halitosis stinks up the room, almost overpowering my ass. I gave Ippolito and Camillo my perfumes and soaps. My bedroom, palatial as it is, only has enough air for one rank butt. I've been skipping on the hygiene. Fra Michel A aims to please no one, particularly the grandmaster, who has relegated this knight to the palace. Brother Superior leaves for another crusade tomorrow, and the grandmaster has decommissioned Fra Michel A. The grandmaster wants us nowhere but inside the armory, finishing the prince's *Annunciation*. Fra Michel A wants to be anywhere but. Now that he's a free man, he wants to pirate the Mediterranean. If he can't buccaneer, he'd like to get booted and suited. He'd like to carouse downtown Valetta and be saluted by islanders and local pros. Aside from the cross clamped to the gold chain around our neck, aside from the white cross on the front of our black linen cassock, Fra Michel A has enjoyed NONE of the perks ensured by knighthood. Grandmaster Wignacourt and Fra Malaspina have been loud and clear about Fra Michel A mooring his ass in the palace so Caravaggio can glorify the Order. Fra Michel A's disgruntlement is my only way off this purgatorial rock.

His disgruntlement has been transubstantiating into tremendous erections, but they're not all Fra Michel A. They're also a little bit me. I've been feeling oversexed since watching Fra Malaspina and Diavolo tangle in their undies. Fra Michel A and I haven't swung the same sword since Mario. These boners are chronic. I'm packing one right now, a mahogany bowsprit jutting from the crotch of my cassock. Ippolito and Camillo don't care to notice. They're earnest students, rounding their mouths, annunciating hilariously discordant o's. I laugh at them. I laugh with them. I feel their subjection. I'm no master myself.

In terms of fucking, my slaves are out of the question. Fucking one's slaves is very much encouraged and highly authorized in the Order's rule book, but mine are ugly and pushing forty years of age. More so, they're not my type, oppressed. After five or six rocky rides through the alphabet, I invite Ippolito and Camillo to sit on the floor while I read some Bruno from my bed.

When the <u>end</u> *comes, you will be esteemed by the* <u>world</u> *and rewarded by* <u>God</u>, *not because you have won the* <u>love</u> *and* <u>respect</u> *of the earth's princes, however powerful, but rather for having loved, defended and cherished one such as I... What you receive from others is a testimony to their* <u>virtue</u>; *but all that you do for others is the* <u>sign</u> *and clear indication of your own.*

Camillo doesn't understand any more of it than Ippolito, but he nods along like a courteous listener. The clacking of Brother Superior's jackboots and his appearance in my doorway conclude our lesson on Bruno. I dismiss my students. Recognizing their captor, they're eager to leave. Ippolito bows and scutters off first. Camillo bows to me, collects my pot, and bows to Brother Superior on his way out.

"Reading your slaves blasphemy. Only you, brother," says Brother Superior.

"I want to make them intellectually useful. They're too small to row in my galley," I reply.

"Not that I have a galley. The grandmaster refuses to place my order at the shipyard," Fra Michel A asides.

Brother Superior laughs away the complaint. He's perma-grinning with wild in his eyes, a rhapsodic resin over the pupils: that keen look killers get beforehand. He didn't get it from the Merisi. We murder on principle, never for money or sport. It must be a Colonna thing. They're descendants of Aeneas, the vainglorious warmonger shielded by the gods in battle, cousin to Hector, and forefather of Romulus and Remus. Lots of men would love hitching their sperm to that lineage. Fermo struck the mother lode. He couldn't have asked for a better son.

I stand to greet him. Luckily, my erection has atrophied. We shake and bump chests.

"Take me with you," Fra Michel A begs.

"My uncle has died. You're down to Cardinals Del Monte, Barberini, and Borromeo. The rest hate you more than ever. Your pardon vexed them. They can't have your head anymore, so they'll try to kill your art. You'll never get another altar north of Napoli."

"And the cardinal-nephew? He's got an inflexible boner for me," Caravaggio says.

"The Vice-God has appointed him prefect of the Sacred Congregation. He has to play politics. Hard to oversee the application of disciplinary decrees of the Council of Trent when you're commissioning a murderer to paint altarpieces. He still wants your pictures, but he wants them for himself. Your pictures will be locked behind the walls of Borghese Palace. The wretched should also observe your genius. Down here in the Mezzogiorno, the churches are all yours."

Caravaggio agrees wholeheartedly. Fra Michel A only hears the hull of his unbuilt galley frothing across flat waters.

"Take me to Byzantium. We rehearsed our crusades as boys," he says.

"How does it feel to be a free man? I remember when the grandmaster had my murder sentence lifted. I felt like Lazarus punching through the walls of his tomb."

"What kind of Knight Hospitaller sits around mixing colors all day?" I ask.

"Knights of merit, not birth."

In the process of slapping my face and kicking my nuts, my brother has put his foot in his mouth. This half-Merisi is only half an aristocrat, only half the knight he thinks. I can't blame him. I can't take his insult personally. He carried me from the chopping block to Malta. When I get off this island, I'll carry him all the way to infinity. He ain't heavy; he's my brother.

"Father, forgive him. He doesn't know what he's talking about," I say.

He tames his wild eyes over me. I mean something to this psycho. I mean more to him than Caravaggio or the hick.

"Mamma wrote me. She thinks you're going to blow this." Brother Superior walks to my bed and looks down at the Bruno book.

"Take me with you," Fra Michel A says.

"I'll be the next Catholic superhero," I say.

"I can't lie to you, brother. It'll be a few years before they let you off the island. It's part of your parole. I stacked books in the library for three years before the grandmaster designated me to a fleet. At least you'll be serving your genius. The grandmaster will get you commissions in every major church. He'll get you in every palace gallery."

"South of Rome," I say.

"Most of the brothers hate me. I won't last three years. Fra de Varayz provokes me. I'm going to fuck him up one of these days."

"He doesn't hate you. He's afraid of you. A few of the brothers resent you living in the palace. You should move into the dorms with them. Let them see your humor. Let them see your sportive side. They'll love you."

"I don't want their love. I want their hate," I say.

"That's your Lombard talking," Brother Superior replies.

"No. *This* is the hick talking."

"How's my weeping Magdalene?" Caravaggio asks.

"My cousin is hosting gallery viewings, sharing her with everyone. She's the heartbreaker of Napoli."

"My aunt was your wet nurse," Fra Michel A says.

"There's some Merisi in these muscles." Brother Superior flexes his biceps.

I squeeze it. It feels very Merisi. Fra Michel A wants to spill the secret. He's always envied our brother's entitlements. Fra Michel A is the better swordsman. He'd be the better Knight Hospitaller if they let him. He would be a better Colonna than this bastard. He wants to let Brother Superior know it, but that's not our way off the island. More so, I could never do that to Mamma's son. Fra Michel A isn't remembering her maternity. He's thinking of himself. He summons the truth to our tongue. Caravaggio is too drunk to cork it, leaving it up to me. I kiss Brother Superior's cheek with the bratty slobbering of an instigative brother.

"Bon voyage. Bring me back a souvenir," I say.

"Don't disappoint Mamma. I know you're tired of hearing it, but she's dispensed a lot of political stock on you. We all have. Don't make us look bad. Keep that boner in your cassock. And take a shower. It smells foul in here. Are you trying to grow another Plague? Are you trying to catch the Plague?"

I forgive his insensitivity. It's easy to joke about the pandemic that killed our father when you're thinking like a Colonna, when you have a fleet of decorated warships at the docks awaiting your every desire.

I lie on the floor of my room reading Bruno until my boner returns. When it's good and ready, I walk it down the hall to the grandmaster's quarters. He's dressed in his designer armor, holding his scepter like an axe, reenacting my portrait with his page, who's holding the plumed helmet with a little more sensuality than I painted.

I genuflect. The grandmaster nods. The page turns away from the general's tent in my cassock. Fra Michel A kneels at the grandmaster's feet, a single tear of frustration streaming down our cheek.

"Please, sir, for the love of almighty God, please deploy me. Let me sail to Byzantium with General Sforza."

"I have deployed you. I've deployed your liberty. I've deployed your genius. I've also militarized it. Not even the Viceroy of Napoli can fortify your stardom with the amount of commissions and recognition I'll provide."

"I'm happy to be a knight instead of a fugitive, but freedom is over-rated for the artist. My genius needs stimulation. It needs sex and violence. It needs wretched company."

"I can understand that. When you finish Fra dell'Antella's Cupid, I'll let you venture into the city."

Caravaggio stands. "Fra dell'Antella's Cupid?"

"Yes. He was instrumental in orchestrating your pardon."

"I'll paint him a fucking Cupid."

"Paint him however you like. Paint him in the raw like you painted your first Cupid."

"That Cupid is *my* Cupid. Nobody gets anything close to that Cupid. Where's my grandmaster?" Caravaggio points my boner to the empty space on the wall where his portrait initially hung.

"I'm having it mounted in the armory. It feels most potent there. I want you to paint me another portrait, like the one you did for Fra Malaspina. I want to be dressed in my habit, sitting at my desk, deep in thought. I'll hang it in place of my other portrait."

"*My* other portrait."

"I'll paint you and Fra dell'Antella a harem of Cupids when I return from Byzantium," says Fra Michel A.

"You're a court artist now. Everything you paint is for the Order. Get that through your thick Lombard skull."

"Your pizza sucks, sir."

"I know you don't mean that." The grandmaster motions a cross above my head with his scepter.

My boner dies. I look to the page. He's hiding his amusement behind the red and white helmet plumes.

"Your John blockbuster has been haunting my sleep. I've been dreaming of it. Flashbacks of Lepanto and the Great Siege. I've decapitated infidels. I've gutted them. I've driven blades of all sizes through every angle of their unhallowed anatomy. But that picture of yours unnerves me in the best possible way. You are the future of this Order. You're our superstar."

"How would Fra dell'Antella like this Cupid?" Caravaggio asks, eating the grandmaster's flattery.

"A sleeping Cupid was his only specification. Something to remind our chaste brother of his vow. I've also been corresponding with the cardinal-nephew. My approbation alone wasn't enough to sway the Vice-God. His holy nephew sealed the deal. I told the cardinal-nephew about the blockbuster. He wants a young John in the Wild."

"I can't paint another John, Juan, or Jean. All johns are dead. I killed them," I say, trying to defuse Caravaggio's exaltation.

"You're a miracle worker. You can bring him back," the page says.

"He's right," replies his master.

"I'll paint the cardinal-nephew a John after I'm done with my new Cupid," Caravaggio says against every fiber of my being.

"And after I have a night in Valetta," adds Fra Michel A.

The grandmaster nods in concession. "Deal. Shall we celebrate on the patio?"

Fra Michel A happily yokes himself to the grandmaster's short leash so he can be walked out of the room. I'm not surprised. His fighting spirit has always come with daddy issues. However, I am surprised to see Caravaggio go shackle-stepping after them. I've underestimated his longing for Del Monte and the cardinal-nephew's idolization. The grandmaster and Fra Malaspina have filled that void. Caravaggio's daddy complex is all tied up with God. I'm done serving them. I won't be marched into the same old unfulfilling and self-destructive habits. If we're going to loop into the same vicious cycle, let's cut the circumference and get to the origin. One of us needs to man up. Our three-legged race toward immortality needs an amputation or we'll rot here on Malta, painting how many Johns and military portraits. That will never get us back to Lena. Halfway to Cecco at the most. Brother Superior expects me to wait three years, but that's three lifetimes in genius age. Another minute in this head, and I'll lose it.

The page follows after Caravaggio, leaving me in the grandmaster's chamber alone. No one notices that I've stayed behind. My emancipation is complete. The defection has begun. My dis-being of being their martyr. I will erect my own ass backward crucifixion.

XLV.

Bent over, I take Grandmaster Valette's bronze hand, steadying myself as Juan Angel has at me from the rear. I remain respectively silent, but his hoarse pleasure is doubling throughout the crypt. His hips are herky-jerky. Fra Michele A's cross bounces off my forehead. It's not good. Juan Angel won't stop talking. He's nervous. Who wouldn't be? He's losing his virginity to the imploding superstar.

Maybe I hear footsteps. Maybe I hear the soft pit-pat of barefoot souls on stone. Probably Ippolito and Camillo. I sent them for some post-coitus Tears of Christ.

"How did you know?" Juan Angel asks.

"Know what?"

"You know."

"I know?"

"You're going to make me say it?"

"The crypt has lovely acoustics."

"Why me?"

"This isn't about you."

"I see."

"Shh."

"Why?"

"Someone is coming, and it ain't me."

My enemy brothers bum-rush our coitus. They're barefoot but fully suited. Diavolo leads the charge with his sword. Fra Valette points a cocked wheellock at my bowed head. Juan Angel unplugs himself from yours truly. I remain bent, clutching the grandmaster's enshrined hand.

"Take your hand off my uncle and step away from the page," Valette says.

"I knew it," Diavolo says.

"Knew what?" I ask.

"That you'd fuck yourself."

"Fuck myself while your page fucks me?"

Fra Valette backhands my mouth with the wheellock. I drop to my hands and knees to spit out the blood. Caravaggio takes a moment to admire their bare feet. Some hairy digits and gnarly bunions. Fra Michele A finally demands that we stand.

Fra Valette tears the cross from my neck.

"Thank you. That was wearing heavy on me," I say.

Diavolo finally speaks. "Take off the cassock. You've sullied it beyond disinfection. The grandmaster will have it burned. He'll annul your knighthood and have you executed for breaking unwritten rule number one."

Juan Angel steps out from behind me. Diavolo hocks a loogie and launches it at his face. He misses badly, tagging Fra Valette's uncle instead. I pull my cassock up over my head and wipe the phlegm from Grandmaster Valette's feet with it, like Jesus pedicuring Peter.

"Have a duel with me. You win, I die. I win, I leave Malta forever," Fra Michele A says.

Diavolo almost bites, but Fra Valette talks him out of it.

"Every brother deserves a whack at his corpse," he says.

I look around for my brothers. No Fra Carafa. No Fra Bastard Lorraine.

"Without the encouragement of General Sforza, your lord and protector, the others won't stand by you," Diavolo says.

Fra Someone walks into crypt, towing Ippolito and Camillo by a chain leash, carrying my flask of wine in his free hand.

The frat boys take my body into custody, reenacting my soldiers in *Christ Taken*. I stand apart from the action, watching over it, elevated on the balls of my feet. The lighting is poor. I take hold of a nearby torch and illuminate my abduction, paying homage to the selfie I painted as the Temple guards carry the son of God from Judas' cold lips.

———

They unshackle my wrists and drop me into the oubliette. The fall is long enough to sing a full *fuck the Order* before landing. I bite my tongue upon impact. Knees buckling, I crumble to the sandstone floor. Fra Michel A absorbs the pain. I swallow the genius' blood. I roll onto my back and stare up at the hatch, a distant square of light presiding over darkness. I see it as God's camera obscura. He fixes my image and the aperture closes. I raise a fist and flip the bird, not that anyone can see it under this total blackout. Fra Michel A starts right in on me.

"You just cost me my lifelong dream of knighthood. You fucking ass-fucker you."

"Shh. On'tday allcay emay atthay. Eythay ightmay earhay," I say.

"They just saw you taking it in the assyay," Caravaggio says.

"You've slapped the entire Colonna family in the face. Brother Superior and Mamma. They put their clout on the line for you," says Fra Michel A.

My tongue is aching and thickened by blood, but I slur my way through a response.

"You were never going to fight a single Turk. You were never going to set foot on a galley, not even your own. They were going to lock us up in that cushy chamber and have the genius make them pictures until the day we died."

"We were free enough. I had them eating from my palm," Caravaggio replies.

"Then why did you let me do it? Why did you let me let Juan Angel do me?" I ask.

"Wait. What? Let *you*, let *him*, do *you*? You're the one who does all the doing around here. You've got the final say. Always have."

"I told you," Fra Michel A says to the genius. "He thinks *he's* the oppressed one. He thinks we run the operation."

"Neither of you have acknowledged my voice in months. You've been trying to kill me since 1604. I thought it was Papa. Then, I thought it was God, but it's been you the whole time."

"Us? Kill you? We hardly exist. We're barely real. We're mostly mental. It's all you. You're the one who's been trying to kill us," Caravaggio says.

"It's all me? I have zero agency. I'm here trying to feed your talent and placate his anger. I've run myself ragged serving both of you. If it wasn't for me, you two would have nullified each other years ago. And how do you respond? By trying to nullify me. You've been ghosting yours truly since Napoli."

"I told you he has a Holy Ghost complex," Fra Michel A says to Caravaggio. "He thinks that you're God, and that he's the Holy Spirit."

"That's precisely what I think."

"You have it backwards," says the genius. "I'm the Holy Spirit and you're the Holy Father. I'm your creative spirit. I paint you, fool. I always have. I don't paint virgins or pros. I don't paint cocksuckers or saints. Every character I paint is you. You're my point of reference."

The genius expects me to believe that. I sit up and rub my aching knees.

"So, let me get this straight. I'm God. You're the Holy Ghost. So that makes the hick Christ?"

"The anti-Christ," he replies.

"You're trying to mind-fuck me. Trying to get me to take the blame for what just happened. For what happened with Cecco. For what happened with Mario. You want me to assume responsibility. I'm your slave. I'm your wretched laborer. But no more! I'm fighting my way out of here. I'm going to win!"

"Win what?" Fra Michel A asks.

"Emancipation."

"Win it from who?" Caravaggio asks.

"The Holy Ghost and Jesus. *The end of all flesh is come before me.*"

"Jesus Christ. Now he's quoting Almighty God," says the Holy Ghost.

"Fucking Jesus," says the anti-Christ.

God's aperture opens. A light from above stamps my back, casting a hunchbacked shadow against the sandstone.

"Keep talking like that, and I'll fill this hole with shit," says Diavolo.

———

I think it's been two days since Diavolo threatened me with excrement. I haven't stopped talking over Fra Michel A and Caravaggio, yet the hatch has remained closed. No food. No light. No verdict. I found a flask of spoiled wine on one of the many shelves carved into the sandstone walls. I drank most of what was left. I have a remarkable headache, but I'm far from sad. My counterparts are grieving, but I've never felt so optimistic. My tremendous erections have returned. The tenderness in my knees is gone. Between soliloquies, I do countless burpees and jumping jacks.

Tor di Nona is a dream compared to the deep darkness of the oubliette, but I'd rather two lifetimes in the oubliette than another year in Magisterial Palace, painting portraits for aging frat boys. The oubliette is a living hell, but no worse than living in this head of mine. It's better than...

"Better than being killed?" Caravaggio asks.

"The grandmaster won't let Diavolo kill you. He won't let the creator of *John Killed* be killed. He could never authorize that. He could cannon blast a Muslim orphanage no sweat. He could behead a fleet of unshielded Ottoman galley slaves without batting an eyelash, but he could never decollate the superstar who painted *Grandmaster Wignacourt and his Page.*"

"This guy is out of his fucking mind. We need to stage a mutiny," Fra Michel A whispers to Caravaggio.

"I CAN FUCKING HEAR YOU!" I down the last mouthful of aged vinegar, burning and sterilizing my tongue.

"He's a masochist," Caravaggio says to Fra Michele A. "Remember my *Christ Whipped*? Remember the gratifying countenance on the Martyr's face. That was all him."

"Oh, so first I was the Holy Father, and now I'm the Holy Son? Make up your mind."

They're speechless. They've run out of lies. I take a nap. I wake up and launch into more burpees. I sing three madrigals and quote some Bruno. I take another nap. After two more naps in the abiding darkness, I find God. I find Him down here in the dank boredom, amidst the mind-blowing monotony of living with myself. God has been hiding there in plain sight since 1604, right under Caravaggio's upturned nose. He's like nothing I've ever thought. He smells like ripe quince and talks like a queen.

"The superstar. The one that shone over Rome all winter. The one you saw in the Raphaelite sky. The one above your killed John. That wasn't me. That was an actual star. It died in 1604. A stellar explosion. It died a spectacular death, but you keep resurrecting it. Stop. It wants to stay dead. It wanted you to flame out with it in 1604. You missed your chance. You opted for Lena. Let the superstar forget you."

I fall to the floor and convulse with ecstatic shivers, His supreme love sluicing through me. I somehow manage to find my bearings and stand. I walk His euphoria off in small, frenetic circles.

"Thanks, but no thanks. At least not yet," I tell God. "I want to make myself feel that good on my own."

I pace the oubliette until dizzy and nauseous. I sit in a corner, somewhere in the far opposite corner of my center being, sobbing with hearty fervor.

"What's wrong with him?" Fra Michel A asks.

Caravaggio twitches, or maybe that was a shrug.

"I'm fucking happy. I've been waiting so long. I had nothing for so long. It's too much all at once."

The hatch opens, the first time in days. I bow my head, saving my eyes from the light. I can smell the grandmaster's displeasure from down here.

"Look at you," he says. "A pig in your own shit, soiling God's beneficence. You disgust me. You shame me. I tried curing you. I put a cross around your neck. You defiled the Order. You're not worthy of decollation. They're building your pyre in the courtyard. Your foul membership will be scorched from the Order. We'll ignite you after morning prayer. By lunch, you'll be nothing more than a charred pile of bones."

Fra Michel A and Caravaggio fall for his clichéd castigation. Their head boils with panic. I sink into them and whisper.

"Don't worry. He's just saying that for the others to hear. He won't set us on fire. He's going to somehow sneak us out of here."

"What about a last meal? A final slice of pizza?" A woeful attempt by Fra Michel A to win back the grandmaster.

"Eat your own cock. That's the only nourishment you deserve," he replies halfheartedly.

The hatch closes. I watch the captured light die against the walls. It's the first time I'm seeing them. They're graffitied with the prayers of doomed men. Someone etched an image of his funeral coach into the sandstone, swankier than Mamma's Hungarian ride. The draftsmanship exceeds that of Baglione's and the majority of my followers, especially the parabolic lines of the charger's stomach and hindquarter. I watch it ride into the brownout. God has left the oubliette. May my darkness inspirit this hole.

———

Sleep is almost impossible with Fra Michel A and Caravaggio shuddering for fear of cremation. Fra Michal A has had his mind set on a steel death. He's already suffered his thousand cuts. The final blade would feel familiar and appropriate. He could almost welcome a rapier through his heart or an axe across his neck. His nerves are still scarred from the stench of Bruno's blistering skin. Immortal Caravaggio doesn't fear the agony of fire. That sociopath feels neither physical nor emotional pain. He's agonizing over his legacy. Fuck *our* body, an uncompleted body of work would be an eternal nightmare. His despair has my bladder in a tizzy. After my sixth piss of the night, I manage to sink into a light sleep. I'm sailing across Navona with Cecco and Lena when the hatch opens. The darkness of the oubliette softens enough to see the walls, but the graffiti remains obscured. It can't be morning. There's not enough light, plus, my morning erections come like clockwork, and right now I'm limp as a noodle.

A ladder is lowered into the oubliette. Its feet land at my feet. I sit up.

"Don't even think of climbing that. Better to rot down here than burn up there," Fra Michel A says.

I stand and grab hold of the rails. I place a foot on the lowest rung. I know what this is. A whisper falls from above, confirming my suspicions.

"Hurry. We're stealing you away. Take flight."

A frenetic energy carries me halfway up the ladder before my arms noodle, the days of malnutrition catching up with yours truly. Fearing for his oeuvre, Caravaggio boosts me up the remaining rungs. I strain my head through the hatch but can't birth the rest of me. Fra Malaspina and Fra Carafa lift me by the scruff, my life quite literally in their hands. I thank God aloud for that. I also thank them. Fra

Malaspina stuffs a crust of bread into my mouth and shoves the parental loaf into my arms. Fra Carafa wraps my bare shoulders with a cloak. Fra Malaspina pulls the hood over my head, packing his precious asset for continental delivery.

I chew fast and walk slow. My brothers tow me at the elbows. We pass a dungeon corridor lined with cages. The smell is septic, but I continue eating. We approach a gate guarded by some Fra Jean who I've seen unsuccessfully sparring in the armory. He says nothing. He doesn't raise a salute. We're invisible. He doesn't look happy about it. We turn down a wider corridor that smells of extinguished torches. My escape has been premeditated by experts. The corridor widens into a lobby. Two orange flames flicker at the far end. The bread has reached my legs. They can almost walk on their own. My gait quickens. We reach a set of iron double doors guarded by two Fra Juans. They don't salute us. They don't even blink at my invisibility. One of the iron doors is ajar. Fra Carafa slides through it first. Fra Malaspina pushes me to follow. I look at one of the Fra Juans as I pass through. He closes his eyes, refusing to see himself turning a blind eye to this fugitive ass-fucker.

On the other side of the lobby is a dark antechamber that also smells of snuffed oil. Fra Malaspina guides me to a large embrasure in the wall. The two-ton cannon has been wheeled back. On the floor below the embrasure is a coiled rope. Fra Carafa holds the end as Fra Malaspina drops the coil out the window.

"Go," he says. "When you reach ground, put your back to the wall and go left. You'll reach the corner of a bastion. There's another rope tied to a balustrade. Lower yourself. There's a dock below and a boat waiting for you."

"Do you mean *ship*?" Fra Michel A asks in all seriousness.

"No. A boat. A fishing *boat*. It will take you to Siracusa. Your old boyfriend awaits."

"Tell General Sforza that I'm sorry. Tell my brother that I couldn't help myself."

"Have another bite of bread. You've got two rappels to make. One forty feet, the other sixty," he answers.

While chewing my last bite, Fra Malaspina hugs my ribs as Fra Carafa lifts my legs, feeding them through the embrasure. Fra Malaspina grabs some rope and anchors himself behind Fra Carafa. I clutch my lifeline and worm backwards out the window. Before lowering myself, I offer my brothers a final thanks.

"Don't you dream of letting go," I say.

They offer no reassuring word or gesture. They're not doing this for yours truly. They're doing it for Caravaggio.

I lower myself into the bottomless night. Halfway down to kingdom come, my arms begin trembling with fatigue. Where I might have let go, Fra Michel A and Caravaggio find the strength. I land on a grass promenade, the moonlight revealing its narrowness. I can feel the remaining altitude, another steep precipice just outside my field of vision. I keep tight to the wall. It dead-ends at the bastion. I feel around the parapet for the rope. This descent is fun. I've let go completely, repelling on the adrenaline of Fra Michel A and Caravaggio.

The ride ends atop a narrow berm of wave-splashed boulders. I maneuver over and around them like a gymnast, surges of tide swamping my arms and legs. The boulders are slimy with moss and spiked with barnacles. I skid and grate my elbows. I skate and slice my shins. The dock is just ahead, but one mistimed slip and this land-loving beast will be pulled into the Mediterranean.

We make it to the dock minus some skin, our blood burning with salt, not a pyre of oak. Fra Michel A and Caravaggio make a run for the fishing boat, but I remain in the shadow of the sea wall. In their mad elation, my two selves don't realize that I've stayed behind. I watch them board. I watch the boat disappear into the oceanic dim. I've finally freed myself of them. Yours truly is finally alone to himself. I sob all over the rocks. I sob into the pounding surf. In the hissing of foam, I hear Fra Michel A broadcasting his confusion.

"Why did you stay?" he's asking.

"Sicily? Mario? It'll be déjà vu all over again. Me falling into unrequited love. Me watching Caravaggio paint for the local nobility. Me watching you fight the local dildos. Same operations. Same problems. I can't go on like that. I need a life of my own."

"I can understand that. I'd emancipate too, but I'm more about this body than you or Caravaggio. With you gone, I'll finally have it to myself. His Genius can live upstairs while I fuck and fight whoever."

"You'll always be a knight of grace in my book. I'll always call you brother."

The surf lulls. Fra Michel A's voice drowns in its silence. There's another fishing boat further up the dock, the vessel that delivers the grand-master his Neapolitan anchovies. I walk from the shadows to board it. The fishermen are preparing their venture into the pre-dawn. They refuse to witness my escape. They're not mad at it. They don't understand, for the behavior of gods is much too complex for the simplicity of men. We sail by the stars, but me and God are the only ones who know that many have already died. We're the only ones who understand the falsity of their light.

XLVI.

Sunset between orange and violet. The sky making a selfie of the sea. My boy and girl knee-deep in it, backlit, more figurative than figure, chiseling mussels from boulders like the Divine One freeing a subject from marble. Their heads are black. Their bodies hot red. Fingers bleeding yellow. Shadowed limbs misshapen and disproportionate. A prolonged arm. An enlarged hand. Adumbrations. Faceless. Sexless. Deathless. The sun is close, so close they could touch it, and it's dropping, no, I'm dropping. I've spun myself free. This existential schism has brought me asylum. I'm free to make unchristian observations. Watching Napoli turn its back to the sun, it's obvious who's been revolving around what. My boy and girl are safe from the sacrilege of Bruno and Galileo. They can't see or hear yours truly. They think I'm in Sicily with Mario and my old self.

This entire sunset has something of me in it, but I'm not looking to make art. I'm not searching for subjects. I'm in absentia watching my subjects live with me. I'm watching my effect over them. I had made myself too available to everyone, Fra Michele A and Caravaggio included. I've taken a lesson from God and made myself scarce. I'm on the run again. Another price on my head. Another open season on yours truly. The Knights Hospitaller lead the hunt with Farnese mercs back in the game, along with yahoo bounty hunters and the Vice-God's stealthiest private eyes. The cardinal-nephew wants me extradited to Rome. He wants to enslave my genius. Everyone is looking for yours truly. Everyone but Cecco and Lena. I'd go to them, but the Swiss guards are expecting me, waiting for me to return like a Vandal. I would never sack my home. I would never burn Rome to the ground, not with Cecco and Lena sleeping inside the Aurelian Walls.

I don't have to reside in Rome. I can see Cecco and Lena from here, from my new cavity in the Gulf of Napoli. I see them in this impressionistic twilight, with these phantasmic eyes. I see them from my newest contraption, through this hole I punched in my head. I'm seeing them through a pane of boredom. I haven't done a damn thing in months. I haven't hurt anyone. I haven't thought of hurting or fucking a soul, not even my own. With no Fra Michel A or genius to mitigate, I've only myself to supervise. And I'm perfect. I'm an angel. I don't sin. God has nothing on yours truly. I offend no one. My ass has stopped stinking. I don't shit because I don't eat. Not anchovies. Not pizza. I want for nothing. I process nothing, of neither body nor mind. I'm a specter having visions. I hide from Fra Diavolo in perceptions of Cecco and Lena, where they're gilded in lunar light, blurred and stylized by memory. These pictures would be revolutionary, but I don't paint them. It would kill my boredom. Boredom is my new patron, and he pays me not to paint. He pays me in visions of Lena and Cecco. My boredom is godly. I owe everything to it. It enlivens me. This boredom is more luxurious than Mamma's coach. I have all the time in the world. Zero interruptions. Just me and my visions. I revel in them, soaking this boredom up out of respect for the world's slaves, grunts, and wretches. I haven't been this happy since those bed-lazed days in Signora Bruni's rental, waiting for Lena's footsteps, for the sound of her jiggling my key, but inside this boredom, I don't need her body. What would I do with it? I'm immaterial. I'm not even of mind. I'm a vanishing god, a dying star. This is my new process, my only process— the slipping away of being.

My boy and girl fill their buckets and leave while there's just enough light to scale the rocks up to the road. Hiding in plain sight, I remain unperceived as they pass. I stare through them to the shoreline. The sea and sky mesh into a modulating field of carbon black. I swim in it, enveloping myself in a canvas darker than my *David with the Head of Goliath*. My monstrous head bobs over the wind-torn swells of distant sins. I'm deterged, slipping away from being in this pure black sea. Color is my sole subject now. Not Virgins. Not pros. No naked lads with wings. Colors are my only context. By day, it's ultramarine skies, ochre cliffs, and verdigris waves. Nighttime bleeds from umber and carbon black. If only art could be so free and easy.

When I return to my cavity, God is there waiting. His quince scent is gone. It's peaches now, but His voice is just as queenie.

"You're not really here. You know that, right?" He says.

"Why do you have to be such a dick?"

"Do you want to know what the hick and genius are doing?"

"Not really."

"They're in Sicily painting for the Dorias, and partying with Mario. They've already made a *Lucy Buried*. She's a duplication of your *Mary Dead*. Caravaggio harvested her from your visions of Lena. Sicily loves her. Sicily loves you."

"What do you want from me?"

"You've been hiding for months. It's crazy. You've nothing to fear. The Dorias have muscled you some breathing room. They've gotten the Knights Hospitaller to stand down."

"You're just saying that because you want this superstar to flame out. You want a stellar death. The Knights of St. John barely drop a knee for the Vice-God or King of Spain. They certainly wouldn't pay Prince Doria any deference."

"They have. You're safe. The other Doria, the archbishop of Palermo, he's related to Malaspina and chummy with Wignacourt. He commuted your sentence. Go to Sicily. See for yourself."

"I am seeing for myself." I point to the black concrete of sea.

"Go to Sicily and paint that. Paint it around another Goliath decapitation, or the background of another John in the Wild, or the armor of another heathen soldier."

"You go to Sicily and paint it. You've always wanted a seat inside Caravaggio's head. I recused myself. It's all yours now. Go to Sicily."

"Me? An artist? I wouldn't live that life if you paid me. Too many feelings. All that heightened consciousness. That's why I made the likes of you and the Divine One. You both failed me, him more than you. I want artists who make something I can't. The Divine One was all caught up in reality. Too much nature in his art. All he did was mimic my hand. I want to see art that bypasses me. I want to see something all too human, the unlocking of primal desires, the reconciliation of ancient follies and systemizing of their resultant personality disorders. I don't want to see Christian symbols. I don't want to see religious illustrations. Let's see that sky and ocean washed in hues of anguish and despair. Let's see you exercise the powers of color. Let's see some emotional geometry. Be mythic. Be transcendental. Shit. Be infinite. Stop painting my creations. Create your own world. Reduce yourself to colors. Strip yourself down. Let's see the bare minimum, and I'm not talking about your ass. I saw that pale heinie in *Matthew Killed*. No, I want to see you, yours truly. I want to see you emanating in colors."

"Are cocksucking and ass-fucking ancient follies?"

"You're not responsible for that. I made you that way. I granted you absolute freedom and moral immunity. I gave you the longest leash. I wanted you to feel everything and then express it in brush-strokes."

"I used to hurt myself to get back at you. I'd sabotage my genius. I wanted to upend your grand plan. You wanted my genius to burn like a wick dipped in sulfur and lime. You wanted Caravaggio to explode like Greek fire. I wanted to smolder like Bruno."

"You're not a total loser. Your art has moved me, more so than the Divine One. *Sick Bacchus* is my favorite. Then *Mary Dead*. *Doubting Thomas* is up there too. You draw your viewers in like Thomas fingering my son's lance gash. Pictures like *Mary Dead* and *John Killed*, you engulf your audience in these immense spaces, and then you draw them in super close. You look them in the eye. You've unearthed human consciousness. You've discovered the modern mind, but why constrain it to the figure? Why not express it with colors? Paint that black ocean! Paint human maladies in expressive color fields!"

"You saw me murder that chicken-plucker right? You saw me kill those pimps. Were you there in the room with Cecco and I? Mario? Juan Angel in the crypt?"

"Speaking of Greek fire, I'd love to see you paint a Greek tragedy tale. King Oedipus but illustrate his complex in abstract geometrics. Maybe a composition of overlapping triangles?"

"Here I am. Here I am in a humid cavity confessing to assfuckery and murder. Here I am proclaiming my sins to Almighty God, and He can't stop talking about art. He can't stop blathering about some kooky, pseudo-psychological abstractions."

"What? You want to be scourged? You want Job-like boils on your pecker? Want me to kill all the firstborn sons of Caravaggio? Nobody cares about your transgressions. I care least of all. I let the men in your family die of Plague. I meant for Mario, Fillide, Cecco, and Lena to break your heart. I let cardinals, nobles, and popes exploit your genius. I wanted everyone and everything to hurt Michelangelo Merisi da Caravaggio so you could aestheticize that suffering in your pictures and bring me to my knees. You're kind of almost there. I'm almost proud of you."

"You know you're not really here, right? You know you're just a figment of my imagination? Like Ovid said, men need gods to exist, so they invent them."

"You are who you are. And you ain't no Savior. You ain't no Holy Ghost either. The genius and hick weren't talking out of school when they called you Holy Father. They needed a higher power, so they invented you. You're it, baby. You're a self-made phenom."

In one vast breath, He disappears. The air turns dry to wet like a manic pro. The ocean foams at the mouth. A gale from the Arabian Desert arrives from the other side of the Mediterranean, bringing a supervening blood rain with it. Sand pellets scour my being. These African storms drive some mad, but yours truly is elated. My ecstatic shivers return. Wind-whipped and stoned by a million pebbles, I black out inside the blackness of my own love supreme.

Many mornings later, I awake in wonder to a song of sun and a washed green picture of sea. My boy and girl are front-lit, singing my madrigal as they harvest babbalucci from tide pools. Today, they're less than figurative. Today, they're largely abstract, their faces creamy swatches of lead white. A yellow plane of breastbone here. An ochre stratum of scapula there. They persist as prisms into the splashy, refracted sunlight of noon. I sail upon this joyous tranquility toward the lighter light of retrospection, searching for Cecco and Lena. I find them sleeping among a golden mist, suffused in the twilight of a far-fetched star. Am I talking about myself here? Fucking duh. I'm the dying star, but I'm dying off the planisphere. I have no coordinates. I'm closer than ever to death. I couldn't feel livelier, dissolving in happiness. I haven't felt this close to Cecco and Lena since the night we snuggled on my three-legged bench.

Cecco and Lena appear celestial in the face, but their bodies don't look so hot slumbering lifelessly inside my psychic landscape. Cecco looks a touch anorexic. Lena is bloated again. Knowing that I'm responsible for their decomposition, this sight would have emotionally torched the old me. It would have inflamed my remarkable sadness. But this me, this defected god, has come to terms with the collateral agonies of his superpowers. The torturing of Job. The mind-fucking of Abraham. The crucifixion of His own son. I'm no better than Almighty God, but I'm grateful for the charitable, undeserving love Cecco and Lena paid yours truly. Not so sure He's capable of expressing one iota of gratitude. Honestly, I don't think He's very happy. Between us, I think He lacks the required faculties for self-actualization.

I spend the afternoon fingering my own psychological wounds like my Thomas probing my Christ. I finally believe in myself. I finally know how perfectly unsound I am. The trick will be not making any art of it.

My boy and girl sit on a rock extracting the snails from their shells with rusty pins. The sun falls on their shoulders. I go out of my way to unsee the shadows it makes of them.

"Carracci died today," God says. "They're burying him in the Pantheon next to Raphael."

The news is supposed to infuriate me. My rival has stolen my spot in the Pantheon. I don't see that way. I see them building an entirely new wing to house my godliness.

"I've been thinking about what you said," I say.

"What did I say?"

"That I was a self-made god."

"Oh that. I've said better shit than that."

"My best feature, my highest accomplishment to date, has been painting in spite of my prodigy. That's my one and only virtue. Would you agree?"

"Look at those two eating babbalucci. Look at what the light is doing to them. They're delightfully unrecognizable. They're just strokes of color. What a painting that'd make! Not a picture. I hate pictures. I want to see paintings. I want to see paintings like that! Think you could paint what I'm seeing?"

"By resenting myself, I've learned to accept and take responsibility for my actions. I've learned to accept the resentment of those I've harmed. Mamma. Brother Superior. Del Monte. Grandmaster Wignacourt. Cecco and Lena. In making art and making love, I went out of my way to make these elaborate errors and commit baroque sins. I did so with many conceits, but I learned to attack my ego. I managed to put him in his place, and I've arrived somewhere, a place pure and simple.

Here I am, a homicidal, lower-cased god fading inside a spectacularly unreal landscape with golden visions of his disappointed lovers. Thank you, Jesus. Thank you, Lord. It's so wonderful. I'm so undeserving. Forgive me, Father, for I have sinned. It's been time immemorial since my last confession."

"Don't repent. Paint. You're my camera obscura. You're the hole inside my cranium. I put killer content in your head. I make all the suffering. I make the wretched and miserable miserable. I make them pay for serving me, for listening to my commandments, for internalizing my sociopathy. You and your immedicable daddy issues! Just shut the fuck up and paint my visions. Paint me some wild abstraction!"

In a rush of warm psychedelia, sunrises meld atop sunsets, vivifying the stop-time figurations of my boy and girl harvesting tide pools. I make no art of it despite God's jangly harping.

XLVII.

"Open your eyes. You've got to see this."

No more queenie tone. There's a trace of Fra Michel A's Lombard drawl in God's voice. His fruity smell is gone too. He carries the fetor of a beast. I breathe through my mouth to avoid smelling him. My eyes were already open. They haven't closed since watching the genius and hick board the getaway ship. My camera has no shutter. The light is always in, capturing energy and motion in their primordial states. Consciousness arrested in space, deeper than a mirror, deeper than Galileo's telescope. My boy and girl have corralled a cuttlefish in a sunrise tidepool. Three creatures struggling for life, splashing in cool hues of skin and sea, dry brushing a line between what is known and what is seen. I've reconciled the two ontologies. I know who I am. I'm the computation itself. I'm the cuttlefish.

"Don't just sit there staring. Paint that shit!" God commands.

"You want me to paint science? You hate science. You killed Bruno."

"Don't put that on me. I didn't kill him. Papa Gout's the one who doused him in oil and dropped the torch."

"And now your Vice-God wants to torch Galileo."

"He's no Vice-God of mine. He's a bureaucrat. You're more Vice-God than him."

"It'd be helpful if you emerged from hiding to tell him that."

"I'm not hiding from anyone. I'm right here all the time. I want my coordinates known. I want my secrets revealed. That's why I blessed Adam with self-consciousness. He asked for it. I gave it to him. The self is the only knowledge worth knowing. It's the lone road to my Kingdom. Science will never locate it, but art can. I wanted Adam to be an artist. I wanted him to paint my location. I wanted him to paint the taste of my apples. I wanted him to paint their impression on him. Adam wimped the fuck out. He and everyone after him deemed self-consciousness a curse. Even yourself. Your fruit baskets are too real, both the ripe and the rotting ones. All that fucking remarkable sadness of yours. You saturated your pictures with it. So many times I wanted to put you out of your misery, but you would have loved that."

"Know what I'd love right now? Some alone time. Jesus Christ, I'm so much happier when you're not around. The loneliness kicks in the second I hear your voice. You and your hokey theories on art."

"What theories?"

"All of them. All this shit about abstraction and expression. I'm out of that game. Va fa Napoli! Go find Caravaggio. Share your theories with him. Art shouldn't have a voice. Neither should God. What happened to being elusive?"

"I'm just painting you an escape route from this unreality you've niched. You've prided yourself on always painting reality, on aestheticizing the wretched streets. Reality isn't bunion feet and crooked teeth. Reality is more mystery than matter. Why not paint it as such? Paint the mystery of existence. Paint the inside of this cavity. Let the world find you. You've nothing to fear. The world misses you."

"Remember that superstar in Rome? The one that shined night and day. Was that you?"

"Nope. That wasn't me, and I can't tell you what it was."

"Maybe I should paint Oedipus slaying Laius on the dusty road to Thebes. Paint the viscera of his patricide in bright expressive strokes. Would that shut you up?"

No such luck. God drones on about seeing with my mind instead of my eyes, telling me to look past my perceptions toward the unknown, toward an ocean of abstracted lines and shapes, and how that abstraction can distill the infinite from the finite and limn the mysteries of His omnipotence, omniscience, omnipresence, and omnibenevolence. In essence, He wants this camera obscura that I've punched into my skull to paint Him a selfie. He has turned my cavity into a dungeon, lonelier than Tor di Nona, deeper than the oubliette. Does He not think I can see Him? Does He not think that I've been seeing Him all along? I saw God there during my murders. I saw Him there when I bounced the dull hatchet off the lawyer's head. He was in the room whenever I entered Mario. He was in the room whenever Cecco entered me. I leaned against Him in the crypt while Juan Angel drove me home to Lombard. My mind can never not see His amorphous omnipresence. I see Him with or without his little birdies and spying superstars. I see Him with or without the symmetry of line, color, shape, or pattern. I see Him on the streets, His galactic weight crippling the backs of laborers and peasants. I've seen and heard enough of Him. It's time to exit this cavity while I'm still feeling blissfully optimistic.

My boy smashes the cuttlefish against a boulder like David beating Goliath's brains in with his sling. When the meat is tenderized, he and my girl collect a bucket of babbalucci and scale the rocks toward Napoli. I apparate there. I find myself at the city gate incomprehensibly naked. I pass the big-eyed customs officers unrecognized. A new wanted poster hangs on one of the columns, an unflattering rendition of yours truly, more akin to Baglione's cock-munching goblin than any of my selfies. I've finally reached a place where I can be happy for my rivals, enemies, and detractors. I'm happy to share my immortality with them. Without the antagonism of Baglione, the artichoke waiter, Pasqualone Esq., Alfonso Alonso, Federico Fallaci, Ranuccio Tomassoni, Ranuccio Farnese, Papa Gout, Papa Beady Eyes, and Diavolo, I'd just be some bratty artist with an unwarranted temper. Jesus had only the one Pontius Pilate. I have at least seven and maybe as high as seventy-six. They're all here in Napoli, waiting to crown me with thorns. I'll never leave this city, not until they bury me in the Pantheon next to Carracci.

It's been twenty-seven months since first I left Napoli, that spell burning through me like an overnight fever. Poof. Here I am with my coolest head ever. No migraine. No remarkable sadness. No growling stomach. And most importantly, no pangs of aggression or creativity. True to its own ethos, Napoli doesn't refurbish itself to accommodate this new me. It's poor as ever, violent as ever, and all the sexier for it. Cecco and Lena like its sultry anguish so much, they've decided to move here. I see them at every abject corner, in every wretchedly teeming square. They're every other face in the city. Lena is the threadbare mother, small-footed but chesty, a colorless infant under her arm. She is the repining nun crawling up the steps of San Giacomo. She's the teenage viscountess promenading in a figured silk dress (pomegranate patterns seem to be the thing this fall). Cecco is the bony lad trying to sell her a basket of soiled rags. He is the ponytailed pimp patting the plump ass of his top pro. He is the old man shouting philosophical obscenities at pigeons. Cecco won't look me in the eye. He exposes his profile only, sometimes obstructed by a shoulder or tuft of hair, but that baroque ear is unmistakable, and here and now, I forgive myself for perfecting it, for perforating it with my brush. I hope it's recording my remorse. I hope it can hear me over all these spatting and soliloquizing Neapolitans.

Through Cecco's florid ear I can hear everything that everyone is saying about me. For every voice calling me a maniacal cocksucker, there are ten more revering me as a supernatural genius sent by God, and for every ten of those, there are ten more citing me as the cultural savior of Napoli. Even the mercs hunting the streets for my head speak highly of me. Even the oligarchs who would soon as surrender me to the authorities once the paint of their commissions dries, even those backstabbers express the superiority of yours truly. My name thunders from the mouths of the masses. They say that I crippled a Knight Hospitaller with my fists. They say that I've reinvented myself in Sicily, that I pulled another Lazarus. That my pictures have discovered yet another realm of human consciousness. They say that God is looking to censure it. I look around to make sure He hasn't followed me here. I look inside San Giacomo for Him. I look inside the Certosa of San Martino. I peek into San Lorenzo Maggiore and the Cathedral of Napoli. No sign of God anywhere. I scan the Raphaelite sky. I'm the only dying star in Napoli. They're already talking about my arrival. They're saying that I've returned to Napoli, that I'm here to erect my final resting place.

I don't know how they know. I'm invisible, more insensible than God. I walk through my most rabid believers without being perceived. I walk through the mercs and knights hunting for my head. I pass policemen and guards. It's deeply satisfying, more so than ramming Duke Dildos at Navona. I pass through the population like a December wind through dilapidated shutters. I'm imperceptible. I'm some kind of dead, but the city is talking about how great I look. They're saying I look existentially swole, like the ultimate version of my best self. This is very true, but who are they to see it? Who are they to enter my netherworld?

"Napoli is your purgatory," God says, His Lombard drawl thick as polenta.

"How so?" I ask.

"You're only here to launder your sins. You'll be in Rome within a year."

I follow Cecco's ear toward the sound of His voice. I still don't know my way around Napoli. I know a church when I see it, or a pizza cart, but I can't remember how I got there. I don't know this square from that square. I still don't know the names of streets. Maybe I don't want to know them. Maybe I've known it all along. Maybe God was lying about Carracci and the Pantheon. Or maybe He wants Napoli to be my Pantheon.

"Open your eyes," He says. "You're in Napoli. You've brought the future of painting with you. Your new pictures are cutting edge. Expressive. Impressionistic. The world is here to witness them. Everyone is here to see them, everyone minus you."

It's quite the thing for God to say as I find myself before the Viceroy's martyr pile. I approach my potential resting place expecting to find the head and limbs of Caravaggio and Fra Michel A, but I discover a crueler dismemberment. The head of Sister Priggy No-Shoes. It crowns the pile of parts like my rosary Virgin rising above the rubble of bald Colonna scalps. Her head is freshly butchered. Her face blue as my beheaded John, but the carnality fixed in her eyes like my pilgrims' Virgin. Sister Prig was a nympho for justice. Judging from her lustful gaze, she took the decollation well, more gallantly than either of my Goliaths.

"Inspired by your pictures, she and some fishermen organized a militia. They were planning a revolt. The viceroy caught wind and made an example of her. Like I said, you're more viceroy than that psycho."

I know what He's trying to do. He's trying to decollate my bliss. This camera obscura isn't working out for Him. He wants to knock another hole in it. I won't forfeit this bliss. I won't let God revoke it. I'll beat Him to the punch by decapitating that Greek gift-giver. He thinks He can Trojan-horse my ego? I haven't wanted a charger or coach since how long? It's time to punch this gift horse in the fucking mouth.

"Tell me again about abstraction. Explain to me how you would have had Adam paint a figurative bowl of apples."

I follow His theoretical jabbering to the German's tavern where his voice finally drops. I stop and look for Him among the lunch crowd loitering outside, blowing smoke and tugging on their balls, waiting for the door to open. I survey them from across the street. Poets, painters, and academics, a few slightly immortal, but no God. Finson and Vinck hold court, imparting the techniques of my chiaroscuro to lesser followers. They've evolved. They wear my intelligence with solemnity. They look good. They look happy. They appear to have Baron Luigi in their pocket. I almost didn't recognize the Carafa. His princely mien has rusted. He looks like a baron now. I don't recognize the Duke Dildo standing next to him in a ruffled linen shirt. His satin cape and breeches match. He's dressed like a femme-fop but doesn't stand with the typical mattarello up his ass. For all his garish fashion, he stoops like a man ducking the police. I know that stature. I'd know it anywhere. I've found God hiding as a femme-fop under the floppiest beret known to man. I approach Him for the kill, well not an actual kill. You can't kill God. The closest thing to death for Him is castration. I have no sword or dagger. I'll have to yank it off with my bare hands or gnaw it off with my cock-gobbling fangs.

I wrap an arm around his throat and stuff a hand down the front of His breeches. This is not the Almighty Cock of God. I'd know this pud anywhere. This garden variety pud belongs to Fra Michelangelo Merisi da Caravaggio.

"Glad you finally came to your senses. Welcome back." Fra Michel A's drawl has worsened in my absence.

Caravaggio draws my hand from our pecker, and places it on the cold iron hilt of our new rapier.

"Stop playing with yourself in public," he says. "It makes you look like an impossibly cocky genius."

I've fallen for the bait. My aperture has transformed into a box trap, the kind Fra Michele A set as a boy to catch hares. It's not dark inside, and I feel more like the box than the hare, Fra Michele's voice phoning through the string.

XLVIII.

A schizo walks into a tavern.

"What will it be?" the bartender asks.

"A glass of your best brandy, and make it a triple," Fra Michel A replies.

We opt for the table in the center of the room, not an inconspicuous corner booth. Finson, Vinck, Baron Luigi, and his bodyguards join us. We don't want to come off as cagey. We want to appear convivial like the rest of the patrons swilling Tears of Christ and talking politics, disserting the failed uprising of Sister Prig and her comrade fishermen. Baron Luigi has a lot to say about the viceroy's taxation of flour and fish. An anchovy pizza now costs the same as a Caravaggio. I voice my anger over Sister Prig's decollation. Fra Michel A and Caravaggio double-take me. They've never heard yours truly sound so authoritative and impassioned, okay, and maybe a little bit haughty, but that's got more to do with the femme-fop disguise. The costume was Fra Michel A's genius. Who would ever think to look for Michelangelo Merisi da Caravaggio underneath a chichi beret? Not even God would recognize me in these flamboyant threads. Everyone in my company is nailing their roles, pretending I'm not me, but that won't discourage yours truly from speaking as myself. If I'm found, I'm found. I'm not hiding from anyone. I want my coordinates known.

I want my identity revealed. I'm captain of this vessel. I'm righting this ship and sailing it the fuck to Eden.

Apparently, I was all the rage in Sicily. I was doing for it what I did for Napoli. I painted the island onto the map. I painted it into the center of the solar system. I painted a nativity fêting the incarnation of Almighty God. I painted *St. Lucy Buried* for the church of Santa Lucia. I painted two pictures of Lazarus raised. I took a razor to the first and resurrected the second in masterstrokes. The picture went to a rich Genoese friend of Prince Doria and his brother the archbishop of Palermo. *Lazarus Raised* earned me a thousand scudi. Mario and I blew the money on wine, poppy, and pros, sharing all of it with the wretched locals of Messina. Without the mediation of yours truly, Fra Michel A and Caravaggio lapsed into worst versions of themselves. Caravaggio strutted around with his cock out, slandering Messina's favorite artists, showing no deference or appreciation to his aristocratic patrons. Fra Michel A was back to his quarrelsome ways, bullying hoity-toity dildos, and splitting the skull of an overprotective schoolmaster who chastised him for staring too intently upon his students touring the navy yard on a field trip. Fra Martelli, prior of Messina, grew tired of harboring an irredeemable monster. He informed Fra Diavolo of my whereabouts and absconded to Firenze with my portrait of him. Wanting to restore the honor of their cocksucking fraternity, the grandmaster has given Diavolo the go-ahead for my head.

Diavolo and his imps caught me in a Messina brothel with my pants down. I leapt three stories to the street and fled all the way to Palermo bare-assed like my *Matthew Killed* selfie, Mario venturing along with me. He'd already ditched both wives in Siracusa so he could reboot his career in Messina, painting my copies, running my shop. For months, Palermo was an artistic paradise but then Fra Carafa arrived with a shipment of slaves. He had spotted Diavolo's fleet sculling into the harbor behind his. He smuggled us to Napoli on a shrimp boat. Mario returned to Messina, to the lusty sales racket we'd left there.

"I don't want to hear about Sicily any more. This is Napoli. Today is the twenty-fourth of October. When is where and vice versa," I say to Caravaggio.

No one outside of my head was talking Sicily. I've put the kibosh on their Duke Dildo charade. I've outed myself to the entire tavern. Yes. The mad genius still talks to himself. The news dismays Finson and Vinck. Baron Luigi can't bring himself to look at the dark side of my brilliance. He looks past Fra Michel A too. He only wants to see Caravaggio. I will not oblige.

"How's my weeping Magdalene?" I ask.

Baron Luigi gathers the German's attention, signaling for another carafe. "Your marchioness arrives tomorrow morning. She's coming to save you, again."

"I only got to canonize her the once," I reply.

The braggadocio is too much for Fra Michel A and Caravaggio.

"She always saw to my gifts," says Fra Michel A.

"And nurtured me more than my own mother," Caravaggio adds.

"But I'm the one who perfected our genius," I say, doubling down on myself.

"Your rosary Virgin misses your brush," Finson says.

"I don't my miss my brush, not one bristle. Haven't dipped it in a year," I reply.

I push my chair back and cross my legs, choking the big idea vegetating in Fra Michel A's pants. Redirecting his thirst, he reaches for the brandy. I nail his palm to the table. The brandy remains untouched. Two more nails to go. Then my supremacy will be complete. In the meantime, no booze or sex. No dulling of perceptions, but in my year of reclusion, I've forgotten how to hear people. After a year of tuning out God's theories on art, I interpreted Vinck's words too figuratively. He wasn't talking about my rosary Virgin picture that I left him. He was referring to my model, my Neapolitan Judith, my counterfeit Lena. Here she comes freewheeling down the staircase in a silk dress fit for a viscountess of a very small fiefdom.

"I need to get myself right. I left my purse in Palermo. Can I borrow a few piastre?" I ask Baron Boy.

He stacks three coins on the table. I signal for three more. He hates giving it to me.

"It's part of my process," I assure him, fisting the coins.

I stand and excuse myself. Baron Boy's ogres rise to escort me. I insist that they stay behind. They look to the boss. He affirms my insistence. The bodyguards are quick in returning to their seats. I wouldn't be gung-ho about defending yours truly either. I meet my counterfeit Lena at the bottom of the staircase, intercepting Baron Boy's carafe of tears from the German along the way. I place my fistful of coins on the small of her back and kiss her neck. She smells like a fresh squirt of civet anus.

Upstairs, before entering her room, I hand her the coins and carafe.

"Can I borrow your room for a few hours? I've got to straighten myself out."

"Anything for the God of the lowly, helper of the oppressed, upholder of the weak, protector of the forsaken, and savior of the hopeless," she answers, quoting the actual Judith.

Fra Michel A leans in to kiss those full lips, but I pull him around into the room, closing the door behind us. Her chamber smells like a civet died and went to heaven.

"So nice to have you back," Fra Michel A quips. "How long has it been? Three weeks? A little over a month?"

"A year," I say.

"Shut. Up. Wow. That really flew the fuck by."

"It was so nice without you in our heads," says Caravaggio. "No moralizing. No micromanaging. No remarkable sadness or anxious tummy. Sicily worshipped us. We were fully actualized there. We finally brought light to life. No more aestheticizing darkness."

"We painted the pictures together, like we did with *John Killed*, rapid and economic strokes but loose, impressionistic. It's like we were painting our psyches and not subjects," Fra Michel A says.

"So that was your drawl I was hearing in the cavity. God wasn't talking to me. God didn't talk me out of my happy place. It was you two profiting off my meditations."

"Yup," says Fra Michel A.

"It was our most lucrative operation yet," says Caravaggio.

"So why lure me back? Why not leave me to myself? You think you were fully actualized in Sicily? I was obtaining god-status in my cavity, and I wasn't some god of the wretched and rich. I lorded over myself. I was god of my own quale. I loved myself, in a healthy way, not your masturbatory egocentricity. I owned my failures and flaws. I reconciled myself with Cecco and Lena. They let me behold them there. I want to return to that realm. I don't want to be here. Why'd you summon me?"

"We told you that you were a god," Fra Michel A says.

"We can't paint that impressionism without you. We painted Cecco and Lena as you were imagining them, but the light was too much. We need your darkness. We need your sadness. We need your anxieties. Your compassion. We need that soft spot of yours. We don't love Cecco and Lena. We don't love the wretched and their filthy features. That's all your mush," Caravaggio says.

"You're ephemeral without me, transients, fleeting figures. I'm the sum of your incompatible parts. It's fuzzy math, but I've constructed a perfect science from it, the science of superstardom. This is my universe. You said it yourselves. I'm God. You're Jesus and the Holy Ghost, two alien outlaws. I've let you reside here, but the free ride is over. No more micromanaging. I'm going macro. I'm done calling you Fra Michel A. You're no knight. You're a street-fighting libertine. And you, we're not painting shit anymore. I'm using these superpowers to enact real social change. No more painting wretches, grunts, and slaves. We're going to free them! We're heading a revolution. We're going to the pier to join ranks with the fishermen. We're going to finish what Sister Prig started. We're going to launch a revolution with no slogan or jingle. Fists and blades! The viceroy is our first vengeance. Who's with me?"

"Do I get to kill people?" Michele asks.

"Can we grab some pizza on our way to the pier?" asks the genius.

I march out of the room, the two of them suctioned in my slip-stream. I pause at the top of the staircase to survey the tavern. The crowd has changed. Finson, Vinck, and Baron Boy have left. The German isn't behind the bar. The rowdy, academic debates have quieted to cynical mutterings.

"This isn't good," Michele says.

It doesn't take a genius. Something is up. The faces of the patrons have the same bookish affability, but their shoulders are tense. Those sitting are hunched over the table. Those standing are slouched into their assholes. When I reach the bottom of the stairs, not a single set of eyes beholds the Earth's greatest artist. When I draw my sword and charge toward the exit, the entire place stampedes in the opposite direction.

Out in the street, I catch Diavolo and the three other Knights Hospitaller off guard. They're waiting for yours truly, but not expecting me to take my assassination to them. I cut through Fra Someone and another before getting to Diavolo. His feints are as trans-parent as ever, but I also have to peripherally contend with Fra Valette's slightly above-average lunges. Four slightly above-average swordsmen (two already wounded) can defeat a great one, and one of those lucky fuckers catches me upside the head, right on my Goliath scar, the same wound struck by Giovan Tomassoni. The death blow is hot and deep but does little to stop me. The death blow unplugs a panicked rage that even Michele never thought possible. It's a whip against a charger's shoulder. It innervates my life. I volt over Diavolo's kill thrust and run my rapier through Fra Someone. Pricked in the kidney, I spin and diagonal slash Fra Valette from armpit to opposite oblique. Diavolo is the only asshole wearing armor. I overhead block his down slash and kick him in the chest. I pull my dagger and plunge it into the fourth knight's thigh. Diavolo is halfway to his feet when I kick him over again. I kick him again, this time in the head. I kick him in the head again. I kick him in the head again and again, the blood of my wound splattering his face like the expressive brushstrokes of a figurative God wanting to paint abstraction.

XLIX.

I sit up so Mamma can change my bandages. My entire head is wrapped, the narrowest slit for the one good eye. The lesion in my skull feels bottomless. I'm thinking that Michele and Caravaggio have fallen to their deaths. I haven't heard boo from them. It'd be a shame if they've died so quickly after our reunion. They hardly witnessed my shine. I brighten even more as Mamma unravels me.

"The newspapers are reporting you dead," she says.

"I hope I stay dead. My enemies can move on from me."

"No chance. The Knights Hospitaller are outside the palace walls waiting for you."

"They were waiting for me outside the tavern. That didn't end well for them."

"Your fans are still raving about you chopping down four knights. They can't stop talking about your volt. Your sword has finally out-storied your brush."

"Did I kill any of them?"

"No, but one is permanently lame and De Varayz will forever speak like a dimwit."

"So, who's left? Who's outside the walls waiting to bag my head?"

"Fra Vincenzo Carafa, prior of Capua. He has a posse of twelve knights."

"This palace belongs to his cousin. Why doesn't he just knock on the door and invite himself in?"

"Every family has an asshole cousin or uncle. The duke hasn't spoken to him in years."

"He's a Knight Hospitaller. They have more authority than a duke, especially the Duke of Mondragone. They have more muscle than the daughter of a Catholic superhero."

"The prior wants a picture. Then he's going to bring your head to the grandmaster."

"He's out of luck on two accounts. I retired from painting and he couldn't best me with a sword if he had eight arms."

"Michele, you couldn't beat me with a sword right now. You're two-thirds dead. This wound might not heal. My dear Lord, you look hideous. You smell worse."

"I want to see."

"Nobody wants another one of your gory, self-hating selfies."

"I don't hate myself anymore. I've learned to live with my sins. They're the necessary evil of a sublime creator, but I've retired from painting. The only thing I want to make now is babies with Lena. I'm going to find her and raise some masterpieces."

"When and if you heal, you're going to paint whatever the fuck I tell you to paint. It's the only resource you have left."

"How bad is it?"

"Everyone but the cardinal-nephew has washed their hands of you. Painting for him is your only hope."

"No. My face. How bad is it?"

Mamma leaves. I'm on an upper floor, in a small chamber, maybe a former servant's quarters. There is a tall window overlooking the sea. If Michele could talk, he'd imitate the voice of God and tell me to paint it as a broad, primal field of thought. I could lean out the window and drop a loogie into the surf, but my throat is dry as sand. My damaged eye has the view of a rainy window, but the good one focuses on the convex mirror Mamma placed before me. An oozy cleft stretches from my temple, just below the far corner of my eye and nostril, to the opposite corner of my mouth. The purple eyelid is swollen shut and bugging. I've lost some top teeth. I won't be gobbling much of anything anymore. The bottom half of my face wants to slink away from the top half. I'm an abomination. I make Goliath look like Mario. This couldn't be a selfie because there's no self here. I'm the other consciousness. I'm out of my mind and perfectly thrilled about it. In a moment of horridly surreal self-recognition, I find myself disoriented and bewildered. What a way to live! The liberty of making no sense. The privilege of fantasy and unleashing one's delusions. It's enough to render any god obsolete.

Mamma reenters and turns the mirror against the wall, somehow managing to avoid herself. The years have deepened her frown lines and blanched her ginger head, but the obtrusion of her breasts defies the physical laws of Heraclitus, Copernicus, and Galileo. A woman of four children can buy herself out of science by paying for a wet nurse.

"You're more morose than ever. Do you miss my father?"

"I'm broken. I'm out of money. I'm out of influence. You've depleted my political favors. I've given you and my sons everything. They're squandering their father's inheritance. The Sforza wrote me off their books. My brother died and left everything to my nephews. I sold my coach. I sold the palace in Milan to the Prince of Paliano. I only have my place in Caravaggio left, and that's because nobody wants it, not even my sons."

"Were you my father's lover?"

"Yes."

"Did you mother my father's blood?"

"What do you want to hear?"

"Why would you protect me all these years? Why would you send me to art school? Why would you sacrifice yourself for your steward's son?"

"I've been asking myself that since I bailed your murdering ass out of Milan."

"Who would have thought I'd be the greatest growing up?"

"I did. Lucia too. But that wasn't the only reason for our love."

"You need money. You need a Caravaggio. What does Mamma want me to paint?"

"It doesn't matter what. Paint anything. Paint what haunts you."

"You haunt me. Lucia haunts me. Lena haunts me. I want her back. I want to make a family of my own with her."

"Her wounds have ruined her. She's in worse shape than you."

"Then I want my weeping Lena back. She's somewhere in this palace. Give her back and I'll paint for you until my wounds get the best of me."

Mamma wraps a fresh bandage around my head, her hasty

knuckles knocking fire into my migraine. She needs that Caravaggio something fierce.

"It's been three years. Why didn't you visit me sooner?" I ask.

"And the Farnese would follow me right to you?"

"What about Del Monte? Why didn't he come for me?"

"He did. He was in Napoli for a few months, keeping an eye on your every move. My big fat little birdie can really get off the ground."

Such a discourteous ghosting would have enraged Michele and Caravaggio, but it jazzes yours truly, enriching the absurdity and bewilderment of my current humor. What a trip! A cocksucking man of the cloth spent a buttload of the Vice-God's resources to monitor my own cocksucking. How cool is that! The man who fathered my genius. The cocksucker who loved me so much that he never even tried sucking *my* cock. I was down here in Napoli painting for my life, and he's around the corner peeping on me! I didn't think Del Monte had it in him. I'm proud of him for ghosting me. I'm proud of Cecco for dumping me. I'm proud of Lena for fucking Ranuccio behind my back. I deserved all of it! That's what lovers do to each other. They make you feel your own depravities. They punish you so you won't have to do it yourself. What about you, Mamma? What will it be? I can't even imagine so I ask her. She doesn't respond. She leaves, bolting, latching, and locking the door behind her, leaving me to my own private wilderness.

L.

Look. I'm sorry to sound so cavalier about this but the death blow is killing me. Figuratively. Literally. It might have killed my other two. Another week has wended, and no word from Michele or Caravaggio. I don't miss them. I'm just saying. I'm barely hanging on. My symptoms aren't subsiding. Migraines. Amnesia (I don't remember Sicily at all). Delirium (I keep thinking I'm some kind of lesser god). Fatigue. Ringing of the ears. Extreme sensitivity to light. How appropriate is that last one? Yours truly, the Dark Prince of Chiaroscuro, getting stabbed in the eyes by a jolly sunbeam, thin as a slat, dust mites twirling like atomic children tumbling down a hill. But!!! There is a BIG but! I'm lacking certain symptoms. I'm NOT experiencing any nausea (biological or existential). I DON'T have any dizziness. I'm NOT depressed. I'm actually quite blissful. I have a HUGE appetite. Mamma feeds me like a baby, foods taxed by the viceroy. Foods unavailable to the wretched. She reads me to sleep like a child, the erotic poems of Marino. She sleeps in my bed, her head on my chest. Under the bandages, my face weeps sweat.

"Have they decided to kill me yet?" I ask.

"They'll only kill you if you start dying. They'll break down the door and make your dying as painful as possible."

"I don't think it can get more painful."

"They're horribly imaginative. They'll rape your ass with something enormous."

"Stop. I'm getting aroused. First time since the Hospitaller crypt."

Mamma puts a soft hand on my utter softness. "Liar."

"Who's coming for me?"

"There are two parties. One party fighting over your pictures. The other fighting over who gets to kill you."

"What party are you?"

"I hate parties. Always have. As a girl, my father wanted me to be the next Catherine de' Medici. He wanted his little debutante attending banquets, socializing morning to night. I just wanted to slack off in my chamber, eating drugs, reading sad poetry."

"*Flame of this heart, sun of these eyes, life of my life, soul of my soul, know that a sunray of your semblants can carve marble and calciner diamonds,*" I say, quoting a poem not yet scribed by Marino.

"*Do not be algae in the light and trembling sea that bends your will,*" she responds in kind.

"Owhay oday ouyay ovelay emay?" I ask.

"You're delirious. I don't speak hog Latin."

"Enthay ingbray emay Lena," I say.

"I told you. I don't understand."

I sprawl across her lap like the Divine One's Christ cradled in his mamma's arms.

After five days without a migraine, Mamma removes my bandages. She washes my scabby face in a bucket of onion water and dries my eyes with the tab of her silk bodice. My bleary pupil has cleared. I'm in a new room. They've transposed me to the attic. It's hot and airless, but I can breathe easy without Michele or Caravaggio around. I also have Lena with me. She's as I left her, crying her eyes out, bemoaning the tragedy I made of her life.

"I brought your picture. Now get painting. Write me a list of materials," Mamma says.

"Tell Baron Boy to punch a hole in the roof. I need light. It has to enter the camera in my skull." I stand from the bed and approach my weeping Lena. "Are you jealous of her?"

"Sure. Why not?"

"Because you love me?"

"Sure."

"Why do you love me?"

"What's not to love? But you have to paint now, or they're going to kill you."

"Who's going to kill me?"

"Everyone." She shuts one eye, extends an arm, and raises a thumb, scaling me to size like a painter. "You almost look as old as me."

"How does my head look?"

"Like someone tried sewing a broken eggshell together. How do you feel?"

"My ears are still ringing, but the delirium is gone."

"Good."

"Not good. Delirium is the obscura to my camera."

"In *Rosary Madonna*, you painted every living Colonna. You've never asked your marchioness to model."

"I never realized how much you resemble Fillide. I suppose that's telling. I suppose I should start painting heads for people. Should I paint the first one for the grandmaster?"

"Wouldn't hurt." The pleasure in her grin is palpable.

"Yes. A sword across the neck hurts less than one upside the head. No pain at all they say, so long as the swordsman has a skilled hand. Who'd you sell your coach to?"

"My princely nephew, and speaking of nephews, the cardinal-nephew is exhorting the Vice-God to pardon you. He thinks you belong in Rome, painting for the Church. Cardinal Gonzaga is of the same opinion."

"Isn't there a Gonzaga staying here at the palace?"

"There are two Gonzagas staying here, and lots of Carafas. A Colonna and a Lorraine too."

"One big happy network. And they gave you the shit job of caring for the sicko."

"That's what I get for rebelling against my father. See, you don't have it so bad. You're a rebel, and you get to live forever. You get to kill and get away with it. You go around smashing people in the face with hatchets and platters of artichokes. When you shit on someone, they bend over backwards to clean it up for you. Nice work if you can get it."

For the past month at Palace Cellamare, an exquisite old gorgon has been emptying my pot, but now Mamma does the unthinkable. The noble daughter of a Catholic superhero carries the heaping pot of a homicidal, superstar genius from the room. She's so dramatic. She's so trying to manipulate me with guilt. But I'm happy to satisfy Mamma! This cuttlefish happily keels into her net. What will Mamma do with me? What party is she working for? I'm too delirious to care. Lena is in the attic with me. I shiver with ecstatic goosebumps. I wait for Mamma's ambiance to evaporate before addressing Lena.

"I'm sorry for immortalizing you. I'm sorry for wanting to love you for myself."

She doesn't answer. I pray she hasn't forgiven me. I pray that she doesn't regret fucking Ranuccio behind my back. I pray that she remains more principled than God and the rest of His picture-hungry cardinals. Of all the lovers to pass through me, Lena wanted Caravaggio least.

It's a shame that I'll be dying soon because I've finally mastered the *craft* of painting. I mastered the *art* of painting somewhere during the preconscious of childhood, strolling the streets of Milan with Lucia. She'd walk me to the market on a leash. She didn't trust our servants to bring home the freshest vegetables. She was a freak about her cos. Milan was hell then. God was punishing the region for idolizing the extremism of Archbishop Borromeo. God parched the crops and poisoned the soil. He infected us with Plague. God's mercenaries, the soldiers of King Philip, persecuted the city's wretched for kicks. The archbishop paraded through the terror barefoot, shouldering an outlandishly large crucifix. The wretched, starved, beaten, and ill limped behind him, some crawling, all of them grinding their rotten teeth as they hummed along to the archbishop's chanting, their filthy soles painted by the gunk of the street. I don't remember witnessing any of that, but I know it taught my unformed mind to see. It pervaded my senses, imbuing the reality of human suffering. It inspired me to paint dirty feet, crooked teeth, and holy terror. Maybe I'm not the first man to ever see it, but I'm the first to paint it. I'm the Adam of art. I'm the Galileo of consciousness. That's my genius. That's the impossibly hard part of making pictures. Craft is just hard. Anyone can learn after a few thousand hours of mixing pigments. Look at me, I taught Michele to paint like Caravaggio. Mario. Cecco. Finson and Vinck. I never thought Michele would become my most skilled follower. I never thought yours truly would become so gratified and blissful that he could admit to just now mastering the craft of painting. I can admit to myself that, until recently, Carracci and Raphael were better craftsmen. Craft shouldn't get one inside the Pantheon. I belong there on creative genius alone. I belonged there after my second picture, *Sick Bacchus*.

While waiting for the Pantheon, I paint some heads. I paint another head of St. John for Grandmaster Wignacourt. I paint the executioner serving it to Salome on a brass platter. He hated having to do it. He frowns upon his craft as I would a fresco painted by Caravaggio. The manly old maid observes the martyrdom with prehistoric gloom. I paint the streets of Campo de' Fiore on her face. A morose Salome looks away, playing her role with a culpable reluctance. Not even John, the lucky recipient of this Christ-level martyrdom, not even he can bear to look at the apathetic viewer. I paint their complicity from memory. I paint it in overruling blacks and tyrannical whites. I'm done painting realism. I'm done painting God's evils. From now until forever, I'll only paint my own. Never again will I subject a living being to the inhumanities of pictures. I will never master another model. I will only master the paint, and even then, my strokes will be broad and generous. I'm mixing every pigment like it's the last mineral on Earth.

Downstairs, the conversations and laughter of the elite carry through the walls of the palace. I hear singing too, Neapolitan love songs from a dramatic tenor with particularly dark tonality. I hear them bitching and moaning about money and politics. They're unhappy with the viceroy for flaunting his villainy during a Royal Commission inquiry into their shared manipulation of grain prices. They're upset with him for executing their adversaries. They think it was too conspicuous. They're also unhappy with their cousin, the Prince of Paliano for liquidating their second castles and curbing their expenditures. No more coaches. No more chargers. No more ostentatious palace renovations. Art is a remunerative investment, the only kind they're allowed to wage without his consent. Lucky for the Colonnas, Carafas, Gonzagas, and Lorraines, there's a supernova locked in their attic. Their rainy day fund has cycloned into a windfall.

It's night. My torches are burning low. I make some hand shadows on the wall. A dog. A bunny. A butterfly. The poormouthing downstairs falls silent, and then there's some lute playing. Then it's the crescendo whirrs of cicadas and nothing else. My ear-ringing is minor but probably permanent. Otherwise, I'm as healed as I'll ever be. I go to the door and push it. It's latched from the outside. I take a few steps back and run my shoulder into it. I bounce backwards onto my ass.

The migraine rears its ugly head. Just as well. I can't leave without my weeping Lena, and I'm not in the mood to unstretch her canvas yet.

I take a nice long piss in my pot and get to thinking about painting a *Peter's Denial*. The chicken-shit coward turned his back to Christ thrice. Now that's a friend! And how did Christ thank him? By making him first Bishop of Rome. It's a shame Caravaggio won't be around to hear Cardinal Del Monte eulogize me at the Pantheon. Del Monte will be first bishop of my oeuvre. I want my friends and lovers to know how much I love them for betraying me. I want this picture to illustrate it. I walk away from my pot with a complete vision of *Peter's Denial*, with Mamma's face as the woman caving to a soldier's interrogation and finking on Peter.

———

"Does it bother you that I'm here?" Baron Boy asks from nowhere.

I don't know how long he's been here, but I'm halfway through *Peter's Denial*.

"How could it? I'm not here. I'm halfway to Rome, painting my way to the Pantheon."

"They finally stopped talking about your volt. They're talking about Salome. They want to know who modeled her. Some think Lena is up here with you. Others think Fillide. I think you painted my aunt."

"You're a true Caravaggio connoisseur, which is why you deserve a *Weeping Magdalene* of your own. You're next in the queue."

"My cousin Marcantonio Doria wants a Virgin."

"I don't do Virgins anymore."

"He wants a St. Ursula. His stepdaughter has entered a nunnery and taken the name."

"St. Ursula? The virgin princess who marched into Cologne with an army of eleven thousand virgins? The St. Ursula who was martyred for refusing the Huns' king?"

"The eleven thousand virgins were killed too."

"I think I might have been there when it happened. If not, I'm there witnessing it now."

"My cousin will pay whatever."

"What am I going to do with money?"

"Send it to your lover in Rome. I hear she's not faring well."

"Why'd you leave the tavern that day? What happened to Finson and Vinck?"

"We went upstairs. I was with your Madonna of the rosary. She said you were in her room talking to yourself."

"Why doesn't your cousin come up here and ask me for a picture? Why don't any of them want to watch the genius in action?"

"They want to pretend that their pictures are being manufactured by a supernatural machine, a divine machine with no human imperfections."

"I've got to get to Rome before my Virgin dies. You've got to help. Write to your cousin. Tell him I need passage to Rome. He can pull it off. He smuggled me out of Malta."

"I don't think he even knows."

"Knows what?"

"That you performed the greatest volt in modern history. He's incommunicado. He's in Africa hunting slaves. He won't be in Napoli until the end of summer, but I'll tell you this. He very much wants you to live, as do I. Painting is the only way to ensure that. My cousin Cardinal Gonzaga wants a picture. He's moved to Rome. He and the cardinal-nephew are working the Vice-God. Keep painting. Your collectors and fans will champion your liberation."

"Can you do me at least one favor? Can you bring me a large platter of artichokes?"

"How do you want them cooked?"

"Drenched in fucking butter."

Baron Boy watches me execute Peter from memory and two weeks later he leaves for my artichokes. I wipe my brushes and sit on the floor next to Lena.

"Don't worry. I would never ask you to model for St. Ursula. I'll never ask you to model anything again. Besides, I have someone else in mind. An actual nun. The last time I saw her face it was bluer than Beatrice Cenci's, blue as moonlight over a winter sea."

I smile at Lena's silent disdain and stretch a large canvas for Sister Prig. I paint her from my concussed memory, through one good eye, with the compassion of my newfound wokeness and bewilderment. She's witnessing her own death, the arrow of King Hun piercing her aorta. I've been there a few times myself, and I put myself there in the picture, standing behind Sister Prig, peaking over her shoulder, her death-white decolorization splashing me in the face.

"This is my last selfie," I say to Lena.

I watch her eyes and wait for a stigmata tear or two. She resists so I cobble some of my own. It half counts as a miracle coming from a recovering sociopath. Mamma enters to witness the phenomenon.

"I have good news and bad news," she says.

"I don't want bad news. Just give me the good news."

"The cardinal-nephew and Cardinal Gonzaga have finagled your freedom. The Vice-God has signed your pardon."

She doesn't look all that happy for me. There must be a catch. I wipe my hands on a rag, cleaning the vermillion from Sister Prig's shawl. I go to the darkest corner of my cell and sit on the floor.

"When can I return to Rome?" I ask.

"When it's safe. When the Knights of Malta set sail for their next crusade. When you finish a John in the Wilderness for the cardinal-nephew and another one for Cardinal Gonzaga. You can't leave until they're done. They want assurances before you go missing."

I stand and go to the window. Baron Boy wouldn't knock a hole in the ceiling, so I built an aperture over the window with pieces of oak flooring. I pry two planks from the wall and scope the Port of Napoli for enemy ships. Nothing. Just a bunch of shitty fishing boats.

"Give me the bad news," I say.

"Your Virgin has passed. She finally succumbed to her wounds."

You'd think I'd want to cry, but it's the opposite. I know that Lena was always somewhat skeptical about living. She must have hated living with broken body parts.

"Your Cupid is still in Rome. He's living in Campo de' Fiori with his parents. Doing quite well painting under the name Cecco del Caravaggio."

"He can't paint with that name. He gave it to Finson and Vinck."

"Think of them all as the children you never had."

"What about the child you never had? What do you think of him?"

Mamma goes to Lena. She tries to pay her a respectful look but fails. I pretend like I don't see it.

"She was too beautiful. Women in Rome still wear their hair like hers."

"She was carrying my child. It died inside of her, which in a way, was better than dying outside of her, in this world."

"Says the blessed superstar with two mothers who sacrificed everything for him."

"To the mother who bought herself immortality with the currency of her genius foster son while locking him in an attic before sending him off to be executed."

Mamma picks up one of the floorboards and javelin-tosses it at my head. I duck. She picks up another and hurls it like Achilles. I dodge. I kick it back to her across the floor. She picks it up with both hands and swings it at my head. I sidestep. She's less predictable than Diavolo. I'll give her that.

"You forgot my pot!"

"You shouldn't have said that," Caravaggio says.

"Ammamay iamay," says Michele.

The fight with Mamma (our first) has reactivated Michele and Caravaggio. They sound like their old metaphysical selves, but their voices are not coming from inside my head. I place a stool in front of the full-length mirror and sit. I can't see them. I still only see my wonderfully bewildered self.

"What? You both hear Rome and presto! Resurrection?" I ask.

"No. Two John commissions. Those were the magic words. I've been wanting to resurrect John since the Knights Hospitaller made us decollate him," Caravaggio says.

"How should we paint him?" I ask.

"Like Cecco with that unbridled satisfaction on his face the first time he made us fade."

"What you talking *us*, cocksucker?" Michele says.

We laugh into a maniacal fugue. The reunion feels good, but we know something has essentially and permanently altered our synthesis.

"I can't see either of you." I widen my eyes on my reflection and stick my tongue out.

"Jesus Christ," says the hick. "How much longer are we going to play this charade? We're not real. You're the god here. You invented us. You invented us to deal with yourself, to forgive yourself for killing men and putting your penis in their mouths."

"We're interfaces," says the genius. "You needed someone to bear the responsibility of genius. You needed to pin your vanity on someone else."

"So I'm crazier than I thought. More delusional than Hercules and Orestes before killing their families."

"Which is why we were digging an escape tunnel. It was a futile effort until that lucky Hospitaller punched a hole in your head," says the hick.

"We saw our opening," says the genius.

"So you escaped, but then came back to help me? To help me fight and paint my way back to Cecco?"

"Ha! In your dreams!" Michele says.

"We've come to get what's owed to us," Caravaggio says. "You've built us these worlds. Dream worlds. Fame. Knighthood. Then you took them away. You've wanted nothing to do with your gifts. But we want them. We were happy fighting and painting for elitists."

Like Cecco, I drew them into a doomed world, but these interns still want to take over the practice. These inmates want to run the hospital. That can't happen. It makes too much sense. It's too kind and contradicts the anarchy I've come to love, the back-stabbing and cut-throating that I've come to embrace. Lena, Cecco, Del Monte, and Mamma found the courage to forsake yours truly. It's high time I shut up and do it for myself. I'll put Michele and Caravaggio out of their misery. I'll do it the most humane way possible. I'll do everything in my power to get Caravaggio to the Pantheon where Michele can preside over the sins of Rotonda Square. If the Knights Hospitaller tie yours truly to a stake, I want my bestial screams to be the only ones in my ears. I'll let them speak their minds and convey their wants in the interim.

LI.

Caravaggio has the idea of painting Sister Prig's Hun as the Divine One. We have his face committed to memory, a portrait by Giorgio Ghisi we once saw in a book. Michele has the idea of placing a dark anonymous hand between Ursula and her killer, vainly reaching for the savage arrow. Michele says it's the hand of God. I don't see it. God would never reveal His incompetence. I see it as the hand of yours truly but keep the opinion to myself. I'm happy that he's happy. I can't get to the Pantheon without him. If the knights get to me before reaching Rome, they'll burn my corpse in Malta, or maybe they'll decollate yours truly and feed my corpse to some unmarked patch of earth.

Painting with my interns is keeping me in check. I keep getting ahead of myself, my thoughts skipping to Rome, fantasizing a reunion with Cecco. He'll see that I've changed. I'm not the same old superstar. I'm more human now, less selfish and kinder. Charity begins at home. I'm learning to be patient and considerate with Michele and Caravaggio. They're not perfect, and neither am I, but that won't stop us from entering the Pantheon. If Cardinal Farnese got Carracci in there, the cardinal-nephew will want the same for his personal artist. Tit for tat aristocrats. They and their silly games, so evil and destructive. I'll beat them at it while remaining true to my new holistic self. The Pantheon is the prize. I'll kill the three of us to get there. It's an egotistical pursuit, but like I said, I'm flawed. Luckily, I have my inmates to keep me real.

I allow their alterations to Ursula, and it fucks up the varnish. I don't dress them down. I don't cuss them out. I remain in our happy place. This attic affords the same latitude as my cavity on the shore. The inmates were right, I alone can enable that perspective. I alone have created these worlds. We scrape down the varnish and apply a new coat, which delays our departure for the Pantheon by a week.

"You mean *Rome*. Not the Pantheon," Caravaggio interjects.

I don't correct him. They have to think that death is an unlikelihood. I don't need any added anguish in the picture. I won't make the same Lena mistake of our collaboration painting Catholic schmaltz. So I busy us with the two new John pictures. The son of Lanfranco Massa, the Doria family rep in Napoli, models for them. His father distrustfully supervises the sessions, two Carafa bodyguards at his side. Caravaggio and I block them out while Michele makes small talk about their shiny new wheellocks. His distraction works. Caravaggio and I manage to sneak my Cupid's cocksureness onto the lad's face. The cardinal-nephew will catch it. He'll be glad to have canvassed the Vice-God for my pardon. I paint the other John with less sauce and minus the ram. I paint Cecco from memory, reclining in my cavity like Titian's *Venus of Urbino*, the picture which taught me how to look at the viewer, but now, finally, my beauty denies the viewer his eyes. I bury him in brown shadow save for his doughy arms and the tops of his supple thighs. I've never met Cardinal Gonzaga, but I've never met a cardinal who wouldn't hang this picture in his private chamber.

Mamma doesn't come upstairs anymore. The beautiful old hag cleans my pot and brings my buttery artichokes. I don't blame Mamma. She's mad at herself, as she should be. I'd be mad at myself too if I had squandered my financial and political blessings on a cock-munching goblin. From here until the Pantheon, I'll do as she asks, even if she pushes me to Rome with a knife in my back. I owe her that. She's been my Lorenzo de' Medici. Perhaps the cardinal-nephew will let her read some Marino before Del Monte eulogizes me at the Pantheon.

The paint on both Johns is barely dry when Mamma enters. Her shoulders are reinforced by the two bodyguards. I've already deconstructed my aperture and stacked the wood in a pile. I already said goodbye to Napoli the last time I left.

"You're leaving today. The viceroy is being impeached. Your safety can't be guaranteed. The new viceroy will execute you and confiscate your pictures," she says.

"You mean *yours* and the *cardinal-nephew's* pictures."

"I want nothing from you. Bring them to Rome. Keep the Lena. The two Johns are for the cardinals. Pack them well. They're your only ticket home."

"Can I have a word alone?" I ask.

The bodyguards advance a step, now reinforcing her great breasts.

"The Knights Hospitaller caught you receiving a cock in the crypt of their holiest church," she answers.

I know she doesn't mean it. I know she's only saying that for the bodyguards, who will report her disdain to Duke Carafa or whoever it is that wants me dead. Her parting wink is more cynical than codified, but I don't take it personally. I'd be selfish too. I'm getting what I want. I'm finally going home.

"You're not going to kiss me farewell?" I ask.

"Angbay, angbay. Ou'reyay morta," she replies.

She turns to exit, catching a glimpse of her frown lines in my mirror, but she doesn't break stride. She's goner than the ghosts of my past.

Come nightfall, the two bodyguards cart me and my three pictures to a small private pier just outside the palace walls. There's a felucca posing as a tuna boat there. They tell me that the felucca will bring me up the coast to Palo. I'll be arrested there by the papal authorities and transferred the rest of the way to Rome, where the cardinal-nephew will receive me.

"What about a sword? I don't feel safe traveling overseas without a blade. Lots of pirates out there," Michele says.

The bodyguards laugh. One of them walks back to the cart and returns with the frailest rapier I've ever handled, slighter than the one held by St. Catherine.

"It couldn't cut through hot lard," says the tall and overconfident one.

I could slice them to frilly ribbons, but I get on the boat with my three pictures. I've already caused Mamma enough embarrassment.

I stash my rucksack and pictures in the hold, wrapping the three rolled canvases in a sheet of heavier canvas. I strap the sword to my waist and return to the deck. The crew of two, a gangly old captain and his knobbier son, wastes no time in shoving off. The bodyguards help with their feet. They wave wry farewells. Michele flips them the bird as I take a seat at the bow.

The bay is black. The sky is blacker. I'd ignore the stars if that was possible, but I'm mostly man at the moment. I can't help but search them for His eye. They all seem to be shimmering. Maybe there are that many dying gods. Maybe I'm one in a million. Wouldn't that be the kicker?

The breeze is barely enough for the sails, but the swells are plenty. We're not outside the harbor when the nausea comes.

At the tip of the jetty, we pass a titanic galleon vilified by shadow.

"The new viceroy," says the captain. "He's waiting for the old one to vacate the city."

"Maybe the new viceroy will lift the tax on fish," Michele says, sensing a proletariat ally.

"No fucking difference to me. I have one client. I sell my entire catch to the Carafas."

"I have a similar arrangement," says Caravaggio.

I turn to net the captain's reaction but he's standing stolid as Charon oaring across the Styx. The son mans the helm as if sailing into a cyclone. They'd rather hump nets than pirate a supernova. Fishermen think they're all that because they brave the surf. They talk up the ocean to glorify their occupation. The ocean isn't so great. It's nothing in fact. It's nothing without the sky. Without the sky, the ocean would have no color. Without the sky's superior vastness, the ocean would have no context. The ocean is nothing but a reflection of the sky, a selfie painted by heaven. That reality is made evident as the sun rises above our slipstream, painting the oncoming waves against their will.

As the morning brightens, Michele and Caravaggio grow nervous. I can't ask them why, not in front of Charon, but I can assume. We're leaving one prison for another. Rome won't be the same. The cardinal-nephew won't let us out of sight. He'll lock us in his palace or villa. He'll entertain our vices, but I don't care to have those anymore. Being a slave of any kind is no life. At best, you're tethered to a lover or friend. A Rome with no Lena. A Rome with no Onorio. If not for the Pantheon, we'd no longer belong in Rome. If the Pantheon weren't there, I'd have stayed in Napoli. Part of me is already missing the Mezzogiorno.

I've never been to Palo, but I've heard there is a large papal fort on its coast with a tower. As the boat tacks for land, as the coastline grows larger in the burnishing daylight, I see no fort or tower, just an expansive wilderness of swamp.

"Where's this?" I ask the captain.

"South of Palo. Too many people waiting for you there. They want us to drop you off here."

It's impossible to see his mouth moving underneath his graying beard, but I know he's lying. I take a long drink of water and stand to stretch my legs. The summer heat is already suppressing the day. The approaching swampland is giving me malaria flashbacks, the fervid muse of my sick selfie. The nausea in this case is worse.

Charon drops sail and we coast toward a derelict dock in the middle of a summer-jaundiced estuary of cat-o-nine tails.

"We're early. They'll be here," says the captain.

This is it. It's looking like Michele will be our last hope for the Pantheon. My nerves are rattling my bladder. As the son ties a line to the dock, I step off the boat to piss. The tide is out. I jump down from the dock onto a mudflat. My feet disappear in the black silt. As my anxious piss stream weakens to dribbles, three figures appear from a thicket of tangled buckthorn atop the beach. They're not wearing Swiss guard red. They're wearing black linen with the white Maltese crosses of St. John.

"At least there are only three of them," I say.

"One for each of us," Michele answers.

"The story of your volt hasn't reached Malta yet," says Caravaggio.

I slowly tie my breeches into a double-tight knot before drawing my Catherine's sword. Michele's aggression is dealt an early blow as the three faces become recognizable. Brother Superior. Fra Malaspina. Fra Carafa. I turn to the boat, but it's already jibing away from the dock, my Lena and two Johns with it.

"They're headed back south," Michele says.

"That's not the way toward Rome," Caravaggio says.

My brother stops ten sword lengths from me. He doesn't look a thing like Fermo. He's looking one hundred ten percent Colonna.

"We're brothers. Real brothers," Michele says.

I don't have the heart to tell him. Let him think it until the end. He too deserves a little hell.

"Michele, you know that's not true," Brother Superior says. "Look at my face. I'm a Sforza. That's just a productive mythology Mamma let you fancy so you'd feel bonded, so you'd listen, so she could protect you."

"Who gets my pictures?" Caravaggio asks.

"Your marchioness," says Malaspina.

"Your value is going through the roof," Carafa says.

"Maybe she can buy her coach back," I say.

"I don't want this," says Brother Superior. "I never did, but you shamed the Order. You've caused dissention. Brothers fighting brothers over how to kill you. The grandmaster has lost the respect of half the Order. You forced his hand. It's better us than Fra Diavolo. He wants you sodomized with a club and burned alive. We'll make it painless as possible."

"So, what? I just kneel here and let you decollate me? Bring my head back to Malta?"

"I'm hoping, brother."

"You know I can cut through the three of you with this nail file, right?"

"Of course. We saw you spar in the gym. We heard about your volt. Wish I'd been there to see it," says Fra Carafa.

"We brought these for insurance." Brother Superior draws a wheel-lock from his belt.

Fra Malaspina and Fra Carafa draw theirs too. I look up and down the beach and give it some thought. I don't owe Brother Superior anything. He's not a Merisi. He doesn't even want to be one. I raise Catherine's sword and step toward the brat. I feel the wheellocks before hearing them. One in the throat. Two in the chest. Michele is the first to go. He never saw it coming. I still have something in me. I could get to them before they reload, maybe take Brother Superior and Malaspina with me, but they don't belong where Caravaggio is going.

I genuflect to the horizon, to that hazy bisection of sky and selfie. The war over this heaven is over. Michelangelo has cast out Satan. I sign a cross and kneel in the lacy sea skim. A surge of tide swallows my thighs. I can't exhale through the blood in my throat. I can't inhale the clot yeasting like bread in my chest. Cecco grabs my hair. My Isaac draws the sword across my neck with the dexterity of my Judith. I'm out of my mind for real! I'm free as Mamma's little birdie. Caravaggio stands and steps away from me. I watch him stumble toward the horizon, headless but determined to get there.

"Go, Caravaggio! Go! Oh my God! Oh my God! Oh my God! Yes! Yes! Yes!"

Acknowledgments

I am forever grateful to Christoph Paul and Leza Cantoral for midwifing the birth of my Caravaggio. CLASH Books will forever be his Rome. I wrote this novel in darkness. A loving thanks to my readers David Schuman and Colette Sartor for being the light of its chiaroscuro. Writing is one circle of hell, and getting published an even deeper circle. I am lucky and thankful to have had Emily Franklin as my Virgil. This Caravaggio of mine is existentially indebted to Megan Barnes for having his back at every street brawl. The warmest grazie goes to my literary mother Elizabeth Searle for always bandaging my ego after said brawls. A very small thanks to Mike and Ned for their laissez-faire Irish American friendships. On the flipside, a big brown bear hug to Mikey Gaga for being my only paesan in Rexhame. A wholehearted shout-out to Amelia English for always standing on tables while cheering for my spiritual and professional success. As an author and recovering neurotic, I owe most of my ethos to Thomas Deininger and our third self. The ultimate acknowledgement goes to Sara and Ronan for being so goddamn wonderful.

About the Author

Eugenio Volpe's stories have appeared in *The Massachusetts Review, Salamander, New York Tyrant, VICE, Post Road, The Nervous Breakdown, BULL,* and elsewhere. He is a former winner of the PEN Discovery Award for Fiction. He teaches rhetoric at Loyola Marymount University in Los Angeles.

Also by CLASH Books

AFTERWORD

Nina Schuyler

DARRYL

Jackie Ess

CHARCOAL

Garrett Cook

I'M FROM NOWHERE

Lindsay Lerman

BORN TO BE PUBLIC

Greg Mania

COMAVILLE

Kevin Bigley

GIRL LIKE A BOMB

Autumn Christian

LIFE OF THE PARTY

Tea Hacic

KILL THE RICH

Jack Allison & Kate Shapiro

THE LAST NIGHT TO KILL NAZIS

David Agranoff

WE PUT THE LIT IN LITERARY

CLASHBOOKS.COM

FOLLOW US

Twitter

IG

FB

@clashbooks